I0817735

SKIPSHOCK

SKIPSHOCK

Caroline O'Donoghue

WALKER BOOKS

This is a work of fiction. Names, characters, places, and incidents are either products of the author's imagination or, if real, are used fictitiously.

First US edition 2025

Library of Congress Control Number: 2024950640
ISBN 978-1-5362-2881-6

25 26 27 28 29 30 SHD 10 9 8 7 6 5 4 3 2 1

Printed in Chelsea, MI, USA

This book was typeset in Dante MT Pro.

Walker Books US
a division of
Candlewick Press
99 Dover Street
Somerville, Massachusetts 02144

www.walkerbooksus.com

EU Authorized Representative: HackettFlynn Ltd, 36 Cloch Choirneal, Balrothery, Co. Dublin, K32 C942, Ireland. EU@walkerpublishinggroup.com

A JUNIOR LIBRARY GUILD SELECTION

To my two favorite salesmen:
Natasha Hodgson, who I crossed worlds to meet—
and my mother, for telling me to go

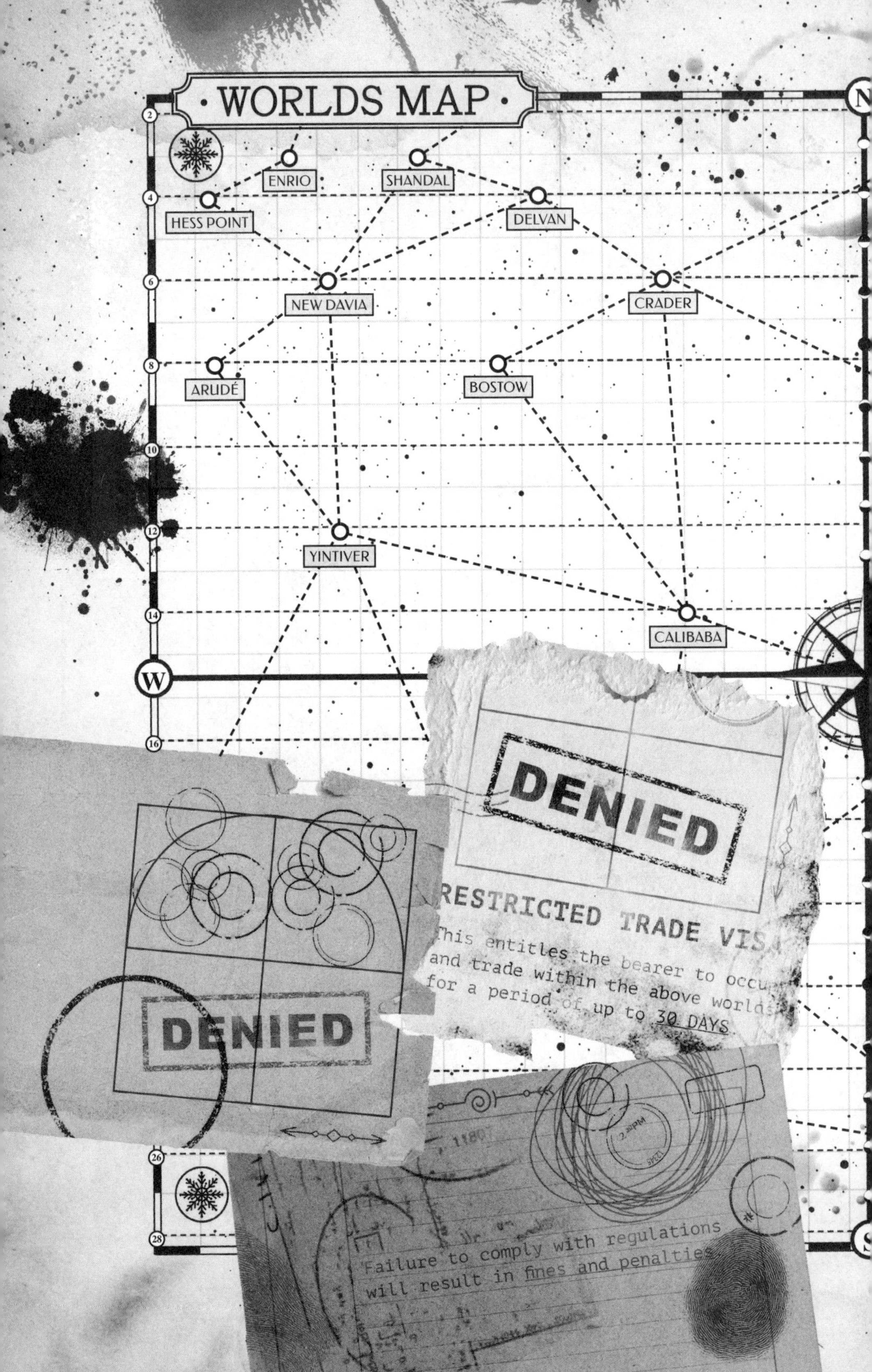

WORLDS MAP
ENRIO
SHANDAL
HESS POINT
DELVAN
NEW DAVIA
CRADER
ARUDÉ
BOSTOW
YINTIVER
CALIBABA
W
2
4
6
8
10
12
14
16
26
28
DENIED
RESTRICTED TRADE VIS
This entitles the bearer to occu
and trade within the above worlds
for a period of up to 30 DAYS
DENIED
Failure to comply with regulations
will result in fines and penalties

DOYOHI
KHAISE
TELLO
BAHAR
ALDERCARR
SOPILKA
E
2
4
6
8
10
12
14
16
18
20
22
24
26
28
00 34 52 04 96
08
30
NAME
SURNAME
AGE
BIRTHP
RESTR
OBS

Prologue
MOON

The most common response I get when I tell people what I do for a living is: I couldn't do a job like that. What they mean is they *wouldn't* do a job like this. Every so often a new gruesome story circulates about salesmen, and what traveling between time speeds does to one's physical health.

We are twice as likely to be alcoholics, three times as likely to die by suicide, and infinitely more likely to disappear without anyone caring at all.

But all I ever say is—you're right. You *couldn't* do a job like this. You couldn't haggle in a language that you don't speak. You couldn't fall asleep anywhere, training your body to relish fifteen-minute-long seated naps in the middle of a busy market square. And you couldn't wake up the way we do.

Salesmen wake up like dogs. Snoring one second, barking at a stranger the next.

I wake up on the train. Somewhere between Crader and New Davia I feel the train car screech against a tunnel, and have the slightly spectral sensation of knowing—even with my eyes closed—that I am being watched. The tangled gari beads are pressed between the seat and the nape of my neck, leaving light indents in my skin.

"Hello," I say, eyes fluttering open. Everything about the stranger tells me she's in the wrong place. First of all, she's a *she*. You rarely get women travelers these days, unless they've got a visa to work a special trade, and she looks too young and too out of sorts for that to be the case. Every detail uncovers a new question. Questions like: Why is she wearing summer clothes, on a train heading this far west? Why is she wearing a man's watch that doesn't fit her wrist? I squint at the glint of light catching the clock's face. It's heavy. Expensive. Silver.

"Hello," she responds anxiously. The longer I look at her, the more her strangeness unfurls like new petals. Frantic green eyes glancing worriedly down at an orange slip, a paper rectangle no bigger than her palm. "You're in my seat."

I gesture around the empty train car, arms wide with emphasis. Evidencing that there are quite a few seats free, and it's rather churlish of her to be protective of this one.

"There is no *my* seat," I reply. "This is the Northwest quad—no assigned seating. Who are you?"

She says nothing. Just shows me her orange rectangle, creased in her nervous hand. I take it from her and read it aloud like I've been handed a story written by a small and imaginative child.

"13:05 single," I read. "Cork Kent to Dublin Heuston."

She looks at me expectantly. "Am I near?" she asks, the hope draining from her speech. "Am I near Dublin?"

I hand the bright stub back to her. I've never heard of where she's from or where she's going to. I choose not to share this information. Salesmen are supposed to know about everywhere. The licensing tests are rigorous. They give you a big empty train map to mark with every world station, and it's 90 percent pass-fail. They want to make sure you know every world so there's less plausible deniability if they catch you in the wrong one with the wrong visa. Perhaps she's a plant. A test. A mole. Some new plan of Semper's, designed to trial our memories, our sympathies, and our resistance to a pretty face.

Pretty face comes to me unbidden, instinctive, the way "sleep tight" might follow a softly uttered "good night." It presents itself to me in a childish way, because even though she's about the same age as me, she reminds me of childhood. The wild hair—red, but nowhere near a natural color. The big eyes. The willingness to show fear to a stranger.

Fear. It's something I've tried to grow beyond. I'm not an idiot, and I don't think of myself as superhuman. I'm victim to the same thoughts and emotions as anyone else. But I do think that in almost all cases you can subdivide large emotions into smaller ones—fear into anxiety, love into affection, empathy into sympathy—therefore protecting yourself from those who will reliably take advantage. In the way insects will cloak themselves to look like their surroundings, I will respond blandly, in the hopes that blandness will cover me and that peace will follow.

It is only very traumatized people, Ves once told me, who confuse stasis for peace.

This person, meanwhile. This person is making no secret of her feelings. She's completely animated by fear, and for a few seconds, I simply stare at her. Her uneasy eyes flitting all around the train car. Her breath running short. Fingers fidgeting at her hair, then her scalp, then at the cuticles on her other hand.

"Why don't you sit down?" I suggest.

We sit, uneasily, in a moment of mutual study. Now that she's across from me, her eyes level with mine, I can feel her digesting my appearance. To be fair to her, it's a lot to take in. The crescent moon that starts above my left eyebrow and hugs around my cheekbone is far bigger than most salesmen's tattoos, its largeness in direct proportion to how much they didn't want to give a license to a Lunati boy. They dug deeply, sharply, and despite their insistence on professionalism and neutrality, with some spite. The scar was violent red in the beginning. Now, six years on, it has smoothed to a papery beige. I watch her watching me. She forgets her panic for a second, because she is wondering how a person could end up with a scar that is so aggressive, yet so precise.

"The answer is yes," I say. Eager, for some reason, to get these private thoughts of hers into the open. "It did hurt, and yes, I was awake. And yes, I gave my permission."

She laughs then, embarrassment briefly overriding terror. "Sorry," she says. "I was staring, wasn't I?"

"Oh, not so much that anyone would notice."

There is a brief trading of apologetic smiles, and then a silence.

Before we continue, I want to say something about that trade and that silence, because it happened so quickly, and no one was there to see it. Among salesmen, there is a practice known as scooping. This means that a salesman "scoops" a bunch of his old inventory into a handkerchief for you at a low price, and while most of it will be useless or cheap or out of date, there will always be something strangely valuable in there. A little gem, or a rare coin, or a kind of glass that you didn't think they made anymore. Maybe the salesman didn't realize he was giving it to you. Maybe he holds you in higher esteem than you originally thought.

That's what it was like with her, during that first train journey. A gemstone was briefly uncovered in silence. She scooped me up, is what I'm saying. Or maybe it was the other way around. The face and the eyes and all the silly red hair. Not red like fire. Red like rust. Red like metal. Red like a chemical spill.

The moment passes. She remembers that she has no idea where

she is, and her breath starts coming short. She lays the palm of her hand across her chest, as though trying to block her own heart from escaping.

"My name is Moon," I say at last. "And I think you're in the wrong place."

PART ONE

NEW DAVIA

one

MARGO

The school pushed for a therapist.

Donna-Anne agreed to it, not because she believed in therapy, but because she wanted to impress upon Margo how serious the matter had become. She had, after all, sold the watch. And not just any watch. *Richard's* watch.

Donna-Anne said it as though Margo had stolen from her mother directly. As if she had purposefully severed her mother's last remaining tie, and only out of spite. But Donna-Anne had many things, including their house, to remember Richard by. Margo had only the watch. It was, technically speaking, hers to sell.

The therapist suggested that Margo had depression. The therapist implied that it was something that was always cooking inside of Margo, even before the crash. That death had stirred up a nature that was naturally morose. Old school reports were summoned and then reviewed. Much was made of comments over her primary school years.

Margo is content in her own company, read one.

Margo often seems a little lost during group projects, came another.

And—this one felt slightly cruel, on review—*Margo has not left much of an impression on the other girls.*

He suggested that there was a link between this early Margo

and the Margo who, aged sixteen, sold her dead father's watch, dyed her hair metallic red, and attempted to run away from home. He thought it was deeper than simply having a dead dad. He said that somewhere down the line, and after more meetings, drugs might be helpful. For the moment, he said, he could recommend breathing exercises.

Donna-Anne took her daughter and left the therapist's office.

There was nothing, Donna-Anne said, actually *wrong* with Margo. If anyone was to blame, it was Donna-Anne herself for allowing the leash to get too long. She had left her daughter to her own devices and it had led to the blossoming of a criminal. The whole thing had gone beyond her mother's capabilities. It was time for a change. It was time for boarding school.

(They got the watch back, of course. The pawn shop owner, a Cash4Gold that took silver, too, had called Donna-Anne after he realized that the third hand only worked when you pushed the timer. The inscription—*Richard Madden III*—made its owner easy to track down. Small towns don't forget plane crashes in a hurry, much less their victims.)

And this is how we find Margo, in the moments before she fell through worlds. A sixteen-year-old failed runaway with a watch and unsuitable clothing. Six days off her next birthday, and on a train from Cork to Dublin.

Thirsty.

So, so thirsty. The summer had arrived late in Ireland, as it almost always does, with hot weather such a rarity that no one knew how to protect against it. She did not bring sunglasses for the immense glare of light through the window. She had not brought her water bottle. Her only snack was a sweating ham sandwich, gluey with heat. She picked at the sandwich and got thirstier by the minute.

The train screeched to a halt inside a blackened tunnel. She waited a moment. A voice came over the loudspeakers, a fuzz of static obscuring the driver's words. Something was broken. He repeated himself, and Margo listened closely. She understood nothing. Then, silence.

When she had boarded in Cork there had been a smattering of other travelers in the train car with her. But they had all gotten off in Mallow, and now she was en route to Dublin alone. She became uneasy. It felt like being strapped into a broken roller coaster, wondering whether her terror was normal or simply part of the ticketed experience.

The open windows, which had been the train car's only air-conditioning, let in nothing but dead heat and a dank earthy smell. There was a faint whiff of piss, and she wondered whether people sheltered in these tunnels at night.

As the darkness pushed in on the train and the loudspeakers continued to express garbled, apologetic sentiments, Margo felt her throat grind with anxiety. There was nothing really scary at all happening, she told herself. She was just dehydrated. This was why she had a headache. This was why she was panicking. There was a shop somewhere on board. There had to be. She needed water. She got out of her chair, keeping her hands on the seat headrests in case the train suddenly started moving again.

As Margo moved through one empty car after another, there was a mounting sense that she was in a problem that Coke Zero could not solve.

Eventually, she came to a shuttered counter that usually sold snacks and drinks. Through the shutters she could see cans winking at her. Margo threaded her fingers mournfully through the gaps, like a mother visiting her son in prison. She looked down at her silver watch, slung low over her palm, and reasoned that she would sell it all over again for a single can.

She was alone on a broken train. A wild sadness rushed through her, not for the situation itself, but because of how much this moment felt like all the ones that had led to it. She had been a clean and well-running thing for so much of her life. She was an only child, and not the kind who had lots of cousins and neighbors to compensate. Their family was a strange and quiet one. Love was gained through achievement and maintained through behaving pleasantly. She had been a good student and she had some friends, despite what those early school reports had implied.

Then her father died. Her habitual insomnia and moody periods became her permanent companions. She was sleep-starved and in shock. She stopped talking to everyone, stopped going to school, and eventually, her friends stopped calling. Life was too hard to put up with for a moment longer, so she decided to run away. She didn't get far. Boarding school was meant to be the compromise. The fresh start.

Yet here she was: stuck, clouded with menace, and alone. No fresh start, and no bad dye job, could change that. She was silly for thinking it could.

The train started moving again. There was a sharp, screeching noise that sounded like metal on metal, and she knew the train was fighting hard against the darkness. Before she even had time to apply this metaphor to herself, the compartment shook and Margo was thrown by the momentum. She steadied herself, one arm clutching furiously to the wall. As the train moved faster and faster, she inched her way to the rubbery airlock between train car doors.

In the airlock, she started to feel sick. It suddenly felt as though all her internal organs were crowding together and looking to escape through her neck. Would she vomit? *Here?* On Iarnród Éireann property? Margo closed her eyes and remembered Cork, where everyone got the bus everywhere. She could no longer keep her balance by holding on to the wall, and instead curled into a ball on the floor, her eye sockets resting on both knees.

As the airlock rocked and screeched, Margo wondered if this was what it felt like to die. She pushed the timer on her father's watch, the thin hand that only ticked for sixty seconds and stopped again. She practiced the breathing lessons that the therapist had taught her. Timing her breaths in ten-second intervals, watching the third hand strike two, then four, then six. Breathing in. Breathing out.

And when she opened her eyes again, the train had changed completely.

Everything was wooden. The industrial plastics had been replaced by dull mahogany. The sticky, piss-soaked air had thinned. It was suddenly cool, like a window was open and letting in a chilly winter. Margo rubbed at her arms in her thin denim jacket, her cheap summer dress soaked with sweat.

She stumbled back to her seat, the car still empty. Although not, she suspected, because passengers had changed for Mallow. The itchy seat coverings that her legs had prickled against just moments before were now a deep red velvet, torn in places, and showing stuffing. Her legs wobbled as she walked.

But one other thing, she realized, had changed.

She wasn't alone anymore.

A figure, a man, was asleep with his head against the window. His suit jacket was draped over him like a blanket, and his shoes—a pair of dark, battered brogues—were on the seat in front of him.

Her seat.

She could sit somewhere else. There was, after all, no one else on board. But to sacrifice 57B at this point was to let go of reality. She needed to talk to someone. Anyone. A grown-up. She watched him, her gaze packed with need, wondering if that alone was enough to wake him up.

His gray eyes opened quickly and fell from her hair to her feet, taking detailed mental notes on each part of her. Margo could do nothing but stare back.

He was not, as it turned out, a grown-up.

What age he was exactly, she couldn't tell. Every element of his appearance both proved and contradicted the idea of maturity. His mess of thick brown hair said *boy*; the gray streaks in it said *man*. His quick, mischievous smile was definitely *boy*; his dark suit was absolutely *man*.

The one thing about him that didn't figure into the algebra of how old he was, was the tattoo that started at his temple and arched around his left eye. The tattoo was the thinnest sliver of a crescent moon.

"Hello," he said at last.

two
MOON

There isn't very much time for pleasantries, because moments after Margo gives me her name, the Pig arrives.

The Pig's mask is iron and takes up two-thirds of his face, which makes me think he was tattooed right at the start of the ban, when things were a little tougher. His right eye, cheekbone, and temple are still pink and fleshy. But his nose is a sculpted snout, his jowls a polished gray. He's making his way slowly down the train car, refilling the paper roll on his ticket dispenser as he does. He's trying to do two things at once, which they're never very good at.

It is sad and probably wrong to hate the Pigs. After the war, when Semper started recruiting Northern workers for the trains, they debated for a long time just how to make it secure. They had to be absolutely sure the ticket inspectors, janitors, and assorted personnel wouldn't use the job as a means to escape to the South. So men—family men, mostly, made destitute by the various collapsed industries affected by the travel ban—lined up to be maimed and plated. Each man's septum deviated by ironwork, grunts peppering their speech where easy breath once drew. We called them pigs, because they snorted, and because we hated them. Then Semper made it official. It has always been in their interest to make travel into a ghoulish thing. They updated their plate designs and turned the pig joke into hard fact.

I look at Margo. "You're really sure you don't have a ticket?"

She brandishes the orange thing again.

"Not *that*; that's not a ticket."

Why am *I* panicking now? This girl is none of my business.

"I was just trying to get to school. My new school."

The Pig drops his paper refill and it rolls under a seat. He sighs, lowering slowly to his knees to fish for it. They must stand up and sit down carefully: their equilibrium is shot from the plates, their inner ear affected by vertigo.

"Do you have a visa?" I ask her, my voice low.

"A visa? Why the hell would I have a visa for Dublin?"

I run my eyes over her again. The thin clothing, the heavy watch, the wild red hair. The accent, melodic and low, and slightly reminiscent of certain Semper house servants I've come across. But richer. Deeper. There are schools in slower worlds that Mid-Axis people used to send their kids to. You can learn so much more in a forty-hour day. Your kid comes back still a kid, but now she's a lawyer, too. I didn't think you were allowed to do that anymore.

"You're from a place called Dublin?" I ask, keeping one eye on the struggling Pig.

"No, I'm *from* a place called Cork." She's indignant about this. "I'm *going* to Dublin. To school."

Whatever brief moment of connection we experienced before the Pig showed up, it appears to have evaporated now. It's as if each of us has been paired up to play a game with a stranger who doesn't know the rules. She can't get over that I don't know about these places, these words. She's frustrated, fuming in a way that implies she thinks she could win if she was with someone who could actually *play.*

Maybe there are open worlds that I don't know about. Maybe boarding school visas are back on. I don't have kids, so maybe I missed the bulletin. Maybe this girl somehow walked onto the wrong train and just needs help navigating her way onto the right one.

"Well, if you can't come up with a visa and a ticket in the next thirty seconds," I tell her, "you're out in the snow." I say it with a touch too much spite, as if trying to remind her that it's *my* game she's not playing properly, and not the other way around.

The poor girl. She looks like she might keel over in panic. She seems to have no idea why you would need a visa to get on the train. And the ticket. She bought it from somewhere, certainly, but not a Semper train. And there *are* no trains except Semper trains. Not for years.

Margo finally notices the Pig lumbering toward us, and for a brief second looks relieved by the presence of a much older person in uniform. Then she clocks the ironwork, and her face pales.

Another benefit of the Pigs looking the way they do: nobody taking a Semper train thinks that anyone on board is going to help them.

"Ticket, visa," he says, first to me, but with a metal eye swiveling toward Margo as he speaks. He's clearly finding her hard to figure out, too. Those clothes? This weather?

My tattoo gives me permission to travel, but my visa informs him where, exactly, I'm allowed to travel to. I can go north. northwest, northeast, far north. Certain worlds along the Mid-Axis. But I cannot go south.

"Sales," I say to the Pig. "Semiprecious raw material; heating sources; dry goods."

He punches the ticket, grunts, and moves on to Margo.

"Ticket, visa," he repeats.

She looks to me, willing an answer, an excuse, praying that anyone will speak on her behalf.

There is a short pause. A pause in which I weigh up several options: what this will cost me, what it is worth, and how many problems it's likely to create down the road.

If she is a lost, rich schoolgirl, then her family will be grateful to me for looking after her. A cash reward. Or, if not a cash reward, a new trade contact, a sponsor for a Southern visa. I need slower worlds on my rota. I am, quite literally, not getting any younger.

If she's *not* a lost, rich schoolgirl, and she's . . . something else, from somewhere else, then this amounts to something far more. It means some of the sealed worlds are perhaps not as sealed as we once thought. That there are avenues of travel that Semper does not yet know about, or does and is keeping secret. It means someone started on one train and ended up on another, which means there is a rupture somewhere.

And where there is a rupture, there is an opportunity.

For Vesna, and for PACT. But most of all for me, the person who delivers this strange girl into their lap.

Option one is lucrative, easy, and gets me out of sales.

Option two is dangerous, deadly, and could help unmake civilization. A civilization that—as Ves often says, and I've agreed with, in a drunk, noncommittal sort of way—desperately needs to be unmade. And in that scenario, there *is* no sales, and so I come out on top regardless.

When you become a salesman you quickly discern the difference between The Rules and The Law. Lying about your quantities is breaking the rules; dodging your taxes is breaking the law. Taking a message from one world to another is breaking the rules; helping an undocumented person cross worlds is breaking the law.

I sometimes break the rules. I never break the law.

Not since becoming a salesman, anyway.

"This is my apprentice," I say as brightly as I can. I take out my wallet and try not to make eye contact with the baton attached to the Pig's pants. "And I can't seem to find her travel papers."

Most people, I think you'll agree, really couldn't do a job like this.

three
MARGO

Wherever she had ended up, her bags had not deigned to come with her. She had nothing except the clothes on her back. Even her phone, somehow, had stayed on the Cork train.

When something bad happens to you, it's normal to comb through your own actions for the moment you signed up for your own doom. In Margo's case, she couldn't locate it. Even Dorothy had wished Kansas away. Margo *wanted* to go to Dublin.

The pig man let them get off at New Davia, accepting the bribe Moon offered him. She kept replaying her memory of the pig man's face. He was short and heavyish, like a club bouncer, only most of his face was iron. Like a mask that was welded onto his skin, or perhaps *instead* of skin. And the mask was . . . well, piggish. Did he have a nose under that snout? Or *was* his nose the snout?

There was nothing to do but follow Moon. He had taken some kind of risk for her. Financial, definitely, but perhaps some other kind, too. Visas were important, wherever she was, and she didn't have one. Could she get one? She vaguely recalled a moment in childhood when her mother lost her passport shortly before a family trip. There were forms and visits to several boring offices, but it was handled quickly enough. She could do that. A visa was just a passport, really, and she had one of those. She didn't know where it was, but it existed, and surely there was a database of these kinds of documents internationally. People were always saying that they were being secretly monitored. Well, here was a moment when this could be both useful and true. She would go with Moon, get warm—it was so cold, it was too cold, it was illegal how cold it was—and then he would show her the way, perhaps even escort her, to the nearest passport office.

The train station was one large room with a shuttered saloon bar. A painted sign read NEW DAVIA CENTRAL STATION.

Below, in smaller writing: NWQ-6—RESTRICTED INTERWORLD TRADING ONLY.

She wanted to ask him to decode this for her, but he was already walking fast, crossing the station at an impressive clip. Margo was left with the unsettling task of trying to decode the sign herself. New Davia she had never heard of. But "Interworld" was far more alarming. She squinted at it, wondering if it was simply a brand name. Amazon wasn't, after all, a company based in a rainforest.

Her focus went back to the train they had just disembarked from.

It was a steam train, and old, but the tracks were the interesting thing. The rickety wooden boards were knit close together on the ground, but as they receded from the station they spread farther apart and curved upward. The tracks climbed higher, reaching toward the sky in a giant curve the way a roller coaster might. The sky was dark and full of snow, so it was impossible to see where the tracks ended. But Margo saw something above the stars. A kind of stitching in the sky, a spot where the air warped and stretched, blurring the edge of the moon's pale circle. For all the world's strangeness, the moon was still the same old familiar silver dollar, hovering mutely before her.

"Are you coming?" He was already across the station. His movements seemed to imply that if she did not keep pace with him, he would simply leave her there to rot.

She ran across the empty station, bursting onto the New Davia streets. Freezing air fell over her, snow falling light and steady. Within moments, Margo's dress was plastered to her skin like tissue paper. The chattering, illegal-seeming cold came harder. It was dazzling pain now, the kind of weather that regularly snapped off the noses of people who were still using them to breathe.

Moon was already halfway up the street. The world was so dark, this strange boy the only visible thing within it. She felt as though she were in a video game, the kind that will load only one step at a time. And like a video game, he always remained several steps ahead of her, just close enough to seem catchable.

"Can you *please* slow down?"

He said something in reply, but it was immediately swallowed by the snow.

"*What?*" she shouted back. "What did you say?"

He did not repeat himself. This struck her as incredibly rude, but as he quite clearly had all the power in this situation, he had the liberty of rudeness, too. She began speed-walking after him, her breath haunting the air in big, hot puffs.

Silently, she began to cry. It made no difference. Not to the snow, or in it.

So she walked on. And the farther she went, the less hope she had for the international database of passports.

Every few moments, a lamppost would cast a gloomy yellow light on the town. Because it *was* a town, she realized: it had shops and houses, and signs that said BREAD and SLIP and FUEL. It was too dark to make out color, but she identified shiny slicks where house paint was, and wormy gray spaces where it had been chipped away. It was not a rich place. It was rickety and frozen. Dull. Dim. Windows were lit by candles and the streetlights were powered by gas.

For a moment, Margo considered that she was not simply in a new place, but in the past, too. Some kind of desolate Siberian township from the turn of the century. But how?

She thought of time-traveling narratives, butterfly effects, and half-remembered YouTube videos about black holes. She attempted moral questions around the killing of baby Hitler. She tried to remember anything about her ancestors, and the possibilities of preventing her own existence. Then she looked up at Moon, who had finally slowed down just as she was starting to match his pace. The baby Hitler stuff had gotten her revved up. They briefly bashed into one another in this new negotiation of speed, her feet tripping on the backs of his shoes, her forehead almost flush with the back of his neck. The path was icy and Moon almost fell, gripping the fence just in time.

"Sorry, sorry, sorry."

"That was you, right?" Suddenly he seemed full of panic. "You crashed into me?"

Margo looked around, unsure if this was a riddle. "Yes. I'm sorry. I didn't mean to."

He kept his hand on the fence a moment, his face empty of emotion. He looked as though he were performing a kind of factory reset on himself. Then he came back, suddenly animated by purpose. He gave her shoulder a strange, reassuring squeeze.

"All right," he said. "All right. On we go."

She didn't quite know what she had just witnessed, only that it was a sort of private dread, and that she should not mention it again.

The moonlight glanced off her father's watch, still ticking reliably. She had taken the 1:05 train from Cork. According to her wrist, it had only just turned two p.m. They twisted off the wide street and onto a narrow path. Then the lamplight cast its beam on something so improbable that she almost laughed out loud at the sight of it.

Oranges.

Everywhere, oranges. Thick hedges, stiff and dense as mattresses, started to curve inward off the road, and the streetlights turned to paper lanterns. Oranges hung off all of them. She was certain that oranges were strictly a tree thing, not a hedge thing, but here they were. Bright and smiling and surrounded by glowing white blossoms. So joyful-looking that they seemed to be tap-dancing their way toward her.

"Oranges," she said, because that was all she could think. *"Oranges."*

He looked at her, bemused. The hedge path had narrowed, pushing their bodies closer together. She gazed up at him. The scar was, obviously, the thing you noticed first. It was the thinnest sliver of the moon, the last wink of the month before the sky became black again. But he looked different outside, and in the dark. He was white, but tinged with something else, something she didn't have a reference point for. His skin was a faint silver, very almost lilac. It felt like a trick of the eye, a color you could only see if you kept it slightly out of focus. His hair had something of the same quality. On the train it was an ordinary sort of light brown, longish and wavy. But under the frosted lamps, strands of his hair refracted light, turning it to silver thread. Not gray and wiry, like an old person's hair. But silver, and very fine.

"You're staring at me," he said as she followed him.

"No," she replied, even though she was. "Is your real name Moon?"

"No." He looked at her like she should have known this. He did not volunteer what his real name might be. "Is your real name Margo?"

"Yes."

They walked on. She put aside her theory of time travel and infant fascists. She did not really believe that she was in the past. The skin, the scar. The fence. The factory reset. If a person like him had existed in any lifetime, she would have heard about it. They would have taught him in schools.

The orange bushes peeled away, and they found themselves standing in front of a large house. Four stories high, cherry-colored, with a porch that wrapped around the whole building. White painted patterns decorated every side, swirls and flowers, birds and half-set suns.

Even though she was cold and frightened and unsure if she had done the wrong thing by following him, she couldn't help realizing that she was standing before something very beautiful. Not just the house, but the whole scene: the oranges and their friendly smell, the lanterns lighting her way, and a sign that said SALESMEN WELCOME—BEDS FOR CHEAP propped up in the window.

four
MOON

Vesna's kitchen door is technically the service entrance, no salesmen allowed, but Vesna started giving me kitchen privileges in exchange for discounts on red salts. I feel in my pocket for the key. Home. Or, home-ish. Home, kind of.

Margo looks cold and confused, and yet something prevents me from asking if she's OK. Perhaps I'm being weird with her. In fact, I'm almost certain I am being weird with her. But I feel a split urge to both get rid of her as quickly as possible and also dry her hair gently with a towel. I have also just bribed a Semper employee, potentially dooming myself in the process. So it's hard to know how to behave.

"Wait here a second," I tell Margo. The snow is catching in her thick hair, settling like a bride's veil before instantly turning to water. I turn away.

The kitchen smells like boiled bones. Ves is at the stove, stirring something with one hand, doing paperwork with the other. Her big green accounts ledger is being quickly filled with numbers, precise little chicken scratches for the dizzying society of sums that live in her head. The kitchen is the engine room of her entire operation. Food preparation is the least of it. There's a desk where she keeps her order forms, invoices, and purchase orders. But because one thing can never have just one job, it is also a station for her sewing, her skinning, and some light smithing. It is not unusual to get a bill from Vesna that is splattered vaguely with animal blood.

"*There* you are," she says. Like I am a button that went missing.

"Here I am," I reply. We do the hug that friends with uncertain fortune give each other. I check how close her bones are to the surface of her skin.

"Your mail was filling up. I was about to throw things out," she says, and her words are a warning. Padding out my panic with friendly bossing. I feel afraid, suddenly.

"How many days was I gone?"

I escape the kitchen briefly to visit the hall shelf, where I find my cubby. There are twenty-two cubbies in all, each for a different salesman. There are a lot of rules for salesmen, and here's another one: you can't have a fixed address. You have to keep on the move, no more than thirty hours in any one spot. Three warnings and then they take your license away. Your mail is sent to boardinghouses. It's a pretty tight network, the places that let salesmen stay, so you get your letter eventually. Ves, tired of having the same old conversations with the same old wanderers, installed a brass slider on each to indicate how much time has passed since her customer last stayed. Each runs to ninety-nine. When you've passed ninety-nine, your cubby is given to someone else, your mail thrown away after it's raided for valuables.

It's not like something dreadful happens to you after ninety-nine days spent away. It's just her policy, a way of keeping admin low. I try not to risk it. It can take a long time for a cubby to open up again.

I check my brass slider, fearing the worst.

Thirty-six.

I whistle.

"How long did you think it was?" she asks, closing the ledger and putting it on the shelf above her head.

"I don't know," I reply, and I don't. I darted around the North for product, then spent some time in the East selling it. It wasn't a hugely successful trip, if I'm honest. Everything in the far North seemed extortionately priced, and no one could fully explain why. Red salts at three times the usual cost.

"And how was it?"

I shrug. "Expensive."

She tastes something with a wooden spoon. "I keep hearing that."

"Yes." I sort through my mail, attempting nonchalance. Vesna and I have the kind of relationship that exists in the gap between friends and family. Or, rather, neither of us has the time for friends, and both of us have lost our families. "How charitable a mood do you think you're in?"

"As charitable as I always am, Mo," she answers, grinding some seasoning with a pestle. "Which is to say: not at all. Are you going to bring that straggler in from the snow, or aren't you?"

"How . . . ?"

She points with her wooden spoon to the rafters, where I see that she has now installed mirrors. Thin slashes of glass, only noticeable if you know they're there. I squint at one and can see through the back window, where Margo's puffed breath is just visible outside.

"Need eyes in the back of my head. You know how it is. Taiyo put them up. Come on, call her in."

"How do you know it's a her?"

Ves narrows her eyes at me, that landlady stare. Like: *don't kid a kidder, I know what you guys get up to*.

Margo stands in Vesna's kitchen, looking so vividly out of place. Her body cold and alert, stiff as a dancer. A rod of panic seems to be keeping her upright, and if she lets go of it, she might just collapse on the floor.

"Moon," Ves says sharply to me, turning back to the stove. "What were you doing, leaving her out there? Her lips are *blue*."

"I thought I'd warn you first. Margo, why don't you go warm up by the fire?"

The enormous grate is burning brightly. Margo doesn't need telling twice. She pulls up a stool.

Ves shoots me a look behind Margo's back: *Warn* me?

Margo holds out her hands, rubbing them slowly back to life.

"I found her on the train," I continue, my tone light. "It was quite a commotion, actually. Imagine, she was on an entirely different train—going . . . where was it, Margo?"

"Dublin," Margo replies. Now that she's sitting down, the circulation returning, the reality of her situation seems to be coming back to her. "From Cork."

Vesna is just confused now. She hasn't realized that neither Dublin nor Cork are worlds that appear on our map. And why would she? She's not a salesman.

"Which is funny," I say, attempting to remain casual, "because I've never heard of either of those places."

I lean hard on the *never*.

Vesna's confusion turns to quick, urgent interest. I sharpen my eye on her, a silent stern expression of *Don't freak the girl out.*

"Huh," Vesna says, fidgeting with the ends of a dish towel. "*Huh*. Knock me down."

Margo looks up from the fire. In the light of Vesna's kitchen I can see that the roots of her hair are growing out, a thick fairish stripe of her original self.

"I'm sorry—where are my manners. Margo, is it? I'm Ves. Vesna."

Ves stretches out her hand, and they shake. Vesna is only about a year older than I am, twenty or twenty-one, but being a landlady has put an armor on her. Halfway between mothering and upper management.

Ves fusses with some food, gives her guest a towel to dry off. She observes Margo, under the guise of helping her. Young, lost, wholesome. Rich kid? Old money, new money?

And Margo, of course, is looking back. And what is she seeing? A big, hot kitchen and two strangers whose words are shot through with ulterior motives. Me and my hideous tattoo, dirty hair, tired eyes. Ves, six foot three with skin the color of rust and a pale, fine braid of blond hair. Vesna is an immigrant, which means her scars decorate her torso, not her face. Two long S shapes scratched under her collarbones.

Margo speaks. "I was supposed to be going to school, but something happened, and . . . I think I fell out of my world, and into yours."

"How . . . strange," Ves says, unsure of what tone to take here. "Well, this is a boardinghouse. We normally host salesmen here, although all kinds are technically welcome, I suppose, not that they ever come. There's a room in the attic you can use."

If you know boardinghouses well, you know that it's unlucky to stay in an attic room. When a salesman is nearing the end of his journey—when either the skipshock or the lifestyle has caught up with him—he will limp his way to a boardinghouse, and he will ask for an attic room. He may stay there weeks or months, but the agreement with the landlady is clear. He's ready to finish. Generally, he doesn't have enough money to cover the costs, and with no family of his own, he will bequeath his travel papers to the landlady, who will sell them on the black market for a tidy profit.

If you're in any way superstitious—and most salesmen are—you do not take the attic room.

"Thank you" is all Margo says, her expression holding nothing but gratitude. Then: "Do you know how I can get to Dublin?"

Vesna furrows her brow, searching her memory. She doesn't know where it is, either. "What time is it there?"

Margo is surprised by the question but looks at her watch. "Two thirty."

Ves frowns. "Morning or afternoon?"

"Afternoon." Margo pauses, tries again. "If you don't know where Dublin is, maybe there's a passport office, or some kind of, I don't know, embassy you can take me to. Maybe a police station?"

Vesna's gaze darts to the mirror at the word *police*. She blinks at Margo, absorbing her hopeful, careful words not so much as information but as brochures for the kind of person Margo is. "Come with me. I'll find you something to wear, and show you where you're sleeping."

"*Sleeping?*" Margo is horrified. "I need to go to school."

"We don't know how to do that just yet," I say as gently as I can. "In the meantime, it seems like you need a meal and some dry clothes. I need to freshen up before dinner. But Ves is good people, and she'll take care of you."

"Your usual room is free," Vesna replies, steering Margo out of the kitchen.

She leads Margo through the enormous house and I head outside through to the converted cellar. It is damp, cramped, and ugly, but it has its own street-level entrance.

Something happens on the way down the steps to my room. I

can't explain it exactly, except that one minute I am at the top of them, my hand on the guardrail, and the next I am on the ground. My chin has opened against the hard concrete, blood pouring into the snow. At first, I think I've been pushed. But if you've been pushed down a flight of stairs, you know it: you feel the nudge, the topple, the slow loss of dignity as your body careers downward. Everybody falls in slow motion, at least to themselves.

No; this is something different. I brush myself down, bruised and embarrassed, and too old for nineteen. What happened, really, is that I briefly lost consciousness. Or: I fell asleep without wanting to, or without realizing that I had.

The room is a bed, a window, and a fireplace. There are some pegs for hanging up stuff. A metal tub for bathing in and a tap that filters the melted snow directly from the path outside. I get undressed and click open my suitcase. Little bags of everything, neatly categorized into a grid with wooden dividers, and loosely alphabetical. Abelbrush, axiom, bronzefruit, damaspring. I wash my hands in the freezing water, then take a pinch of dama and rub it into the cut on my chin. Blood congeals around the orange powder, scabbing up quickly. A teaspoon of this stuff will set you back thirty-five gens, and the margins are *tiny*, so I can't afford to fall down a set of stairs every day.

"It won't be every day," I say to no one at all. Then, louder: "I won't do it *ever* again."

I follow my finger down to S for salts. Red crystals that smell of offal and sweat. They are, I realize, almost the exact same color as Margo's hair. I pour some into my palm, crushing the hard flakes into dust, then sprinkle it into the water. I swirl it around with one hand, watching it dissolve, turning the water pinkish. In two minutes, it will be hot enough to take a bath in.

But two minutes, it turns out, is exactly enough time for me to think about the scab on my chin.

Six years I've been doing this job. Seven if you count my apprenticeship with Mitwatch. The average length of a sales career is about a decade, give or take some bad assignments.

After that you either ascend or decline. You get into procurement. You get yourself an office, or a shop. That's *if* you have enough savings. If you don't? Well. You keep it up as long as you can. Maybe you make it to twelve years, or fifteen. But a salesman on the road for too long is like a dog the owners just won't put down. The skipshock is deep in the bone then. Your memory shot. Your nerves shattered. Your vision so confused from years of unreliable light patterns that nothing quite comes into focus properly. Stomachaches. Bleeding bowels. It manifests in everyone differently, but here's how it starts.

It starts with passing out on the stairs.

No, Moon, you're kidding yourself again. It *started* earlier. The vertigo last month, the bleeding gums last week, the moment at the fence with Margo less than thirty minutes ago.

I lift the tray of product out, where another layer to my briefcase sits. The money from this month's sales. It's not much. Not enough to buy my way out, anyway, which is the only thing that matters now that I'm in the falling-down-the-stairs stage of my career.

How much will PACT give me for Margo? Vesna could tell right away that she was valuable. She's even given her a free room. Vesna's livelihood is too slim for that kind of charity. Vesna will get the local leaders together—she has the pull to do it—and I'll help them realize just what an opportunity this is. The trick, I suppose, will be in affirming that Margo is mine to sell. There's always a risk that they'll just convince Margo and she'll join them on their own merits. Then

Taiyo will turn around and give me a smug *The Revolution thanks you for your trouble* and I'll have risked my life—and bribed a Pig—for nothing.

A change of clothes, a shaving kit, and a bottle of something brown and strong that I do not remember the name of. The bath is hot now, and I inch slowly in, the water lapping up toward my throat. The gari beads around my neck fall into the water. Thirty beads light as raindrops.

I worry at the beads with one hand and cradle my drink in the other. Alternately praying to the goddesses and swigging in spite of them. The beads are starting to warm up, little hot bugs between my fingers. In a few days, the Wash is due, their thirty-day wait finally up.

I pray to the moon and each of its phases. I pray my savings are bigger than I remember them being; I pray the skipshock hasn't gotten to me too much already. I pray my parents will forgive me.

I sit and I prune and I weigh up all the evidence, and as the water gets cold, the hope does, too.

five

MARGO

Vesna led her past a closed door hiding male voices. The corridor smelled badly of cigarettes, the smoke funneling out from the room of men and pushing itself against paintings, peg hooks, and wallpaper made from sheet music. Margo glanced around for plugs, outlets, photographs. Where there should be technology, there was instead heavy utility. The peg hooks weren't just holding hats and jackets, but briefcase handles, dangling memo pads, bags of cutlery. With her every movement, she seemed to disturb something. Vesna led her up the staircase.

"Where did you say you were from again?" Vesna asked as they reached the first landing. A narrow crop of bedrooms, some occupied. From a hook she plucked a pair of boots that were dangling by the shoestrings.

The Cork and Dublin conversation had been a dead loss, so Margo decided to go wider. "Ireland?"

"How long is it there?" Vesna handed the boots to Margo. "Here, these should fit."

"Thank you," Margo said, doubting they would. "Sorry? How long, did you say?"

"How long?" Vesna repeated. Margo began to notice that Vesna was watching her reactions very, very carefully.

"I mean, it's a small country, I guess. Compared to the UK. My dad said you could drive the length of it in half a day."

Vesna nodded, understanding nothing, but the *fact* of understanding nothing clearly of interest to her. They reached a landing, where a dark-haired girl was sitting on a padded cushion in the window, sewing buttons onto shirts.

"Ani," Vesna said. "This is Margo."

"Hey," Ani said, glancing up with interest. Ani was brown-skinned, very pretty, and strangely dressed up for sewing in a window. Her eyes were heavily lined with black pencil, her red skirt billowing and ruffled. She looked to Vesna.

"You can't have two of us," Ani said, territorial. She had an accent, but Margo couldn't place it.

"Relax," Vesna replied. "No one's replacing you."

Vesna picked up a stack of laundry and carried on escorting Margo through the building.

"You speak Traders," she said to Margo. Not a question but a comment.

"What do you mean?"

"You speak the Traders Language even though . . ."

At this, a very thin man suddenly emerged from his room. He looked like he had just washed his hands and was anxiously pressing them against the legs of his pants.

"Vesna," he said, eager to catch her. "Can I speak with you privately?"

"After dinner, Heckley," Vesna said, depositing one of Ani's freshly sewn shirts into his hands. "Can't you see I'm with someone?"

The man looked past her, his fingers fluttering in a nervous wave. "Hello." He nodded quickly to Vesna, embarrassed to have taken up her time at all. "After dinner. OK." Then he disappeared back into his room.

They ascended two more floors, depositing shirts as they went, until they were in the attic. There was only one bedroom.

"The dinner bell will go shortly," Ves said, not bothering to show her around. She handed her the remaining clothes in her arms, a shirt and a pair of pants. "Big. But dry, at least. I won't come this way again, so I'll depend on you to change your own sheets."

Sheets? Surely she wouldn't be here long enough to necessitate a change of sheets?

"What do you mean, you won't come this way again?" Margo said. She felt like a missionary being left to convert a far-flung nation. Wasn't this Vesna's house?

But Vesna was already halfway down the stairs, her steps light and quick.

Margo knew she should be grateful for the bedroom and the clothes. She was, after all, simply a lost person, relying on the kindness of strangers. But all the same, she hoped no one asked her how she liked it, either. The room was depressingly bare, with not even the sheet music wallpaper that she had admired in the hall below. The cooking smells and tobacco smoke had risen through the house to merge here, making her feel nauseous. There were two pegs and a single bed and nothing else except the clothes Ves had given her.

She unfolded the white shirt and dark pants, both threadbare, both miles too big for her. She knew she was expected to attend a dinner very soon and couldn't wear the pants without them pooling around her ankles. Nor could she wear her damp summer dress. It was soothing to focus on this one small problem, to keep out all the much larger ones, and so she sat on the bed and started methodically ripping the polyester dress at the seams. Then she tore it again, the cheap material parting pleasingly in her hands, before rolling it until she had a long purple rope to use as a belt.

So she was dressed. The huge pants were now drawn at her

waist, the shirtsleeves pushed past her elbows. She looked like an accountant on a pirate ship. The boots fit, sort of, although they were ugly as hell.

A slow drip of horror came over her, as though it were a leak trickling onto her head from the ceiling. Donna-Anne had a keen sense of decorum, and everything Margo wore had always been washed and pressed. Donna-Anne, who had cried when Margo dyed her hair. There was no situation where Donna-Anne would allow her to look like an accountant on a pirate ship, and this, for some reason, made her burst into tears.

She didn't cry for her own confusion or for the frigid cold or the strangers who seemed to be both helping her and stripping her for parts. She cried because she should be arriving in Dublin by now. And that by being here instead, she had activated a chain of events that would end in her mother realizing that yet another person she loved had vanished.

To pile another thing on Donna-Anne like that. She wouldn't be able to take it.

Her mother had been hugely in love. She knew that. Richard was almost an obsession for Donna-Anne, even before he had died, and his frequent business trips meant that there was always something they had to be on their best behavior for. The house must be kept nice, because Richard was going away. Or, he was on his way back. Or, Donna-Anne couldn't make a real decision without him, and so Margo must wait for him to return before asking if she could go on the school ski trip. Margo must be good before he left so he could miss her; she must be good while he was gone so that he might bring her back a present; and above all, she must be good on the days after he returned, because he was so tired.

The dinner bell rang. She heard an internal shift from within the house, the moving of several sets of feet. She doubted whether she could even handle going downstairs, and be confronted with yet more faces whose eyes lit with confusion every time she communicated the merest fact about herself. But she went anyway. There was so very little choice in the matter.

In the second-floor hallway, she passed a mirror. Margo looked so unlike herself that she thought she was careering into a stranger. She tried to pose so her clothes it at least looked like a choice, not a bundle of odds and ends, and in doing so reached her hand into the pants pocket.

The time difference between hemispheres meant that Richard often returned home at odd hours of the night. These memories all had a fond fuzz around them. Padding her cold feet across the hall floor, blue morning light streaming quietly in from the front door. Her tiny hands in the pockets of his coat and suit, searching searching searching for whatever had collected there during his time away. Stamps from the Japanese subway. Ticket stubs from Singapore. And sometimes presents: tiny tchotchkes, colorful bracelets.

Now, don't bring these into school, he would say. *These are for home only.*

As if she would bring anything into school. As if any of her real self belonged there.

Now the tchotchkes and ticket stubs were long gone, and Richard two years dead. She wondered if they really were as precious as all that, or whether he didn't want anyone at school to correctly identify it all as airport junk.

Now here she was. Knuckles deep in her own suit pockets, the material rough and hewn instead of the silk puckering of her father's. And just like when she was four years old, she pulled out a train map.

It was a flimsy bit of paper, printed on one side only. The stops all unfamiliar, the various colored train lines all crisscrossing on top of one another like veins in an arm. She looked for even one word that meant something to her, that at least gestured to a familiar location. *New Davia (6). Crader (6). Hess Point (4). Shandal (3). Khaise (2). Aldercarr (12). Yintiver (12).* She ignored the numbers, instead sounding out the letters, searching for familiarity.

Her eyes eventually zoomed out to see not just individual place names but the whole pattern of the map. First, that the map was split into four quarters. A compass symbol sat in the bottom left corner, indicating that these four quadrants represented North, South, East, and West. So New Davia, which she found in the top left quadrant, was clearly quite far north, and very far west. Immediately, her brain crowded with more panic, more questions. North of what? West of *where*? She searched again for an anchor point, a place she may not have been but had at least heard of. Belgium, for example, or Finland. Nothing. She tried to recall names of cities and towns, as far from her home as she could think of—Osaka! Kuala Lumpur! Delaware!—then scanned the map to see if they existed. Margo knew, even as she squeezed her eyes shut and thought very hard on the word *Milwaukee*, that she was playing a child's game. She could not manifest familiar words onto this train map, because she was not in a familiar place. She gave up and went downstairs.

As if to prove her point about the lack of anchors to her own reality, the first thing she saw on descending the stairs was an orange. It was sitting on the hall table, turning around and around over a small candle, like a pig on a spit. A hot citrus smell wafted over her. She was dazzled, confused, her brain turned inside out at the sight. She wondered why she had never seen anything like this before, then wondered if an orange *would* do this in her own world. She pushed at the leather skin, expecting resistance, and her finger fell through as though it were made of wax. Drops of something thick and oily dribbled out, and the orange smell became so strong it made her nauseous. She drew back, wondering if she had just broken an ordinary orange or a special, possibly priceless, one.

She wanted to flee the scene, to get away from the ruined orange, but didn't know where to turn. She was faced with four closed doors, and had a crippling bout of shyness about opening the wrong one. Margo put her hand on the kitchen door and listened to Vesna bark orders.

"Ani, are you out of your mind? Here, look. This is still cold. Did you not keep the lid on? And this—this has a skin on it. Are you trying to put me out of business? Are you? Here, bring this out—quick, *quick*, for god's sake."

Her voice was urgent, cold, and wildly different from the gentle hospitality Margo had just experienced.

". . . I will put you out on the *street*, Ani, if you show up here with dirty fingernails again. That is not a joke. Moon—why are you in here? Get out. No salesmen in the kitchen. Especially when I'm trying to get dinner on."

"I'm the exception. Remember?" Moon's voice was easy, softened out. "Hey—relax—"

"Are you drunk already?"

"I have a light buzz on, yes. Relax."

"*Relax?* Your little arrival means I'm behind on—"

"I'm sorry, would you rather I take my *arrival* elsewhere?"

Margo stood stock-still at the closed door. In the two years since her father had died, she had been made to feel like an inconvenience many times. By her school, by her mother, by her ex-friends. These people had just met her, yet her New Davia reputation was already boiling down to her Cork one. She was a problem that other people were always trying to sort out.

Margo heard the door to the dining room swing, and Vesna spoke again.

"Not in front of Ani," she snapped in a low whisper. Margo had to strain to hear now, her ear wedged to the door. "Let's talk about this after dinner."

Vesna seemed to be piling up after-dinner appointments. When did she sleep?

"I don't want Taiyo suddenly arriving in a blaze of glory."

"Taiyo doesn't need a blaze of glory."

"I just want us to get some terms straight. Now, preferably."

"Moon, you know I don't have the authority to release funds. I'm not the fucking treasurer."

"You have a vote, though. A strong vote."

"I swear to g—"

"Just tell me you'll do your best and I'll leave you alone."

"I'll do my best, OK? But you have to admit, it's hard to discern right now how valuable she actually is."

Margo's blood froze. He was selling her. This strange boy she had followed off the train, who she had trusted simply because he was roughly the same age as her and didn't have a pig mask melded to his face. He was trying to offload her on the owner of a boardinghouse, on a woman who also wasn't much older than herself. These were her peers, in a way, and they were selling her into servitude.

I'll depend on you to change your own sheets.

Was that the game, then? She was going to work for Vesna? For how long? Forever?

It dawned on Margo how trapped she truly was. She had destroyed her one outfit, her single tether to her old self. All she had in the world was a sodden denim jacket with two euros in the pocket that she had planned to buy a drink with. Her handbag and luggage she had left on the original train, the one she had so casually lost track of, despite never disembarking. Margo heard everyone file into the dining room. She could use this opportunity to make a dash for the door. The train station wasn't far away. She had a map. She could make it back there and run onto the next train, find another pig person, explain herself. If she explained her situation to enough people, she was sure that someone would help her. She would explain that she had fallen into a network of people who posed as rescuers and then sold their victims into domestic servitude. God, how stupid she was. It all felt like the plot of a tacky film where a man's daughter is stolen and he goes on a rampage to get her back. Only for this tacky film, there was no father, and no clear way back.

But the Pig had taken Moon's bribe. So maybe the whole system was corrupt. She had been alive long enough to know that most systems were. Potentially, she could escape this scenario and find herself tied up in a worse one.

She considered all this, staring bleakly at the front door—*run, run, now, NOW*—until suddenly Moon was right in front of her.

"There you are," he said. "I'm so sorry. I should have come to get you. Not very gentlemanly, I suppose."

Margo shrank back from him. The corridor was narrow, and she wanted to get as much space between their bodies as possible. What would he do if she bolted? Grab her? Run after her? She could stamp on his foot, knee him in the crotch—

"Your pants," he said. "Are they being held up by rope?" His hair was wet and combed back off his face, the color lighter. A little fair, a little gray.

She hooked her thumbs into her gaping waistband. "I tore off a strip of my dress."

"Practical." He smelled of soap and spices. He had a new, small cut on his chin, presumably from shaving. "We tend to be superstitious about real belts, anyway."

"Who is we?"

Of all the questions that needed answering that day, this felt most pressing of all. There had been a moment on the train when they had felt in sync with each other, and when Margo was sure Moon was on her side. That they were at the dawn of a tentative *we*. Now she didn't know. Vesna and Moon were the real *we*, and so, probably, was this Taiyo person. She was on the outside. She was the thing that the *we* interacted with, and that made her feel, among other things, extremely lonely.

"Listen. I understand how you feel."

"Do you?"

He let his eyes drift downward. Rattled some change in his pockets. She could see the sharp parting of his hair as he examined the floorboards. "I had a big family," he said at last. "And so the first time I was by myself, I found it very strange."

Had a big family. I found it *very strange*. She was not about to press harder on that revelation, though she filed it away.

"Right." She was already beginning to doubt the conversation she had overheard in the kitchen. Was he selling her or befriending her? "So what did you do?"

"A lot of things. Not all of it clever. Not all of it good." He took her hand then, tucking it into the crook of his arm.

A third option emerged: was he *flirting* with her?

"But I learned one important thing. Which is not to turn down a free meal."

Despite her strong suspicion that Moon had kidnapped her—was, in fact, still in the process of kidnapping her—she allowed herself to be taken to dinner.

SIX
MOON

If you are staying at Vesna's place, then you are probably here for the food. Or rather, the dinners. There are plenty of other boarding-houses in New Davia—cheaper ones, too—but the way Ves puts on dinner makes everyone feel like they're part of a grand old society, rather than stuck in a chilly world at the edge of the northwestern quarter.

There's four people already at the table, including Ves herself. Ani is the only native New Davian among us. If the authorities come asking, Ani's role is to help with the dinner service and mending clothes for the salesmen. And while she does technically do these things, her main hustle is sex, which Vesna allows her to do at the house in exchange for the laundry and waitressing stuff. No tattoo. Doesn't need one. Doesn't travel.

The salesmen are more or less familiar to me. Heck: thin, nervous, a figure eight tattoo carved on the back of his neck. A sign he was born in an eight-hour world. Domingo, four X's on his chin betraying his four-hour one. My moon tattoo is unique in that it betrays not just where I'm from, but who I am. The Lunati: a race of people who, before the travel ban, followed the full moon from world to world.

They are here to rest, to sell, to needle each other, to undercut, to bargain, to brag.

And they all stop when they see Margo.

"Everyone, this is Margo," I say. "Margo, everyone."

"Sit next to me, Margo," Vesna says with false cheer.

"Nice legs." Ani.

"How do." Domingo.

"We met in the hall." Heck.

"She's my apprentice," I tell them when I feel their scrutiny deepening. There aren't very many apprentices around. You've got to sponsor an apprentice, pay tax on them, teach them, ensure they pass their test, book their tattoo appointment, all of it. And for what? A helper for a couple of years, someone to raid your suitcase when you die. But it's the nearest thing most of us come to having a legacy, and new salesmen have to be made somehow.

But before anyone has a chance to pounce on this, a burst of cold air travels from the corridor to the dining room, slipping under the doorframe and curling its way around our ankles. A door slams quickly, rattling the plates. My stomach seizes and I think: *Here they are*. Already, the Pig has decided that my bribe wasn't enough, and he's ratted on me to the Northern Guard. Double prize money for him. I study the door to the kitchen and wonder if I could bolt through the house and make it far enough into the wilderness before they charge in here and shoot me in the head.

"Who's there?" Vesna calls.

"Only me, only me."

Etan's voice, smooth and unaccented. I'd know it anywhere. So distinctively indistinct. He comes in, shaking the snow off his overcoat, hanging it on a free hook. Etan's more delicate-looking than the rest of us, his skin dark, jawline tight, eyes unlined. He was born in the South—some poor merchant's kid, from what I understand—but because most salesmen are Northern, he has a kind of aristocratic air that he plays up for anyone who will let themselves be charmed by it. Which is quite a few people.

"You know I don't let latecomers into the dining room," Ves says sternly, finding him a plate anyway.

"You'll never believe this," he says, sitting down. "But I'm late for a reason."

"Well, everyone is always late for a *reason*," Vesna replies.

"A good reason, I mean. The Six is closed."

Everything stops.

"What do you mean, the Six is *closed*?"

Etan pauses before answering, taking a drag from his cigarette holder. Salesmen always smoke from pipes or holders. We touch enough poison every day to be fastidious about our hands.

"I mean: I was changing from the Eight to the Six in Arudé, and they told me I couldn't get on it, because the Six was closed. That there was a rupture between Crader and New Davia. So I had to get to New Davia the long way around, by doubling back and getting on the northeastern line." Etan's eyes flick around the table, taking in his company. His gaze settles on Margo. "And who might you be?"

I don't let her answer. "The train lines are never *closed*. I just came in on the Six an hour ago. How can it be closed?"

"Perhaps you cast some kind of Lunati spell on the thing." Then he puts his hands up. "Joking! Joking. All I know is that there was quite a bit of confusion, the Pigs going crazy, the NoGa checking everyone. Strange business. Very, *very* strange business."

Heck speaks up, nervous. "And are they going to . . . fix it?"

Etan tips his ash, enjoying the attention. "They seemed confident that they could, but that it might take a day. The tracks just fell from the air. Can you imagine that? Falling right out of the sky. They'll just have to hoist themselves up there and replace them, I suppose. Though who knows where they'll get that kind of technology in New Davia."

"I don't like this," Domingo says. "I don't like this at all."

Sometimes very stupid things can make you a good salesman, and for Domingo it's stating the fucking obvious. In all the years I've been doing this, the tracks have never been broken. And now here they are, broken, on the same day that Margo turns up. Vesna and I exchange a look, which Etan seems to catch but does not comment on.

"I don't like it one bit," Domingo goes on. "Not on top of everything else."

"Everything else?" Etan raises an eyebrow.

"The prices. Surely you've noticed? Everything's gone up."

The economics of the salesman profession is that basic resources—anything that helps with heat, light, growth, whatever—develop faster in the far North, but because it's difficult and dangerous to get there, you buy it cheap and you sell it at a markup. The margins are small, but enough to make a living. Now the prices of commodities are rising, and I'm not the only one who has felt the pinch. I'm relieved in a way. I had assumed that people were jacking up the prices because I was Lunati, but it seems by the three nodding faces that everyone's been getting the same treatment.

"*Everything,*" Etan agrees.

"Thickening agents for rice and grain, even," Heck says, tetchy.

"That gluey stuff that makes the meal bigger?" Etan quips. "I'm sure we'll see plenty of it tonight." He nods to Ves, who at that very moment has started ladling out a cheesy rice porridge that's laden with the stuff.

"Oh, shut up, Etan, go somewhere else if you don't like it."

"I'm fine with it. I love it, even."

"They say Semper is trying to edge freelance salesmen out of the game," Heck adds, rubbing his palms on his pant legs. "They want to get rid of us."

"I don't like talking about politics," Domingo adds nervously.

"He didn't say a word about politics."

"All the same. Talking about Semper like that." Domingo's eyes slide to the kitchen and parlor doors, as if a SoGa spy is about to burst in.

Ves serves food in the Davian way, which means everything is on the table from the beginning of the meal, but you work your way down to it, left to right. Cheese rice porridge at the far left. Gloopy with thickening agent, just as Etan said. Then bone broth in a tureen, then small slivers of boar, then citrus, then a kind of dried fibrous oat thing. Then a shot of slip, then more slip until we all pass out. It sounds opulent, until you realize it's the only meal of the day.

"Are we *ever* going to be introduced?" Etan says, finally putting his cigarette holder down to start eating.

"I'm his apprentice," Margo answers. And you've got to hand it to her: she doesn't sound nervous, or like she's lying. She sounds like she's always been here, always at this dinner or dinners like it.

"Your *apprentice*."

"Is that so strange?" I ask.

"A little, yes. They say these sorts of things always happen in threes. I wonder what will happen next."

"Are you a Lunati, too, then?" Ani asks Margo, her New Davian accent strong and bouncing. "Will you get a crescent tattoo, like Moon's? Such a shame. It will ruin your lovely face."

"Gosh, two Lunati salesmen," Heck says. "And a woman! Terribly, terribly rare."

Margo begins to interrupt, but I cut across her. "Margo isn't Lunati."

Officially speaking, there's supposed to be no trade until Vesna clears the table. It's just too dangerous to have open briefcases while people are still eating. Eventually, though, cutlery starts to drop and the smoking gets heavier.

I sell small-batch chemical compounds that are usually for boring household stuff: red salts to heat water, axiom to start fires, bronze-fruit to knit fabric. And the silver seeds, of course. Only Lunati people can make silver seeds, which is the only reason I could get a sales license in the first place.

Finally, the table is cleared. The briefcases are hung on wall hooks, each case fitted with hairpin legs that extend to the floor and turn it instantly into a shop.

"Who is going first?" Heck clearly wants to get it all out of the way. There's some murmurs, some hand waves, a general sense that he is free to have the floor. Heck is both the worst salesman I've ever met and the most widely traveled. Which is a real shame for him, and a real privilege for the rest of us. He will go anywhere. And generally, he'll bring back something insane that he has absolutely no idea how to sell. His general appearance and demeanor don't especially help: his long face, his reddish skin that always looks faintly scalded by hot water. His hands, always wet. You shake his hand and feel like you're getting a fistful of shrimp.

He plucks a small jar of something greenish and glowing and presents it to the table. He passes it around.

"Now this," he says. "This is *really* magnificent. Limits infant progression for six to eight weeks. With just a daub of it nightly on the forehead, your baby stays plump and gurgling, before the trials of toddlerhood take over."

"Your baby stays *plump and gurgling*," Ani repeats. "I think that's the most disgusting sentence I've ever heard."

"Stunting baby growth," I reply, inspecting the jar when it gets to me. "A new low, even for you. Where did you get this?"

Heck gives me a small, proud smile. "Somewhere very far away."

I know immediately I can buy a liter of this for half-nothing and resell it as antiaging cream. This has not occurred to Heck yet, and I don't think it will. But before I can come in with a lazy offer, Etan swoops in.

"Put me down for six jars," Etan says, writing in the small notebook that he keeps in his breast pocket. "Six jars at five gens each."

He rips the note out, folds it in half, and flicks it toward Heck.

"This is a very rare product, Etan," Heck says, already crestfallen.

"The baby goop?" Etan looks up from his notepad. "The ingredients are probably rare, yes, but easy to make in batches, and probably you can only make it in big batches, so I imagine you have a lot of it."

"Twenty a jar," Heck retorts. "That's all I can do."

Heck takes a swig of slip and slams the short, thick glass down heavily on the table. It might have been a convincing show of confidence if he did not hold on to the glass for quite so long, and if his hand did not have a slight tremor.

Etan whittles down Heck's price. When he's got it low enough, we all buy a few jars for ourselves. After that, I pitch my inventory. Everyone buys a little of something. I even buy some ivory medicine pots from Dom, which I will decant the baby goop into and sell at a markup.

In all this, I almost forget about Margo. Everyone else does, too. Sales is a profession mostly made up of lonely men, and very few of them know how to talk to women. But I see the color suddenly drain from her face, and that she has become deeply unmoored.

"Are you all right?" I ask in a low whisper.

Margo gets up from the table and walks, trancelike, toward a beam of sunlight trickling through a gap in the curtains. She pulls the curtains back. If everyone wasn't drunk already, I'm sure they would shout at her to get away from there. Vampires that we are.

But no—not vampires. Nothing nearly so glamorous. Just a bunch of rapidly aging young men with hard lifestyles and a preference for longer days.

"Margo," I whisper sharply. "Sit back down."

She's still, as if the morning light has turned her to stone. I get out of my chair, and with one hand on the small of her back, turn her toward me. The pupils of her eyes suddenly contract to the size of pinpricks, and I see that her first bout of skipshock is settling in.

"Come on," I say, nudging her again. "Let's go to the kitchen."

I can feel a scene coming. Feel it like a thunderstorm. Vesna sees it, too. Margo was not expecting the morning. Not this soon. Not by a long shot.

I get her to the kitchen just in time for her to vomit into the sink.

After Margo gets sick, we can't get her to sit down again. She wants to go outside. She wants to prove to herself that it really is morning, and not an illusion.

The wraparound porch surrounding Vesna's house sparkles in the dawn light. I can see Margo's thoughts so clearly, feel her brain burning with confusion. We have just finished dinner, and it was not a long dinner. How is it now morning? She arrived at Vesna's house in the evening. We ate not long after.

Yet here we are. Me, Vesna, and Margo, outside and breathing in the morning.

A fat little bird perches next to my hand on the porch banister, cold breath escaping his beak in tiny puffs. The sun is rising quickly now.

"What time is it, in your world?" I ask Margo.

"Four in the afternoon."

I've been in this situation often enough to understand. The nausea, the panic. The sense that a whole handful of sand from your life's personal hourglass has been thrown out the window. It's a big weight to shoulder, even when you know the system you're getting yourself into. Margo, on the other hand, knows nothing.

The New Davian day, Ves explains, is six hours long.

Six hours *ahead,* Margo corrects.

No, says Vesna. Six hours long.

"And how many hours in your . . . your native day?" Vesna asks.

"Twenty-four."

Vesna and I look at one another, not quite sure what to say.

"But there's twenty-four hours in a day everywhere. Because of the . . ." She tries to find an explanation. ". . . sun?"

"Respectfully, Margo, there are not twenty-four hours in everyone's day."

How can I tell Margo that she's the wealthiest person either of us have ever met? Without being terrible about it, that is.

"What? Is that bad?" Her eyes flit from me to Ves, not knowing whose truth can be relied on. "Am I in danger, or something?"

"No, no," says Ves. "It's just . . . interesting."

"It doesn't make any sense," she says. "How can you fit a whole day into six hours?"

We look at her with an expression that probably says: *with great difficulty.*

Margo reaches into her pocket—or, not *her* pocket, but the last salesman who wore the trousers—and pulls out a train map. She holds it out to me, her hands firm, indicating that I may look at it but not touch.

"New Davia, six," she says. "That's what? Six hours?"

"Right," I reply, relieved to have a prop. "So the farther north you go, the shorter the days are. The farther south you go, the longer the days are." I run my fingers up and down the line in the center of the map. "The farther west you go, the colder it is, the farther east you go, the warmer it is. We're in the Northwest."

"We're in the Northwest," Margo repeats back to me slowly. "So it's cold, and fast."

"Exactly."

"So *my* world . . . would be Southern, right?"

A silence. Ves and I both look at each other and think: *Duh*.

"When you say different worlds . . . do you mean different planets?"

"What?"

"Like space travel? Do you go into space?"

It feels like a strange, almost philosophical question for a person at this stage of a panic attack. "I mean . . . we're all in *a space*, aren't we?"

"No," she replies, clearly frustrated. "How can you be going to different worlds if you're not going into outer *space*?"

It's difficult, because I want to reassure Margo, but I also cannot follow the logic of her questions. I decide to talk to her as though she is a very clever child. "Because that's how it is. That's how it's always been. There are separate dimensions—worlds—that sit on top of one another. Each one is different in time and temperature. Ancient mathematicians plotted their locations and then ancient engineers connected them."

This is too much for Margo. It's as if her brain is a walled city and this last piece of information has crumbled the old stone. Her face screws up in agonized confusion, and she paces the porch trying to make sense of it.

"Look." I put my hand on her shoulder. "All I want is to get you home. Right? So does Ves. So just tell us everything you know about *your* world, and we'll work backward from there."

She stares at me a moment. Her pupils shrink a little, and her shoulders become rigid and square. Maybe this sounds dramatic, but I feel like I'm watching whatever slight bond we formed on the train become severed. A string, replaced with a wall.

"I need to lie down," she says. Then looks blankly at Vesna. "Do you mind if I go do that?"

"Go ahead," Ves says. Margo goes back inside. We listen to her footsteps fall away, and then Vesna starts pacing.

"She's spooked," I say.

"Of course she is," Vesna replies. "She doesn't have a clue where she is. So what do we think? She's from a sealed world?"

"A world that has been sealed for such a long time that it's not on a single map. She doesn't even know the *name* of it, I don't think. She's clearly from some kind of single-world system that has no relationship to anywhere else."

"But how did she get here?"

"Either she *did* something, or she *is* something. Something . . . innate, that makes her travel between worlds."

Vesna is silent for a moment. Then: "Taiyo needs to meet her."

"Do you really think he can use her?"

But she doesn't have time to answer, because just then, we hear the front door slam. Ves stops pacing.

"Ani," she calls. "What was that?"

But Ani must have already cleaned up and gone home, because Heck is the one who appears at the kitchen door.

"Are you ready to talk now, Vesna?"

"No," Ves says bluntly. "Where's Margo?"

"Margo . . ."

"The girl. Moon's girl."

"Oh. She left. Went out the front door," he says. Then Heck looks at me. "I suppose she changed her mind about being your apprentice."

seven

MARGO

In the clear morning light, Margo could see that the sign above the station—NWQ-6—RESTRICTED INTERWORLD TRADING ONLY—was the tallest point in the town, and so she ran toward it.

All I want is to get you home.

When she had *heard* him! She had heard him talk about prices and treasuries, about someone called Taiyo, and her supposed value.

Margo had come to accept that she was in a very different world. Time moved strangely. Days passed quickly. People were regularly maimed for reasons that were still largely mysterious to her. But it was this last bald-faced lie from Moon that finally pushed her out the door. These people—their values, their morals, their perspective on goodness—were not like hers. They were disparate on a soul level. Ves and Moon would walk her off a cliff if she let them.

So she ran. She ran like an escaped prisoner into the streets of New Davia. She had not been running long before she felt the thud of steps behind her, and knew without turning that Moon was within reach.

The street that had been completely dark just an hour earlier was now flowering with life. It was a market day. No matter where you are, regardless of the world, you can feel out a market day like good music. There was energy and cooking smells, awnings and hot plates. It would have been lovely, if the market wasn't so plainly obscuring her route to the train station. The makeshift streets made up of stalls and sellers were divided up by wooden gangway planks to keep the gray melting snow from soaking their feet. It bottlenecked the market, making it hard to move with any velocity. She bobbed and weaved, then heard a familiar voice behind her.

"Margo!"

She ducked and dodged. She felt people push up against her, heard them scold her and swear. She looked like a criminal. Someone on the run.

"Margo, come *on*, where are you even going?"

Margo fell upon a row of tents that sold old clothes, and spied a clear opening to the train station. She could make it. But so could Moon, annoyingly, because he was close to her now. He was lean and fast, and he knew these streets better than she did. Well, so? What was he going to do? He was a boy, sure. Stronger and bigger than her, yes, but not so much so that he could knock her out, or drag her back to Vesna's without attracting a lot of attention.

She came upon a wide bench of old boots, and an older woman who couldn't be deterred from showing them to her. The woman spoke a fast, spiky language that Margo didn't understand. It had a sharp, rasping quality, like French spoken backward and in a hurry. She saw Margo's face and switched quickly to a broken English.

"Good quality," the woman said. "Hardly worn. Look."

The woman shoved the boots in Margo's face, and suddenly she felt his hand on her arm. "Margo," Moon said again. "What the hell are you doing? These people will eat you alive."

"*These* people?" She gestured wildly to the boot seller. "Oh, *these* are the people I should be afraid of?"

Moon grabbed her roughly by the collar. The shirt was so big on her that she could still pull away, the white linen billowing out like a sail.

"What are you trying to do?" he asked.

"Get away from you."

"Yes, but why?"

"Who the hell is *Taiyo*?"

He paused. "Excuse me?"

"You're *lying*," she said, at last. "Because you told me that you want to help me get home, when I know for a fact that you're looking to palm me off. You're a salesman, right? Isn't that it? I'm just another thing in your briefcase."

"You're not . . ." He was agonized for a second, deeply insulted. "You're not a thing. In my briefcase."

"I'm not a thing at *all*."

"No. No, of course not." He covered his eyes with his fingers briefly, as if the sight of her was distracting from the subject. "It's just. Remember what I told you about being alone?"

I had a big family. I found it very strange.

"Yes."

"Well, something I learned in those early days is that there aren't many advantages to going through the world alone, because people are suspicious of anyone who's alone—alone and traveling, anyway—and so you learn to be a different person in different company."

"What? What does that have anything to do with—"

"So if you heard—or overheard—something that seemed unusual to you . . ."

She looked at the young salesman and thought, suddenly, of the moon itself. How the shadows on its surface could be mistaken for a face. But there was nothing there, nothing except water and rock.

"No," she said, tearing away from him. "I'm going."

And maybe she would have, if the whistle hadn't come straight after.

eight
MOON

Peep!

Every ear in the market pricks up. Weavers stop weaving. Stall owners stop yelling. Even the woman with the boots stops her constant stream of chatter about how new they are, and how good.

Peep!

A pause. And then.

. . . *peeeeeep!*

Then I see the uniforms. The Southern Guard uniform is orange, their black boots creaking on the wooden planks. No khaki, no navy, no olive green. They want you to know that they're coming. And they want you to shit yourself first.

It's not just about seeing the SoGa. It's about feeling them. It's realizing that everyone around you has gone ramrod straight. It's knowing, on an instinct level, that every person in the vicinity has an illegal side business. It is the high metallic scent of fear, the tingle in your nerve endings sent from your body to remind your brain that they are armed, while you, simpleton, merely have arms.

There are two main police forces that report to Semper. The Northern Guard, who are awful, but local. They can inflict terror, but they still have to live here. It tempers them, somewhat. Then there's the Southern Guard, who Semper trusts with the stuff they actually care about. Their secret police. Their private army. They almost never come north, unless there is something—or someone—highly specific that they are after.

Strange things, as Etan said, often happen in threes.

Here, at last, is the third thing.

Of course, I think it's about me. You live this kind of life long enough and you adopt a certain level of protective self-absorption. Every raised alarm, every abruptly closed door, and everyone with a gun is somehow about you. I bribed a Pig yesterday. I took a girl with no visa off the train.

Then I cast my mind back to last night, and Etan's late arrival at dinner. No. I'm being paranoid. They're here about the Six being closed. Of course they are. It's a huge deal for a train line to suddenly not be working, and it makes perfect sense that Semper would send the SoGa to see if it's some kind of guerrilla attack.

I take another look at Margo. The wild red hair, the ill-fitting men's clothes. Everything about Margo sticks out in New Davia, even her body language. She's all open and coltish, not drawn in and hidden away like most people.

If the SoGa are looking for answers in a marketplace, there's no doubt they'll find them in a Lunati salesman standing around with a strange girl.

"We need to move," I murmur.

I shuffle her toward a table filled with mismatched clothing.

"A scarf," I hiss at the girl sorting it. "For my wife."

She looks mutely around, blinking at the assortment. "I'm not sure if we . . ."

"*Anything* then."

She holds out a ream of blue fabric and I give her a coin. My eyes swivel in the direction of the SoGa, still making their way through the market. Browsers clear a spot as they barge through, and I can see them stopping at every stall. Two, three questions, abruptly spoken, and then they move on.

I throw the material in Margo's face. "Come on. Cover yourself."

Margo is immediately enraged, and throws it back at me. "You're not my savior, Moon," she hisses, turning her body toward the SoGa.

Oh god.

"Margo." I pull the material around her head. "I accept that I'm probably not your savior. We can talk about that later. But *these* guys aren't going to help you. In fact, they have the capacity to make things a lot worse."

The SoGa have stopped at a musician, playing his guitar at the end of the gangway. Three of them crowd around him, looking under his blanket, into his hat full of loose coins. It's illegal to make money this way, technically, though the NoGa wouldn't enforce it. They are in the mood to punish someone, and perhaps today they will choose him.

"How could it be *worse*?" She genuinely doesn't believe me. She's still pulling toward them, training her eye at the trim orange uniforms. I realize that Margo is a person for whom authority, armed authority, is reassuring. "So who are they? The police?"

I'm at a loss for words, because *police* is such a mild term for what these people are. Her expression curdles. "Well, no wonder *you* don't want me to talk to them."

She still thinks I was going to sell her into servitude or whatever it was. "Please, Margo—" My eyes slide over to the clutch of orange uniforms, fifty paces away. The SoGa are getting irritated by the musician now, who is still clutching his guitar.

"I won't rat you out, don't worry." She wrenches herself away from me. "Look—thank you for your help, or whatever it was. Maybe you thought you were helping, I don't know. But I'm going to talk to those men and start finding a way home. OK?"

Margo takes one last look at me, and I think—*Let her go.* For a few hours you thought this girl might be your ticket out of sales, but now it's looking like she might be more trouble than she's worth. If the SoGa want her, and she wants them, then intervening will only kill you faster. Margo moves away from me and I give up. Good riddance.

But just as I'm making my peace with this, right as I'm ready to let her go forever, the musician must say something that the SoGa don't like. There's a flash of orange sleeve as one of them raises his rifle and quickly slams the butt of it into the musician's face. There is the hideous squish of flesh opening, like meat hitting a counter from a great height. A hollow *clang* as the guitar falls to the ground. Margo's small figure, now only mere steps from the scene, stops moving.

I watch her as she wraps the scarf slowly over her head. Margo turns back around, and our eyes meet through the chaos. The line of threats in Margo's head reshuffles, and she decides that perhaps I am not the most dangerous person here.

I keep my gaze still, moving my chin slightly, beckoning her back. There's no victory in it. I'm not smug that I've been proven right, or that the SoGa decided to be savages at exactly the right time. To tell you the truth, it feels awful. Like I'm killing a child's last faith in the fairness of the world.

But Margo changing her mind doesn't mean that we're safe. The second she's back at my side, head covered, I realize that another band of orange uniforms is coming up the opposite gangway. We're trapped. They're talking to everyone. Which means, sooner or later, they will talk to us, too.

"What do we do?" she whispers fiercely. I look down at her face. Flecks of the musician's blood are on her chin. That's how close she was.

"*Fengari.*"

The voice is soft and comes from nowhere. Or rather, from below. I look down and see the white shine of an eye, looking up from a hole in the wood. Taiyo.

"The chandlery," he says. "Under the incense urn."

The chandlery is a gloomy little shop that is three doors away from us, and the moment we step inside I realize that I can't simply walk into a business and ask to see their incense urn. But it doesn't appear to be necessary. The old man behind the counter changes his expression the moment he sees us, his body language flipping from attentive shopkeeper to a keeper of secrets.

"This way," he says, ushering Margo and me through rows and rows of candles toward a rich, fragrant alcove at the back of the store. And sure enough, there is an incense urn.

Under the urn is a rug. And under the rug is a board. And under the board is a hole. And in the hole, there is nothing.

"Get in," the old man says. "Now."

I travel too much to ever get a good grasp on who, in any given community, is a member of PACT. I have sold to this man dozens of times over the years, and not once has he ever alluded to being in PACT. Or having an escape hatch.

There's no time to judge the height of the drop. All we can do is plunge into the blackness. Margo's scarf has now fallen so far forward that she can barely see, and it's probably better that way. I land hard on my feet, my knees aching with the impact. Margo, clearly, is feeling it, too.

"Are you all right?"

"Yes," she replies, pulling the scarf off her face. It doesn't do much good. The hole is dark, and getting darker as the old man re-covers the opening with his rug and incense urn. "I mean, I can't see, but other than that."

"I can fix that."

The Wash is still a few days away, and I'm down to my last two silver seeds, jangling in my pocket like loose teeth.

"Have you got any jewelry?" I ask. "Or keys?" You can stick seeds to metal, if you wet them down a bit.

Margo lifts her wrist. "Only this," she says, offering the watch.

It's so dark that I can't quite examine it, but the weight tells me everything I need to know. It's solid silver. How many seeds would you have to smelt down to make a thing like this, so chunky and heavy? I wet my fingertips with the edge of my tongue, then roll the seeds between them until they're warm and can stick to the watch links. We're toward the end of the month, so the seeds are old, and need waking up a little.

The seeds up the shine from her watch. Bluish light darts around us, the PACT tunnels revealing themselves to us in every direction.

nine

MARGO

So many new and frightening things had now happened to Margo that it was becoming gradually easier to accept that they would keep happening and she would just have to think on her feet and deal with it. She was terrified, but she also felt strangely weightless. It was like losing all your possessions in a fire. She was starting from a place of absolute zero. She understood nothing, recognized nothing.

Which is why it was so alarming that she knew the silver seeds.

"I know these," she said, touching the bluish teardrops of light. "I know them from somewhere."

It was like the memory of a dream, or a TV show watched as a child while half asleep. Even the weight of them against her finger, strangely heavy for their smallness, felt like a surprise she had experienced somewhere before. Had her father shown them to her? She associated them with him, and she didn't know why. Perhaps it was just the presence of small precious things that did that.

"Silver seeds," Moon explained. "A Lunati specialty. Do you mind if I wear it, just while we're going through the tunnel?" He let her fasten the watch onto him. In doing so, she felt the underside of his wrist, the skin pale and soft as an eyelid. "Just as, you know, a torch. I won't—Are you OK?"

"Yeah." She shook her head but, in the shaking, felt a great wooziness come over her. The spray of blood, the heavy sound of the musician dropping his guitar. He was too covered by bodies for her to see what happened, but she knew it wasn't good. Suddenly, her knees felt weak and porous. She felt herself sway. It was as though the world were spinning in one direction and she was facing another.

"Sit down," he said, guiding her to the dirt floor.

"What is happening to . . ."

"You're having a little skipshock, that's all. It will pass. You've come from a place with twenty-four hours in the day, right? Now you have a quarter of that. Your body is confused by the days passing in a different way. The light is changing too rapidly for your brain to keep up with it. Your body is aging at four times the speed. I promise you, you won't feel it after a few days."

A few *days*? People kept speaking about her time here as though it was going to be this protracted era, a whole section of life, and not just a stopover. She couldn't stay here. She would die.

"You're going to be fine."

She looked up at him from her spot on the floor, dizzy and unconvinced. He began to pace the narrow opening, her watch on his wrist, cascading light like a disco ball.

"How? How will I be fine, Moon? Because nothing about this feels *fine* at all."

Margo suddenly felt aware of another presence in the room. The silver light on Moon's wrist bounced off the walls and onto a boy. A boy who was remarkable for his lack of interference: no tattoos, no scars, no ironwork. He had arrived silently, and in shadow, his hands navigating the marks and indentations on the tunnel walls. He was dark-skinned, the same as Ani, and presumably New Davian also.

"Taiyo," Moon said flatly. "You got here quick."

"This is Margo?"

"This is Margo," Moon replied. Then, seeming to remember

that Margo thought Taiyo was going to sell her into servitude: "But she's made it very clear that she's not a 'thing' in my briefcase, so I'll let her speak for herself."

Taiyo was mapping the room slowly, keeping his hands on some invisible indentations on the wall, his gaze fixed on Margo. He had a wild thatch of black hair, instantly putting Margo in mind of Donna-Anne, who would say Taiyo looked as though he'd been dragged through a hedge backward.

"Oh, she's definitely not a *thing*."

He loomed closer to her. If she had known he was this . . . tall, maybe she wouldn't have run into the market with quite so much energy.

"Are you sure you don't want to be a thing? Things have purpose. Things don't die. You ever hear of a brick that died?" He spoke English, although Margo could tell it was not his first language. "There's a certain timelessness to things."

Margo got the sense he was taking the piss out of her.

"*You* be a thing, then."

Taiyo smiled, as if babysitting a younger cousin. He fixed his eyes back on Moon.

"Did you hear anything else?" Moon asked.

"Not much. Just a girl. They're looking for a girl with a lot of red hair, which presumably they got from the Pig. He didn't say she was with a Lunati though, so you got lucky today, Mo." He looked Margo up and down. "A redhead seems to me a far more dangerous thing to be than a thing. Sure you don't want to revise your answer?"

"I'm sure," she replied, though faintly. New wafts of terror were settling over her. These guards, who had attacked an ordinary street musician with no provocation, were on the hunt for her. Why?

Because she didn't have a visa? It was ridiculous. She hadn't done anything wrong.

Dim memories of her own world came back to her. Stories about people being stuck at borders, of dying in transit, of kids in cages. For the first time since she arrived in New Davia, she realized that her existence there would not be treated as an honest mistake. That she was, in effect, an illegal immigrant.

"Now considering that Margo is a wanted criminal, don't you think we should be on the move?"

"After you," Moon said, gesturing to a dark opening that led to a narrow passageway. "I won't have potency in these seeds for very long. We better make use of the light."

They began moving through the tunnels, all of which smelled like they were once used to store food. It was a moldering stench, like blue bread, or potatoes left too long in a cupboard. Taiyo led the way, the space only big enough to allow them to travel single file.

There were spots where they had to fall silent, or stop moving, or crouch low, and Margo would hear the sound of boots thudding overhead. Low tones of interrogation, followed by hurried assurances. The occasional clatter of furniture. The thick walls of the underground tunnels muffled their speech, but words like *where* and *please* and *no* sometimes melted through. She listened to invisible forces searching for her, horrified that anyone could care this much.

The tunnels became steeper, as did the sensation that they were walking farther underground. Her calves grew heavy in the constant downward momentum. The voices and footsteps faded away. It was silent as a tomb when she finally asked where they were going.

"Through the city, down to the sea," Taiyo replied cheerfully. "They're patrolling the harbor, making sure you don't stow away on a fishing boat or what have you. But we'll keep clear of all that."

Why was she so important to these people? If she was breaking the law by being there, that was one thing. But shutting down the market? Patrolling the *harbors*?

Frankly, did no one have anything better to do?

Every time she opened her mouth to demand clarification, she heard the light stomp of human activity, and became too terrified to speak again.

Some of the tunnels led nowhere. Some led to open pits. Moon shone the watch into them, and Taiyo peered into a deep abyss. "Bodies," he said. "Sometimes they fall in."

They came to a wood panel, glowing rose from the warm light behind it. Taiyo knocked twice sharply and waited. No sound returned. He pushed against the panel, and she heard a heavy sound of old hinges. It was, finally, a room. A room in someone's house.

There were shelves lined with jars, holding some kind of pickled vegetable, and sacks of animal feed on the floor. Margo turned around to realize that the door they had come through was, in fact, a pickle shelf. A pickle shelf that Taiyo was now securing back in its place.

Taiyo busied himself, trying to find the next trick shelf that would lead to another endless tunnel. She looked to Moon for reassurance, before remembering that she had spent the morning trying to flee him. So why did it matter how he registered things, how he reacted? Why did she keep glancing at him like he was her compass? *You didn't trust him ten minutes ago,* she reminded herself. *So don't start now.*

"Onward," Taiyo said, before carefully leaning his body weight against another wall, which swung open. More tunnels, more basements. More pickles and pickling equipment. Hay. Animal food. As they were moving between basements—Moon leading the way with the watch light, Margo in the middle, then Taiyo—Moon lost his footing. The salesman fell backward all of a sudden. Margo shot out her arms and caught him. He was stiff all over, his spine rigid. His eyes rolled back into his skull, their whites shockingly bright in the tunnel's dim surroundings.

For a brief, terrible second, she thought he was dead.

"Damn it, Moon, what's going on?" Taiyo called irritably from behind her.

Moon's eyes focused again. He looked up at her, his face upside down. She was holding him under both armpits, her wrists dragging.

"Tripped," he said, and quickly got to his feet. "Thanks, Margo. Sorry about that."

They kept moving, the event unremarked on, to the point where Margo felt she had dreamed it. Moon had passed out. This was not an accidental fall. This was a complete loss of consciousness. He carried on, his pace even more hurried than before, his shoulders stiff and determined. She remembered the night before, when she'd briefly knocked into him on the way to Vesna's. How scared he had been. For all his confident patter and quiet charm, Moon was hiding something. Something that made him both susceptible to, and afraid of, falling.

They went through a dozen more basements. In one there was a young woman not much older than Margo. She was peeling potatoes.

"Ela," Taiyo said with a nod. "How are you settling in?"

The woman didn't seem very bothered by a gang of people walking through her basement. She pushed a mass of curly brown hair off her face and shrugged. "I haven't been outside in five weeks, Taiyo. How do *you* think I'm settling in?"

And on they went, to the next house, the next tunnel, the next basement.

"Is anyone going to explain who that was?" Margo asked. Was this the plan for her? Would she also be peeling potatoes in a locked basement?

"Sure," Taiyo said brightly. "That's Ela." And that was it.

Eventually, they stopped at another storeroom to rest. They sat cross-legged on the floor, and Taiyo pulled pears from his pocket. Margo could smell salt in the air. The floor underneath her was damp.

"Next stop is the sea," Taiyo said. "And we're out in the air again."

"How's the skipshock holding up?" Moon asked.

"I need to know what's going on," she said, not answering the question. The best way, it seemed, to get over skipshock was to keep walking and talking and not focusing on the rollicking evil at work inside you. "Why am I so important to these people? Why are they tearing this place apart trying to find me? Why are they guarding the *harbors*, for god's sake?"

Taiyo and Moon looked at each other as if cordially waiting for the other to go first. Then the silence went a beat too long, and she realized there was no politeness in it at all. This was the glance of two people who weren't particularly intimate but were still attempting telepathic communication.

"Just tell me," she said, irritated now. "I'm stuck in here with you two, and there's people looking to either arrest or kill me, so it's not as if I'm going to run again."

"Here's the thing, Margo," Moon started. "I know as far as you're concerned, you're just a girl"—he corrected himself—"woman"—then again—"*person* who has found themselves in a weird situation, and you just want to go home. And I *want* you to go home."

Margo opened her mouth to speak, because she already knew this wasn't true, but he corrected himself again.

"But the facts of the case are this: you're important. I know you don't want to be, but you are."

"How? How on earth could I be important?" She gestured at them wildly, showing her two open palms, demonstrating the nothingness her presence brought to any given situation.

"Because we're at the beginning of a war," Taiyo said grimly. "And whoever gets you, wins."

ten
MOON

Here's something you need to know about Taiyo. Taiyo will say anything, literally anything, to get what he wants.

"Whoever gets *me*?" Margo repeats, sounding as though she has received a script for the wrong play. "I don't understand. How could I be any use? I don't even know where I am."

"If you want to understand why you matter, you first have to understand the nature of the war."

It's not just the revolutionary stuff that puts me off Taiyo. It's Taiyo's inherent drama that I can't stand. The way he adopts these little characters to put on and take off as he sees fit. There's Taiyo the Revolutionary, Taiyo the Smuggler, Taiyo the Local Kid, Taiyo the Lover. They all feel as fake as the other, all rehearsed scripts that you can feel him dreaming up even as he's talking to you. You never know who the real Taiyo is, and that unnerves me.

Thankfully, it seems to unnerve Margo, too. She looks to me, terrified.

"All right, Taiyo, less of that," I say, though he's already stepping toward her with a face full of destiny. "Let me try to explain in a more . . . uh, normal way. Let's say the average human lives for twenty thousand days. Right? And it doesn't matter if that day is six hours long or twenty or fifty, a day is a day."

"What do you mean a day is . . . still a day?" Margo says, puzzling it out. "I mean, I'm seventeen in six days. Six . . . of my days, I guess."

I'm not sure what to say to her. I let her do the math by herself.

"Five days," she whispers, her voice laced with terror. "Five of *your* days?"

"Five days is five days. A day is a day is a day. How long your life is depends a lot on where you are."

Taiyo fizzes silently next to me, his excitement bristling like static. He can really believe it now, that a girl has fallen from the sky to save him. Margo doesn't have to do or say anything to prove she's special. The fact that she *doesn't* know any of this is what makes her unique.

I explain it all. How, in the South, families and fortunes are allowed to grow big and bloated. Fruits and vegetables grow better with dozens of hours of sunlight a day. Technically they grow here, too, but it's different. An orange doesn't even have time to develop individual segments, instead filling its skin with oily mush. Industry and fruit and power and money and just about *everything* can thrive better when there's more time to do it.

"Why wouldn't you just live somewhere like that?" Margo asks. "With more hours?"

"Good question," Taiyo says to me, as though this were some kind of two-person show that we do all the time. Me, the straight man. Him, the clown. "Why wouldn't we live somewhere like that?"

"Well. For a long time, you technically could," I answer. "The South was always expensive, but you could save up money and go there, or you could find a job as a servant or something. Everybody could go everywhere. That train you came in on? Fifteen years ago, it would have been standing room only."

Talking about time and the wasting of it makes Taiyo anxious.

We get up to move again, plodding through New Davia's underside, assaulting Margo with the facts of our existence.

"And where do you think they got their labor force from?" Taiyo says, keeping one palm on the left-hand side of the tunnel. "Here. The North. They got their coal here, too. Fuel generates quicker where the days are shorter. But they abused their servants—chattel, really—then they imprisoned the miners, the coal miners, for protesting. So we revolted."

We? "We" were children, Taiyo and I. But if he wants to take credit on behalf of all revolutionaries, then who am I to stop him?

"We'll skip the various war crimes for now," I add. We need to get through this potted history, and I'm not quite in the mood to discuss how the Lunati fared in all of this, which was not well. "But Semper—which is one of the Southernmost worlds—got sick of it, got sick of Northerners demanding to be treated like human beings. So they swooped in and decided, you know what would make this better? If we had one streamlined government, controlling everything. No more local worlds doing their own thing."

"And then what happened?" Margo asks, rapt.

And then what happened? Well, what didn't happen. A faceless dictatorship that smothered us almost overnight. They shut the sacred caravan trails that allowed the Lunati people to move. A whole culture—my culture—was forced underground. They banned all travel, they cut trade. Thousands of Northerners died of famine or preventable illness, simply because their economies had been relying on imported goods and medicine. Thousands more killed for insubordination. Work camps in worlds where the days passed in minutes. Red-blooded revolutionaries who became withered overnight.

And now: this. This half-life of poverty that dozens of worlds attempt to gracelessly survive in. A police state of Northern Guards and Southern Guards and maimed citizens who are mistaken for pigs.

We describe all this to her, Taiyo and myself taking turns, neither of us remembering key events or dates or even good reasons for why any of it happened, except that it did, and we were kids for the worst parts of it. Kids in different contexts, and living through different time speeds, but children regardless. And as we're explaining it, I look at Taiyo and realize that we are a kind of case study, but for what I'm not sure. For people who are doomed to grow up in interesting times, I suppose. Him, a revolutionary. Me, a guy who sells powders from a briefcase. Both ultimately out for ourselves. Neither strong enough to rest your whole weight against.

It's hard to know how much of this Margo is really processing. She squints at us in concentration, gasps in horror, but ultimately her face says: *Yes, but what does any of this have to do with me?*

"So, now, unless you're a salesman, or have some kind of special visa, you can't travel. And if you can't travel, you can't mobilize. If the North can't communicate, we can't ever unite against the South. That's where PACT comes in," Taiyo says, sounding a little too proud of himself. "The People's Action for Common Travel. We steal food shipments, munitions, ammo. We built these tunnels. We smuggle revolutionaries from one world to another. Ela back there? Her family owned a printing press in Crader. Ela and her husband were printing and distributing anti-Semper pamphlets there. Not even *anti*-Semper. "Semper-critical" is probably more accurate. Anyway, they assassinated her husband. They were coming for her next. We got her out."

It's been unclear how much Margo has been taking in as we explain the various problems of our lives. But this information, for some reason, hits like a ton of bricks. "That girl back there?"

Taiyo nods, taking Margo's hand briefly to skip over a narrow pit beneath us.

"But she's . . ." Margo is astonished. "She was *my age*."

She doesn't seem to know where to begin with this: the assassination of Ela's husband, or the fact that she *had a husband*. Margo almost loses her footing with the shock of it.

"So you see, Margo, life is quite tough for us," Taiyo goes on. "But here you are. No visa. From a world nobody has heard of. Granted, no one knows why or how yet. But you have bounced between worlds undetected. You've found some kind of travel corridor, and Semper is panicked. And that—that's what I mean by you being a weapon. If we can learn how you did it, we could do it, too."

We're near the exit now, the sea's breath coming cold through the final tunnel door. The passageway finally widens enough for us to all stand beside one another.

"I know you think I'm useful," Margo says, her hair blowing lightly off her face as the breeze whistles through the final door. "But I don't know what happened on the train. Please believe me. I don't know why I'm here, or how I got here."

"I know, Margo. I know," Taiyo says, heaving his shoulder into the door, his weight against the wind. "But I just think you could help. That's all."

By the time we emerge, the sky is streaked with peach, the cool bleeding sun sinking swiftly under the water. The town slopes toward the ocean, the series of interconnected basements hidden in a swamp of smoking chimneys and patchwork roofs. We're standing on an ugly strip of beach, the tide coming in, the sea beginning its slow hug on the land.

Margo looks back at me, her thrill at seeing the ocean dimming instantly.

"It's evening," she says.

I nod.

"A whole day went by while we were in those tunnels."

I nod again.

She doesn't cry this time. She moves away from us, scarf tight around her. We watch her walk the cold beach, staring out at the horizon. Taiyo smokes a black-market cigarette, the packet lettering in a language I can't understand. He offers me one, and I shake my head.

A mile or so down, the harbor is still busy, cratemen from the train loading their goods onto ships that will sail to the rest of New Davia. Margo watches them, peering for the people who are apparently waiting to snatch her off the shore. We watch her in silence until she comes to a wet stone wall. Margo clutches the stone, wind whipping against her face, and leans back. For a second it looks like she's appreciating the sea air, but then she crunches forward, waist folded over the edge.

"Is she gonna jump?" Taiyo says, his eyebrows raised. "Is she trying to drown herself?"

The depth wouldn't kill her, but the cold might. We rush forward, getting ready to save this girl who would rather die than live like we do.

But then we stop, and realize that Margo is not about to drown herself. She's vomiting. She's upchucking her guts into the Davian sea. I'm impressed that she has anything left, after this morning. We watch her for a moment, both of us laughing in an empty sort of way.

"Listen," I say, a strange pang of guilt coming over me. I am, after all, the person who took her off the train. "She's a human being. She's a kid, still. Just get her home. Get the intel you need or whatever, but send the kid home."

All we can see of Margo is her legs. She's completely bent at the waist, hurling into the sea.

"I'll try," Taiyo says.

"That sounds dazzlingly noncommittal."

"Well, it's not up to me to commit. I'm a foot soldier. I don't get to see the big picture. If PACT decides she's too useful to let go, then who the hell am I to argue?"

"You've been talking an awfully big game for someone who claims to have no control and no idea."

"I didn't *say* that."

Taiyo juts his chin into the air, his handsome face curling like a bulldog's.

"Listen, Mo. I need to tell you something. Something that is strictly PACT intel. Something you can't repeat."

Ah, Taiyo the Spy. This is a new one.

"Sure. Hit me."

He takes a long drag of his cigarette. This is more of it: making a big production of steeling himself to deliver bad news.

"Something bad is coming."

A big wave crashes against the sea wall, the spray hitting Margo. She straightens herself, one hand on the gray brick, woozy on her feet.

"That's it?"

"I'm serious. People think these travel restrictions are as bad as it's ever going to get, just because it's been this way for so long. But it's about to get much worse."

"Uh-huh."

"Come on, Mo, don't look at me like that. Listen. You've noticed it, haven't you? Things getting more expensive?"

I blink at him. "Clearly you've been talking to Vesna. Those salesmen dinners are supposed to be confidential, too, you know."

"This isn't anything to do with Vesna." He scowls. "Listen. Let me put this in a way you'll understand." Condescending Taiyo now. "Things are getting more expensive in the North, right?"

"Right."

"Because they've got SoGa up there, buying up resources to start a war. A real one. Not a vague 'war of ideas' sort of war."

"*What?*"

Taiyo takes a weathered notebook out of his breast pocket, flipping it open. "Three hundred tons of rice. Two hundred tons of red salts. Four hundred tons of axiom," he reads, then closes it. "Food, energy, ammunition. They're buying it in the far North, and they're making confidentiality agreements with their sellers. Basic supply and demand means that it all trickles down until you're paying three times as much for axiom and you have no clue why. Well, soon you'll know why. When there are soldiers marching into New Davia and putting a rifle to Vesna's skull."

Is any of this true? Is any of it serious? PACT is notoriously a means-justify-the-end kind of organization. Which I don't hold against them, unless it specifically pertains to Taiyo lying to my face.

"And why, exactly, would they start a war? What's in it for them? Why now, after all this time?"

Taiyo shrugs. "Because PACT is too powerful. Because the North is getting strong. Because they're sick of itty-bitty loose-endy little salesmen when they could have a complete monopoly themselves. You pick. I don't know."

I don't even have the energy to be offended by *itty-bitty loose-*

endy. What he's saying is technically plausible, but it could also be a classic case of putting two and two together and making five.

"I think I will take that cigarette, Taiyo."

I take a black-market cigarette, washing my hands in the ocean first.

"So what do you want?" I ask. "Say this theory is real. What's a kid like Margo gonna do about it?"

Taiyo shrugs, briefly abandoning his many characters. "I don't know. All I know is, she's special. She needs to get to Alder."

I choke on the smoke from my horrible cigarette. *"Alder?"*

Aldercarr is a very old, very busy world with an enormous market city. Copper mines in the mountains. It's one of the few Northern worlds with real, free-moving money in it, and where that money hasn't been completely hoarded by the South. They have a royal family—useless, all of them—but they have just enough Southern cousins that the South leaves them alone. Four different train lines meet in Alder. It's a junction of sorts, a place where many people change lines to go to different worlds.

"AlderPACT is the most powerful chapter in the North. They need Margo. I'm headed there anyway—you just have to convince her to come with me."

The cigarette tastes like dirt and amber. I forgot that I hate cigarettes. I keep hold of it anyway and watch Margo through the gap in my wedged fingers, her face right in the crosshairs.

"How are you headed there?" I retort. "You don't have a tattoo. Or a license."

"You think I can get people out of worlds but I can't get myself into them?"

He shakes his head like a pony shaking off a bridle, and I see that he is currently reading the script for Taiyo the Smuggler.

"You have to convince her," he says. "Please? Just get her to trust PACT, because she sure as shit doesn't trust me."

She doesn't trust me, either, but he doesn't know that.

"Why should she trust PACT? Why should she care about any of this?"

"Just because *you* don't trust us, doesn't mean she shouldn't."

"Uh-huh."

Taiyo takes a step back, rubs at his hair, and attempts to change tack with me.

"Listen. Vesna told me about what happened with PACT when you were a kid. The fire and everything. I get it. But that was—"

I remind myself not to tell Vesna anything ever again.

"That's neither here nor there, Taiyo. Just tell me this: Why should I help you?"

"Because you don't want a war."

"Right," I say, my tone flat.

He sighs. "And because we'll pay you."

Our voices drop low, our chins tucked, careful that the wind not take our thoughts to Margo.

"How much?"

Taiyo shrugs. "I don't look after the money."

What kind of person would take money for manipulating and trafficking a lost schoolgirl? And not just any lost schoolgirl, but Margo?

"Five hundred," I say.

This makes him break character, and I'm glad. Taiyo stands back and looks at me, shock on his face. "Are you *high*?"

"Two hundred and fifty finder's fee. That's what I'd expect anyway. She wouldn't be here if it wasn't for me, right? And two hundred and fifty for getting her to Alder."

The incident in the tunnel was too close a call. My skipshock has already advanced to the point where I've passed out twice in a two-day period. That's not good. It's probably too late to reverse the damage of this lifestyle, but I have the tiniest window of opportunity to prevent it from getting worse. I can buy my way out.

"Three hundred," Taiyo counters.

"Five."

"Three fifty."

"I said *five*."

A shop in New Davia. Clean windows and fair prices. They don't mind so much about the Lunati around here. They might let me get on with things.

"You do realize this is a revolution you're stealing from?"

"I'm not stealing from anyone. I'm charging a business a sensible going rate. I should be charging expenses, too, for bribing that Pig. I could lose my license. And now that the SoGa are involved, I could lose my life. I know *you* don't have the money, but PACT absolutely does. You have donors. There's money in the kitty for stuff like this."

Taiyo sticks his hands in his pockets, sulking now at the thought of the conversations he'll have to have to release this kind of money. "We don't have a pricing list for random girls found on the train."

"Well, you should. That way you wouldn't be subject to the whims of people like me."

He ponders. "I could give you nothing. She's stranded here anyway. It's only a matter of time before she comes around on her own."

Margo starts slowly walking back toward us. We both drop our voices to a whisper.

"She bolted this morning. Ves told you that, right? She could bolt again."

He blanches, peers at her. Her pale face looking a little harder, a little older than it did this morning. I'm running out of time to haggle.

"Four hundred and twenty-five, final offer."

"Deal," he says. "But one condition. You're in now. None of this fence-straddling stuff. I know you're looking to get out of the profession and I respect that, Moon, but while you have a working travel visa, we need to be able to use you. I can't budge on that."

I think about it. "I will work for PACT. But for Margo stuff only. I'm not going to smuggle knives in my pant legs, or whatever it is you have in mind."

"Fine. Get her to Alder, Mo. Drop her off there with PACT, and the money is yours."

"You willing to sign on that?"

"I'll sign and I'll swear on Aante," he says, holding up his hand.

I clamp my cigarette in my teeth as I take my notebook out and write the sales agreement. MARGO TO ALDER, it reads. 425 ON DELIVERY. Taiyo signs it. I rip it out and give it to him, leaving the carbon copy in my records.

She looks at both of us, her hands deep in the pockets of the men's pants she inherited from the attic bedroom Vesna put her in. Her face is pinched, tired. Yesterday I thought this face was going to make me rich. Now it's beginning to stand for a whole lot more. Margo, the girl I met while we all teetered unknowingly on the brink of war.

"You didn't see that, did you?" she asks, her voice a little bashful. "Me getting sick?" The wind runs through her, and a faint, hot stink of stomach acid wafts over.

Taiyo claps an arm around her shoulder, giving her a squeeze. "No one saw a thing."

Margo points to the sea, and to the blurry line of hills beyond it. "What's out there?"

"More shit," Taiyo grumbles. "Shit on shit."

"New Davian shit? It's all New Davia?"

"Hick town, then miles of snow, then more hicks." He takes his cigarettes from his breast pocket. "Do you want one of these? For the smell?"

She takes one, her hands trembling. Taiyo lights it. And there we are. A salesman, a smuggler, and a schoolgirl, standing at the edge of history, our backs to the sea.

eleven
MARGO

"Much as I'd love to stay," Taiyo said, walking away from them, "I've gotta go see a man about a box."

"A box?"

"Yeah. One about *this* high." Taiyo gestured to the top of his own head, where his jagged black hair met his palm. "And *this* wide." He opened his hands at his sides.

"So, a coffin," said Moon.

"You pick up fast, Fengari."

"Why a coffin?" Margo asked.

"Gotta leave this world somehow. Your boy can explain."

Moon sighed. "I really don't want to."

Taiyo pulled his black coat against the biting wind. "I'll see what the status is on the SoGa's search party. In the meantime, keep a low profile, Margo. Don't get in anyone's way."

He took one last look at her, and his black eyes shone in the vanishing orange light. "Maybe be a little less . . ." He waved his hand in front of his face.

"What?" she asked, wondering what was wrong with her face. "A little less what?"

"Conspicuous," he said. "Not a lot of redheads in New Davia."

And he was gone.

A puddle of melted snow revealed a dim reflection. Margo had become streaked with dirt in the tunnels. Her hair was damp and coated with a light frizz, puffing around her face like the ears on a cocker spaniel. Suddenly it became clear to her how dangerous it was to go through this town looking like Margo Madden.

Moon appeared to be having the same thought. He studied her, his eyes flitting up and down her body.

"What should we do?" she asked.

He reached forward and held a length of her hair. He brushed his thumb along the damp wool of it. "What are you prepared to do?"

She hesitated. Terrified at the thought of losing yet another connection to herself. Nervous that a boy was holding her hair. "Where would we even find scissors?"

"I can't get us scissors." He thought for a moment. "But I can get us a knife."

What he got, in the end, was a meat cleaver.

There was a parade of shops near the shore, all weather-beaten, all flinching against the sea. They were also all closed. A squat blue butcher's shop sat empty, its window filled with gleaming metal trays that had not been filled in some time. MERRY MEATS was picked out in gold lettering, along with a fading illustration of a pig.

"Merry Meats," he muttered, locating a back-door key in a flowerpot. "Moon and Margo. *M* might be a lucky letter for us."

Moon let himself into the disused butcher shop as though it were his own home. The place was freezing and filled with rusting meat hooks, along with a large wooden slab stained pink from old blood.

"How . . . ?"

"They closed down last year. Not many people can afford meat around here," Moon said matter-of-factly. "I used to sell the guy flintoil. For his blades."

"And he just told you where his key was?"

"Oh. No. I took a guess."

Moon rattled around the shop, which consisted of a tiny back room and an open counter space, looking for anything that could feasibly cut hair. He looked through empty drawers while she sat on a high stool, the one remaining piece of functional furniture in the room. She felt awkward, and shocked yet again to be in a location that had absolutely no continuity with her day.

"Uh, I'm sorry by the way."

Moon found the meat cleaver and started examining it by the window's light. "Hmm?"

"I ran away from you this morning because I thought you had, like, kidnapped me off the train just so you could use me, or sell me, or whatever."

Moon's eyes widened in alarm as he held the preposterously large knife aloft. She continued, trying not to think of it being anywhere near her skull. "But I see now that if I had stayed on the train, things could have got . . . really, really bad for me."

He lay the knife down on the butcher's block. It was a horror, a cartoonishly brutal thing. Moon looked at it a second, and then at her.

"Yeah, well. Don't thank me too much." He began looking under the sink, where he found a narrow tray of rusting, discarded tools. "It could be an out of the frying pan, into the fire sort of situation. I've saved you from the SoGa, but I've put you in PACT's line of sight. Which might be worse."

"Worse? Why worse? Aren't they, you know. Freedom fighters? The good guys?"

He shook the tray of tools noisily. She watched him pick through it, and realized he was avoiding eye contact.

"I don't know how long you're going to be here, Margo," he said. "But while you are, try not to get too preoccupied with good guys and bad guys."

Moon raised his gaze to her. Him, on the floor of the abandoned butcher's shop. Her, on a stool, feeling like a judge in court.

"Why?" she pressed. "Which one are you?"

He didn't answer. The moment became stiff, intense. She got the sense that he wasn't staying silent because he was a villain, but because claiming he was a hero felt like a step in a direction that was far too extreme. And he did not like extreme things. His life was, above all, a failed attempt at being a measured person. Funny how she could tell this about him, but it might take him years to get there himself.

She picked up the meat cleaver.

"You could kill a man with this thing."

"Perhaps we should take it with us," he said. "We might have to."

She shivered. Fear, partly; but also just the cold. This was, after all, a place where dead things were kept cool.

"Here," he said, taking off his coat and putting it around her. His touch was strangely warm against her, his fingers hot as batteries. He eased the cleaver out of her hands as he guided her arms through the sleeves.

"Thanks. Won't you be chilly?"

He shrugged. It was night now, and his skin was humming silver through his shirtsleeves. He was a boy with his own lighting crew. With his coat off she could tell how thin he was. How the brackets of his shoulders were all wide sinew, his genetics fervently wishing for more fat than his resources would currently allow.

"You better get your head on that block."

He was holding the cleaver again, this time with frowning purpose. His thumb ran along the blade, testing its sharpness.

"You can't cut my hair with *that*," she said, cowering in his black coat.

"I checked the tool tray. There's nothing else." He looked at her, and then at the butcher block. "Do you have anything to tie your hair up with?"

Like all girls over the age of nine, Margo had an elastic band perpetually cutting off the circulation on her wrist.

"Yes."

"If you tied your hair up high," he said thoughtfully, "you could tilt your head back. It would be easy."

She felt as though he had just asked her to run through the street naked.

"The Southern Guard are looking for you," he continued patiently. "They have a description."

"But it will look . . ." She groped for the right words. "Bad."

He tilted his head, disappointed. "You're very young."

"Excuse me?"

"You realize they could kill you, right? That they could, and would, do that?"

She touched her cocker spaniel hair. "Stop it."

He tilted his head, as though amazed at her reticence. "I'm not going to *hurt* you. It's just hair."

"Have you done this before?"

He blinked. "Well, no. But you're in New Davia, Margo. It will grow back before you can even think about it."

She was not convinced. She did not feel good about this. "Can't Vesna do it?"

"Vesna is in her house," he said, gently. "And that house is two miles away. To get there, we have to walk through the town. And in the town . . ."

"There's SoGa. I get it." She wondered whether anyone she had ever gone to school with had been faced with this kind of decision.

"Unless you want to lose another day through the tunnels."

"*No.*" She felt queasy. "What do I have to do?"

"Tie your hair up high. Lean your head back on the block."

She looked between him and the block, scandalized. "But there's *blood* on it."

He gave her a disapproving look. Despite everything, she wanted to be tough in front of him. "Fine," she said, and tied her hair up high in the elastic band. Margo leaned her head back on the butcher's block. It already felt terrible. The stool was the wrong height for this kind of activity, and her back and stomach muscles roared from having to hold herself horizontal. Suddenly she was looking up at him, his scar a perfect crescent, his face her whole sky. But then she saw the knife again as Moon took practice swings in the air.

"I can't do this," she said, sitting up. "No."

"Margo, we don't have time for this."

"You'll cut my *head* off."

"Only if you keep moving like that. Stop squirming around."

She was shaking, she realized. Her entire body was trembling like a whippet.

"Listen. Lie down again. Just get comfortable. I'll only do it when you say it's OK."

She laid her head on the wood, feeling like a wife of Henry VIII.

"I hate this."

"Just talk to me." He put both his hands on her shoulders, his fingers on her collarbones. They still radiated warmth, like hot little coals against her frozen skin. He pushed her body down, sternly aligning her bones with the butcher's block.

"Why are you so warm?" Her voice came out in a whisper. The intimacy of the act had almost winded her.

"Lunati live outside, traditionally, so we don't feel the cold so much."

That word again.

"I don't want to be rude, but I feel like if I don't ask, it's just going to keep coming up, and I'm going to keep getting more confused."

"What?"

"What's Lunati?"

He laughed. "Of course. You don't know. I'm sorry. I'm just used to everyone knowing. Or thinking they know, I should say, and making assumptions from there. Lunati follow the full moon. We follow it from world to world."

"The same moon?"

She felt his hand on the base of her ponytail. He tugged on the elastic slightly, creating a larger space between her crown and the hair he planned to ax.

"Ow," she said, though she didn't mean *ow*, she meant something else. She meant, if anything: *oh*.

"Sorry. I'm trying to be careful," he murmured. "Where was I?"

"The moon."

"The moon. Right. Every world has its own moon. But because of the time speeds, it's full at different times. So, say you're in a place with a two-hour day. The full moon comes around every sixty hours. But in a three-hour day it comes around every ninety hours. So in the old days, if you timed it right, you could stay near a pretty fat moon almost all the time. You would spend the year moving from the far North to the deep South. Our big holiday actually used to be in Semper, ironically, because the full moon lasts so long there. That was before the war. Before the travel bans."

She was still horizontal, still on the block. Still carrying on as if this were a normal way to hold a conversation. Margo got the sense that the only reason he was allowing her to ask so many questions about his life was because he needed to cleave the hair off her head, sooner or later, and that something needed to be traded in the process. He was a salesman after all. "So your family, you'd travel from world to world. And what? You'd just get the train?"

"Well, traditionally we would use the caravan trails. We went on foot."

"What are they? Caravan trails?"

"Temple gateways that are linked to one another. They were closed down years ago. They were the first thing to go."

Margo furrowed her brow. "And they *killed* people for worshipping the moon?"

"The moon part isn't really what people tend to focus on."

Her abdomen quaked with the effort of leaning back on the stool. "Are you going to cut my hair, or what?"

A moment's pause. "Yes. Hold still."

The cleaver came down, the blade hitting just beneath where her ponytail began. There was a horrible thump, and she screamed slightly, feeling as though she must have been beheaded. Her eyes watered, blurring the boy who had butchered her.

But then she sat up. She felt the top of her head. Instead of the familiar heavy weight of hair, there was a feathery crop of short strands.

"Oh my god," she whispered, holding up the now homeless length of coarse, red hair. "Oh my god, oh my god."

"That was terrible. I am never doing that again."

She sat up. "Does it look OK?"

He surveyed her, reaching his hand out to fluff her stubby cut. "Yeah. You look good."

Margo was certain that she did not look good. But she was talking to someone, she realized, who had clearly lived through a number of terrible things, things that were far more devastating than a butcher-block haircut.

"It's just hair," she said. Then louder: "It's just hair."

Moon closed up the shop carefully when they left, replacing the tools, the stool, and the cleaver. Margo, for her part, threw her red ponytail into a bush. She wondered if a bird might make a nest of it. She examined herself in the empty window of Merry Meats. She looked like someone who had escaped from an asylum, but at least she was no longer a redhead.

The moon, fat but not full, began to rise in the distance. She looked at it a moment, yellow as cat's eyes.

"You said that people didn't hate you for worshipping the moon. What did they hate you for?"

"Because we can make our own money," he replied.

"*What?*"

"See? Look. You're suspicious of me already."

"Sorry. But how?"

They were in the middle of the city, and walking briskly uphill. The bricks a weak yellow, the buildings tall. He was in the rhythm of talking about himself now, and she wasn't sure when an opportunity like this would come up again.

"Lunati is an old religion. Older than the rails, even. Our goddesses know that it takes a lot of time and energy and community to be so nomadic, so they gave us this monthly ritual where we harvest silver seeds that we can sell for clothes or shelter or what have you."

"A month . . . anywhere?"

"When it's been thirty days or so, the beads start to warm up to tell me it's time. So I find a full moon. I do a silver Wash, and my silver seeds are replenished. It's why the salesman life was so appealing. I can always find a moon when I need one."

"So do you try to stay near a full moon all the time?"

This made him uncomfortable. She had overstepped, somehow.

"I did in the beginning," he said, his pace getting slightly faster. "But it's hard. You know. You've gotta go where business is. I never miss a Wash, though."

This affected him. He was ashamed of this, this way that he lived, a life of being observant of his religion but not devout.

"It does sound nice, though. Like, nicer than all the other religions."

"It would be fine if Semper didn't make it so difficult. There's a full moon here in New Davia in a few days. That's why I was coming to Vesna's in the first place."

"Are there other people like that, here? Who follow the moon, too?"

Suddenly the lightness vanished from Moon's face. "No," he said. "No, there aren't very many Lunati people left, I'm afraid. We make people suspicious. A whole race of people with their own travel, their own ways of making money, their own goddesses? We were a tiny community, and because we moved around so much we were easy to pin things on. Disease outbreaks, looting, hunger, theft. It was all supposedly because a Lunati family had either just been or were on their way. It was very effective. And then they closed the caravan trails down, years before the travel ban."

"How?"

Moon shrugged. "I'm not sure how. I was so young. People said we were carrying diseases or attacking civilians. Semper was trying to legitimize the travel ban, so they planted all kinds of stories like that."

They had stopped walking without her realizing. They stood in the alleyway, the gabled roof of another red shrine jabbing at her. "That sounds like a terrible thing to live through."

"Some of us didn't. A lot of us didn't. The Lunati who are left mostly live in disguise. Dyeing their skin and hair, doing their monthly Wash in secret. I've got a cousin . . ."

He broke off. Whatever he was thinking about, he didn't want to say it out loud.

"How come *you* don't live in disguise?"

Moon tilted his head, showing the scar on the left-hand side of his face. "Don't have much of a choice, do I?"

"You can't pick your own tattoo?"

"No."

He was getting tired of her questions now, she could tell. It cost him a lot to answer them. She kept on pushing, anyway.

"Didn't the Lunati get bad skipshock? From all the traveling?"

"Not really. Because we moved slowly, north to south, going from a four-hour world to a five-hour one, spending a month there, then going to six. You don't feel it when you travel that way." He patted his trouser pockets and took out a thin wad of bills. "You hungry? You want me to get us something?"

She looked around the empty street. "Sure. Where?"

"Night bakery."

Down a series of alleyways, he described what a night bakery was. Like all businesses in New Davia, it had to have multiple uses, or else risk going the same way as Merry Meats. A night bakery was a bakery, yes, but it was also a brothel. And you could gamble there.

Margo stood outside the completely ordinary-looking bakery wondering if he was trying to take the piss out of her.

"It doesn't *look* like a brothel," she said, as if she knew what they looked like. "It *looks* like it sells bread."

"There's a back entrance," Moon explained. "For . . . non-bread needs."

"Ah. Non-bread needs." Margo cocked her head. "Do you *not* buy bread often?"

He stuck his chin out indignantly. "I don't pay for Not Bread."

"So no Not Bread for you?"

"When Not Bread *happens* to me, I partake in Not Bread. But I don't *buy* Not Bread."

The whole conversation made her brain feel addled and her face hot. He was a little older than her. No—*younger* than her? She couldn't figure out the math, considering he had spent much of his life traveling between time speeds where a day could be four or six or thirty-six hours. The only pertinent marker of age seemed to be experience, and he'd clearly had some. A *lot* of it. She flushed to think about it. The cleaving of her hair was the most intimate act she had ever shared with a boy. She could still feel his fingertips flattening her shoulders against the wooden block. And here Moon was, sleeping with everybody.

Moon jingled the change in his pocket. "Right. I'm gonna get us some actual food."

He disappeared into the bakery. Which, of course, was when the SoGa decided to arrive.

There was a drunk, sloppy edge to them. They were bored and cold and talking about how boring and cold it was to be there. She tried to shrink back into the alleyway, treading lightly on the wet paving stones.

"What was *that*?"

Suddenly Margo's vision was filled with a man in orange, his face flat and fair, his jaw wide. He seemed more pillar than person. No blood or bones, solid all the way through. He took her by the collar—Moon's collar—and dragged her into the street.

Perhaps it was because she had grown so used to how people generally looked in New Davia—worn in, like old, friendly slippers—that the SoGa's freshness was disorienting to her. He was big and broad, with a ruddy glow drawn from the cold unfamiliar climate. Cool blue eyes, empty as currency.

"What are you doing here? Why are you dressed like that?"

Margo briefly looked down at the jumble of men's clothes. "They're my clothes" was all she could say.

The officer observed Margo, and she thanked god that she had laid her head on that butcher's block when she did.

"Show me your hands. Both of them."

"Excuse me?"

"I said *both of them.*"

Margo stuck out her hands, the sleeves of the borrowed coat cutting just under her thumb. He rolled back each, inspecting her wrists, his grasp tight.

"Take off the coat."

She did so. The officer fished through Moon's coat pockets and found nothing.

"Turn out your pockets. Your pant pockets."

She felt a brief awkwardness at having nowhere to put the coat while she turned out her pockets. The officer, annoyed already, grabbed the thick black material and flung it to the ground. It dropped into a puddle. Margo winced, thinking of the battery warmth that Moon's body had given the wool that was then given to her.

The officer went back to the hands again.

"Why are your hands so soft?" he asked. He was furious now, intent, irritated. "And what are you doing here? In the street?"

"Waiting . . ."

This was apparently maddening to the SoGa. His hands shot to her neck, and she felt the back of her head touch the stone wall behind her. He lifted her off the ground, her feet kicking uselessly, her breath cut at the throat.

He held her like that. Just watched her a moment. He looked far away all of a sudden, like he had forgotten why he came to New Davia and was just enjoying the feeling of burning an ant with a magnifying glass. She felt the blood in her head become trapped there. Her skin reddening. *He's going to kill me,* she thought. *He's going to kill me, and there won't be a thing I can do about it.*

"*Waiting*? For who? For what?" he asked. He did not free her throat to let her respond, so she continued to dangle there, watching him. He had no lines on his face, the SoGa. Not a forehead crease, not a stamp of crow's feet.

Slow world, she thought instantly. He came from a place where the time passed like long summer days, where the weather was mild and the sunshine forgiving. He was from a world where you swam outside any time of day, many times a day, all year round. He was from a place so lovely that it terrorized ceaselessly in order to protect itself.

Suddenly, everything made sense. Moon made sense and Vesna made sense and Taiyo made sense and the panic of the setting sun made sense. The excitement of her arrival, the notion of a person who could slip through undetected, made sense. The fear around a train line temporarily closing made sense. Everything flowed, logically and brutally, forming deep cuts in her brain that would never mark this man's plain face.

He set her back down on the ground, the skin of her throat burning. "Do you know who I am?" he asked. Margo did not respond. "My name is Captain Halvpas. I've been sent here to investigate the Six closure. Do you know anything about that, young lady?"

She shook her head. "I've heard about it," she answered. "But I don't know why it's down. We're all so worried."

Margo worked a little plea into her voice. She pretended briefly to be Ani, who had grown up in New Davia, and imitated her quasi-French-sounding vowels. She hoped her eyes weren't black anymore. That skipshock giveaway that might make Halvpas smell a rat.

"I'll bet," he said at last. "I'll bet you're all worried."

There was a pleasure in this, a private joy, a sense he knew something that she didn't. He was a sadist, this Halvpas, and he needed to inflict a certain degree of cruelty every day to make his life worthwhile. The personal satisfaction he took from frightening her, from choking her, from knowing something she didn't—today, it was enough. He was full.

"Do you hang around here a lot? Skulking in alleys, and that kind of thing?"

Again she tried to imagine herself as a normal New Davian teenager. "A little."

He looked her up and down, assessing the mismatched bag of rags, the fabric belt. The black coat, sopping in a puddle. "You're not in school," he said. Not a question, but a comment. "You beg, don't you? You beg, and steal, and thrift, and pickpocket, just like every other runt in this town."

"No, sir."

"You don't have to lie."

His tone was different now, the choking business quite forgotten. He wanted to know her secrets. He wanted a street urchin, and it was her job to give it to him.

"All right," she said. "I won't."

"Has anyone new come to town? Anyone unusual? Before the Six closed, I mean."

She pretended to think about it. "There was a commotion in the market this morning," she said. "There were some soldiers I didn't recognize. They found a musician—"

"Not them," he snapped. Halvpas grabbed her shirt collar less rough this time. He pulled her chest close to his. The gold buttons on his uniform dug through her thin clothing, pressing down hard on her heart. Keeping one hand on her collar and one on his lapels, he slowly opened his jacket.

"Look," he said. "Look in my jacket. What do you see?"

She was crushed against him, his huge pillar of a body. One of her shoulders was completely immobile, pressed hard against his chest, and the other exposed to the street. The second officer, whoever he was, had started to smoke and watched the proceedings with curiosity.

"My jacket," he repeated. What do you *see*?"

The inside of Halvpas's jacket was made of a glossy maroon silk. It had an inner pocket, and in that pocket she saw a wallet stuffed with bills. She also saw something else: a gun, a white revolver with a carved head, strapped into a holster that hung below his shoulder.

"I see a wallet," she replied. "And I see a gun."

"That's correct." His voice was very soft now. "A wallet and a gun."

She thought of grabbing the gun. Of tearing it out of his holster, pointing it into his stomach, and blowing him away. But what would that solve? Even if she could use a gun, his friend was behind them, smoking and laughing. And besides: she was Margo Madden.

She was a suburban kid from Ireland. She was not about to shoot a police officer with his own gun, whatever world she was in.

Halvpas looked down at her and smiled, knowing what she was thinking, knowing he was the one who put the thought there. She was wrong about his appetite for cruelty. It was not the kind of thing he could ever be full of. The more he ate, the more he wanted.

"Get the wallet," he said. His voice was soft and slippery, like the lining of his jacket. "Get it."

Somehow, this was worse than when he was choking her. Margo reached inside the pocket. She felt the cool leather nestled in silk, Captain Halvpas's heart beating steadily behind it. Her body crushed against the hard gold buttons. Whatever fond memories Margo had of fishing in her father's pockets for presents were ground down instantly to dust.

She found the wallet. It was thick with bills, blue and lilac and red, rolled tight until they stretched the dark leather.

"It feels good, doesn't it? That much money in one place?"

She didn't say a word. Anything good about having money was erased as she felt the sticky, strange perversions of someone who had not precisely done anything sexual but had violated her nonetheless.

"I'm going to be here, in New Davia, while we fix this Six issue. There's someone here that I want to find. Someone your age, or a little younger. A girl. Thirteen or fourteen. She'll be confused. Scared. So I want you to keep me informed. Is that understood? Anyone new crops up, you tell me. You can choose the wallet. Or you can choose the gun."

He let her go, plucked out a bill, and put it in her hand.

"Choose wisely."

And that was it. Captain Halvpas left her with cash and a wet coat, and the feeling that she would never quite be the same Margo ever again.

twelve

MOON

Realistically speaking, there is nothing I could have done.

As we walk back to Vesna's, I try to think of all the possible scenarios where I leave the bakery and defend Margo. It's not pretty. Nine times out of ten, that ends with my brain splattered against the shop's windowpane.

And if they *didn't* kill me? They would have hauled me in for questioning, tortured me, and taken my sales license away. I am, after all, the one who bribed the Pig. I am the only salesman with a moon carved into his face. The only Lunati with a license, and possibly the only identifiable Lunati in New Davia.

The gari beads rub at my skin, and it feels like my mother telling me off.

You let that poor girl be picked up by the throat, Lev. You watched him choke her.

Then, my father. *We don't do that. Lunati are not a by-standing people.*

But would they really have said that? Or is it just easy to ascribe saintly lectures to your parents long after they're dead? They were survival-oriented. They did so much to preserve our way of life before our way of life was made completely impossible. They didn't concern themselves much with the lives of people who didn't travel, who didn't follow the moon like we did.

Then I remember my mother, every time we pitched up in a new world. The big canvas awning that extended out from one of our wagons, the soup she gave away in clay bowls. You had to drink the soup there, because of the bowl scarcity, and in the time it took for someone to drink she would speak to them, softly debunking every terrible myth they had heard about us. She would even laugh, sometimes, when they told her what they had heard. "Rich!," as if hearing this accusation for the first time. Then she would take them on a tour of all the wagons and show them how rich we weren't. "I understand why you'd think it, though—if I heard of a people who could make their own silver, I wouldn't trust them, either!"

But she would have. She trusted everyone, until she had a reason not to.

She would have thought of something to do. She wouldn't have let Margo hang there from a SoGa's hands. She would have made a commotion, provided a distraction. Diffused the situation somehow. She would have done more than I did, which was nothing.

We walk back to Vesna's in silence.

"I'm sorry," I say again, eventually. "I guess you understand now, why we needed to cut your hair."

She touches the remaining thick clumps, sticking up as though in shock.

"He gave me money," she says. "He gave me money to keep him informed." Margo looks like she's about to get sick again. "What do I do, Moon?"

"What do you *want* to do?"

"I want to go home. I want to get out of here."

"I understand. I would, too."

She looks at me, her face so young and new that I feel like I'm ruining her just by knowing her name.

"I know that Taiyo is trying to use me."

She pauses, as if waiting for me to contradict her. I do not. She carries on. "And I'm afraid. I'm afraid that I'll do what he says, and then I'll just end up in another random world, even farther away from my own, and by then the path will be so long that I won't be able to find my way back."

"Of course."

"But I can't just wait around here for someone to get me," she says, arguing with herself. Then she looks at me hopefully. "Can I?"

I think about this. I try to be as honest as I possibly can. "Well. Halvpas has given you money. He's going to want a return on that investment, eventually."

"So?"

"So he'll come looking for you. The haircut has bought us a little time, but how long before people start noticing you? Even if you never leave Vesna's house, the city is small. Word gets around. Which means we have to be out of here before he does. Which means, sadly, that we have to work with Taiyo."

Returns on investment. Like the note in my pants pockets that promises me a return on Margo.

"You don't like him," says Margo. "Taiyo, I mean."

I shrug. "He's fine. It's not personal. Or rather, it *is* personal, but that doesn't mean you can't like him. I'm not big on any of these PACT guys, if I'm perfectly honest."

"Why not?"

"I find their dreams . . . unrealistic. Crushing Semper? Opening up all the travel borders again? Come on. I'd rather take my chances within a bad system than waste my life trying to destroy it."

Margo seems to think about this very carefully. "I get that. But why can't you appreciate what they're trying to do, even if you don't want to join in? I mean, there are people in my world who fight for stuff, and sometimes I feel bad that I don't fight, too. But I'm glad *they're* doing it, at least."

It's a perfectly reasonable point. I'm just not in the mood for it. Where would I start with PACT, and where would I end?

"Back when things were getting bad, PACT and the Lunati made a deal. PACT could use our caravan trails to smuggle ammunition and people, to help get around Semper. PACT took advantage, and then the caravan trails got shut down. Then thousands of Lunati were imprisoned, or killed, or forced underground. And do you think PACT lifted a finger to help? After everything the Lunati risked and sacrificed?"

Margo is silent. A respectful silence, but also an expectant one. I'm bleating political facts at her, all of them true, all of them valid. All the same: we both know I'm holding back. That no one would be this furious unless they had a more intimate history with the subject matter. It is a history I do not plan to give her.

"We need to get you to Alder," I say instead.

"Alder? What's that?"

"It's an old world, and it has the largest PACT chapter of anywhere. They're powerful; they have money. They're the only people this side of the map who are likely to know anything about where you're from, and how to get you back there."

I feel confidence rippling through me like a drug. I know, in moments like this, that I look taller, and that my features are sharper, and that the threadbare suit doesn't look cheap or battered but sleek and discreet. I was twelve when Mitwatch found me. I've had my license since I was thirteen. Shoot me in the middle of a sales pitch, and I know the bullets would bounce right off.

I'm giving her exactly what she wants. I *will* help her get home.

But there's a way of helping Margo that also means I get to make a small fortune and potentially live till thirty.

"The only problem is . . ." I go on, puzzling it out slowly, "travel papers. Only salesmen and people with registered tattoos can travel. We need to get you a fake apprentice license from somewhere. I'm sure Taiyo can help with that."

"How is Taiyo traveling? He doesn't have a tattoo."

"He'll bundle himself into a crate, bribe one of the import guys, something like that. But they won't take a stranger, or a woman. They're too nervous for that kind of thing. We find you a fake apprenticeship license, we get you on a train, we get you to Alder. We send you home."

Margo nods slowly. "Alder," she says. "We're off to see the wizard."

"Pardon?"

"Where I'm from, we have this old story. A girl lands in a strange new place, and everyone says: you have to go see the wizard, in a faraway city called Oz, and he'll help you get home."

"Right. And does he?"

She turns to me, still wearing the sopping coat that Halvpas threw in the puddle. "He doesn't," she says, her green eyes sharp and fierce. "It turns out he's a fraud."

I can't tell whether this is *meant* to be pointed. She becomes unreadable to me in that moment, the light in her eyes dim and untrusting. I can see why someone like Halvpas might single her out as a spy. There's another place Margo goes in her head, a place you can't reach her, and that feels like it would stand up to questioning.

We've reached Vesna's house at last, weaving through each corner of her hedge maze, the gravel crunching loudly underfoot. Vesna was smart to build this maze. She told everyone that it was a Sopilka custom, and they all believed her. What she really wanted was an early threat-detection system: she can hear people coming, five minutes before they're even able to reach her door.

We finally reach the end of the labyrinth. Before I can take my usual sharp left to the kitchen door, I see that the front porch is illuminated against the dark night. The front door wide open. Vesna is sitting in the doorway, knees tucked under her chin, a bottle of slip next to her.

"Heck died," she says.

The story goes like this.

After Margo bolted and I followed her, Vesna received word that the SoGa were in town and raiding boardinghouses. Heck asked to speak with her. She told him to wait. She set about hiding any evidence of either PACT membership or the multiple crates of stolen goods she was currently acting as a fence for. That's when Taiyo showed up. He tried to get her to store more black-market rum and heard all about Margo. And then Heck asked, again, if he could speak with her. Again, she asked him to wait. She instructed Taiyo to go to the market and act as a lookout for us. Then the SoGa, finally, did show up. They raided the house, insulted some people, pocketed some money, and were gone. By now exhausted, Vesna helped Ani prepare dinner, rang the dinner bell, and noticed that Heck had not come downstairs.

"So I went up to look for him," she says, her voice trembling. "And the second before I knocked on his door, I knew. I knew without even having to go in. But I did go in, Mo. I did."

I cradle her, her strong body feeling so strangely brittle in my arms. "It's not your fault, Ves."

The mere physical presence of a friend seems to send her over the edge. She collapses into tears, her shoulders shuddering with regret. There is a broken rhythm to her crying. A series of short, sharp inward breaths—*hup! hup! hup!*—and she's done.

We take her into the kitchen, Margo and I. We drag stools in front of the fire, tin cups filled with dark tea.

"Where is he now?" I ask. "The body, I mean."

"Dom went down the road and found the mortician. He just left, carted him off toward the woods. Can you believe that, Mo? A whole life. Now he'll have some salesman's grave that no one will visit."

My eyes travel to the fire where, on a milk stool, Heck's briefcase sits. The coarse white stitching along the lid is fraying and uneven, like a shattered lifeline on a palm. It's the loneliest sight in the world.

Ves covers her eyes, embarrassed by her own emotion, but too in touch with it now to let go. "He just wanted to talk to me. And I wouldn't. I was too busy, too paranoid. He didn't even do it himself, you know. It looked like a heart attack, something like that. He must have known he was dying, and wanted to warn me. Can you believe that?"

I meditate on everything I knew about Heck, and sadly, I can believe it. He was not a bad man, by any stretch. A bad salesman, but not a bad man. But he was one of those vanishingly rare people who got into sales because he loved to travel, and he would do anything to do it. The selling part was always unnatural to him. He was shy and strange and he liked to notice things. He did not, himself, like to be noticed. And so when he finally requested real and genuine attention, it went unanswered.

This is what is killing Vesna. Not because she was a friend to Heck, or even because she liked him. But because she is a consummate host, and her guest's wishes went unanswered.

"Ves," I say gently, holding her knee. "He traveled a lot. It's what he loved to do. He knew . . . he knew what that meant."

I have known too many dead salesmen to mourn every passing too deeply. They don't stick in my teeth the way they used to anymore. Now, when a person like Heck goes, I just think: *You're next, Mo. You're next.*

"Will there be a funeral?" Margo asks. Ves just shakes her head.

We are quiet while the fire crackles and settles again. A silence that has movements and parts to it: first reverent, then reflective, and that finally turns to resentment. Vesna's body language shifts, her hands clutched to her knees in rage.

"We can't go on like this," she says, her teeth gritted. "But we keep going on like this. On and on like this."

Vesna turns to me, the fire making her red skin appear molten. "Is this how you want to go, Moon? Some landlady riffling through your stuff before she boils your bedsheets clean?"

"Ves," I say quietly. "Even if the borders were open again, Heck would still have died. He loved to travel. It was his . . . his calling, I guess."

"Maybe," she says fiercely. "But Heck could have traveled without having to live a horrible salesman's life. There's another version of Heck's life where he had a real life, and a real home, and traveled when he wanted to. And if—*if*—he still died of skipshock, he might have had a wife and children, and a community, to mourn him."

Her points are good, and yet I feel an iron wall springing up within myself. Resistance, retreat.

"Vesna," I say, trying to keep my tone level. "Stop."

"Why?"

"Because it's rude, Ves. It's rude to call someone's life horrible. And besides, this is all academic to you, isn't it? *You're* not going to die of skipshock, after all."

I level my eyes at Ves, telling her without telling her: *But I am.*

Vesna looks at her hands.

"Something's coming, Mo. Something bad."

"Stop it. That's just Taiyo's crazy theory."

"I don't think it's crazy," she replies, voice quavering.

"Of course Taiyo thinks there's a war coming," I say quickly. "But he would, wouldn't he? When you're the big self-styled romantic revolutionary, every nail needs a hammer. He probably thinks there's a war brewing in the fucking bakery. It's cracked."

"I don't think it's cracked," Vesna says. She fiddles with a dish towel, running it nervously between her fingers. "Things *are* getting weirdly pricey, hard to get ahold of. Then there's the Six. And Margo suddenly appearing. And the SoGa showing up, terrorizing everyone in the streets. I know none of it really adds up to anything, but . . ."

Vesna's face smarts with worry. I know her well enough to know exactly what she's thinking.

"It's not that, Ves."

The dish towel is crunched into a ball. "I just don't want to miss the signs. Not again."

"The signs of *what* again?" Margo asks.

Margo is beginning to understand—we all are, I think—that this odd moment in her life is going to amount to more than just a handful of strange days in a strange place. On some level, she has to invest in this.

Vesna looks dead at Margo. "Margo, do you know what a sealed world is?"

thirteen

MARGO

Needless to say, she did not know what a sealed world was.

"A sealed world," Moon said carefully, "means no one can get in, and no one can get out. It's taken off the train map. Blacked out of the history books. No one trades there, no one goes there, and if you have family there . . ."

His eyes went to Vesna, who had turned to face the wall. At first, Margo thought that the landlady was too upset to continue, until she plucked a piece of sheet music down and placed it in front of Margo.

"My mother is a composer," she said simply. "All the music in the house was written by her. She was famous, inasmuch as Northern composers are ever famous, and she traveled a lot. She came back with stories, with presents, and I was the eldest, so I looked after everyone. My three sisters and me. Then when things got hard, and most people weren't allowed to travel anymore, my mother was still offered all these special dispensations. Special visas. So she could play for the elite. And we were proud of her. Isn't that nuts? We should have been worried. Worried that first Lunati couldn't travel, then far North people couldn't travel, then all Northerners. And we were worried, but we thought it was temporary, and look—*our* mother was exempt."

The house creaked, the old wood moaning in chorus.

"We all played music. We all thought we'd be like her. It's disgusting to say it, Margo, but we really didn't care about other people or what they weren't allowed to do. Everyone in our family had always been exceptional. Above the law. And Sopilka was . . . Sopilka *is* one of those places that was always exempt, you know?"

Moon guided Vesna into a chair, as though she were an elderly family member who he was afraid was exerting herself. He laid his hands on the tops of her shoulders as she sat and looked blankly ahead, her face desolate.

"Vesna is right," he said softly. "Sopilka is Northern, but near enough the axis to not really count as Northern. An old, very artistic, very cultured place. It has the oldest university in any world."

"But where you get universities," Ves went on, "you get students. Then you get thought, and where you get thought, you get rebellion. There were demonstrations, which were ignored, and then attacks, which . . . weren't."

Vesna wasn't even speaking to Margo anymore. She was settled in memory now, like a dog that has paced around its bed enough to finally lie down.

"And then my mother came back from a concert she had played in Semper and she took me aside and said: Vesna, we need to get you a visa. She knew that something was happening. About to happen. But even when I got permission to emigrate, I always thought I would be coming back. It was an economic thing. Work abroad, send money, come home."

Vesna touched the scars on her chest. "Salesmen get marked on the face. Immigrants—when there was such a *thing* as immigrants—got it on the torso. That was more humane, they decided. Immigrants should get the option to cover it up. The embarrassment of being from somewhere else." She sighed. "And now I look like a giant cello, and I'll never see my family again. That's what happens when a world gets sealed. The infrastructure is removed. Train lines, gone. No way in. No way out. Collapsed economies. Riots. Famine. And for years, I've thought: if I had just read the signs more clearly, paid attention to things—I could have been prepared. I could have gotten my sisters out."

"I'm so sorry, Vesna," said Margo.

Ves just nodded. A silence fell over the room. The coals hummed with orange light, low and soft.

"You think I'm from a sealed world, Ves," Margo said, the information finally clicking in her brain. "You think where I came from has been sealed, sealed so long that nobody knows about it."

Vesna sat very still, holding on to her own arms. "Yes."

"And you think . . . if I'm here, here in New Davia, then there must be a way out of sealed worlds. That's why you're letting me stay here, isn't it?"

Vesna didn't need to answer this. She just looked at the kitchen wall, where her mother's music used to be.

Later, alone in her room, Margo sat in a bath near the window. Vesna had given her a packet of red salt that was meant to make it hot. She followed Vesna's instructions, gazing at the pink water as it swirled and briefly bubbled. Margo soaked in the tin tub, warm and naked, her knees nudging the sides. She even tried to wash her hair using an old enamel jug, attempting some kind of style on her freshly amputated head.

Outside, the sun was starting to rise again. Another dawn in New Davia was breaking, and already an old version of her felt like it was dissolving in the hot crimson water. She thought of Vesna, who left her own home with reasonable faith that she would be able to return in due course. Then it was sealed. Margo pictured an entire populace drenched in waxy fluid. It was a horrible way to think of your home. And yet, it was the way Vesna and Moon thought about hers: their theory that she was from some kind of sealed world, spinning alone and forever out of context from this vast interconnected landscape that Moon traveled between.

The thought made her feel incredibly lonely. Or rather, it seemed to explain a kind of loneliness she had felt her entire life. Her entire civilization had been orphaned so long that it didn't even know it had extended family.

When she finally got out of the bath, her skin hot and red, she lay on a towel on top of her single bed. She had never been a good sleeper. Even as a baby she hated it. She wasn't afraid of how things looked at night, the piles of clothes that might be mistaken for the shadow of a monster. She was never bothered by nightmares. It was the feeling of sleeplessness that frightened her. Of acres of time spent alone in bed. The next day half-dead before it had even started, the life already choked out of it by insomnia. Then her mother in the morning, waking her up for school, Margo's eyes already dry and alert. It was a kind of torture, she found out later. Depriving people of sleep.

And so her father coming home at strange hours was always a thing to look forward to. A reward system. It broke up the long nights, talking to him. It never occurred to her to be frightened by air travel until his crash. She was born too long after 9/11, and she had always had to take her shoes off at the airport.

Margo lay in bed and thought about her father's plane going down after Shanghai. It crashed, eventually, into the mountains around India. The location of the crash site was not found for days. The bodies dragged off by animals by the time it was.

Dragged off by animals.

"Tigers?"

She would always remember where she was, the first time someone suggested her father might have been eaten by tigers. She was at a house party and Dua Lipa was playing. How could toffee schnapps and Dua Lipa and house parties all exist in the same world as the Grimms' fairy tale where her father was potentially eaten by tigers?

This was the kind of thing that kept her up, in her old life. Here, at least, was an advantage to living in New Davia. For the first time in her life, Margo fell asleep instantly.

When she woke again, the room was dark. Not dark the way her own bedroom at home was, which always had the blinking light of an electric toothbrush charging somewhere in the room. This was pure dark. The dark of heavy furniture and thickest night.

She felt a kind of manic energy, a sense that she had to regain her lost time. She got dressed quickly, and found that fresh clothes—still men's, but altered to her frame—had been put out for her. She did the buttons quickly, trying not to think about how all these clothes she was wearing probably belonged to dead men.

Hurrying down the stairs, she reasoned that she had probably missed dinner. She was getting to know this house and its rhythms now. It never completely slept. There was always someone up and around, someone dozing in a chair, someone demanding that they needed something. She passed rooms with doors ajar, seeing various salesmen engaged in the little activities that salesmen got up to. The bedrooms weren't so much for sleeping as they were little offices of privacy. Places to count your money, to arrange your inventory, to die in peace.

In the kitchen, she found that dinner had come and gone. Vesna was still doing dishes. Taiyo was, curiously, sitting at the kitchen table, a bundle of papers before him. She had clearly interrupted something.

"Margo," Vesna said. "We saved you dinner."

Taiyo looked up at her. "How's the skipshock holding up?"

She was handed a bowl of rice porridge topped with thin slices of hard beef. Margo took a bite and felt her stomach churn. It wasn't just her brain that was getting confused about the light and the length of the sun's workday. It was her body, too. She felt both heavy and hungry, weighed down with rich, gluey food, and also like she hadn't had a speck of fiber in a week.

Vesna must have seen her expression, because she actually laughed. "You've moved on to stage two, I see."

"What's stage two?"

"Constipation," she said breezily. "Taiyo, check Heck's case. He probably had something in there for that."

Taiyo dutifully began searching the case, and Margo wanted—very earnestly—to die.

"The interesting thing about salesmen," Taiyo said, examining various bottles and containers from Heck's orphaned bag, "is that half the stuff they sell seems to be remedies for *other* salesmen, to fix the symptoms of living as a salesman."

"I'm fine. Really. Where's Moon?" she asked, her face turning red. She wanted, very badly, for this conversation to end before he arrived. No one ever wants a boy to know about their gut health, but the notion of Moon knowing was unimaginable.

"Sleeping pills, waking-up pills, eye drops, enemas . . ." Taiyo carried on, rootling through. "It just doesn't seem worth it, to me."

"I don't need anything."

"Who's getting an enema?" Moon's voice from the kitchen door.

"Nobody!"

"Oh. You're awake. Feeling OK?"

"I'm feeling fine," she answered, taking a huge bite of her meal to prove it. "Have you all been waiting for me?"

"We've been arguing about you," Vesna said grimly.

"About me? Why?"

All three of them exchanged a look, as if inviting the other to go first. Moon finally went for it.

"There's a problem," he said. Arms crossed, his body leaning against the doorframe. "And it's to do with the apprenticeship plan. The Six is still closed for repairs. They still don't know what's going on with it. The Northeastern and Northwestern lines are open, but . . . well, they're being strict."

"No sales licenses under a year old," Taiyo said. "No apprentices without tattoos. Special dispensations are being triple-checked. They're being fierce. They've got some psycho military captain, checking everything."

Margo sat down, still cradling her hot bowl of sludge. "Captain Halvpas," she said.

"So forgery is out," Moon carried on grimly. "For the time being."

For her entire life, she'd shuttled between school and home and the shops. When her family went abroad, she showed her passport to the person in the glass booth at the airport. She felt the strange excitement of having the border control agent look between her and her photo and back again, wondering if they found something missing in the translation from person to image. But she had never *worried*. Not like Taiyo, Moon, and Vesna were. Not like she was apparently expected to now.

"All right. So what does that leave?"

Again, their eyes darted between one another, trying to decide who would break this next piece of news.

"Well," Taiyo said. "It leaves impersonation."

"Of who?"

Vesna extracted a slim wallet from her apron and handed it to Margo.

"Spring Heckley," Margo read aloud. "Traveling salesman."

"Keep reading."

"Born: Tello, eight hours. Coloring: white/fair," she continued, touching the newly exposed mousy blond hair. "Eyes: green. Height: five foot seven. Tattoo: Neck. Eight symbol, three-and-a-half-inch length, two point four centimeters below hairline. Then . . . a stamp."

"His visa stamp," Ves said gently. "Which is the same Northern visa as Moon's."

"How tall are you?" Taiyo asked, peering at her. "Five six? I'd put it at five six, five seven. Listen. We can put big shoes on her."

Margo's eyes lifted from the page. "I'm not a boy."

"Look closer. It doesn't specify gender."

"Salesmen are very rarely female," Taiyo said. "So they don't bother specifying."

Margo looked at the visa again. She kept her fingers on the base of her neck, rubbing the skin. She pictured the scalpel going in, and in the moment of silence, everyone else seemed to picture it, too.

"No," Moon said. "We'll find another way."

"Does it hurt?" Margo asked.

"Yes," Vesna said bluntly. "And it's permanent. So think carefully."

"I could get you drugs," Taiyo said. "For the pain."

"She's not doing it," Moon said sharply. "She'll be scarred for life. The kid only has one neck. And besides, it's bad luck."

"Salesmen and bad luck! *Life* is bad luck, Mo, so don't start with that. And anyway, you've scarred her for life already, with that godawful haircut."

The notion of being scarred for life didn't frighten Margo so much as everything else. Her list of fears, from smallest to largest, were thus:

That she would lose weeks, possibly even months, of her life to the New Davian day.

That she would have to see Captain Halvpas again.

That she would never get home.

That she would let everyone down.

Even as she listed these fears in her head, she was surprised at their running order. These people, who she had run into the street to escape on her first day here, had slowly revealed themselves to be among the most fascinating individuals she had ever met. Perhaps fascinating was the wrong word. They had all done terrible, brave things, and lived through terrible, brave times. Suddenly, she could not bear the thought of disappearing back to her own time line without having contributed anything meaningful to their lives. Margo could barely get her head around the various things they were suffering, the doom they all thought she was a portent of, the future they were afraid of. But she had been held by the throat by the SoGa. She had seen the gun in Halvpas's holster. Their lives were not long, not long in the way that hers would be. She could not do nothing.

"I'll do it," she said, digging her fingernails into her neck as she spoke.

There are certain phrases, she realized, that functioned like spells. They changed the energy in the room. They had metaphysical power. Air changed its direction of flow. *I'll do it,* in this room, had that kind of power. Suddenly, they were not three people exchanging glances around Margo; they were four. They were a team.

fourteen
MOON

The seriousness of what we're doing only really hits me the following evening, when Vesna closes the boardinghouse for dinner.

"Margo," she says, once Margo has gone through several iterations of *Yes, I'm sure I want to maim myself for your cause*. "I need you to knock on everyone's door and tell them that we've had some kind of cooking emergency. The stove isn't working, or something. I don't know. Tell them they'll have to eat in one of the pubs in town tonight, and that I'll take it off their bill."

"They won't like that. The SoGa are still holed up in town."

"I don't care what they like."

It's not so hard: there are only seven guests at Vesna's right now, including me. But she charges twenty gens a night, bed and dinner. Will she have to give half back, if she doesn't provide dinner? Even if she gives five back to each customer, it's a luxury she can't afford.

"Moon," she says, snapping her fingers at me. "Can you change the sign in the window? I have a closed sign *somewhere*, I think."

I go to turn the sign, and there's Domingo with a packed case, getting ready to leave.

"It's just closed for dinner, Dom," I say. "You don't have to check out."

Domingo's eyes scan me grimly. "No, no, I don't think I'll be coming back, old man."

His jaw tightens, the row of X's on his chin furrowing in the process.

"You don't want to be here after Heck?" I offer gently.

"That," he says. "And I don't like the tone of how things are going, around here."

There's a short, strange look between us then. A strange, muted warning. *I know something shady is going on,* he seems to say. *And I'm not about to get tangled up in it.*

"Well. I'll see you, Dom." I shake his hand, see him out the door, and wonder if he'll ever speak to me again. Then I turn back into the kitchen, where Margo sits. Waiting.

The only reason I got taken on as an apprentice in the first place was with the understanding that I gave my salesman, a cranky old drunk called Mitwatch, the yield from my monthly silver Wash. So I did. You're supposed to get thirty seeds a month, but that's only when the faith is strong, and when there are enough people left alive to practice it. At that time, I usually got about fifteen. Every month I handed over the seeds. Every month he accused me of keeping some back. And every month, I asked him if I was ready for my license yet. He would always find a reason. I didn't know enough yet, or I acted like I knew too much. His reasons changed all the time. He didn't want to lose me as a son, he said, before admitting he didn't want to face me as a rival.

The men file out the front door like surly children. Vesna locks it behind them. She shutters up the kitchen windows and summons Margo and me to the table. Ves takes down a new bottle of slip, pours us all a glass, and we wait.

"Will he get in trouble?" Margo asks. "You said pain relief was illegal."

"Everything Taiyo does is illegal," I reply. "But this, probably most of all, yeah."

The back door clatters open and Taiyo appears, looking like he has braved a little too much in getting here. He produces a small glass bottle of pasadol and places it on the table. "I'll be shot in the head if they find out about this," he says cheerfully.

"And I won't feel anything?" Margo asks nervously.

"Well, you'll feel something. Pressure, maybe. But not sharpness. It won't feel anywhere near how it's supposed to feel."

A silence, then, that Vesna eventually breaks. "Margo . . . you don't *have* to do this."

"That's right," I add. "You really don't."

I hate myself in this moment. Like if I present enough easy exits for Margo, enough chances for her to say *No tattoo for me, actually,* then I will have absolved myself in all of this. Every moment since the PACT meeting, I've been hearing Taiyo in my ear, like a song caught on a loop. *Get her to Alder, Mo. Drop her off there with PACT, and the money is yours.*

Because the thing is, there really is no route home for Margo unless she gets on a train again. That's a fact. We can't just expect her parents to show up at a random boardinghouse in New Davia to claim her, given that they live in a far-off world no one has heard of.

And Alder really is the best place to bring her. It's such an old and porous world, and AlderPACT really is the most powerful rebel faction in the North. Those are facts, too.

Further: I really will be risking a lot. I'll be traveling with her, after all, even though she'll be under the guise of the now-deceased Spring Heckley. If they catch me with an undocumented person traveling under a dead man's name? I'm done. Cooked. Over.

These are all facts. This is all true. But the overriding soul truth of the matter is that PACT, a freedom-fighting organization that I am not even a member of, will give me 425 gens for doing it. For dropping her off like a sack of potatoes, and washing my hands of the situation forever. I am merely stage one of Margo's journey, and AlderPACT will engineer stage two. She doesn't know this. Anything could happen at stage two, and it will no longer be my business. I will just be the salesman, and after I have been paid, I will be expected to go.

"Where should I sit?"

I'll admit it. She impresses me. Margo sits in a hard chair by the sink, her eyes fixed determinedly on the eaves in the ceiling, while Vesna carefully injects the pasadol into her neck. She watches Ves calmly as everything gets laid out: the measuring tape, the scalpel, the needle and thread. The gauze. The towel for the blood. There will be a lot of blood, I expect. I've already promised myself not to leave the room. I may be making deals behind this girl's back, but I will not look away while she goes through this. That much I can do.

The drugs take about ten minutes to kick in, and Vesna traces the outline in ink. She uses a measuring tape to do so, following the diagram on Heck's license precisely. She tests the skin every minute or so with a sewing needle. Pinpricks of blood begin to emerge on Margo's neck.

"Pressure or sharpness?" Vesna asks.

"Sharpness," Margo answers dutifully, and then we wait another minute, nobody speaking. I sit across from her, watching her gaze become soft. Slowly, she untethers from herself.

"Pressure or sharpness?" Vesna asks again.

"Pressh . . ." Margo's eyes begin to close, her body falling forward a little in a dozy haze. "Pressure."

From where Taiyo is standing, I know he can see the pinpricks of blood that have already emerged from the sewing needle. His face turns pale. For all his swagger, he's still a local kid. He's heard about salesman tattoos. I've even caught him staring at mine. But here he is, with a front-row seat to an illegal branding and he can't really take it.

"What if you guys run into people who knew Heck on the road?" he asks, eyes fixed to the ceiling.

"She'll go by Spring. Most people didn't even know Heck *had* a first name."

"And if they look at her papers?"

I blink at him. The only time you should show your papers is when a Pig asks for them. If you're showing them to just anybody, you're already in big trouble. I wonder, not for the first time, whether Taiyo should really be in a position of this much authority.

"They won't," I reply. Perhaps too firmly.

"You don't have to be cranky. It's a normal question."

Margo starts to wobble. Her head begins to droop, shoulders slumping like a broken toy.

"Keep her upright, Mo," Vesna says, poised at her neck.

"I'm off," Taiyo says, getting up. "People to see."

I would empty my wallet to go with him. Instead, I hold on to Margo's shoulders.

When Mitwatch finally got around to taking me for my license, he didn't even bother to stick around for the tattoo. He told me he would wait outside. I remember the excruciating pain, the stink of my own blood drying in the dirty room. The shock of the scalpel's incision, then the horrifying burrowing sensation of metal digging deep and scraping bone. I fainted twice, and remember thinking, as I came around each time: *Oh, it's still not over.* When I finally came out, holding an alcohol-soaked handkerchief to my eye, I couldn't find Mitwatch anywhere.

"Margo," I say quietly. She's flopping forward now, a dreamy, blissed-out rag. "I need you to sit steady so Ves can work. Can you do that?"

Her eyes struggle to focus, but they lock, eventually, on mine.

I never saw Mitwatch again, after my tattoo day. About a year ago, I heard from another salesman that he had died. Stabbed in a bar brawl.

"Look," I continue, trying to be as gentle as I can with this newly doped-up Margo. "Why don't you rest your elbows on your legs, huh? Like this? That way your neck will stay in place."

I mimic the pose I'm trying to get her to do, spreading my legs, resting my elbows above my knees, my arms creating a bough across the middle. She does it gamely. "Now, drop your head, so Ves can get to the back of your neck."

Margo drops her head. Just as I think she's completely out of it, she speaks. "The floor is making me dizzy," she says. "The wood keeps moving."

My tattoo is so close to my left eye that sometimes, when I've been drinking too much, the scar becomes swollen and blots the corner of my vision. A dark circle hovering just to the left of me, and I think—*There you are, Mitwatch.*

Is that how Margo is going to think of me, after she goes back to her own world? Imagine her, years from now. A woman with a life and a person she loves. Maybe she wears her hair long, to cover the scar. And maybe, every now and then, she wears it up. A fancy place, a real occasion. A long neck in an elegant gown. And maybe she catches sight of her neck in a mirror and thinks: *There you are, Moon.*

I'll be dead, of course.

Just like Mitwatch.

"Keep her talking," Vesna says quickly, trying not to lose her nerve. "We're lucky Heck's tattoo was just a figure eight. Imagine if it was one of those complicated ones. Imagine if it was yours? I'd never get the crescent right."

The scalpel is poised above Margo's skin, ready to cut down.

Get her to Alder, Mo. Drop her off there with PACT, and the money is yours.

Suddenly, I smell copper in the atmosphere, and I know Ves has made her first incision. There's no turning back now. I quickly look up at Margo's neck, a trickle of blood spilling onto her collar. I grab a towel and hold it there, Vesna moving her scalpel deftly, trying to find a middle ground between speed and precision.

Margo makes a noise, but her words have started to mush together. All I hear is: "Fluh . . ."

"What's that?"

"The fluh *moving.*"

She starts to sway again, her upper body trembling from being held up by her elbows. "I can't look at *fluh,*" she says desperately.

"Oh, the *floor* is moving." I'm not sure what to do. I can't change the floor.

"I can't . . ."

"OK, OK, hold on," I say, getting up. An idea comes to me quickly. I lie on the floor, my head between Margo's feet, my eyes looking into hers. It's a strange way to look at a person, upside down, on the floor. But in a way, it's the sort of perspective on Margo that I needed. Her face jumbled up, her green eyes flaring. A funny little puzzle.

"Hello," she says.

"Hello," I respond. I remember the moment at the butcher block. "Why is it we're always looking at each other upside down like this?"

And despite her high, she gets it. "Because we're always doing fucked-up stuff to me." Then she sighs, exhausted, like this is something she has privately come to terms with. "But it's OK. You've all been through terrible things. So this is my turn."

Ves stops working briefly. I can't see her face, my eyes so full of Margo, but I know she doesn't feel great about the aforementioned *fucked-up stuff*. Margo goes on, her mouth numb, her words slurring. "Now we're all even."

There are many terrible reasons to mutilate a person. Some of them are government-issued. That Margo might be doing this simply to *fit in* with us, with me and Ves and every other sorry soul that walks through this boardinghouse, might be the most terrible of all.

"I'm going to get you home, Margo," I say. "I promise."

Do I promise, though? And where does this promise intersect with the bill of sale in my pocket from Taiyo? Vesna, who feels very far away now that I'm lying on the floor between Margo's feet, coughs loudly. Her way of saying *I heard that*.

The blood flowing down her neck is thicker now, darker, the smell hot and oily. I can feel the towel becoming sodden. A drop of it splashes onto my cheek.

"Is that me? Is that my blood?" Margo's dreamy tone is crossed with faint worry.

My coping mechanism for dealing with terrible things—and I count the blood of a freshly maimed girl spilling onto my face as quite a terrible thing—is to zone out. To busy myself, to count invisible inventories in my head. But I do not have that option here. I need to be here for Margo, in spirit as well as in body.

"I like your new hair" is all I manage.

"You do?"

"You look like a duckling." Now I sound like the high one. I'm just trying to distract her. I think. Although I do like it, and she does look like a duckling. The new haircut is feathering around her face, covering her eyes, and there's something terribly sweet about it.

"A *duckling*!"

"Almost done," Vesna says quietly. "I just need to sew it up."

Vesna uses the special dissolving thread that the government uses. God knows how she got it, but it will ensure Margo will both heal quickly and scar for life.

Eventually, the smell of blood is replaced with the cold odor of antiseptic, and Vesna steps back.

"I'm done," she says.

Then she bursts into tears.

fifteen
MARGO

The day Margo realized that she had missed her seventeenth birthday, she was working in the parlor. The salesmen had all gone to bed, and she was packing up the chess set as Ani stacked up empty glasses of slip.

A note fell out of her apron pocket. This happened all the time now. She spent her healing time working for Vesna, and was secretly slipped notes by whatever salesman was near.

beautiful

and

I love you

and

I take water with my slip. please remember.

Today, however, the note was quite remarkable.

Come to bed with me. Will pay. 40 gens.

The man had a tattoo of an elephant's tusk on his cheek. He signed the note with the same symbol. Considering the horror with which salesmen talked about their tattoos, they took great pride in signing their names with them.

"More presents?" Ani said, rolling her eyes.

Margo handed her the note wordlessly.

"You should go for it," Ani said after examining it. "He's not bad, you know."

By now she was quite familiar with what Ani did for money, and that she often went straight from the night bakery to the boardinghouse. It wasn't so shocking, really. Multitasking was important in New Davia: you ate while working, dozed while talking, and evidently, made money while screwing. Ani seemed very untroubled by it. And if she was troubled, Margo knew that she was too poor to find an alternative.

Ani might be the only sex worker—a term Ani herself found strange, and quite rude in its directness—but she was not the only one having sex. There were at least two salesmen who were sleeping together. Margo also suspected that Taiyo and Vesna might have a thing going on. It made her think of her own sex life, or lack of, and whether everyone in the boardinghouse would find it shocking that she was almost seventeen, and a virgin.

That's when the panic began.

"Ves," she said, coming back into the kitchen. "How long have I been here?"

Ves did not look up from her ledger.

"Nine days."

"Excuse me?"

"Nine days."

Margo sat in the chair by the fire, her head in her hands. "I missed it."

"You missed what?"

"I missed my birthday."

She didn't weep. She wanted to. She wanted to cry for herself, and for her mother, who must have been falling apart with worry, and the boarding school, which in some way must have felt responsible.

A day was a day was a day

was a day.

And she had missed her seventeenth birthday.

"Oh, Margo," Ani said, and both she and the landlady put their arms around her. "I'm so sorry."

"It's OK," Margo said. "It's silly."

It was silly. But. They still presented her with a cake that night, and Ani sang a kind of "Happy Birthday" song in New Davian. Margo looked into the blade of the cake knife and said that in just nine days she had become a person that no one would recognize. She meant her hair, but she meant everything else, too. The three of them were silent, and Margo felt bad. She didn't want to sound sad or ungrateful. The cake was expensive.

"Well," Vesna said, taking out a pair of scissors. "You might as well look good, if you're not going to look like yourself."

The landlady snipped carefully, turning Moon's butcher-shop job into a neat boyish cut. Margo's eyes, still black from skipshock, looked enormous.

"Now *that*," Ves said when she had finished, "is a salesman."

The night after her fake birthday, she woke up in her chair by the fire. Moon was gently shaking her.

"Margo? Can you wake up?"

Moon always looked different at night. She'd noticed it the first day, standing in the orange maze surrounding Vesna's house. His skin glowed. It was like there was a small star nestled inside him somewhere, its light obscured by blood and bone but never quite extinguished.

"Hey," he said. "You still wanna do this?"

She nodded. His face was so close to hers. There was a cool, mineral atmosphere around him. The calm that came with snow.

"Here." He held out his hand. "Let me help you up."

It had been days since the drugs, yet the first moments after waking still felt like living under the surface of very deep water. Her eyes began to focus, and finally she saw that Ani was there, too. She had just come in from the cold, her dark hair under a red scarf.

"Ani," Margo said blearily. "What are you doing here?"

"You need to go," Ani replied. "Now."

Margo stood up wearily. "Why? Why now?"

No one had given her a schedule, exactly, on the Alder plan. Her scar had healed quickly, but she assumed that there would be some kind of tutorial process on being a salesman, on inhabiting the character of Spring Heckley. But no. Apparently the time to go was now. *Right* now.

"That psycho Halvpas who held you by the throat," Ani explained, taking her scarf down. "He came by the night bakery. Usually he goes right upstairs, but tonight he was in the parlor room, blowing off steam. I slipped some of the leftover pasadol from your surgery into his drink. He's gonna be out for the count for at least four hours."

"So it's never," Moon said. "Or it's now."

Margo blinked. Was everyone in New Davia somehow in on this secret plan to smuggle her to Alder? "Halvpas was at the night bakery?"

"In my experience, powerful men always have a major vice," Ani said with a sly wink. "And if you're planning a revolution, you better hope it's women."

"Ani's been monitoring his movements for us," Moon said, counting out cash. "And she's been a wonder. Thank you, Ani."

"Are you in PACT, Ani?" Margo asked blearily. "Is everyone?"

"I'm in the cash-under-the-counter business, not the PACT business," Ani answered. "Like our boy here." She pulled at a lock of Moon's wavy brown hair, a little flirtatious. A little too flirtatious, really, for Margo's comfort.

Moon scowled and gave her the money. "I said *thank you*, Ani."

"Much obliged." She turned to Margo, her eyeliner smudged heavily under her eyes, disappearing into the fine lines beginning to develop there. "Good luck, girl. You've been a real ticket to have around."

Ani kissed Margo on the forehead. It was astoundingly tender, given how little time they had really known each other. It occurred to her that, if the trip to Alder was successful, she would never again return to the boardinghouse. She had swept the floors and wiped the tables and vomited in the garden. Yet she might never see it again. A strange dread came over her. She wasn't ready. There was too much to do, and too much to miss.

"Where's Vesna?"

Ani and Moon shot each other careful, pained looks. "Ves doesn't do goodbyes," Ani said. "Not after last time."

Of course. The Sopilka sealing. The musical notes pasted to the walls.

Ani grabbed some sewing that had been left in a pile by the door.

"I'm taking these to the window upstairs. Light's better. Oh, and Margo—Vesna found you a suit. I made the amendments. I went by eye, so I'm not sure how good it is."

She handed Margo a heavy cloth bag, her expression strangely shy. For a few seconds, Margo was certain she was seeing all of Ani, her complete soul, and in that soul she saw an earnest teenager who liked to be helpful and make sure her friends had the best things. But both girls blinked, and the moment was gone again.

"I hope it fits," Ani said, then disappeared from the room.

It was just her and Moon now, standing on the precipice of whatever came next.

"I can wait outside while you get changed." He gestured to the bag of clothes.

"It's OK," she said, and quickly slipped the pants on under her loose smock. It was good to have clothes feel so close to her body again. It reminded her that she had one.

Moon gamely watched the ceiling while she did up her shirt buttons, but was forced to look back again while she fixed her suspenders. All salesmen wore suspenders, and so Margo would wear them, too. Belts, she had been told, were unlucky. Too many salesmen had been found at the end of them.

The suspenders became twisted, and Moon had to fix them so they lay flat.

"Uh . . ." He fidgeted with them. "They sit differently on . . ."

She looked down. Moon had run into the problem of Margo's breasts, sitting primly under her new suspenders. Margo knew this was her cue to straighten them herself. To take this delicate responsibility away from him. She didn't. She stood there, watching as the straps rolled against his thumbs, her body almost flush with his. Something about the woman-shaped hole that Ani had just left in the room made Margo eager to prove that she was a girl, too. A girl who wanted boys. Maybe even *this* boy. Her new hair and suit didn't change that, and something inside her needed him to know that. To admit it. To write it down, if at all possible, in his salesman notebook.

He paused. Scanned her briefly, appraisingly. It was so quiet in Vesna's house that she could hear a tiny, and deeply satisfying, intake of breath. He shook his head, trance broken, and stepped away from her.

"And finally. The notebook."

Moon handed her a black spiral-bound notebook. A black pencil tucked in the rings, each sheet paired with a carbon copy so you always had a record of what you'd written.

"Welcome to the profession."

They left through the front door. Margo felt rushed, out of her depth. She couldn't just go. Not like this. She respected Vesna's distaste for goodbyes, but she did not share it. She had lost her father very suddenly, the way you lose a button. She couldn't just *go.*

"Wait a second." She took out her brand-new notebook and paused, wondering what on earth she could write that might sum up her time in this strange house.

I'm going home, she wrote quickly. Then, underneath: *You next.* She was about to sign *Love, Margo* until she realized that she wasn't supposed to use that name anymore. She signed with the number 8, then stuck it to Vesna's wall, underneath her mother's arias.

At the train station, the sign she'd read on her very first day beckoned them in. NEW DAVIA CENTRAL STATION. NWQ-6—RESTRICTED INTERWORLD TRADING ONLY.

"Just do everything I do," Moon said, handing her one of the suitcases. The suitcase, she realized, that once belonged to Spring Heckley.

"Is that wise?"

"No. But do it anyway. We're getting the northeastern to Alder. That's all you need to say. Then show him your papers."

He went to hand her money, and Margo remembered she already had some. The bill that Captain Halvpas had given her to keep him informed.

Perhaps it was wrong of her to keep it. The heroine's thing to do would be to burn the money, or give it away. But this was not the place for grandstanding. She needed money, any kind, and Moon didn't have a lot to spare.

There were two armed SoGa at the entrance to the train station. They had been in New Davia for over a week now and seemed to be losing morale. They drooped at the doorway in orange uniforms that were already beginning to fade in brilliance after the constant snowfall. One appeared to be completely asleep. The awake one nodded at Moon and Margo, yawned as he checked their papers, then let them through.

Margo looked at the map on the train station wall. She knew salesmen were expected to know every world. New Davia was there, on the left-hand side, and the Six line ran from west to east with several other worlds dotted along the way. The northeastern line had more stops, and curved across the map in a snake shape.

Alder, she was thrilled to see, had twelve hours in a day.

"Twelve hours in Alder!"

"Try not to make obvious statements like that. They'll smell a rat. Head down, papers up."

The Pig in the ticket booth barely looked at her as he sold her the ticket. She turned around to show him the 8 on her neck. It was a few seconds, ten maximum, but eras seemed to pass within it. Yet everything was fine. He stamped her visa, then noted her details in his own ledger. Then he waved them both through the barriers.

They walked to the platform quickly, deliberately not making eye contact with each other. Terrified that any signal of excitement or relief between them might be caught by the Pig who had already forgotten they existed.

Her gaze followed the curving tracks as they climbed into the sky. They were early. Their train was on the way down, a black steamer chugging steadily from its place in the clouds. She could dimly see the warped, airy blur where New Davia's barrier began. The train spiraled gracefully, then started to meet the ground.

"This is us," Moon said, gathering their things. "Let's find a seat. It will probably hold here for a few minutes, so . . ."

"What are you doing, asleep?"

A voice burst fatally through the sleepy station. Thick, masculine, infuriated. There was a sharp cry that made them both look over. One of the dozing SoGa had just been hit in the stomach with the butt of his own gun. And the person holding it was, unmistakably, Halvpas.

Even through the fog of steam, Margo could see the thick, terrifying pillar of Captain Halvpas.

Perhaps you needed many skills to become a captain within the SoGa, but here were his: he stood up well to a drugging, and he knew when he was being looked at. He seemed to feel the heat of Margo's and Moon's notice and, like a robot, turned his head to face them. He squinted. Margo knew, instantly, that he recognized her. That this was the street urchin he had first choked and then given money to. For information, he said. Now here was that same girl, pretending to be a salesman. And with a dead man's papers.

Halvpas began to stride purposefully toward them.

"Moon. We have to go."

"It's coming." He was trying to keep his voice level. Their train was coming, but not quickly enough. It was still slowly chugging toward them, its pace sluggish as it pulled into the platform.

"We can't just get on this. He'll see. He'll jump on."

Moon made some quick calculations. He looked around. There was another train waiting on the opposite platform.

"Come on," he said, grabbing her elbow. "Follow me."

Halvpas was beckoning the Pig over, demanding to be let through the ticket barriers.

The train next to them was going to Hess Point. She could not remember where Hess Point featured on the map, but she knew it was nowhere near Alder.

"It's going to leave in one minute," Moon said, grabbing her case. "Margo. Get on this train."

"To *Hess Point*?"

"Just run through the cars. He'll follow you. You're faster. Smaller. Just stay ahead of him, a train car at a time, and then run off when it's about to depart. He'll be stuck on a train to Hess. Here, give me your jacket. You'll move faster."

He tugged the suit jacket off her. She felt oddly exposed in her shirt and suspenders.

"I can't do that," she said, panic rising sharply in her. "Mo, I can't. Don't make me do that. I can't outrun him."

But Mo had already pushed her on the train. "Go, Margo, *go*."

The moment her foot was in the almost-empty car, she could hear Halvpas's voice, almost as close as she could hear Moon's.

"Stop that girl," he roared. "Get that girl off that train."

She started to run. She heard Moon say something, something like *What girl*, and she bolted through the car.

The train shook as one foot thudded heavily after the other. These were not like the trains back home, everything plastic and inorganic. These had wooden floors that creaked underneath her. The narrow train car sounded as though it were about to split in two.

It wasn't long until she felt a second pair of feet behind her, rattling the fixtures.

"Get back here!"

But she wouldn't. She would do exactly as Moon had told her. She would run and run until she ran out of train.

The Hess Point train had thin, accordion-style doors between each compartment that slid back to open. She bounded into the second car, slamming the door shut behind her.

The second train car had people in it. Four. Salesmen she did not recognize, clustered together with their cases open. She bounded past, feet slapping on the floor. They glared at her, their disapproval quickly turning to horror as Halvpas followed, heaving in his orange uniform.

"Get back here," he roared. "This girl is trespassing on this train. Do you hear me? She's without a license."

The four salesmen seemed to find this interesting, but clearly it was not an aberration to them, the way it was to Halvpas. How many people tried to run onto trains without a license, she wondered. How usual or unusual was this crime?

The sliding doors meant she had to stop every couple of feet, find the grooves of the handle, and pull them backward. Turn around, then pull them shut. Every time she went through a new door, Halvpas gained on her. The head start she began with was starting to close.

By the time she reached the fourth door, he was inches away.

Margo briefly turned her head to the window, her breath already failing. She was, quite literally, running out of road. There was only one car left. The platform was coming to an end and if she did not get off within the next ten seconds, she would be stuck on this train with Captain Halvpas indefinitely.

And he had a gun.

By the fifth train car, there was less than ten inches between them. The seats loomed before her, with only one passenger on board. A heavyset man with dark hair and a row of X's dotting his jawline.

Domingo. From her first night. She had not seen him again, since he decided that everything had become too political for him. She had assumed he had moved on to a different world. But no. He had stayed in New Davia; he just didn't want to be at Vesna's anymore.

She bolted past him, feeling like she could not keep this up, that no one could. That Halvpas would win every time. That feats of strength or speed had never been her wheelhouse, so why would they be now.

The final sliding door was just ahead. She could feel Halvpas's breath on the back of her neck.

Sometimes being part of a revolution means risking your life and neck for the cause. Sometimes it means sleeping with an officer and drugging him so your friends can escape.

And sometimes, it's a matter of sticking your foot out at the right time.

Domingo, who had no political affiliations one way or another, was prepared to do this. And because he did, Halvpas briefly buckled and fell, enabling Margo to get clear ahead of him.

She bolted to the sixth car, Halvpas still getting to his feet. She didn't even bother to shut the sliding door after her. She knew she had made it. And as she pulled open the train doors and leaped onto the platform, she heard one long howl as the service to Hess Point began to pull away.

She watched him, hammering the window where she had trapped him like an insect. A strange instinct from childhood reemerged within her that she felt honor bound to obey. She gave him the finger.

She hoped that nothing terrible would happen to Domingo. She realized with sickening fright that she would never be completely sure. But as Halvpas screamed at her through thick glass, she swore she could make out the shape his lips were making.

A word he should not know, and yet was saying, again and again.

Margo, he screamed. *Margo.*

PART TWO

ALDER CITY

sixteen
MOON

The Hess train is already slowly moving off the platform. Margo opens the final set of doors and, without a second to lose, leaps from it. One toe pointed behind her like a dancer, the other arching forward in a runner's lunge. There is a brief, excruciating moment—whipped by wind, face red, breath short—when I am sure she is the most beautiful thing I have ever seen.

She collapses into me, and I drop the suitcases just in time to catch her with both arms. Her body warm and writhing, the white shirt sticky with sweat. I want to just stand there a moment. To hold her, and praise her, and revel in the fact that Captain Halvpas is stuck on a train heading north. Her heart is beating like a drum, the whole organ overcooked, and I should keep both arms firmly around her until she simmers down.

But these actions would all take time. Time that we do not have, especially as the Alder train is about to leave.

"Come on," I say, pushing Margo onto yet another train. My hand between her shoulder blades, her whole body trembling like a spooked horse.

Surely they won't just let the train *go*? After a SoGa captain chased a girl through a six-carriage train, his voice roaring through the empty station like a siren?

But Captain Halvpas made a terrible mistake in the moments

before pursuing Margo, and it was attacking his own men. The soldier with the rifle butt in his stomach took too long to get to his feet, and the other one had to help him.

I peer back through the window of the moving train. The chase happened so suddenly that no one in the ticket hall seems to understand yet what went on. Their view of the trains can't even be that good. They don't seem to realize that Halvpas is gone, and that he will not be striding back down the platform anytime soon, issuing new orders.

And so Margo and I get our train. Breathless, shaking, sweating. But we make it. We flop into two empty seats. Wild-eyed. We are lucky. For the first time in my life, I am lucky.

"Are you OK?"

She nods mutely, then closes her eyes. A bead of sweat falls from her forehead as she tries to parse the last five minutes. Then her eyes snap open again, green and clear and brash.

"He said my name," she says. "He said Margo."

"What?"

She starts to gnaw anxiously on her thumbnail. "Why does he know my name? I didn't tell him my name. When he caught me, I mean."

I rest my mouth on my knuckles, considering this. "Someone at the boardinghouse," I say at last. "Someone talked."

I go through them in my head. Everyone Margo has met, everyone who knows her name. Etan. Domingo. Ani. Taiyo. Ves. We only ever used Margo's real name on that first night. The traveling salesmen who have passed through since have simply known her as *the new girl*.

Margo screws her face up in disbelief. "Domingo helped me on the train just now. He stuck his foot out. Tripped Halvpas."

I shrug. "Etan, then." A likely candidate. He is, after all, still from the South. And why should you trust a Southern salesman?

But. Halvpas has been in New Davia for almost the same length of time as Margo. If someone from the boardinghouse was an informant, then wouldn't he have broken down Vesna's door days ago?

The train rises toward the heavens. The altitude is making Margo's ears pop. She winces, tugging at them in pain.

"Are you trying to look like a rookie?" I say, and I'm not sure where the sharpness comes from exactly. Maybe it's because I can still feel my heart in my throat. *You almost lost her there, Lev. You almost lost her forever.*

And then: *That's the goal, isn't it? To lose her forever?*

"Sorry," she replies, and places her hands back in her lap. I can tell I've made her feel chastised, and frightened, and small. She *should* feel frightened. Why does a captain in the Southern Guard know her name? Why is he after her?

We burst through the world barrier, and the train is briefly shrouded in darkness. Margo yelps softly, then starts to fidget with her watch. Rolling its loose links up and down her arm, the nervous habit of a lost girl.

"Where'd that watch come from anyway?" I ask.

"My dad," she says shortly, still smarting after the rookie comment. We sit in silence as the train passes into the next world. Crader again.

"I was sent to a doctor once. A therapist. For my mental health."

She says it searchingly, the way she does sometimes, checking if these words exist in my vocabulary. I nod to indicate I understand the theory of mental health.

"He said I should try to externalize my internal thoughts. Get out of my own head. Like if I start to panic, I should start counting things in the room. To calm me down. But that didn't really work, so instead I started to use the watch."

"Use the watch how?"

She cranes forward, showing me the face of the watch. It's a beautiful thing, with a glass screen in the center to show the whirring of the inner dials. "It's got this broken third hand, you see, and it's a stopwatch. It goes for one minute. And so when I feel anxious, I hit the stopwatch and breathe in and out for sixty seconds, just watching the hand go around."

"And does that work?"

There must be something revealing in the way I use my voice. I might sound a little too interested in the idea of calming down.

"Why don't you check?" she asks, and slips it on my hand. I do as she says. I click the watch, and observe the thin arm rotate around the dial.

"Breathe in and out," she says. So I do. In. Out. I've never thought about breathing so much before. I don't know what I'm supposed to be thinking about, but inevitably, I think about Margo.

When I first met Margo, she was a problem. Then she became a product. A payday. I didn't think much about her past or her future because those things would make her feel too real, and me too involved. But then the tattoo happened. You can't deny someone's reality after you've lain on the floor and their blood has trickled onto the flat of your cheek.

Somewhere in the last week Margo has become the dominant *she* of my life. Every day I wake up thinking, *What is she thinking, where is she going, what will she do?*

And most importantly: How would she feel if she knew that, technically speaking, my first priority is not to get her home? That this trip is, in essence, a delivery mission for me. Drop off Margo.

Collect 425 gens. Maybe there will be a second, follow-up mission; maybe they will thank me and tell me to piss off.

I keep picturing a world where I walk away from Margo. *See ya, kid*. How is that supposed to happen? After everything?

The copper mines in Alder have made it rich, famous, and, crucially, ugly. Everything is bronze. Not just the carved angels watching us from the eaves in the train station, or the huge clock looming in the foyer. But everything: the floor is a dull brown. The ceiling, though prettily fixed into a glass dome, is lined with dark brown filigree. It's undeniably very grand, but the mud-colored metal sucks the light away. Then there's the spots of festering, swampy green where the copper has oxidized, giving the place a feel of stale bread. It's hard to come here and not feel poor and depressed.

"*Hey.*" Margo breathes hard, struggling with the weight of Heck's case. "Wait."

"Sorry. Time is precious," I mumble, rooting around for my ticket. "Get ready to show your pass again. Barriers ahead."

The place is bristling with admin, with people going and checking and buying and leaving. It's a busy day, with a half dozen horses being trotted through the building. Bahar thoroughbreds, Yintiver stallions. Serious horses. Racing breeds.

Margo is clearly bewitched by it all. She can't resist staring at the glass ceiling, where the train tracks wind toward the sky.

"I just keep thinking," she says, "how my world should have this. But it doesn't. Why?"

She sounds as if she's been screwed out of some inheritance. Which in a way, I suppose, she has. I shrug.

"You're thinking about Halvpas, aren't you?"

She nods. "Maybe no one from my world is *supposed* to know about any of yours. Maybe that's why he's after me the way he is."

But the moment we turn away, we hear a loud *thunk* from above. Then another:

thunk.

thunk.

thunk.

Two hundred people all look up at once. Huge wooden planks have started to plop down from the sky, hitting the glass. The roof is made for heavy weather, so at first, it doesn't seem likely that a few wooden planks could do too much damage.

But then the planks start falling faster, a blizzard of them coming at once, and the glass starts to splinter. Breakages start to spread, spiderweb style, across the station roof.

It takes me a full minute of watching the glass splinter before I realize what's going on.

The train tracks are falling.

So this is what it looked like in New Davia. Why Etan was so shaken when he showed up for dinner at Vesna's.

Margo left the train in New Davia and managed to close the Six line for almost a week. I had been ready to write that off as a coincidence. Or, if not a coincidence, then a series of symptoms that came from an old, fracturing train system that has been toyed with by Semper too much, and for too long.

But Margo is not a symptom. Margo is the cause. She gets on trains, and then those trains break down. The sole mode of transport that Semper uses to control the flow of people, of capital . . . and Margo alone can disrupt it just by coming into its orbit.

What are you supposed to do with information like that?

One of the senior Pigs starts bellowing through the loudspeaker for everyone to get out. The half dozen horses get spooked, the loudspeaker and the falling tracks enough to upset their delicate horsey brains. They start to rear and pull from their handlers. Whinnies echo through the grand copper station, their panic bouncing off the walls.

"What is going—" But she can't finish her sentence. People are starting to rush for the exits, and an older crateman has just knocked Margo off her feet. She trips right over her suitcase, lands face-first on the polished floor.

"What the *hell*, man." I push back against the crateman who knocked her.

"You do this, Lunati?" is his immediate response. Ah. Here it is. It only takes a minute, two minutes maximum, before someone blames the Lunati. "Trying to pinch the horses, you Moony scum?"

Blood is starting to bloom beneath Margo's nose. Oh, *shit*. Not the teeth. Anything but the teeth. Cuts and scrapes I have the medicine for, but I've got nothing to fix teeth. I crouch, trying to help her up.

"*Answer me*, you freeloading little shit."

Freeloading! Wonderful. That's just wonderful.

"You've knocked my friend over." I try to stay calm. "So you can apologize to her and help me, or you can fuck off, but if you stand around insulting me, we're going to have a problem."

The crateman is older but not old. He has gray hair, but it's all still firmly on his head. His temples are decorated with small nicks, right near the hairline. The kind you could theoretically grow your hair out and cover, were you to leave the profession. Cratemen get these kind of luxuries. They work for big companies, giant Southern importers. It's only freelance salesmen who get the honor of true disfigurement.

"What did you say?"

Margo has gotten to her feet and—thank god—it's just the skin above her lip that's bleeding. Her front teeth are still firmly in place.

"I said, apologize to my friend"—I should not be insisting on this apology, but we're here now, and the racket of the station has brought out the boldness in me—"or we'll have a problem."

Crack.

"Moon." Margo tugs at me. "Let's just get out of here."

The splinters in the glass have finally spread enough that the whole ceiling might give way at any second. The crateman doesn't notice, or doesn't care. "It seems we have a problem then, Moony," he says. I hear another crack, louder this time. A crack that splits the world open. I look up, idiot that I am, and in that instant I feel a pounding thud in my gut. The crateman has punched me, hard, in the stomach.

It winds me. My vision is spotty for a few seconds, my breath gone, the pain thudding through to my spine. Margo steps in front of me and starts screaming something indistinct at the crateman. All I can see is Heck's 8 on the back of her neck, the skin shiny with healing.

"That's enough of *that.*"

The voice is familiar. I look up and Taiyo has leapt onto the crateman from behind, locking both arms behind him. What the *hell* is he doing here?

"Now, sir," he says, a song in his voice. "Did my friend upset you somehow?"

Taiyo twists the crateman's arm behind his back, and he yowls in pain.

"Can't leave you two alone for five minutes, can I? Margo looks like a prizefighter and you're wheezing like an old lady. Now. Who's this?"

I glare at Taiyo. *Don't say her real name, you idiot!* Margo is supposed to be going by Spring Heckley now.

"Just some prick," Margo says, daubing her white sleeve to her bloody lip. "He called Moon a thief."

"Well, that's not polite, is it? You wanna punch him, Mo?"

I'm not given any time to decide. A Northern Guard, splendid in his emerald-green-and-gray uniform, decides to take control of the room.

"Everybody *out*," he screams. "Back through the platforms, onto the street."

He is listened to. Partly because he is a government employee, and partly because he is aiming his gun at the crowd.

The pavilion outside the train station is filled with statues of great men and good daughters. Anemic-looking princesses, weak-chinned noblemen. The station doors close, and everyone spills outside to make sense of what just happened.

No one knows that this exact thing happened in New Davia ten days ago. So few people are permitted to travel between worlds anymore that news travels extremely slowly.

Out of a tight knot of conferring cratemen emerges a boy who looks about fourteen. He had, up until now, been held in place by his colleagues, subdued by the grip of four men. He wrestles away from them with a bloodcurdling scream. He starts beating his fists against the walls of the shuttered train station, the heavy bronze doors absorbing his fury.

"They're *sealing* us. Can't you see? This is how they do it. My god, this is how they *must* do it. They're going to keep us in here like rats."

One of his colleagues attempts to subdue him. "Stop that. Stop that nonsense now."

But clearly, not everyone thinks it's nonsense. Panic is bubbling, threatening to turn a crowd into a mob. The boy starts throwing rocks at the station, and some people start to join him.

"We need to get out of here," I murmur to Margo and Taiyo.

"You get hit in the face, too, Fengari?"

"What? No?"

Taiyo leans forward and tracks his finger under my nose, then draws it away covered in blood.

"That crateman gave you a bloody nose."

I pull a handkerchief out of my inner pocket. This is not a bloody nose, the kind you get in a brawl after some idiot punches you in the face. This is a nosebleed. This is what happens when skipshock slows down your body's natural healing processes.

"How did you get here, anyway?" I ask him.

"I told you. I went to see a man about a box."

"The *coffin*? You were serious about that?"

"I'm serious about everything." He glances at Margo. "Love the new suit, by the way. Very sharp."

"You're telling me you crossed worlds in a coffin?"

"Not my favorite way to travel. But. There you go."

"How did you get *out*?" Margo says, equally as horrified as I am. "Without anyone seeing?"

"I'm highly skilled in the art of escape."

She looks at me, and neither of us have the energy to figure out whether he's joking about the coffin. Or, for that matter, about the art of escape.

"I suppose you have an address written down somewhere, Taiyo?" I say, dabbing at my face. "Perhaps some very particular people we have to meet?"

"Yes. Yes, I do."

He palms me a tightly folded piece of paper.

"I appreciate you want to be secretive," I say flatly, unpicking the folds in front of him. "But actually this draws *more* attention to us, me having to unfold your dumb note."

"Can't you ever just be *grateful*? I just saved you from getting your head caved in."

I finally unpick the note. The address reads *Chariot Theater, Radius Eight, Diameter Three*. Then on the other side, there's just one phrase: *Ghost story.*

"Do you know where it is?" Taiyo asks, and I realize he has no idea how Alder City works, and would have no hope of finding this address if there wasn't a salesman here to show him. This, then, is how I'm supposed to be helping PACT. Not just by delivering Margo, but by helping small-town revolutionaries locate the addresses that aren't just obscure. Alder addresses are quite literally moving targets.

I scrunch up the note. "I think so. Come on. Follow me."

And they do. Taiyo looking like a lost child, Margo with a cut lip. Me with a nosebleed.

If we're the three people who hang in the balance between war and peace, then peace is fucked.

seventeen
MARGO

They got away from the train station just quickly enough to watch the roof shatter. It was a bright, crisp day in Alder, the sun shimmering off the fractured glass, and finally the dome could hold no longer. Everyone seemed to realize it at once. A terrible hush came over the crowd, and together they watched the glass curl and fall toward the ground. She would never forget that. The silence, the awful nothing, as they waited for the glass to hit the hard metal floor. The floor that still had, in addition to many other things, a small amount of Margo's blood on it. The sound was like hard rain.

The three of them stood in silence. Margo didn't know a thing about Alder, but she knew this train station was clearly old, clearly important, and now it had no roof. It would take weeks to fix, probably—and that was before you even started on the train line they had just arrived on. The train line that had spontaneously shed its tracks moments after Margo had stepped away from it.

"Did I do this?" she said, looking to Taiyo and Moon standing on either side of her. "Was that . . . me?"

She waited for either boy to say it was a coincidence. They were such different people, Taiyo and Moon, that if one of them thought it wasn't her fault then the other would definitely think it was. But neither said a word to contradict her.

Finally, Moon spoke.

"All we know is that the train track broke in New Davia after you arrived, and now . . . now it's doing it again."

That was it. That was as close to a diagnosis as anyone was prepared to offer.

"Right," he said, picking his case up. "Let's go."

Moon led the way, head down, stride long, pace fast.

"This guy," Taiyo said, breath a little short already. "Does everything have to be a race?"

She laughed, then instantly felt disloyal. The crateman at the station had pounced so quickly on Moon, his face twisting with glee when he realized a Lunati salesman was in the building. Maybe Moon's obnoxiously fast walk wasn't about saving time. Maybe it was about saving his own skin. How quickly could you identify a crescent scar when it passed by you in a blur?

Moon led them to a large square archway where a dozen or so people were also gathered. They were clumped together like they were sheltering from rain, even though the day was bright and fine. A couple of people chatted, but most kept quiet, or read while standing. They were waiting for something, but Margo had no idea what.

It was comforting, having Taiyo there, a partner in having absolutely no clue how other worlds worked. They cut eyes at each other, made *Your guess is as good as mine* faces, and then fell under Moon's disapproving glare.

She wished he wouldn't be like this. Just as she had seen a flash of the real Ani that morning in the boardinghouse, she was routinely treated to flashes of the real Moon. He was funny and strange and had feelings so strong that they cooked in his chest. He was a wavy-haired boy with night-lit skin, and he made her want to run up right against the edges of decency. *Past* decency, even.

But then there was the other Moon, and that Moon had learned very diligently to survive impossible odds. That Moon was the fast walker. He was also the one who fussed over the rules of his profession. The one who frequently became impatient with Taiyo, who did things so showily. Both Moons, she reasoned, were real. One she just preferred more.

She stared at a tall, smart building on the other side of the archway. It felt like a fancy person's house, with its glimmering gas lampposts and wide shining steps. The ground was paved with ordinary gray cobblestones, with deep bronze furrows that looked like tramlines.

Suddenly, there was a whirring sound of machinery and the landscape swung around her. The smart building with the gas lampposts whirled past her as though on a moving walkway. Margo looked down at her feet in disbelief. She was still underneath the archway. She watched in shock as several people stepped away from the arch and onto a completely new street, this one filled with Victorian-looking offices. Through a long window, Margo saw a man copying figures from one huge book into another.

"Business district," Moon said. He held her arm firmly to indicate to that this was not yet their stop.

Just as soon as the business district had settled in her vision, the world moved again. Everything in Margo's eyeline moved about half a mile to the left, the diligent bookkeeper carried far away.

A new street emerged. This was another huge bronze building, another onion-shaped glass roof. Here she saw stained glass depicting sheep, cows, and vegetables.

"Market district," he said. He said it quietly into her ear, his breath warm on the healing skin of her neck. He dragged on the way he said it, like he was very aware of how close they were standing, and for a few seconds the Survivor Moon melted away again. It was strange how the murmuring of two words—*market district*—could do all that, but it did.

More people left the moving platform, until it was now just the three of them. "One more rotation," Moon said, back in his normal voice.

"What *is* this place?" she asked.

"It's a movable city. The buildings run on tracks."

Moon pointed to the horizon. There, Margo saw a strip of buildings slowly inch to the left. She followed the line of it, turning all the way around to chart their progress. A hundred buildings or so were on a rotating band, all moving counterclockwise to the faint hum of whirring machinery.

"Each neighborhood is on one of these concentric circles, you see? Like the rings on a tree. And at planned points in the day, they move."

"But *why*?" she asked. Taiyo was saying nothing, but he looked grateful that Margo was willing to ask the stupid questions.

"They had some king a hundred years ago, this brilliant engineer guy, who made it all happen." Moon started patting down his inner coat pockets, taking out the address that Taiyo had given him. "His big theory was: people run out of time, but buildings don't. Buildings have all the time in the world. Right?"

"Right . . ."

"So why should the people move? The city should come to *them*."

She felt like her brain was simmering with this new information. A city that *moved*?

They rotated once again, and Moon led them through a large, open street where four grand theaters stood facing one another. Like all theaters, they did everything to communicate to pedestrians that they were buildings of huge cultural importance. They had columns, and steps, and big curved roofs to aid the echoing of important words, meaningful sounds.

There were enormous posters, hand-painted and crackling with drama. They had titles she did not recognize but dynamics that she did. Lovers clutching one another, a disapproving parent figure in the background. Lovers clutching, an evil wizard in the background. A woman in one man's arms while another looked on in despair. It was all about love.

Maybe everything was.

Moon led them past the huge open parade of theaters and into a set of narrow, winding streets. Margo heard a faint crank of machinery and looked over the squat roofs into the distance. Another rotation had begun. The ruined train station moved out of her view and briefly blocked the sun.

These streets had theaters, too, but smaller, and plastered with aging posters. They were crumpled and yellow, advertising plays and dance performances. They mostly seemed to concern themselves with women, some of them dancing, many of them topless. They each had initials pasted in the left-hand corner—NN, PN, FN—and she asked Moon what they meant. This was a question that Taiyo was able to answer, and he did so gladly.

"No nudity, partial nudity, full nudity."

"So they aren't real plays? They're just strip shows?"

"Oh, they're real plays, all right. Three acts and an intermission."

She had learned in New Davia that people in Northern worlds multitasked as much as they possibly could. Alder, moneyed yet still short on time, elaborated on this: you got told a story while enjoying some tits.

The shows were all in progress but barkers were standing at

each theater door, tempting them in. "Latecomers welcome," an old man in a boater hat urged. "Three seats, all together. No one minds, come in, come in."

Moon ignored him, pushing past into the next street. But the boater-hat man caught Margo's curious eye and moved in on her.

"Ladies welcome, gentlemen welcome, the show is for everyone," he insisted. She moved away, following Taiyo and Moon into the next set of streets. "*The Tale of Orpheus*," he called to her desperately. "A favorite of the ladies."

Margo stopped dead. Her brain briefly swam back to school, to an English class or a history class or a history of English type of class, she didn't know. But she had heard of Orpheus before.

"Excuse me?"

The boater man saw his opportunity and grabbed Margo by the arm. "A young man journeys to a Northern world to find his love," he said temptingly. "Eurydice, captured by Hades."

Moon appeared again, having doubled back to find her. "What's going on?" Then he saw the boater man's hand on Margo's arm. "Leave her alone. Come on, we have places to be."

He dragged her away, the coins in her mind's piggy bank still rattling around. Eurydice, Orpheus, and Hades. She knew very little about Greek mythology, except that it was extremely old, thousands of years.

There had been customs and dishes and habits in New Davia that were common to her own world. The cheese rice porridge, for example, was a kind of bad risotto. Birthdays existed. But any culture can land on the idea of risotto; everyone can stumble on the notion of a birthday. Trees produce wood and everyone everywhere understands what wood is for. But cultural ideas, stories, Jesus Christ, space travel, *The Wizard of Oz*, phones, plugs—all the things that were native to Margo's world were completely absent in Moon's.

Except this. Except Orpheus.

They were finally at the Chariot, a shabby gray building with a plaster cast of a charioteer at the entrance. Taiyo and Moon went in ahead of her. Margo lingered at the door, staring at the charioteer. He had two horses pulling him in different directions, one black, one white.

Margo didn't know what was waiting for them inside the theater, but she knew that she couldn't go a step farther until she had processed the Orpheus thing. Moon came back out and stood quietly next to her until she spoke.

For all of Moon's bluster and urgency, he had calm habits, and she liked that about him.

"We have Orpheus," she said.

"What do you mean?"

"Do you know the story of Orpheus?"

"Of course."

"Well, what is it?"

Moon leaned against the charioteer, the plaster hand already crumbling at the reins. "Eurydice is a Southerner," he said. "And is stolen to a Northern world by Hades, who's king of this particular world. Orpheus goes to get her."

"And where does the story come from?"

"Semper. All those stories come from Semper."

"We *have* Orpheus. And Hades."

"What do you mean, you *have* them?"

"They're part of our myths. And if they're part of Semper's, too . . ."

He nodded, finally getting it. "So at one point in time, Semper and your world were linked."

"Even if it was hundreds of years ago. Stories have traveled between worlds before, and if stories have, then people have, too."

They had long held the theory that Margo's world was one that had been sealed so long ago that no one remembered it. But it had always only been a theory. Here was the proof. A postcard from her own culture, sitting in an Alder street as though it were a bookmark in an old paperback. Lightness came over her. If Orpheus had found a path here, then there must be a path back.

Moon raked both hands through his hair, pulling at the skin on his temples. Margo caught a rare sight of the top of his tattoo, the tip of his crescent moon intersecting faintly with his left eyebrow. They had dug too far into the brow when they carved up his face. You could see a scratch of white, where the hair refused to grow back.

She was suddenly taken out of her Orpheus problem. All she could think about was a visa worker digging into Moon's face with a knife. No painkillers. No anesthetic. She knew what that meant now. She still couldn't lie down without hurting her neck.

"What are you looking at?"

The stare had gone on too long. The eyebrow had, for whatever reason, become fascinating.

"Nothing."

There was a moment of nothing, a nothing so large and empty that it went right back around to being something again.

"Come on. What are you thinking?"

"I'm thinking: they could have blinded you, they went so close to your eye."

Moon shrugged. "I guess they could have."

"And that was for a salesman license. What will they do to you if they catch you? Forging my tattoo. Taking Heck's license. Helping PACT."

Her anxieties rushed out then, epiphanies strung together with panic. The realization that Moon mattered to her. And that, for a combination of reasons pertaining to who he was and what he did for a living, Moon would not be treated kindly when caught.

Captain Halvpas would kill him instantly. And how many Captain Halvpases were there out there? Waiting for them?

"They'll kill you." She had heard the sentiment before. Felt it, even. The day of the haircut. The evening of the tattoo, all anyone could talk about was what Semper might do to them if they were caught. But for some reason, the shard of white skin in his eyebrow made the idea real to her. They would have blinded him. They really would have.

"Margo . . ." He took a step toward her, hair resettling on his forehead. He was not much taller than her, really. Maybe half a head. For once, they were close without either of them being upside down, or on drugs, or on a butcher's block, or running to a train station.

"You're . . ." He started. Stopped. Tried again, but then became distracted by her hands, which had somehow become threaded through his. Always so warm, his hands. Their knuckles lined up like sloppy stitches.

"What? What am I?"

Margo leaned her body against the theater wall and waited for him to close the gap. Instinct really. She had kissed enough boys to know when to create space and when to fill it.

"Young," he finally said.

Then he stepped back, and let go of her hand.

"Excuse me? No I'm not. I'm probably older than you."

"That's not what I mean. You know what I mean. You're a kid, still. You live with your mother. You need to get back to her." The words seemed to sober him up, turned him back into the brusque young man who was always scolding revolutionaries for dreaming too big. "Margo, I think it's probably wise if we don't have a physical relationship."

The insult of it. Breathtaking.

She had never felt so ashamed in her life. Never so ashamed, nor so ugly. Nor so dumb.

"Come on," he said, looking embarrassed for her. "We're not gonna figure anything out standing here."

And he went inside.

eighteen
MOON

idiot idiot idiot

Fucking *IDIOT.*

???

What is wrong with you???

WHY DO YOU SAY THINGS?

WHY ARE YOU ALLOWED TO SAY THINGS???

The girl wanted to be *kissed*, Moon. When's the last time someone wanted to kiss you like that? When's the last time you wanted to kiss anyone? I don't mean falling into bed with some girl in a boardinghouse. I don't mean a sloppy tryst with a housewife after a sale.

This was not just a trick of the light. This was a spark.

And you killed it.

It's dead.

Well, that's good, isn't it? That simplifies it. We're back to business. Business being, handing Margo over to PACT without all this lousy sexual tension and guilt getting in the way of things.

While Margo and I were outside ruining our friendship, Taiyo had collected our tickets. I don't know what he said to the lady in the booth, but it seems to me that our seats are deliberate. A set of three together on the edge of an empty row, far from the door but right in view of the stage.

There's a sharp, damp smell in the theater, like mildew and carpet. There are maybe forty people in the audience, watching some kind of ghost story. I can't follow the plot. Perhaps it's obvious, the way all ghost stories are obvious, but all I can think about is Margo. I can't make out her face. Why did I say all that stuff about her being young? What did that have to do with anything? But even as I'm scolding myself, there's an uneasy truth to it. Age isn't about days or years. It's about what puts lines on your face, pressure on your organs, fear in your heart. I have too much of that kind of age, and Margo doesn't have enough.

Is that true, though? I think of the girl who jumped off a moving train. Who sacrificed her hair and her skin for a cause she has no loyalty to. What was *that*, if not experience?

"Two people have gotten up and left since we came in," Taiyo whispers to me, breaking my train of thought. "Ninety seconds apart. Exactly."

"Huh?"

He spreads all ten fingers in his lap, folding them down as he silently counts. Five fingers. Four. Three. Two. One—

A woman in front of us gets up and leaves the theater. Slight, with fair hair in a bun. Wisps of it are briefly illuminated by the lobby light as she pulls open the door and disappears.

"Maybe they just don't like the play."

Halvpas knowing Margo's name. The tracks breaking twice. This Orpheus thing. Too many coincidences are following me around, like stray dogs I've been stupid enough to feed.

The characters in the play have had enough of their ghost and have paid a Lunati priestess to get rid of it. Lunati people always turn up in bad plays, either granting wishes or playing tricks or handing over their monthly silver Wash to some poor orphan.

"Oh, come on," I say, rolling my eyes. Someone from behind shushes me.

The fake Lunati woman is dressed in silver rags, a weird approximation of the Wash robes my mother and father used to wear each month.

"We must feed the ghost." She beckons, then looks toward us. "But who can satisfy his hunger?"

The stage is just two sad, lonely steps above the audience, and she hops down to select her prey. Smoke billows around her, smelling thickly of axiom. Huh. I write down a reminder to myself in my notebook: *Sell axiom to theaters?* And when I look back up, she's standing in front of me.

"You three," she says. "You have the look of the goddess about you. You will be my Unda, my Tempus, my Lux."

Even Taiyo seems to see how embarrassing this is for me. "I don't think we do," he says.

"No. No, I'm sure of it."

And with that, we're dragged onstage. The two other actors onstage, who have been fairly wooden so far, are suddenly very realistic in their surprise. They look at each other, a genuine *huh?* communicated between them, and the Lunati priestess babbles more nonsense.

More axiom smoke rises, and suddenly there's another crank of machinery. Briefly, I think it's another Alder rotation, turning dimly in the distance. But no: this sound is coming from the stage.

From under us.

We fall. Or rather: we are dropped. A trapdoor opens and the three of us are deposited into the basement of the theater, where we land on a straw mattress.

"Jesus *Christ*," yelps Margo.

"So sorry," someone says. My eyes quickly adjust to the dimness.

It's the fair-haired woman who left the theater moments ago. She's all slender sharpness, like a knife for opening letters.

Taiyo is rubbing at the small of his back. "Do we really need this rigamarole?"

"We had to verify you. To check whether you were followed."

"And were we?"

"If you were, whoever followed you is currently watching the third act of the worst play ever made. I'm Aska. This is Margo, I suppose. Who are you two? I suppose you're the salesman?" She nods to me, or rather, to my tattoo. "And you're the smuggler?"

"Word gets around fast," I say suspiciously as Aska leads us from the basement to an abandoned dressing room. There's a mirror and an array of cosmetics, along with yet another long silver cloak, presumably for the inclusion of a second Lunati character.

Aska, to her credit, looks slightly embarrassed.

"I don't write the plays," she says, dragging a stool out for each of us. "In fact, I hate the theater. But here we are. Margo. Before we begin, thank you for coming all this way."

It's hot in here, sticky and airless. I shrug off my jacket, laying it on top of my briefcase.

"You're welcome," Margo says levelly. "I didn't have much of a choice."

"Is that how you feel about it?"

"I feel like I've been trapped in this world, or worlds, and the SoGa are trying to kill me. I *feel* as though I have to trust everyone I meet, even though there's no real reason to, except that they tell me I should."

My conversation with Margo outside, the one in which I doomed my chances of kissing her forever, has hardened her against all of us.

She's stiff, unimpressed, a wall up against any kind of further feeling.

"Fair enough," says Aska. "What can I do for you to make you trust me a little more?"

"Not much."

Aska sits forward, elbows on her legs. She looks at each of us with yellow wolf eyes, absorbing every detail, every dynamic, every time one of us looks at another.

"All right. I'll rephrase. What can I do that will make you more positively disposed toward helping us, so I don't feel like I'm selling a child bride into marriage?"

Margo's eyebrows shoot up. The words *child bride* and *marriage* are unfortunate, given the aborted romance of ten minutes ago. But still, you've got to admire Aska. She wants this to be Margo's choice, and she's confident she can talk her around until it *is* her choice.

"You can send me home."

"Right. Of course. And where's home?"

Suddenly, it feels as though Taiyo and I are the bodyguards at a diplomatic meeting. Margo a reigning queen, Aska some kind of new president.

"Home is . . ." Margo balks. "It's Ireland. It's Earth, I guess, although I don't think that's the word I'm looking for. It's twenty-four hours."

Was that really it? Was that everything that made home *home*?

Aska nods vigorously.

"Right. All right. OK. Well, I don't know it, but that probably doesn't surprise you, does it?"

She waits for Margo to respond. "No," Margo says, though the question did seem rhetorical. "But . . . I do think my world used to be joined up to yours. I really do."

Margo carefully explains to Aska about Captain Halvpas, about the track closures, about the Orpheus problem. Aska listens, though I get the impression she knows at least some of this information already. Like Taiyo and his various revolutionary characters, I feel as if Aska has perfected an excellent Listening Face. A front she puts up while her mind whirs on, like the machinery of her enormous city.

"I didn't know it was Halvpas," she says when Margo stops speaking. "That's unlucky. He's a bloodhound. But you say he's in Hess Point now?"

"Yes. We trapped him on the train there."

Aska breaks into a grin. "That's great. That's really fun."

The word *fun* surprises us all, but Aska keeps rolling.

"I'm with you, Margo. You've got to go home. You've got a life and a family, I'm sure. And as I say: I don't know where you live. But just because I don't know, doesn't mean somebody else doesn't. What I *do* know is that after Semper took control, they confiscated or burned all the old maps. That's part of what makes sealing such a terrible punishment. You're not just physically isolated, you're eventually forgotten, too. Spiritually, intellectually, creatively, and so on."

"When you say that somebody else might know," Margo replies, "what do you mean?"

Someone knocks on the door. "Who is it?" Aska calls.

Some words in Alderian, a rough, pointy sort of language with lots of g-sounds in it.

"Come on, then."

A man with a port-wine birthmark covering two-thirds of his face enters the room and sits down. Annoyingly, the birthmark only seems to draw attention to how handsome he is, with a big chiseled jaw and the same fair Alderian hair that Aska has.

"This is Sonne. He's the archivist at the palace library. Sonne: Margo, Taiyo, and Moon."

I go to shake his hand, at which point I realize he only has one arm, and I have reached for the wrong one. He smiles gamely, pumping my other hand with his remaining one.

"He's got access to the libraries. He can work on finding Margo's world, and on finding her a route home."

Sonne smiles, as if slightly embarrassed by this.

"You speak Traders?" Taiyo asks him.

"Very well," Sonne answers quietly. "And only when necessary."

I squint at Aska and Sonne in disbelief. "Are you telling me that PACT has found a way into sealed worlds?"

Aska hesitates. "It's not easy. But it can be done."

"Worlds like Sopilka?"

"Not Sopilka. No. Too recent. Everything's been severed, nothing's had a chance to grow back."

"I'm sorry, what?" I've never heard of anything sealed *growing back*, as though a world was just a deadheaded rose. "Grow back?"

A glimmer in Aska's wolf eyes. "I thought Taiyo would have told you."

"The way New Davia's been lately, I wouldn't say my own name out loud," says Taiyo.

"Fair. Well. It's a new thing. We don't know very much. But it would appear that new openings are forming in certain worlds. Presumably it's what brought Margo to us, and why Semper has become so skittish lately. All the weapons buying and so on."

And so on is a big phrase for Alderians. A conversational tic rooted in their own self-importance and belief that they are the most dominant Northern world. Their way of saying: *Of course I know everything, I just don't have time to tell you about it.*

"Semper is terrified that the North is going to find and use these new openings. They want to make it seem like there's only one way in and one way out of every world, but you know that isn't true, Moon, don't you?"

Aska settles her gaze on me. "The caravan trails were built by the Lunati, which is why Semper tried so hard to get rid of you. You had travel routes they couldn't control."

I suddenly feel extremely exposed. "I'm quite familiar with the crushing of my people, thank you."

Aska backs off. "I know. I'm sorry. I'm just saying. There are a few old worlds that can be accessed—very Northern worlds, mind you, most too dangerous to spend much time in—that were sealed off so long ago that new openings have formed. We've been trying to find and use those entrances. My suspicion is that Margo is from an old Southern world where a new opening has formed. Think of it as someone getting too big for their clothing, and the material is starting to burst at the seams. Margo has fallen through one of those seams."

Here, in the basement of a horrible theater, my entire understanding of existence is unwritten. I turn to Taiyo. "And you knew about this?"

Taiyo smiles slyly. "There's an opening between New Davia and Enrio." Enrio is northwest of New Davia. A tiny world with a three-hour day, and so cold that the only trade is in seal blubber. "It's not good for much, except keeping black-market beef fresh before I move it on. The locals don't even know it exists."

"You're telling me there's a split in New Davia and you use it to make *money*???"

"Yeah." Taiyo shrugs. "Wouldn't you?"

Sonne interrupts. "If we find Margo's world on a very aged map, we can find ways back to it."

"It's not a guarantee," Aska warns. "But it's the best chance you have."

A light comes into Margo's eyes. Finally, she's allowing herself to become excited. "You're saying you can really send me home?"

"Potentially. It will take time. Sonne is the only one who can access the palace archives. Then there's actually finding an opening, which might mean going through several other worlds first to get there."

Margo sits back on her stool, pressing her back against the wall with a faint groan. "Right."

"And in the meantime . . ." Again, Aska gives Margo that narrow, appraising look. "You can do something for us."

"Right. I figured that was coming."

Aska doesn't waste any time. "We need you to go to Khaise."

"Sorry," I interrupt. "You're not sending Margo to Khaise."

"Where's Khaise?" Margo asks.

"You don't want to go there. It's a Northeastern industrial desert. It's got a two-hour day."

"*Two!*" Margo turns back to Aska and Sonne. "Sorry, I'm not going to Khaise."

"I understand. But it wouldn't be for very long. You just need to buy us more time."

"How?"

"You break trains, Margo. That's your power. Surely you understand that by now. You go somewhere and the tracks fall out of the sky. We need you to break the tracks in Khaise."

"Why Khaise, of all places?"

"Because the SoGa are there right now, shipping two hundred tons of explosives back to Semper."

"*Explosives?*" I can feel my skin prickle. "Why?"

"Because there's a war coming," Taiyo says, with a silent *like I said.*

"I don't know if it's a war," Aska says, her tone suddenly grim. She trains her eyes on the fuzzy damp carpet in front of her. "A war sort of implies there's two well-equipped sides. I think they want to annihilate us. They have the numbers, the weapons, the resources. The trains. We have ourselves. We have these new world openings. And we have Margo."

She looks to the teenager in a man's suit. The one I told was too young to kiss me, but apparently old enough to save the world. Or some of them.

"If you'll have us," Aska says, framing it to Margo like it's a choice. Like any of this is a choice, and like there aren't wheels of commerce moving without her knowledge already.

Margo sighs. "I guess I'm going to Khaise, then."

nineteen
Margo

Shortly after this, the play ended. Weak, short-lived applause briefly scattered over their heads like hailstones. Aska quickly examined a pocket watch and motioned for them to follow her.

"You can leave your suitcases and jackets here," Aska said, and Moon immediately looked as though this was going to be a deal-breaker for him. "I promise they'll be safe. We'll have someone collect them."

Margo assumed they would be ejected back into the moving streets, but instead the five of them—she, Taiyo, Moon, Sonne, and Aska—burrowed deeper into the building. Aska led them to a service elevator with iron railings that pulled right across, designed to deliver heavy props to the stage above.

"Arms and legs all inside?" Sonne asked. Before anyone could answer, he pulled an enormous lever that plummeted them instantly into the depths beneath.

The sound was awful. Metal on metal, scraping and sawing. It rattled her guts. Heart in her pelvis, knees in her throat. She lost her footing, yet even in the panic she knew instinctively not to reach for Moon. The humiliation was still too great. On one level, she understood the reasoning, and could see how their already complex relationship may not stand up to the further complexity of, e.g., kissing up against the wall of a theater. On another level, though—and clearly, they were descending through multiple levels today, physically speaking—how dare he? He had sent signals. Lingered his eyes, brushed his hands, hushed his tone.

And so she grabbed Taiyo. They dropped another, terrible floor, as she gripped the smuggler around the arm, and he gripped the wall. The light was gone now. It was impossible to see whether anyone but Taiyo noticed, or even cared.

Taiyo kept an arm on Margo's shoulder, stabilizing her.

"You all right?" he whispered, and Margo just nodded in the dark.

Eventually, there were no floors left to plummet to. They came to a bottom level that was surrounded by hard concrete on every side. Margo reached out through the iron bars of the elevator, feeling the cold gray blocks on every side.

"No one will hear you," Sonne said pleasantly, and Margo had to remind herself that Sonne had never seen a horror film, and did not know this was a terrifying thing to say.

Despite there being no discernible exit, Aska pulled the huge, clanking doors open.

"Moon? I hate to stereotype, but you wouldn't happen to have a few of those silver—"

Moon produced a cluster of seeds, casting teardrops of light into the narrow shaft.

"Thank you. All right, kids. Hands and knees."

Arms and legs. Hands and knees. Aska and Sonne were like two highly menacing primary school teachers educating them on body parts. Aska dropped to the floor and located a narrow chute carved into the concrete. It was just wide enough for a human body.

Margo, who was not naturally claustrophobic, felt panic rising in her anyway. "No. Surely not."

"Sadly, yes. I'll see you on the other side. If you freak out, just remember: it's technically wider than a coffin."

"Why would that calm *anyone* down?"

"Because you're not dead yet. This is bad, but it's an improvement on death. That's something, isn't it? That *has* to be something."

Aska crawled into the narrow shaft and disappeared.

"I'll go last," Sonne said, his tone even and polite, as though telling them he would wait for the next taxi so they could all ride together.

Taiyo stepped forward. "And here was me, thinking I'd done the coffin bit already."

"Wait," Moon said. "Take one of these each."

There were only four silver seeds in Moon's hand. Margo knew that he needed to do a monthly silver Wash to get more, but didn't know exactly when that was coming up in Alder. This was a precious resource.

"You sure?"

"Yeah," he said, not quite meeting her eye. "Take it."

So she did, attaching it with spit to her watch like Moon had done on her first day in New Davia.

The tunnels had been one thing. The gradual, calf-aching feeling of descent as they crossed into one basement and then another. This was a more violent nausea. They each crawled through the cement, single file, the air heavy. The ground underneath Margo's bare hands was so cold that she felt her fingertips, and then her palms, go entirely numb.

She thanked the Lunati gods she did not know for her lone silver seed. Her one light against the enveloping, terrible darkness.

Finally, they emerged from their spiraling coffin into a large room with low gleaming ceilings. There was a thin orange light here, fuzzy and phosphorescent. As Margo's eyes adjusted, she began to see that this light came from a series of bronze statues scattered seemingly randomly across the empty room. Each standing on a fat marble plinth, each spotlighted by an overhanging lantern. They were the first statues that Margo had seen in this densely statue-populated city that were not of people. They were bears.

"The Hall of the Seven Bears," Aska announced, flaring her arms like a circus ringmaster. Margo almost expected them to come to life.

"What *is* this place?"

As promised, Sonne emerged last, dusting himself down as he straightened up.

"You've heard of the copper mines in Alder, yes?" he asked in his gentle, schoolteacher way. "Well, they used to be in the city, too. These rooms were once great quarries. When the copper was all gone, they moved the mining into the mountains, and Roman the Builder had miles and miles of cleared space under Alder to build his vast clockwork that rotates the city. But some spaces were left empty. Given to the quarriers as rewards for their service, or used to store royal treasures."

Neither Moon, Taiyo, nor Margo could resist pacing the enormous room, examining each brown bear. One juggled, one balanced on a seesaw that tilted over a large ball. Others did regular bear things, like eating fish or sitting down.

"Don't get lost, you three," Aska called. "We're not there yet. Come to the whistling bear."

Whistling may or may not have been the sculptor's intention for this particular bear, but Margo could see why Aska called it that. The bear had his paws on his hips and his snout raised to the sky, as if in a children's illustration of the perpetually carefree.

"I like this bear," Taiyo said as they trotted toward it. "I feel a real affection for this bear."

They all agreed that the bear had a certain something.

Aska directed them to each grip a part of the statue. Within a few moments, the whistling bear began to rotate. "Hold on," Aska said.

Margo looked to the ceiling and found that the gleam above her head was not filigree or some kind of royal detailing. It was cogs. The room was built on the underside of the city's turning dials. The realization was dizzying, euphoric, like discovering as a toddler that there are numbers that run past ten. Right now, the city was turning and rotating above them, various districts and neighborhoods being broken up and remade anew. And here, a second city echoed it.

Alder's dream self. Its shadow side.

As the whistling bear moved like a chess piece, the room shrank from a large rectangle to a squat circle, and another opening lay before them.

"Onward," Aska said. They passed through several more rooms and corridors, many of which had water damage, were completely flooded, or were blocked by more concrete. Aska and Sonne navigated each turn deftly, sometimes murmuring a few words in their own language to each other, until they arrived at a dead end.

"Shit," Aska said, rapping her knuckles on the concrete. "This is new."

"Every so often the NoGa tries to block an entryway," explained Sonne grimly.

"So they know you're here?" Margo asked.

"Of course. But it's too vast for them to be really effective. Nobody knows the labyrinth like PACT does. They just do this to show Semper that they are doing *something* about us."

Sonne turned to Aska. "The Room of Cats?"

"The Room of Cats," she repeated, by way of agreement.

They doubled back, waded through a slightly drowned room

where the water came to Margo's shins, and then into a pitch-dark room with caved-in ceilings. She felt something small and sleek rub against her legs.

Despite the phrase *room of cats* being repeated at least three times between Sonne first saying it and that moment, Margo still squeaked in shock.

"Something wrong?" Sonne asked.

"There was . . ." she began, then felt foolish. "A cat."

The light from her silver seed was fading rapidly. She held up her watch and caught the gaze of a dozen cats. All small, all thin. Mostly tabbies. A tortoiseshell sat loaf-like above them, swatting the cave wall angrily with her tail.

"These rooms connect to the sewers," Aska explained. "And are under the market district. The cats wait here for the crowds to go home so they can dart up and eat all the scraps."

The cats did not look like they had much in the way of scraps. Clearly competition was stiff. The human party passed through, every glowing set of eyes trained on them. Margo felt as though the cats would gladly devour her.

Finally, they came to an enormous hall with very low ceilings. It wasn't wet, dark, cold, or filled with cats. Because it shared all of these rare assets, Sonne and Aska announced it as simply the barracks.

The huge room was filled with columns supporting the roof above. The columns were the only thing that gave the place any sense of perspective, as they slowly shrank farther and farther back into the dark horizon. Seven or eight columns down, Margo saw a cluster of people crowded around a table. Candles lined the walls, leading the way.

As they went closer, Margo saw that most of the action was happening around a long banquet table crowded with documents, maps, knives, and the occasional cat skull used as a paperweight. In an eastern corner were some straw mattresses where people were either dozing or having close, intense conversations. On the opposite side was a kind of makeshift pub, goblets stacked on top of wooden crates.

"Welcome, welcome," Aska said. "Welcome to the middle of the middle."

Later, when Margo tried to remember the Alder catacombs, she found herself often tripping up over how many people were there, and whether they spoke to her, or if she spoke back. It could have been fifty people, but she would not have contradicted Moon or Taiyo if they had said a hundred. There was a continuous state of flow, of people coming and going, eating and talking, none of them speaking English, many of them arguing with one another.

Even Taiyo, a fully committed PACT member, seemed astonished at how many conversations seemed to be happening at once. He stuck near Aska, his eyes wide.

"What's going *on*?"

"It's busy today, I'll give you that," Aska answered, seeming to sense their collective shock. "There's a big horse race tomorrow. A qualifier for the Forty-One this summer."

"So . . . ?"

"There's a cohort of Semper bigwigs who are here for the race. You know. Ministers who like to brag about having a racehorse. We're trying to get as many eyes on them as we can while they're here."

A large and very dark-skinned man approached them, holding out his hand to Margo first. It was so strange to her, being treated like the special one again. It made her feel like they were expecting some other Margo, some wise and brave person who she had no power to summon.

"This is Dimanche," Aska said, introducing her. "President of PACT."

"Dimi," he said, pointing to himself with a kind of kingly humbleness, to indicate that Margo could use his nickname.

Dimi was bald and wore gold-rimmed glasses, kept firmly balanced on the end of his nose. He said something to her in Alderian, which Aska promptly translated.

"He says thank you for taking such a long journey to come meet with us."

"Oh," fumbled Margo, who had never spoken via a translator before. "That's OK."

He spoke in Alderian again. Margo didn't know whose eye contact she should be meeting, his or Aska's.

"Dimi was a young man during the First Northern Wars," Aska explained. "Education wasn't exactly a priority. He doesn't speak Traders."

Dimi smiled apologetically at Margo, as though he was used to hearing this explanation of himself, even if he did not technically understand it. Margo's heart strained against this terrible unfairness, this cutting of contact from worlds that were once so connected. Dimi spoke again, and this time she was sure to keep her eyes on his.

"He says that he wanted to say hello at the theater, but he had to go."

"Oh, that was you?" Taiyo said. "The first person who left!"

He spoke again, made a gesture to his size, and then laughed. Aska and Sonne laughed, too. A lot.

"He said he would have journeyed with you here, but the crawl space from the theater can't fit him anymore."

They all laughed a little awkwardly, each knowing that he was obviously too important a person to crawl on his hands and knees through a cement passageway.

Dimi turned to Moon then, sticking out his hand.

"Ah!" he said with great, expansive friendliness. "Lunati."

She wondered whether anyone in these worlds was capable of meeting Moon without bringing up the Lunati. Despite his still very recent rejection of her, she felt for him. It must be so strange, to be singled out like this so often.

Dimi spoke quickly then, his face apologetic. Aska's translation took on a regretful tone.

"He says he is sorry, he did not mean to be rude, just that it has been years and years since he has met with the Lunati. It makes him happy. That it was such a tragic thing that happened to so many of you. He says he respects the culture very much, and that all PACT members do. The Lunati value freedom and movement above all else, and we take inspiration from them."

Moon smiled, and she could see the white nick of scar tissue in his eyebrow quiver. He spoke some short, careful words in Alderian. Quite formal, and rather unmoved. The words were something like: *I appreciate that. Thank you.*

More smiling. More talking. More fast Alderian, more translating.

"But what is *most* unusual to him," Aska went on, "is that after so long without meeting any Lunati, he has now met two in the same week."

Moon went absolutely still. "Excuse me," he said slowly. "What was that?"

twenty
MOON

At first, I think I've heard him wrong, or that he's misunderstood something.

"Taiyo isn't a Lunati," I say, gesturing to him. "We're not related or anything."

Truthfully, I've felt a little bad for Taiyo throughout this exchange. Dimi hasn't acknowledged him yet. It's a bit painful, considering Margo and I are lukewarm on PACT, whereas Taiyo has been dreaming about this moment for most of his life.

"No," Dimi says. "Another."

"Is he saying there's another Lunati around? Are there Lunati in PACT?"

"We have a Lunati trainer helping us," Sonne explains. "Undercover. For the Forty-One."

My breathing stops for a moment. I swallow hard. "A trainer?"

"I can take you to meet her, if you like?"

"No need," Aska interrupts. "I think she's here."

Before I can respond, Aska is loping across the room toward a series of low archways where people are drinking and playing cards. She moves too quickly for me to stop her, calling out to the group. Her voice rings out across the cavernous room, bouncing off the thick walls.

"Hey, hey, is Yaz here? Yaz? You over here? I've got someone I want you to meet. Or maybe you've met already. I don't really know."

Yaz is here.

Yaz is *here.*

Yaz is *here.*

Then, all of a sudden, there she is. Small, round, fierce. Two long dark braids wrapped around the crown of her head. And that face. That familiar, scrunched-up expression of a little dog trying to guard a big house. Suddenly, I hear my mother's voice, echoing from a decade ago.

Levi, just let Yaz do what she wants, she says. *It's easier that way.*

What had we been fighting about, for my mother to give me that advice? Probably nothing. Whatever kids fight about. Whatever little cousins want from big cousins, I wanted from Yaz.

Yaz sees me. Furrows her brow. Then her stomping, determined walk, the walk that hasn't changed since she was a kid, and that propels her until she is right in front of me.

"Ahoro, Fengari," she says.

"Ahoro, cuz," I reply.

Nervous. I sound nervous.

Yaz reaches out—reaches *up,* because she's so short—and hugs me.

I'm not sure if she's doing it out of genuine warmth or because five people—including the president of AlderPACT—are watching us. But she holds on tight. She smells of horses and warm straw and home.

People think that Lunati don't have homes because we move around so often, but that's not true. Home is a moving target, because home is one another. And now that there are so few of us, that *home* feeling is so rare it's unsettling. It's painful. You see one Lunati and you're reminded how culturally excruciating it is to see just one Lunati, when we are supposed to travel in packs, in groups. In families.

Maybe that's why I can't quite make my interaction with Yaz feel natural, or comfortable, and why everyone else seems to sense it immediately.

"Shouldn't you be in Bahar?" is all I can say. It sounds rude, bizarre, like I'm accusing her of stalking me. "I mean, how did you get a visa to Alder?"

Not: *How are you?*

Not: *It's so good to see you!*

Not: *How did you come to arrive at this underground rebel hideaway, and are you a rebel yourself?*

Just: How did you get a visa?

Yaz's eyes slide to the others, to Aska and Sonne, to Dimi, then back to me again.

"Always the same, with this one. Salesmen," she says with a laugh. "All they're concerned with is money and paperwork."

Everyone else laughs along, grateful to Yaz for defusing the tension. She drapes an arm around me and guides me away from the group. I'm a foot taller than her, but still I'm the baby cousin.

"Come on. Let's talk."

"I can't leave—"

But *who* can't I leave?

I look back to Margo. To Taiyo. To Aska, Sonne, and Dimi.

I have technically done my job. Margo is with PACT. I have an invoice of 425 gens to fulfill, and once I've done that, I'm one major step closer to getting out of sales. No more nosebleeds. No more fainting attacks. No more skipshock.

Aska nods at me. "Catch up with your family," she says, before adding under her breath, "We'll talk later."

Margo's back is already to me. She's looking at something at the other end of the room, pointing it out to Taiyo.

She's still angry about earlier. Well, let her be. I feel terrible enough that I'm about to cash in on this job, and I'd feel a lot worse if I'd spent the earlier part of this afternoon with my hands in her shirt.

And so, with no one to say goodbye to, I follow Yaz to a corner. Despite the endless open space, people have set up private areas for themselves using the huge pillars as dividing walls. A straw mattress is next to Yaz's pillar, with an apple crate for a bedside table. Her only possession, that I can see, is a grooming kit wrapped in a leather bundle.

We sit down. She's on the mattress, and I'm on the floor. I cannot think of a single thing to say, so I start looking at the brushes and curry combs.

"These your dad's?" I ask, examining the silver handles.

"They are."

"Nice. That's nice."

"How are you, Lev?"

At some point in the last seven years, my given name became a limb too tender to rest my weight on. All the other salesmen called me Moon because I was the only Lunati salesman around. I learned to like it. When you can't hide from who you are, you have to make it the headline act. I didn't have to worry about exposing Levi, the malnourished runaway with an arson charge against him. I was just Moon. Silver seeds and small-batch household resources. Reliable if surly. Friendly if temporary. It's been a good mask to live behind. Until Margo, that is.

"I'd rather you not call me that."

She has to make a big effort not to scowl. "Why?"

"You know why."

"No one's looking for Lev Evreleri anymore. It's been years."

"All the same. I'd rather not chance it." I put the brush down. "Why are you in Alder?"

"The Qualifier. Mr. Rundy thinks he's got a winner this year."

Mr. Rundy is Yaz's employer, a big trainer from Bahar who has come up with a few winners over the years.

"Right. And you couldn't have stayed with him?"

Yaz starts unfurling the two braids from the crown of her head, so that both locks fall heavily around her ears. She unpicks them with her fingers, carefully not making eye contact. The room is dim enough that my skin is starting to percolate, the wormy light blooming through to the top layer of skin. Yaz's skin, I note, does not do this. She washes with a deep carbon soap that dulls her skin, and dyes her hair black with axiom. If you didn't know she was Lunati, you'd have no way to guess.

"I could have."

"But you didn't," I counter, the point rather obvious. "You're here. With PACT."

"Why are you acting surprised?"

"Why are you trying to get yourself *killed*, Yaz? What's the game, you sneak into the Ministers' Box between races? Steal their secrets, pass them on?"

Yaz frowns. "You're forgetting something, Lev. You're here, too."

"That's different."

"How?"

Because I need money, and soon. Because if I don't get it, I'll die of this strange salesman's disease that's already doing god knows what to my internal organs.

"Because this is about the money, for me. I'm here on a job, and after I leave, it's over. I'm not about to jump in front of a bullet for a goal that's completely unattainable. You can't beat Semper. You can get *around* Semper; you can play ball with Semper; but PACT thinks they can bring the whole thing to its knees, and I'm not about to die for a noble idea."

"You'd rather live with no principles than die for freedom."

"Yes. One million times, yes."

Suddenly, I remember a time when Yaz was eight and I was four, and all the Lunati came together for the Red Otter festival in Doyohi. The blood moon high in the sky, its shadow the perfect outline of an otter with its tail up. Everyone covered in red dusty clay. All the kids staying up to dance. The big swim in the morning, trails of red streaming in the water behind us.

There must have been a thousand people at that festival.

"PACT is deeply respectful of the Lunati, you know. Many of the founding leaders were—"

"Yes, I heard all about it. Our free way of life. We weren't exactly a priority for PACT when they started locking us up and killing our parents, were we?"

"What could they have *done*, Lev?"

I stand up so quickly that I let the set of horse brushes fall, clattering to the floor.

"Which is it, Yaz? Because from where I'm standing, PACT is either a deeply powerful, ambitious organization who had the power to save the Lunati and chose not to, or they are a useless bunch of well-meaning cowards who happen to have wonderful underground real estate that they are kindly allowing you to sublet in exchange for state secrets. Neither makes me want to fight or die for them, and it shouldn't make you want to, either, but I guess we're different."

"Yeah," says Yaz shortly. "I guess we are."

In this sudden moment of bile, I realize that I've never had a problem with Taiyo, not really. My problem is with an organization that turned me away, dropped me like a hot stone once they realized I was a wanted criminal. I was twelve years old and PACT, who claims to accept everyone, who pretends to love the Lunati, decided I had too much heat on me to let me in.

My problem is that salesmen are seen as filthy, transient, and criminal, yet they are the ones who saved me. Not PACT. Not an ideology, or a whispered wish for freedom. Commerce saved me from a life on the run. Business.

"I have to go."

"*Where?*"

I suddenly realize that my only other option is Margo, who hates me, or Taiyo, who's probably busy kissing PACT's ass.

"I don't know."

Yaz gets up. "Well, come with me, won't you? I think you need to get out of the ground for a while."

So I surprise myself. I follow her.

twenty-one
MARGO

Margo watched Moon leave, and had a sudden feeling that not only would she not have a physical relationship with him, but that going forward, she would have no relationship with him at all.

At that precise moment, the room shook, and there was a deafening clatter overhead. The column next to her vibrated, buzzing against her arm. Candles flickered. The whole world seemed to shake as she watched Moon leave the room.

"What was *that*?"

"The train," said Aska, sitting down. "We're under the train station."

"The train station?"

"It's the only part of this whole city that stays still."

Aska steered Margo and Taiyo to a table, where they were given a plate of cold food and a glass of warm spirits. Not as bitter as slip; something closer to hot, thin caramel. The food was a kind of cold mincemeat dumpling. She poked at it with a fork, trying to discern what animal it came from.

"I'll let you two eat and get comfortable," Aska said, excusing herself. "I'll be back shortly, and we can go through the plan."

All of a sudden, she had gone from a guest of honor to just another person eating in a crowded room.

Margo swayed a little, dizzy. She couldn't tell if it was skipshock from the new time speed, or shell shock from having recently been quite a pointless person to suddenly being a vital one. She had an immediate picture of herself as she should be: in boarding school, in Dublin. Her watch, which was still set to her own world's time, had just struck five p.m. What would she be doing now? Changing from one set of clothes into another, from a uniform into gym clothes, or from gym clothes into jeans.

Perhaps she was happy in that world. But whether she was or she wasn't, nothing depended on her. Certainly not thousands of innocent lives.

For the first time, Margo considered that perhaps she wasn't a person who was stumbling and tumbling through worlds at random. Maybe she was not just a victim of bizarre circumstances. Maybe she was in exactly the right place, at exactly the right time.

"You OK?" Taiyo asked, tearing apart the dumpling on his own plate. "You seem a little . . . shaken."

The room was filled with a hundred low-burning candles, a soft glow over everyone within.

"So where would you go?" she asked Taiyo, breathing through her nausea. "If PACT got their way, if all the borders were broken. Where would you live?"

Taiyo finished his drink before answering. "Oh, I expect I'd stay in New Davia."

"Really? You'd risk your life to *stay* in a six-hour world?"

He settled his dark eyes on her. "It's my home. I would want to travel, of course, and see other places. But it's not about . . . PACT isn't about me, or where I want to go. Do you know there are four times as many Northern worlds as there are Southern ones?"

"I did *not* know that."

"There are more Northern worlds, but they tend to be smaller. Two million people in New Davia, maybe five million in Alder. Families are smaller when people have less time to have them. I think there's fifteen million in Semper, or something. But if you packed all those Northern worlds together, especially the sealed ones, we'd overwhelm the South in a heartbeat. That's why they're afraid of travel. That's why it's the first thing we fight for. Oh, we could campaign for better trade deals, or relaxed visa rules. But at the end of the day, Semper will always hold the cards while they have the trains. They know we can't unite against them if we can't physically get to one another."

Margo felt the brown drink burn in her throat. "And you've always just . . . been part of this? Part of PACT? Who got you in?"

He shrugged. "It's what you do."

She couldn't help herself. "Not Moon, though."

"Moon's a law unto himself." Taiyo sighed, filling their glasses up again. "You're not in love with him or anything, are you?"

"No." She said it quickly. Too quickly.

"Right." Taiyo clinked her glass. "Cheers. To lying."

Margo laughed, long and nervous. She knocked her drink back, gasping on the sweet fire of it. "I'm not lying," she said. "And anyway, if I did . . . feel that way, or any kind of way . . ."

She broke off. Taiyo just nodded a silent *go on*.

"He doesn't want me."

There it was. Out loud.

Taiyo laughed. "Oh, I wouldn't say that. I've known the guy years now. He's gaga."

When Margo didn't look convinced, Taiyo cupped his hand around his left eye, making it look like a crescent moon. He made his voice deep and dour. *"Taiyo, I don't have time for your shit right now. I'm not in the revolution game. I'm in the buying and selling game."*

He took his cupped hand away, the Moon impression apparently over. "That's literally all the conversation I've gotten out of Mo, as long as I've known him. But now . . . he's invested. He won't admit it, even to himself, but it makes him furious. He's always looking at you, to see how you're taking things, how you feel. The day you got your tattoo, Margo. You'd swear he was in the delivery room with his pregnant wife. That's how anxious he was. Pacing and growling at everyone."

Margo remembered almost nothing of her tattoo day, except the fuzzy vision of Moon lying beneath her. She reflected the next morning that she could never really regret the tattoo, because the memory of his face between her feet was too lovely. A picture in the perfect-size frame.

"He rejected me." Margo was eager to close the conversation. The memory, which had felt so sweet to her, was becoming bleached out by her un-kissed lips outside the theater. "So your theory doesn't exactly hold up."

Taiyo was a little drunk now. So was she. They had, without noticing, gone through three glasses of the Alderian liquor. It was far harder than slip, which you could drink a lot of and not feel much. This was serious, serious booze.

"He did?" Taiyo ran his hands through his black hair. "Well. Listen. I guess he's got a bit more of a moral backbone than I thought."

"How do you mean? A moral backbone?"

The train rattled again overhead. The table shook, the vibrations making their drinks waltz. Taiyo beamed at the ceiling. He was excited to be there. To be in the middle of everything.

By the time the train had passed, Sonne and Aska were back.

"Are you finished with your dinner?" Sonne asked, but Aska was already pushing the cold meat dumpling away to make room for an enormous map.

"OK, you two," she said. "We need to talk about Khaise. We're still waiting on the details—where the SoGa are stationed, what they're up to—but we might as well give you the basics now."

"Shouldn't we wait for Moon?" Margo asked.

Sonne, Aska, and Taiyo all silently cut eyes at one another.

"We can fill Moon in later," Aska said, her voice careful and even. "But it's really important that you and Taiyo know what you're doing."

Margo's face felt hot and confused. "Moon is *coming* to Khaise, right?"

Silence.

"Is it a deal-breaker for you if he doesn't?" Sonne finally asked.

"Pardon?"

"We only mean," Aska interrupted, "that technically speaking, Moon's job was just to get you here. To us."

"His *job*?"

"His role, I mean."

Margo tried to puzzle this out through the thick fuzz of drunkenness forming at the front of her skull. "Is it a job or a role?"

"To clarify," Sonne said, in his eternally patient tone, "you will not do this without Moon?"

"I didn't say that," she answered defensively. "I was just under the impression that we were doing this together. He's coming back, right?"

"Of course he's coming back." Aska was getting impatient with this now. "We just dropped off both your suitcases, so he's not going to get very far without that, is he?"

"Our suitcases? Where?"

"In the sleeping area. We put you guys next to his cousin. Now, Margo, we really do need to go through this."

"OK," she said, still agitated. "OK. Go on. But it seems pointless, considering you'll have to explain it all again, to him. And who is this cousin, anyway? He didn't say anything to me about a cousin."

Aska smoothed the map where it was beginning to curl at the edges. "May I continue?" She did not wait for an answer. "So you'll arrive in Khaise and the train line will break. There's only one line in and out of Khaise, so the SoGa are going to be marooned there."

"Won't we be marooned there, too?"

"Aha! You should be, except that we have an opening in Khaise that leads to its neighboring world, Doyohi. We'll come to fetch you through that opening, bring you back via Doyohi, and you can take the train to Alder from there. Simple."

"And then you'll send me home."

"By then, yes, we will hopefully have located your world on one of our old maps."

Sonne nodded. "It will be my number-one priority."

Margo felt a cold sweat climbing under her clothing. She was struggling to believe that this really was their number-one priority. Suddenly, she felt the future as though it were a psychic vision. She would do endless errands for PACT. Each one would feel more vital than the last. They would always be so close to finding her world, and while they looked, she would do job after job.

Or not job.

Role.

She needed Moon here. She needed someone she could trust, to lay out their problems and priorities again. Halvpas was still pursuing her, after all. She needed to feel like she wasn't alone in this. Margo needed Moon's good, clear sense. Ironically, she needed his profoundly unromantic stance on things. PACT was a noble organization, but did it really care if she ever saw her mother again?

The physical relationship thing—whatever. It was embarrassing, but she could put it behind her. She just wanted her friend back.

"Margo? Does that sound OK to you?"

Suddenly, Taiyo's words came swimming back to her.

Well. Listen. I guess he's got a bit more of a moral backbone than I thought.

"Where did you say our bags were?"

Sonne and Aska exchanged another worried look, then pointed to their assigned mattresses. "Between the third and fourth columns."

Margo got to her feet and made her way to the dark makeshift dormitory in the center of the room. There, she found Moon's suitcase and jacket, lying in a pile. She picked up the jacket, the folds releasing the faint, warm smell of his body.

Its weight felt uneven. The right pocket had a heavy drag to it, and once again she found herself going through a man's pockets. His sales notebook. She opened it. The pages were already running low. He would need a new one soon. But the black carbon copy pages were still there, holding a record of everything he had exchanged in the last month.

She looked at sales receipts from before they had met. Deals on axiom, bronzefruit, damaspring, abelbrush. Sales on silver seeds. He didn't get very much for silver seeds, despite how beautiful they were. She moved through these days and came finally to the Margo Period, with a receipt she recognized from her first day in New Davia.

X 3 BABY GOOP—30 GEN—HECK.

Poor Heck. Could she really afford to doubt PACT? She had already witnessed a man die while in these worlds. Was that not enough for her?

Drunkenly, she flipped to the next page.

MARGO TO ALDER, it read. 425 ON DELIVERY.

And it was signed, she saw, by Taiyo and Moon.

twenty-two

MOON

We leave the PACT hideout through a storm drain, and emerge at the Alder racetrack. By now it's deep night, and nobody at the stables gives me a second look as we pass rows and rows of resting horses and step into Mr. Rundy's box.

Rundy is nowhere to be seen, of course, but instead there's his latest protégé. An enormous black Bahari thoroughbred called Biography.

"Biography?" I say, keeping a safe distance, my back pressed against the stable door.

"Oh yeah." Yaz takes her brushes out and starts rubbing him down. "Because this horse is going to be the story of his life."

"Right."

If Bahari horses could talk, their standardized greeting would be *Hey, loser.* They're beautiful, but you wouldn't want them on a farm or anything. Bahari horses have their own kind of character. They know how good they are. They like to win, and they like to be among winners. They'll nip at the people looking after them, despising any air of downtrodden behavior. Even right now, Biography is attempting to take a bite out of Yaz's shoulder.

"Hey," she says sharply, grabbing him by the nose. "Less of that."

After the caravan trails closed, some Lunati kept moving anyway. Or at least, my family did. We used the trains, even though people hated us, even though we had to ride with the livestock. But other families—Yaz's, for instance—settled wherever they could. They chose Bahar, for the horses. In the summer, the humidity and the rainstorms grow the grass high, fattening up the foals quickly. The winter is the dry season, the soft orange earth perpetually dusty but firm enough for a constant battering of hooves. They sweat the fat off in no time. By six months, they're racing fit. By two years old, they're monsters. At five, they're usually dead.

Yaz and I grew up together, traveling as a big community, until the trail closure made our respective families go separate ways.

"So what are this guy's chances then? Realistically?"

"Biography? Who knows. He's good, he's mean, but he's untested. You know how Rundy gets. Falls in love with an idea. Loves potential. But if something doesn't look like it's living up to potential, he scraps the whole animal."

"You've hung on with him long enough. Are you living up to your potential?"

She snorts. "Not nearly."

"You should go out on your own."

"I keep trying, but Rundy always outbids me whenever I find a colt worth looking at. There's one in Bahar right now, coming up for auction. I'd die to have him. I've lunged him a few times. I know exactly what he needs to make him a winner."

"Well, maybe you can overbid before auction. You're getting good money from PACT, right?" I ask. "Tell me you're getting paid, Yaz."

She narrows her eyes. "Are they paying *you*?"

It's as fair a question as any. But the money I'm getting for Margo is starting to feel like a curse, like an immovable weight that is constantly sitting on my chest.

"Yes," I say eventually.

"For what, exactly?"

I don't answer. Yaz doesn't push it. Instead, she works out a clump of dirt in Biography's coat.

"How's your Wash?"

My last Wash was just after Margo's tattoo. I produced only eight seeds out of a possible thirty.

"Not good."

She nods, still working out the dirt with her brush. "The faith is too weak. Not enough people are practicing it anymore. We're going to keep producing less and less. Remember the old days? The big Semper feast days. All of us together. Thirty seeds each. Even the kids. The ponies would have them sewn into their manes."

I'm not sure what she's getting at with all this. "Yes, I remember that," I say stiffly.

"Are you doing anything for the Ekleip this year? I'll be in Bahar. You should come visit. We could celebrate together."

The idea of this. Yaz and me celebrating Ekleip as two lone Lunati, when the celebration is meant for hundreds. Her, staring at me across a makeshift altar. Her, knowing I'm responsible for some of our missing family members.

"No thanks."

"So what? You don't give a shit about keeping our customs alive?"

"Alive for *what*, Yaz?"

"For whoever comes next. When you have kids. When I have kids. When the others, whoever's left, have kids, and those kids come looking for more Lunati. Then what will we tell them? That we can't remember the Nati word for *silver*? For *hello*?"

It takes me so completely off guard that I actually laugh. "Are you pregnant?"

"No."

"So why are we having this conversation? I'm not going to have kids."

"And you know that? You know that for sure, at your big age?" Yaz spits, in full fury now. "You're nineteen years old, Mo. I know you've seen a lot of things as a salesman, but you haven't seen everything."

The way she says these last three words, with pauses between each. *Haven't. Seen. Everything.*

"What haven't I seen, Yaz? Go on. Tell me what I have yet to see. Because I've seen men die of old age at twenty-seven. I've seen teenagers line up to get their faces iron-plated. I've seen my parents' burned bodies. I've seen the people who murdered them. And I've lived with the fact that it's my fault. So tell me—*Ahoro, Fengari*—tell me what I have yet to see?"

Yaz is silent a moment. She lets my words float into the enormous warm stable air and become nothing.

"It wasn't your fault, Mo."

I remember the night I found them. It was the coldest winter the North had ever seen. My father's beard had been cut off in rough clumps, so his killers could sift through it later for silver beads. He looked so young without his beard. People always said I looked like my mother, but the older I get, the more I see his face in mine. Or rather, I see his dead face in my living one, and feel like the last Lunati ghost left wandering.

"You should talk about them," Yaz says gently. "They were good people. Their memory deserves to be kept alive."

"Yeah, but my memories don't. Why don't you talk about them, Yaz?" I say, with a cruelty my cousin doesn't deserve. "Why don't you tell Mr. Rundy how great my parents were? You can't, can you?

Because then you'd have to tell him that you dye your hair and skin so that no one can see you glow in the dark."

Yaz gives me a wan, disappointed look. "I can think of one thing you haven't seen," she says softly.

"Go on."

"Change. You haven't seen change."

Her voice is so low that Biography cranes his neck around to disapprove.

"Hah."

"I'm serious. Things weren't always this way. They had to change to get this bad. So who says they can't change again? And for the better this time?"

"You don't actually believe that, do you?"

"I do," she says. "And you know what else? I think you do, too."

"And why is that?"

"Because the SoGa are after you," she answers calmly.

"Who says?"

"They must be, if you're working with PACT. I know you wouldn't do it just for the money. It's too dangerous, and you're too chickenshit. So go on. What are you doing it for?"

Of course. Yaz is a horse person, and horse people miss nothing.

"There's a girl," I say at last.

"Go on."

"She's lost. And she's . . . well, she's got some kind of power. She breaks the train line, wherever she goes."

Yaz stops brushing. "Are you serious?"

"Swear on Unda, Tempus, and Lux," I reply, raising my hand. "I brought her here for PACT. They want to use her to stop this war that Semper is allegedly planning."

Not war, I think. Annihilation. That's the word Aska used.

"That's why I'm here. They're giving me a small fortune to hand her off to them, and now they're expecting me to make myself scarce. But I can't, Yaz. I can't leave her. I can't—"

My vision blurs, and I think, *Here we go.* Another lost moment. Another fainting attack. The third in two weeks. Add that to the nosebleed from this morning, and what do we have? Just another dying salesman.

But the world doesn't blot out or blacken away. I am resolutely conscious. The blur is not skipshock.

It is me. Crying.

"Lev . . ." I can feel Yaz panicking. She expected a fight. She did not expect tears. "Oh, come here. Sit down."

I find myself sitting on an upturned grain bucket, my cousin's warm arms around me. Blood runs hot in our family. We can withstand anything.

Or. Almost anything.

"Levi . . ." she says, rocking me slightly. I hate myself for this. I'm already fast-forwarding to the next time I see Yaz. The shame I'm going to feel, knowing I cried in her arms like a child. "You love her, don't you?"

Can you love someone you barely know? Can you love someone you're exploiting? How am I expected to parse any of this out, when I am simultaneously trying to protect Margo and also relying on her to save my life?

And most importantly: Could they ever love you back, when your entire relationship is founded on a lie?

"Lev," Yaz says. "It's all right. It's all right to be in love. It's good, even."

I cover my face with my hands. "Why, Yaz? Why is it good?"

She sighs, patting my back like she's soothing a spooked horse.

"You're a great salesman, Lev. And you know why you're a great salesman? Because you always make sure to have no skin in the game. You always put yourself in a position where you can walk away and feel nothing. That's why you've survived. Thrived, even. But it also means that you cut out anything or anyone that makes you feel uncomfortable, or exposed."

Her speech slows a little here. I can hear the crack in her throat. She doesn't want to say what she's thinking, so I finish the thought for her.

"Like you."

"Like me," she says softly. My cousin. My big cousin Yaz.

"And I'm proud of you. Ten years ago, a Lunati salesman would have had stones thrown at him in the street."

"That still happens sometimes."

"But the point is: what makes you a great salesman won't always make you a great person. Or even a happy one. You need skin in the game. That's what being in love actually is, at the end of the day. It makes the strong parts of you weak, and the weak parts of you strong."

There's a long silence then, when it's too hard to say anything. It's too much to go through.

"You sound like you know," I say eventually. "Like you're in love, too."

"Nah," she says, getting up. "It's just horses for me, I'm afraid. You spend your life loving strong, horrible, fragile animals and you end up learning a few things."

Suddenly, I have a brain wave. "Speaking of horrible fragile animals," I say. "I have an idea."

twenty-three
MARGO

He was different, when he came back. Happier. His features brighter, his step lighter. For the first time since she'd known him, he seemed like a teenage boy. He returned to the PACT headquarters with his arm around his cousin's shoulders, looking like a protective elder brother.

"Hey!" he called to Margo, his face a sunbeam. "Margo, get over here. I want you to meet someone."

And so she met Yaz, who was friendly and interested in her. But not, it felt, as the newfound messiah of PACT. Yaz was interested in Margo vis-à-vis Moon. She asked her questions about what it was like traveling together, and whether Moon had told her about Lunati customs, or whether she had ever been to a monthly Wash.

"You haven't taken her on a Wash yet?" she scolded Moon. "Next one, Margo. You have to come. More people is always better, even if they're not in the faith."

It was all deeply confusing for Margo. She had found the purchase order in Moon's notebook. She was armed with all the information she needed to confront Moon, to tell him she knew what he was doing, what he had done. Yet here was Yaz, blindsiding her with these questions about her cousin.

"Have you had a nice time?" Moon asked, as though they were at the end of a formal dance. "I'm so sorry for leaving. I haven't seen

Yaz in a really long time. We needed to catch up. You didn't mind, did you?"

"He's handsome when he smiles, isn't he?" Yaz said, teasing him. And he was, which was the painful thing. Moon as a stone-faced salesman was intriguing. But Moon happy, in the dim light of the underground room, his skin a lunar plate? It almost winded her.

"You look like you've come into money," Margo said flatly. "Which I suppose you have."

That was it, wasn't it? Soon he would be rid of Margo, with 425 gens in his back pocket. She knew just enough about the currency to know he was making a fortune off of her.

He was confused by this but just pressed on. "Yaz trains horses, and she has her eye on a colt in Bahar coming up for auction. I thought, let's give her some of Heck's baby goo, right? She can smear him with it in secret, make sure he's looking a bit runty, then go in with an offer before auction day. Get a real bargain. Genius, right? And I thought Heck's potion was useless. Where's our stuff?"

Margo pointed to the corner where his suitcase and jacket sat waiting for him. Yaz bounded over to it and immediately started searching through her cousin's bag for the fabled goo.

"Great." He patted his pockets. "Where's my notebook?"

"Here," she said coldly. And with that, she took it out of her own pocket and gave it to him.

Finally, Moon understood that something was wrong. "Is everything OK?"

"Four hundred and twenty-five gens," she said. "If I'd known I was worth so much, I would have asked for a nicer suit."

The light inside him seemed to dim instantly. "Margo. It's not what you think."

Margo was sure to speak very carefully. "You accepted four

hundred and twenty-five gens to take me to Alder, and your plan was to dump me as soon as we got here. Or, wait—what was the exact wording, again? *Margo to Alder. 425 on delivery.* It doesn't really matter what happens after that, does it? Where I go, or what they do with me? Just as long as you get paid. Is that it? What part am I mistaken on?"

"You're not mistaken on the facts," he said softly. "Just the context."

"That's it? That's all you have to say? The *context*? What possible context could you have for literally selling me to PACT?"

"Can we sit down and talk about this?"

"I don't see why I should trust anything you have to say. Because you know the worst thing about you, Mo? You don't even believe in anything. You don't have any principles. I can't even hold this against Taiyo, because Taiyo would put his body in front of a moving train if it meant Semper went down. But you? It's just money, isn't it? Just stupid, cold, boring money."

He ran his fingers through his hair. The eyebrow again. Why, with all the extraordinary things about Moon's appearance—the glow, the scar, the fact that his skin never went cold like hers did—did she always gravitate back to the tiny fleck? That blade-thin slice of white skin where the hair wouldn't grow. She wanted to lay her finger flat on it. She had a perverse urge to touch it with her tongue. All of her intrusive thoughts seemed to come back to that tiny nick of pale skin.

"Margo," he said, "I'm dying."

A train passed overhead. There was no choice but to simply look at each other while it passed. To watch Moon's expression as the joy drained from it, and was replaced by that old sad look of inevitability.

"What are you talking about? What do you mean you're *dying*?"

"It's the skipshock. It's advancing on me. If I don't—"

"*Skipshock!*" she trilled. "We've *all* got skipshock, Moon. I'm the one adjusting from a twenty-four-hour day to a six-hour one, now a twelve-hour one. Soon a *two*-hour one, by the sounds of it."

His voice was dead calm now, with a chill wind that felt like it came off the sea. "Yes, Margo. We've all got skipshock. But you have traveled in three time speeds in two weeks. In the last three months, I have been in and out of twenty. In the last seven *years*? I can't even count. Don't you understand? It's an illness that *accumulates.* It starts off with a stomachache or a bit of insomnia, but it becomes . . ."

He broke off, his face agonized. Margo did not quite believe, yet, that Moon was dying. But she was starting to believe that he believed it.

"Remember the first night at Vesna's? I had a cut on my chin? That was because I passed out trying to get down the stairs."

She balked. "So?"

"So that's how it starts. Then the next day, in the tunnels—"

She blinked, remembering. "You fell backward."

"Yeah. I fell backward. My nose wouldn't stop bleeding this morning. Remember that? My blood isn't clotting the way it should. They're all signs, Margo. I'm surprised that it's taken this long to get as bad as this. Maybe it's because I'm Lunati. We're built for travel. But if I keep at this job, I'm going to die. And not in a dim, distant way. I'm going to die soon."

Margo shook her head violently, like a cat refusing to be picked up.

"It won't even take very long, Margo. I promise you. I'm not saying this to get your sympathy. You can be angry with me. You *should* be angry with me. But this is the context I'm talking about. The context is: if I don't get out of sales, I will die, and quickly. And the only way I can get out of sales is to save enough money to buy a permanent visa and a business license for some nice world where I can let my body heal. That is why I took you off the train. That is why I struck the deal with Taiyo."

"I don't believe you. If it was really as bad as all that you wouldn't be in sales at all. You're too smart."

It hurt, to give him a compliment when she was so furious with him, but it remained true.

"Not that smart," he said miserably. "I'm a Lunati, Margo, and a criminal. When I first got into sales I was a wanted criminal. Arson."

"Arson?"

"Right. When you burn a building?"

"I *know* what arson is."

"You sounded confused." He rubbed at his temples, eyes closed, exhausted by her. "Listen. Margo. If you don't believe me, have a look at your fucking sales papers. Do you remember the night Heck died? The way Ves pulled out his papers like magic? Because salesmen die all the time. It wasn't some genius sudden idea on her part. A salesman dies. Someone buys his papers. Then eventually they die, too."

Margo felt the 8 on the back of her neck, the scar tissue raised and cool. Suddenly, she realized why Moon and Vesna were so concerned about her regretting this. This small scar that meant very little to her, because it didn't really hurt. But now she understood. It wasn't just a scar. It was like jumping into a man's tomb. Her fingers curved around the shape again and again, and she stopped associating it with the number eight. It wasn't an eight at all. It was an infinity symbol, a loop that went around and around, dead salesman after dead salesman, and never stopped.

Moon stepped toward her and placed his warm hand on the back of her neck, his palm covering the scar. He seemed to know exactly what she was thinking, his thumb tracing the shape of it. Around and around. Year after year. Body after body.

She didn't know whether she forgave him. Decisions like that were arbitrary now. The fight had gone out of her. She leaned her forehead against his chest and breathed hard. Moon held her. His hand the only comforting thing, the only thing that felt like it was holding her spine upright.

"All salesmen?" she asked after a moment.

"All of them. Eventually. Unless we can get out. And they don't make that easy, either. Or cheap."

"Hence the money."

"Hence the money, yes."

Suddenly, she understood something. Another piece of this vast universe that she was expected to save came into focus for her.

"That's why they let you do it," she said, her forehead still connected to his chest. "Why Semper let salesmen travel. Why they don't see you as a threat."

He paused before answering. "Yes. Yes, I suppose so."

She thought of Moon's life, through the eyes of someone like Captain Halvpas. What did it amount to, for him? A dog's life? A mouse's? Or something far smaller, an ant or a fly?

Could she forgive Moon? That no longer seemed to be the most important question. There was only one thing on her mind now, one question that took the place of all others.

Could she save him?

twenty-four
MOON

It's different between us now. Not romantic, exactly. It feels broader, wider, airier than that. It's a release. The falling away of secrets. The layers that have formed to protect twelve-year-old Lev Evreleri, to separate him from Moon the Salesman, are evaporating so quickly that I don't know who I am in front of Margo now. Where to look, where my hands normally go. Flush with my pants pockets, usually? Right? I don't know how to stand. How to *be.*

Thank the gods for Yaz, puncturing the moment. She drags us over to a crate in the drinking area, the hum of revolution all around us.

"So will this *actually* work?" Yaz asks. She holds up the glowing jar of Heck's final sale. My hands are still shaking from talking to Margo. I knock back two glasses of Alderian rye in trying to remember.

"The guy who sold it to us certainly thought so."

"Limits infant progression for six to eight weeks," Margo says. "A dab on the forehead and your baby stays—"

"Plump and gurgling," Margo and I both say together, snickering a little. A shadow in our eyes. Heck. Poor Heck.

Yaz laughs. "Didn't realize you were a two-man operation now, cuz."

I don't know where to put my hands again. Margo answers.

"Yes," she says, her voice very firm. "We are."

We all laugh then, filling up our glasses, and the candles are burning so low that you could almost mistake the room for a church. Margo asks Yaz about her work with the horses, and Yaz explains the racing scene in Bahar, the excitement of it all. Yaz tells her that I was good with horses, too, back in the day, and that I should have done *that* instead of sales.

We talk, and we drink, and time blurs. Suddenly, the world seems divinely simple. Which I suppose is why people go to church in the first place. To reduce the complexities and the frailties of being human to the divine. To the simple.

Beat the bad guys.

Save the girl.

Live till thirty.

"You drunk?" Yaz shakes me, pouring me another glass of sweet brown liquor.

"No," I reply, my forehead resting on my fist. I am drunk. I always forget about Alderian rye. But it's fine. It's nice.

Yaz teases me, but Margo comes to my defense. "It's been a big day," she says. "A weird day."

I zone in and out of conversation, focusing on the space behind Margo's ear where her short hair is starting to grow out. When she first came to New Davia, it stopped at her lobe. It tickles her jawline, curling slightly. I find myself wondering how many times it would go around my finger, if I tried to wrap it.

Salesmen will blame almost anything on skipshock. Lateness, cheapness, violence. Eating too much. Not eating enough. But what I do next, I cannot blame on illness. I can only blame myself.

I lean forward. And I curl Margo's hair around my fingers.

“Hello?” she says, and I can’t tell whether she’s going to burst out laughing or smack me in the face. “Can I help you?”

“Just checking,” I murmur, not quite holding on to my words. “Just checking.”

It’s over for me then. Yaz and Margo are creaking with laughter, realizing how completely wrecked I am.

Yaz. “Excuse me, aren’t you supposed to be a big tough salesman?”

Margo. “Aren’t you meant to be hardened from your legendary life on the road?”

Yaz. “Is this the dangerous world of sales? Three drinks and you’re out?”

Margo. “Is this why you were never in the parlor at Vesna’s? Can’t handle your booze, Mo?”

They laugh and they laugh, and I get to my feet. I get to my feet a little *too* quickly, because I kick out the stool I’m sitting on and hit the table behind us. The revolutionaries drinking there give us a dirty look. Yaz and Margo laugh harder.

“Put that guy to *bed*,” someone says sharply.

“*You* go to bed,” I snap back.

“All right, all right,” Margo says. “I’ll take him.”

Suddenly, my weight is being balanced over Margo’s shoulder as she hoists me over to an empty mattress.

“You’re deceptively strong,” I slur suspiciously. “You in the NoGa or something?”

“Thanks. I was in the rowing club at school.”

“What? What’s that?”

“Never mind.”

When I eventually flop down onto a bed, it’s the most comfortable I have ever been in my entire life.

"Margo. You've gotta try this." I am completely horizontal. Margo is perched at the edge of the mattress. "Come on. Seriously. Not in a weird way."

"OK," she says, lying down. "As long as it's not in a weird way."

Then there she is. Simple as that. Next to me on a straw mattress in a crowded room. No anxiety, no artificiality. Just the ease of being with the person you most want to be with, in the very moment you want to be with them. When does a thing like that even happen? Once in a century?

"It's *narrow*," she says, wiggling slightly.

"Shh. Come here." I pull her onto my chest, and find myself amazed at how she just *fits*. Her head tucked under my neck. Her arm across my body. "This is good, isn't it?"

She laughs and presses herself closer. "Yeah. It's *really* good."

Oh, thank the gods, I think. She's drunk, too. I press my lips into the crown of her head, not kissing it exactly. Just holding it there, breathing in the smell of her. Of her, and of everything we've been through. The ash in the tunnels below the theater, the warm rye. Under that, the raw Margo smell. Clean and cool, like new bedsheets.

"I thought you said," she whispers, "that we weren't going to have a physical relationship."

"I said it would be *best* if we didn't."

"What do you call this then?"

"Being friends. Being really, really good friends."

I don't know how long we're awake for, after that. But we stay friends through all of it. We lie there, talking nonsense into the ceiling, and every time a train rumbles above us we seem to inch a little closer together. We find new gaps and spaces to fill. We align our hands together, her small fingers ("stubby"—her words) only reaching as far as my knuckles.

It is not *not* sexual. It is not *not* romantic.

But before it is anything, it is friends.

And that's how we fall asleep. As friends.

I wake up hungover to find Margo still tucked under my arm. Which would be fine, nice even, if I didn't also have Taiyo and Aska standing over me.

Aska speaks first.

"We have a problem."

I ease myself up, my bones rickety, my back against the column. Margo's in a similarly delicate condition, her arms draped protectively around her knees.

"What kind of problem?"

Aska drags a crate over and sits on it.

"The Southern Guard are here."

"What?"

"Yes. I'm not sure who, and I'm not sure how many, but the Khaise plan might need to fast-forward."

Margo looks around as if Captain Halvpas might pop out from under a crate. "Where *are* they?"

"Sonne sent a message back from the palace libraries. A group of them arrived before dawn, asking to speak with the palace dragons."

"I'm sorry, the palace dragons?"

"Sorry. Not dragons. That's just what we call them. They index and archive Alder's treasure, from the various royal dynasties."

"Treasure?" I blink. "They must not be here for Margo, then."

"Maybe not. Maybe they're trying to liquidate the palace assets to fund their war. Either way, I don't like it. Alder is still technically a Northern world. What are they doing up here? If they want their hands on some ancient sapphire, why not do it through the NoGa?"

Aska pauses, her eyes darting from Margo to me, steadily clocking our sleeping arrangements versus how many clothes we still have on.

"I'm afraid this means that everything has been moved forward. We need to get you on a train to Khaise today."

Margo gets to her feet, holding her head slightly. "*Today?*"

"I know, I know. Best-case scenario, you want things planned and precise. Worst-case scenario, you just want things done. And I'm afraid we're edging toward a worst-case scenario here. If the SoGa get ahold of you, Mars, that's our biggest asset gone. Do you understand what I'm telling you? You need to get on a train. Today."

Mars. This is no slip of the tongue from Aska. I know enough about sales to know a rebranding when I see one. Margo is a schoolgirl with a funny name. Mars is a legend. A revolutionary. A martyr.

"I'm going with her," I say, putting on my shoes.

Aska winces. "I can't pay you any extra, Fengari."

"I don't want any extra. I don't want the four hundred and twenty-five to begin with."

"Yes, he does," Margo says blearily, fastening her suit jacket on. "Moon, don't be deranged. We need that money."

We. We are a *we* now.

Aska still doesn't look satisfied. "I don't like it. Let Taiyo go with her. Moon, stay here. They'll come back, and in the meantime you can make a killing in the Alder marketplace."

"Why don't you want me to go, Aska?"

She massages the bridge of her nose for a second, like she's insulted to even be asked what her motivations are. Aska looks at me, her yellow eyes penetrating.

"Because you're too conspicuous, Moon. People notice you.

You're the only Lunati salesman who anyone knows about. You've got a fucking *moon* carved into your face. Which has its uses, and I'm very excited to talk about how you can best serve PACT, but right now I cannot in good conscience send you to Khaise on a mission where thousands of lives—"

"—hang in the balance, I know. All right, well. What does Margo—sorry, *Mars*—say?"

We all look to Margo in expectation. Perhaps it's the hangover that has sanded the edges off her nerves, but for the first time, she seems ready to fit into whatever new role PACT has written for her.

"Sorry, Aska," she says. "We're a two-man operation."

She narrows her eyes at Aska. "Now pay him."

"Margo . . ." I interrupt.

"We can't be a two-man operation if one of us is a dead man."

"Right. Wouldn't want a dead-man operation."

"We certainly wouldn't."

There's a standoff, then. An honest-to-god standoff. Aska simply stands before us with her hands on her hips, waiting for either one of us to give in. To relent. After a few moments, wherein she realizes that she simply does not have time to waste, she sighs and drops her hands.

"All right," she says. "Get ready to leave. Let me get the funds."

Margo and I grin at each other. Taiyo looks like someone who has just walked in on two children who have drawn on the walls.

"Oh, don't look so *pleased* with yourselves," he says sulkily. "And if it's going to be the three of us, don't think I'm going to share a room with the two of you."

Yaz bounds over, dressed for the racetrack. "You're heading off? To Khaise?"

"Looks like it."

"Well, listen, look up Saffy when you're there, OK?"

"Saffy. *There's* a name I haven't heard in a long time."

"Your mother *loved* her, she'd roll over in her grave if she knew you were in Khaise and didn't visit. She's your teyzi you know."

"Lunati don't have teyzi." I resist the urge to say: *and my mother doesn't have a grave.*

"I know, but Khaise do. She's your Khaise teyzi. You have to visit."

Yaz hugs us all goodbye as Aska sulkily returns with a stack of bills. "I knew I was paying you," she says, handing it over. "I didn't know I couldn't get *rid* of you."

"What happened to PACT being a friend to the Lunati, Aska?"

She scowls in return. "Follow me."

Taiyo nudges me, his face all smiles. "Aska stupid question . . ."

And despite everything, I laugh. I'm dehydrated and dirty and I'm going to a two-hour world for an undisclosed amount of time. But I'm going with Margo, and with Taiyo. I clap my arms around them both, feeling like a unit. Like a family.

"What's gotten into *you*?" Taiyo asks.

"We're going to Khaise," I say simply. "To save the world."

twenty-five
MARGO

"OK, you three. Follow me. I'm going to be talking the entire time, because there's a lot to get through. When I'm *not* talking, it is not an invitation for you to speak. I am intentionally not making noise because we are in a delicate or thin-walled part of the infrastructure, where someone aboveground could potentially hear. Is that clear?"

Taiyo, Moon, and Margo looked at one another, unsure of whether this was a test of their ability to stay quiet.

"Please say 'I understand' if you understand," said Aska impatiently.

"I understand." They all felt very sheepish, and very young.

Aska led them through another labyrinth of tunnels, drowned rooms, and passageways, a constant stream of speech the entire way.

"Obviously, we're right below the train station, but never, ever use any exits that lead there. We blocked those ourselves. The risk of being followed, or caught emerging, is too huge. So we're going to come out at the market, cross through, and go to the train station on foot."

They came to a solid wall. Aska stood in front of it and checked her pocket watch in silence. They all waited, obedient and speechless. Within a few minutes, the wall moved, revealing a narrow passageway that was filled with discarded pottery shards. They shuffled through, their steps clacking noisily as Aska resumed speaking.

"As soon as we arrive, we will split up. Margo: move toward the left wall. Moon: right wall. Taiyo: down the center. Take a circuitous path. Talk to people. Buy something, if you have cash on you. Market traders are going to try to sell you things, and you should let them. We have eleven minutes to get across the market hall. Use them. Do not look at, or for, one another. If we all do exactly as we're told, we should be at the main exit by 3:05. This will let us catch the rotation that will put the train station next to the market hall. It will stay there for five minutes. If you miss that rotation, that means you miss the train. The next one isn't until much later. I can't afford to have Margo hanging around Alder that long. Not while SoGa are around. Is that understood?"

They came to the Room of Cats, where a shaft of daylight from the upper world had cut the room in two. There were far fewer cats now, and the ones that remained seemed elderly. They sunbathed, eyes lightly focusing on the four intruders.

There were subtle footholds that were carved into the walls of the Room of Cats. Aska scaled them easily, and posted herself through the letterbox-shaped window. The cats each looked up as this dagger of a woman briefly blocked their sun.

"Mars. You come next."

To her own surprise, Margo didn't hate the nickname Mars. The phrase *two-man operation* floated back into her head again. Moon and Mars.

Aska took her hand and helped hoist Margo to the window. When she finally emerged aboveground, she almost gagged on the smell. Suddenly, the location of the cats made sense to her. The narrow street they arrived at was filled with blood and fish carcasses.

"Yeah. I should have mentioned," Aska said, brushing down her clothes. "This is the rubbish tip behind the market. Where all the bad fish go."

Huge, filthy bins disguised the narrow opening to PACT's underworld, which Aska pushed back to allow room for the two boys to come up. Margo reached down and helped Moon out, both his hands reaching for her.

His grip was familiar to her now, the precise sensation of how his touch felt on her. They had not, technically speaking, "done" anything the night before. Or at least, nothing that the girls in her school would have classed as "anything." But that didn't mean that things hadn't changed. Between the two of them, yes, but also between Margo and herself.

For the first time in her life, she had a person. She and Moon had been born in different places and brought up in different ways, but regardless, one thing was very clear to her. They had each spent most of their lives lonely. Her in a cold house; him in a cold world. They were houseplants that people forgot to check on. And now they had each other. There was a feeling of boundlessness, of growing, of feeling like you could do things. Somehow, she didn't need to wonder if he felt this way, too. She *knew* it.

"Thanks," he said, his smile dreamy, until he caught the smell of fish. "Oh, *shit.*"

It was still too early in the day for there to be many fish corpses around, which somehow made it worse. The smell was baked into the atmosphere. It was there *all the time.*

Taiyo came next. "My god. What is *that*?"

"Fish," they all answered at once. "Dead fish."

"Is that what we are? Dead fish? It's not a very morale-building exit, Aska."

"We're not in the morale business," replied Aska.

"Really? Silly me."

But there was a glimmer between them, and Margo briefly wondered if she and Moon weren't the only ones who got drunk and cozy the night before. She wouldn't put it past Taiyo. According to Ani and Vesna, he slept with pretty much everyone.

They wove through the rotten smell of bins and found the market hall through a side door, propped open with a brick.

"OK," Aska said, looking again at her pocket watch. "Let's stagger this. Moon, go. Bear right. Eleven minutes."

"All right. See you on the platform."

He smiled at Margo and disappeared.

"Taiyo, go. Down the middle. Be inconspicuous. But not *too* inconspicuous."

Taiyo went, saluting briefly with his fingers to his forehead.

It was only Margo and Aska in the alleyway now.

"OK, Mars. Our great hope. You know what to do. Or, rather, just do what you've been doing ever since you arrived. Break the damn train line."

Margo paused at the door. "Aska . . ." She didn't know what to say, exactly, except that she needed to communicate to Aska that she shouldn't be placing too many hopes on her, or too heavily. To make it clear that she was just a teenage girl with a dead dad and a spotty, unclear history with mental illness. "I'm just . . . I'm in school, did you know that?"

"Pardon?"

"Just, you know. I'm a schoolkid. I was on my way to boarding school when Moon found me. I just don't want you to think I'm some big hero or something. I know how important PACT is. I don't want to give you the wrong impression."

Aska listened to this carefully, nodding all the time. "You know who I'm supposed to be right now, Mars?"

"Who?"

"Mrs. Sam Donnerstag."

"What?"

"Sam Donnerstag. His family owned the sheep farm next to our sheep farm. I was supposed to marry him. Consolidate the family interest. But I'm here instead. There are no perfect candidates, Mars. Just people who can, and will. Can you help us?"

Margo thought about it. "Yes."

"Will you?"

"Yes." Quicker this time.

"All right. Let's move. I'll stick with you. Two ladies on a shopping trip. How about that?" Aska checked her watch. "Now."

They entered, keeping to the left-hand wall. The market hall, like everywhere else in Alder City, respected seniority. There were hundreds of sellers, the bulk of whom were local market traders, who had their stalls near the front, with freelance salesmen joining at the back.

There was a fashionable, louche air to the people of Alder. She spotted a man in a smart black suit with a skirt of peacock feathers gathered around it. A woman in a sculpted gray hairdo, like an ornate version of a barrister's wig. There was a tailored flamboyance to almost everyone: of being dressed up, but as a joke.

They had eleven minutes to get from one end of the hall to the other. It should have taken six. They dawdled, and their dawdling attracted interest.

"Ladies! Slate pottery, terra-cotta, fire-burned Waldram clay—"

"My darlings! Self-cleaning linens, for the busy housewife—"

Margo wanted to play along, but it was hard when almost everything that anyone tried to sell her was for someone in charge of a household.

"Young ones at home, missus?"

A squat man with a cheerful face was standing in front of a colorful market stall, selling rainbow-bright paper. Stationery. Margo could pretend to be interested in stationery.

"Beautiful writing paper. Ideal for schoolwork."

Her fingers brushed against the heavy, velvet grain of the paper. "How much?"

"Thirty gens for a bundle of five."

"*Thirty*? For paper?"

Aska smirked at her, enjoying Margo's quite genuine shock at the cost. Then her gaze traveled over Margo's shoulder. She frowned in concern.

Margo turned around. Someone was badgering Moon. He was too far away for her to see what, exactly, was the tone of the interaction. But Moon was taking out his briefcase. He was opening it on an empty table.

"For you, miss, twenty gens for five sheets."

The market seller was not letting her go. "I don't think so. It's just paper."

He kept on talking, but Margo's eyes went back to Moon. What was Moon doing, taking out his briefcase? Selling, when they only had ten minutes to get across the hall?

Margo looked at her own watch. Six minutes to go.

"Margo," Aska said sharply. "You're being *spoken* to."

There was a glare in Aska's eye, and Margo remembered that she was not meant to be looking at, or for, anyone. She went back to the seller. "What?"

"I said, you haven't seen what the paper can *do*."

At this, he laid a square of indigo paper in front of her and, with an eye dropper, let a single drop of water fall. The paper folded itself into a crane. It hopped around the table for a moment, beating its wings, and then became still.

The self-folding origami scrambled something inside Margo's brain. She had seen it before. She was sure she had. She stopped dead, forgetting for a second where she was, or why she was there. A flood of deep sensory recollection came to her. Not just of images, but of sounds and smells and the feel of silk pocket material against her fingers. She was in her house again. Seven or maybe eight years old.

"You see, lady," the seller said with some satisfaction, "this is quite special. Especially if you have small ones at home."

She had a sudden vision of her old duvet cover, decorated with pink clouds. She had insisted on going to bed with the paper crane, because she was not allowed pets, and she had heard of dogs that slept at the end of your bed. If you had something in bed with you, a friend, you would never be lonely again.

"Here," Aska said, her tone still light. "I'll buy you a sheet, seeing as you're so bewitched by it."

You can take it to bed, her father said. *Just don't take it to school.*

She made it dance on the duvet, then fell asleep grasping it delicately in her hands. When she woke up, it was a crumpled ball.

Aska handed the seller a few coins. "Red? Orange? Blue?"

"What do you think?" she asked, turning to Margo.

"Um. Blue?"

Where did her father get the crane? Did they sell them in Shanghai, too? Or Hong Kong? Or wherever it was that he had been, that time?

They moved on, and Aska looped her arm through Margo's.

"Don't look," she said. "But your boy is having some trouble."

"What?"

"Nothing serious. But the market sellers know him. He's a salesman, after all. They want to buy stuff. Don't look."

"Stop *saying* that. I'm not looking."

The origami paper twitched in her pocket, aching to be folded. Here was another thing that Alder had in common with her own world. The self-folding paper crane, and the Orpheus play.

They had four minutes remaining until the platform rotation.

"Taiyo's moving fine. It's Moon who's the problem. I told you, Mars, he's too conspicuous. I get that you're a team, or whatever, but part of being on a strong team is accepting that—"

Aska pushed her on, moving through the market, chastising her choice in teammate. Margo couldn't focus. What if Moon didn't make the rotation? What if something happened? At the train station, a random man had picked a fight just because Moon was Lunati. Her stomach grinded away with anxiety. What if the stress of all these possible obstacles played on Moon's skipshock, and he collapsed right there in the marketplace?

"Don't panic, Mars," Aska said firmly, her grip tightening at Margo's elbow. But Aska didn't sound calm herself.

What was the thing about Orpheus again? That he had to lead Eurydice out of hell, but he couldn't look behind to check if she was still there. It came up again in the Bible, somewhere. The same sort of idea. All these heroes who just had to trust that their person was behind them, without ever knowing for sure.

She had never sympathized with these stories before. But now her body ached and stiffened with the effort of not turning around. Moon was behind her now. She knew that. But how far behind? How badly was he caught in the belly of the market?

"Three minutes," Aska said, motioning to the clock at the top of the hall. "Taiyo is at the doors already."

Something in Aska's tone seemed to suggest that it would be better, for all involved, if she had fallen in love with Taiyo instead.

"We have to go back for him," she whispered to Aska fiercely. "Aska, he's not well. He's got skipshock."

She could hear Aska's teeth grinding slightly in resentment. "All right. Go to Taiyo. Let me see if I can loop back and pick him up."

Aska left her side and went back through the market. Her narrow body swept through market sellers and browsers. She moved like oil, somehow never nudging anyone, never making herself known. Margo ached a little watching her, knowing she could never be so graceful, and certainly not under this kind of pressure.

She watched Aska grab Moon, watched his face flood with relief as she pulled him out of the knot of buyers who had formed around him.

"It's fine," murmured Taiyo, his hand on her shoulder. "Look, she has him. We've got time. We're going to make it."

She watched Moon's shaggy hair and hunched shoulders move through the crowd, Aska's hand firmly on his wrist. Moving quickly, weaving effortlessly, even though this time their movements were tracked carefully by the people around them. The market sellers who murmured *Lunati* under their breaths. Who used their fingers to draw moon shapes on their own faces, nudging one another.

But it didn't matter. He was inches away now, his eyes brightening as they saw her, the relief rushing through as he felt for her hand in the crowd.

He said something to her that she couldn't hear. The rotation had begun, the cranks pulling and cleaving into one another, all sound reduced to a mechanical grind. Her knees trembled with movement, one hand on the wall for stability. They had made the rotation.

As they waited for the doors to open, she could feel the eyes still on Moon, the people who were amazed that he had people to meet, people who were glad to see him. Margo felt an irrepressible urge to give them a show: to tilt him backward and kiss him extravagantly, like a flamenco dancer in an old movie. She settled, instead, for wrapping her arms around him. She slid her hands boldly under his suit jacket, against the smooth cotton of his white shirt. Aska wouldn't like it, but in less than a minute Aska would be seeing them onto a train, so what did it matter? Margo faced the market traders, her head on Moon's shoulder. The few who were still looking at her grimaced; one even spat on the floor.

Margo felt a cold gust as the doors opened behind her. Suddenly, everyone in the market hall turned toward the train station entrance, their faces switching quickly to horror. Moon's body tensed, his hands suddenly active and firm against her.

Then Margo heard the whistle, and she knew exactly who stood on the platform.

twenty-six
MOON

I've never had much luck in Alder. The city is so precise and industrious that they tend to reserve a special resentment for the Lunati, who they regard as free-floating spongers who don't contribute because they can make their own money. So much of Lunati hatred comes from the misapprehension that we have limitless self-made wealth, instead of a stipend of a dozen silver seeds at the end of a month. A dozen silver seeds that most people don't want to buy, because Lunati hands have touched them. We're unlucky. We're freeloaders. We're scum.

So no one is more surprised than me that Alder suddenly wants my business.

"Mr. Moony!" an old supplier of mine bellows. Big Bronze is how I always think of him. Creatively, because he's big, and he deals bronzefruit. He's older, red-faced, and with a little white moustache that feels incongruous with the size of his pillowy face.

"How are you, sir?" I ask politely.

"Very well, my good man, very well. You're looking *sharp*." Big Bronze beams at me, with what feels like genuine warmth. "I'm very glad to see you today. Yes. Yes."

Up ahead, I can see Margo and Aska weaving through the market. Taiyo, doing a terrible job of appearing to look interested in buying stuff, is almost at the end of the hall.

"Yes, you too," I say hurriedly. "Bit of a rush today."

"Of course. I just wanted to know if you had any of those fantastic little seeds you're so good at making. There's quite a demand for them, these days."

"I don't think so, sir."

"You don't have any? Aren't you a Lunati?"

His voice is so big and booming that other people are starting to look. I remember then the new seeds that Yaz insisted on giving me in exchange for Heck's goop jars.

"A Lunati salesman with no seeds? What are you even doing here?" He laughs loudly, but the question, along with the repeated mention of the word *Lunati*, draws eyes.

"Of course. Of course," I say, snapping open my briefcase. "How many?"

But now everyone seems to want seeds, and a bidding war opens up that quickly goes beyond my control. Three or four different traders overhear and join, and suddenly we're going to sixty gens for a handful of seeds they usually wouldn't pay ten for.

It's the fuel shortage, I realize. The SoGa's war stockpiling has limited everyone's access to light and heat. How long have they been doing this for? And why did it take me so long to notice?

"Listen, gents," I say to the small crowd. "I'm in a hurry. Your highest bids now, please."

But they resent this, because who am I, a foreigner from a weird religion, to set the terms of my own sale? Murmurings and grunts from the bidders, and the energy starts to turn sour.

"Jacking up the prices when times are tough," a woman who isn't even part of the auction says loudly. "That's the loonies for you."

I'm running out of time, and I don't know what to do. The wrong step could turn this into a riot. Times are hard, as she said. And hard times welcome an easy target.

I turn to Big Bronze. "Sir. Does sixty sound right to you?"

"Sixty is twice what you did last time."

Never mind that someone else is offering eighty. Never mind that.

Aska, with a face like thunder, weaves back through the crowd. "Loony," she says loudly. "Give me everything you have, seventy gens, or I call the Northern Guard."

People appreciate this. Appreciate that someone local is taking the situation in hand. They part, and I follow Aska, hearing grumbles as I go.

"Come on. We've not got much time," she says, pulling me behind her. "In fact, we have less than a minute."

We dart around sellers and stalls, my heart beating, my breath short. Taiyo and Margo are there at the heavy carved front doors, waiting for us.

Margo holds me tightly and any doubt I might have had about last night—whether Margo was drunk, whether it was all a bit of silly fun—falls away. Whatever happens in Khaise, we're in it together. Whatever happens after that, we're in that together, too.

And we would have made it. If the doors had not opened, and the SoGa had not been standing on the platform.

They surge into the market, the force of them pushing everyone and everything back. The four of us are guttered into the stalls to the left of the doors. There are so many SoGa officers that the act of them entering the market lasts the entire length of the rotation. The doors close again as the market moves counterclockwise, taking us two miles from the train station.

Now we have not only missed our train, we are stuck in the Alder market hall with a hundred SoGa.

At the top of the hall is a large brass bell, which is rung at the open and close of every market day. They line up in front of the bell, arms behind their backs, gazing coldly at us.

There, presumably fresh from his journey to Hess Point, is Captain Halvpas. He strides in front of his battalion and hits the bell sharply, the brutal sound ringing across the hall. As if he needs a bell to get a room's attention. As if everyone's not already looking at them, their backs ramrod straight, their hands quivering.

Halvpas strikes the bell again and again. Usually, it tolls for a couple seconds, and the person who does it has a light, business-like way of conducting proceedings. The more Halvpas rings it, the sicker the room feels. The thick brass brushes our bones, burrowing into our skulls.

"Good evening," he says finally. "I'm so sorry to interrupt your business. I know this market is an important hub for salesmen."

He says *salesmen* like he's humoring us. Like it's a name we call ourselves, but not what people like him call us in private.

"My name is Captain Halvpas," he says. "And I'm looking for a very particular object, an item that was stolen from one of our most high-ranking members of government, and must be returned as quickly as possible."

An object?

"The item," he continues, his voice booming across the hall, "could easily have ended up in a trade center such as this. I must stress that whoever has it, the SoGa will presume to be totally innocent as long as it is given up willingly. I do not pretend to know through what channels salesmen receive goods, and I know that thorough background checks are not always carried out."

No one speaks, but I can feel the ripple of offense through the room. Basically: *We know you thieves deal in stolen goods, but we're willing to look the other way. Today.*

"The item we're looking for," Captain Halvpas concludes, "is a watch."

In that moment, Margo and I aren't salesmen. We aren't even really people. We are two hunted animals, our eyes fastening together, helpless as prey.

"A silver watch," he continues. "With three hands: counting hours, minutes, seconds. It was last seen in New Davia."

Margo is looking down at her sleeve. Thankfully the suit we gave her is too long on the cuffs. But I can see her puzzling it out. If it wasn't the soldier who picked her up by the neck, she would volunteer the watch here and now. I don't think it even means very much to her. She let me wear it for days in New Davia, barely noticing.

Captain Halvpas observes the silence and then looks at his own watch. "We have about twenty minutes before this rotation ends," he says. "Please, go about your business, and I will come speak to you individually. But I would very much love to leave your great city today with one silver wristwatch, and no blood on my hands."

Could we just drop the watch and leave? Scatter it to the floor, wait for someone to find it and call out to the captain?

The four of us look to one another, desperation written on all our faces.

"To think," Aska says, her tone light but her eyes steady. "To think, some government watch ending up here!" She is asking us silently: *Do any of you know what the fuck this is about?*

Government watch. No: watch belonging to a high-ranking member of the government.

Margo is looking at me like she's praying I have a plan. If we drop the watch now, the SoGa gets off our back. But why is the watch so important? Why do they even know about it? The watch was given to Margo by her father, who died in her own world years ago.

Richard Madden III.

Margo would sell this watch in a heartbeat. Use it as a bribe, if she needed to. But the fact that they want it has erased any chance that she could give it to them.

Captain Halvpas is making his way through the market hall. It's all too much like the market day in New Davia, when we followed Taiyo into the tunnels.

And then Halvpas held Margo up by the throat.

But he let her go, didn't he? That was the strange thing, the thing we didn't talk about, the thing we chalked up to SoGa idiocy. They were supposedly looking for a girl. They probably had a description of Margo and everything. But they had her, and they let her go.

What if they were never looking for Margo?

What if they had been looking for the watch?

The watch that, at that time, I was wearing. In the bakery ten feet away.

There are enough SoGa in here that they could check every wrist, pocket, and suitcase if they need to. I look to Aska in desperation. "I don't suppose you have a contingency plan for this?"

"None springs to mind," she says, a slight tremor in her throat.

"Margo? Taiyo?" I ask. They each look back at me, mute with terror. Captain Halvpas is moving through the crowd, no more than a dozen feet from us. In a moment, he will recognize Margo. The girl he choked, paid off, then chased onto a train in New Davia. Here, in a salesman suit, with an apparently precious watch on her wrist.

I open my briefcase. There isn't much left but pinches here and there, each nestled in their compartments.

A is for axiom.

I tear a piece of notebook paper in half. I get a fistful of axiom together and stick it in the paper with some red salts.

"What is *that*?"

"This," I say, rolling the mixture into a tight paper fist, "is a bomb."

And *this*, I think as I throw it in the air, is rebellion.

twenty-seven

MARGO

Fire bloomed instantly, catching the paper bags that were used to wrap fruit in. A burst of orange tickled and spread, pushing back a herd of screaming people who were trying to deal with the threat of war and the threat of fire all at once.

Moon pulling her by the collar.

"Come on," he said. "Run."

They would have to escape the SoGa by going back the way they came, via the small waste door, and through the Room of Cats.

Axiom and red salts: a combustion agent and a heating agent, neither designed to be particularly strong, and not especially potent from spending weeks in a salesman's briefcase. But it was enough to frighten everyone, and enough to make Captain Halvpas order his men to fire shots into the room. They came, short and punchy, and too drowned out by panicked screams to tell if they had actually hit anyone.

The soldiers pressed toward the double doors. Against all better judgment, Margo looked at her watch.

The watch?

Two more gunshots. A bullet hit the roof, and Margo wondered if her short stay in Alder would lead to the destruction of not one but two enormous glass ceilings.

Everyone was running now. She hoped that there was too much

of a rush and panic to tell if Aska's, Taiyo's, Margo's, and Moon's running looked out of place alongside everyone else. The path to the waste exit was blocked by a cluster of garment stands. Huge bolts of slippery fabric had been knocked over, dominoes of thick material piling up like rolls of carpet. The four of them climbed like children, Taiyo losing his footing on a length of singed velvet. Margo stopped to pull him up and caught a look at Captain Halvpas, who was advancing toward them.

Halvpas, crucially, looked back.

The recognition was instant. He knew her face in a crowd, any crowd, because he had trained his mind to identify Margo's looks, movements, and ultimately, her meaning. The alley outside the night bakery. The train to Hess Point. The way he had roared her name through the closed doors of the compartment.

He knew her, and he would follow her to any world to take what she had.

It wasn't her, after all, that he was after. It was the watch.

But *why*?

Margo ran, knowing he could follow her. Knowing he would never stop.

They veered toward the alley's side entrance, the door clipping them on the way out. They wove around the market garbage, feeling the stamp of feet behind them. Taiyo briefly attempted to push the trash cans over, to create a barrier between them and the advancing SoGa.

They found the storm drain that led to the Room of Cats. They squeezed themselves inside, each of them lowering into the room below. Aska came last.

"We're in luck," she said, breathless. "The rotation is just about to start again. The fish alley is moving away from the market."

"Aska. Halvpas is up there. He's seen me. He wants the watch." Then she held her wrist up. "*My* watch."

Aska looked, dumbfounded, between Margo and the watch. It seemed as if she was quickly reevaluating everything she knew about Margo.

Once again came the sound of machinery cranking. The game board of Alder resetting itself.

"We need to move," said Aska. "It will take them a few minutes to figure out the storm drain is really a door. Some of them are big, too, so it will take them a moment to fit. Especially with those guns. We've got to trap them."

"*Trap* them?"

"Right. Ten of them, maybe twelve. But how many of us?"

"Four," Taiyo said, panic rising. "And we're not armed."

"Wrong." Aska grinned. "There's a hundred of us, at least, down here. And *we* have guns. Quite a few, as it turns out. I quite like those odds, don't you?"

"But they'll find your location. They'll know where PACT is."

Aska bent down and pulled something gleaming out of her boot. A dagger, short and sharp, was released from its leather binding.

"That's why it's important," she said patiently, "that we don't leave survivors."

The sound of soldiers came closer. They had hit a dead end. Margo heard confusion, disbelief, rage. They heard the beginnings of a search, and the words—*look for entrances, openings*—in Captain Halvpas's familiar voice.

"Margo," she heard Aska say. "Now is not the time to panic. Stay behind me."

Aska sprinted into the labyrinth. They had no choice but to follow her. No guns, no knives. The route was beginning to feel familiar to Margo, and led them eventually to the Hall of the Seven Bears. Aska went immediately to the juggling bear.

"Taiyo," she ordered. "Give me a boost."

Taiyo took her foot in his hands. He pushed Aska's body up to the lantern that swung, low and orange, over the bear's head. She fumbled a moment, then plucked two revolvers from inside the lantern.

"Mo," she said, seconds before throwing one. "Safety's on."

Moon caught it. "You didn't say anything about guns."

"Yes, I know. I assume you can shoot?"

"Yes," Moon said, looking as though he'd rather not.

"Yes," Taiyo answered, like he wasn't completely telling the truth. Aska threw him the other gun.

"Mars?"

She considered pretending, then thought better of it. "No."

"Well done for being honest," Aska said, her pocket watch out again. "If even *one* of these clowns is telling the truth, then my guess is we can hold them back for three or four minutes. Five, if your man is a surgeon with a pistol. I need you to go to the barracks. Bring in reinforcements, and so on. Get everyone. Do you understand me?"

Margo began to protest. "I can't *leave*—"

"Well, you're going to have to," Aska snapped. "Now listen to me carefully. I'm going to tell you the way to the barracks. When the balancing bear's door opens, you're going down a passageway, and you're keeping your hand on the left-hand wall, OK? Eventually, you'll feel an opening." Aska broke off, retracing an imaginary map in her head. She bit her lip. "I'm sorry. This is not a great time of day. You're going to have to swim."

"Swim?"

"Yes. So take that left, then left again. You're going to see a tunnel beneath you. The water in there will come up to your chin. You have to swim through. Can you swim?"

Margo could hear the sound of the SoGa getting closer, their boots hard, their calls rough. They had moments, only.

"Yes," she said hurriedly. "I can swim OK."

"Great. Swim through, then there will be some loose bricks on the right-hand side that you can push in and will lead straight to the barracks. Get Dimi, get reinforcements, get back here, and pray that we're not all dead. Is that clear?"

The sound of boots fell closer. She heard gunfire, practice shots aimed into the labyrinth. The SoGa were shooting in every direction, in the vague hope they might hit someone hiding within the depths.

"Mars," Aska said. "Are you with us or not?"

Moon's gun was already trained on the door. He seemed alarmingly comfortable with it, his grip firm and precise.

"I'm with you," she said.

"Then consider me your commanding officer. Repeat my orders back."

"Balancing bear. Left. Left again. Swim. Bricks on the right-hand side."

"Atta girl. Go."

Margo looked aghast at Moon. "Go, Margo," he said. Then: "Wait. Take this."

He reached into his pockets and found a single silver seed.

"That's all I've got. My last one. Put it in your watch."

She did so, rolling it between her fingers.

"Don't die," she warned, turning to go.

"I'll try."

"Don't be an amateur," Aska yelled, and Margo made her way to the balancing bear.

The balancing bear stood atop a bronze plank, that itself was on top of a bronze ball. Margo darted to it just as the room moved, revealing a dark, narrow passage.

Margo ran straight into the blackness, keeping her hand on the left-hand side. She turned, went left again, and found the pit of water that awaited her. She had to stoop to get there, and found a slope leading to the drowned corridor. It was only about three inches taller than she was, and if she put her arms out long, her fingertips grazed the sides.

Margo felt the water. It was freezing and filthy, grimy sediment passing between her fingers as she withdrew. She stood back from the pit, the words *Don't be an amateur* echoing in her head. An amateur would swim in a full suit, trapping cold water in the pockets of their clothing. She took off her jacket, her shirt, and her shoes. She stepped into the tunnel wearing just her undershirt, a bra, and a pair of men's pants.

The cold bolted through her like an iron rod through the spine. Her feet scurried under the water, feeling the slimy brick beneath. Her arms could not reach wide enough for a full breaststroke, so she had no choice but to dog paddle. More than once, her head went under. More than once, she felt salt water on her lips, and realized that this room was tidal, the water rising and falling throughout the day. There was nothing to say she couldn't drown in a wave.

She kicked and beat against the water, emerging eventually on the other side. Had the SoGa reached the Hall of Bears? Were Aska and Moon and Taiyo holding them back? Could all three of them be dead already? *Don't be an amateur.*

She pushed the bricks and emerged, soaking, in the back sleeping area of the barracks. Ahead, she could see Dimanche standing over a long table, deep in conversation. Margo ran to him, frightened, dirty, and wet.

"Margo," he said. Then a stream of words that she could not understand.

"Where is Aska?" someone said, intervening. "We sent her to the station with you. Where is she?"

She looked around, breathless in a room of strangers.

"The SoGa are here. They're in the Hall of the Seven Bears. They followed us from the market. Taiyo, Aska, and Moon are in there."

A man she did not know spoke to her. "How many?"

"I don't know. Maybe ten, twelve."

Quick, sharp Alderian words followed. The long table was moved, and so was the rug underneath it. A floorboard was hinged upward to reveal crates of more weaponry, of long and short guns that Margo did not know the names of. People scurried around her with great purpose as she stood, not knowing how to speak to any of them.

The crates went back, the rug and table replaced. Dimi stood on a crate and boomed a list of instructions in Alderian. Margo carefully watched his body language to try to guess what he was instructing them to do. She watched him illustrate channels and directions with his hands. He divided the revolutionaries into sections with one slice of his palm. He seemed to be telling them that they needed to hit the Hall of Bears from a number of pathways. There were perhaps forty people in the barracks, all armed, and they were each grouped together and sent in different directions.

"Dimi," she said. "Give me a gun."

She made a gun with her fingers.

He looked at her doubtfully, and spoke in slow, deliberate Trader's. "You can . . . shoot?"

She considered this for a moment and realized that if she wanted to progress further, it was her job to lie, and his job to believe her. "Yes."

He put a gun into her hand as though passing a guest their coat. "*Komm,*" he said, indicating that she should follow him. They went down another dark pathway, joined on every side by PACT Alderians. Each of them fierce, armed, and young. They waited for a door to open and Margo turned to a redheaded girl who stood beside her. The girl looked her up and down, as if she didn't really rate Margo's chance of survival. "Keep low," she said, her accent heavy.

The door to the Hall of the Seven Bears slid open.

In the short time Margo had been gone, four of the seven bears had been eviscerated by gunfire. Thick, chalky smoke clouded the room. The bears were plated with bronze but were clearly made of some kind of plaster underneath, and now it was crumbling all around her. The rattle of gunshots, so close and loud that they deafened her, separated her mind from her body and briefly made her think that she had been shot. She followed the redhead's instructions and ducked low to the ground, crouched behind the marble plinth that held the whistling bear.

Two trenches had formed between the eastern and western sides of the room, the SoGa pitching behind one side of the remaining trio of bears, Moon, Aska, and Taiyo behind the other. Moon's body was flat on the ground, his head and chest shielded by a pile of rubble, his right arm outstretched and firing a revolver.

Relief rushed through her. Moon could shoot. Thank god, Moon could shoot.

The ground was strewn with orange-clad bodies, three or four, none of them moving. She felt a strange burst of pride, a menacing darkness from deep within her, a genuine *glee* that these soldiers had died at the hands of her friends. It was a black tar of feeling, something that contradicted her every vague concept of war that had led up to this, which was that violence was never right and never good. Violence *was* never right and never good, except when it was in defense of the people she loved. Person she loved.

The new strain of PACT members fell on the room like a wave, their gunfire fresh, their movements sharp and springing. Margo watched the redheaded girl dive on a man's back, slit his throat, and take his gun in one fluid movement. They had been waiting for this. Training for this. They knew the Hall of Bears better than anyone alive. Knew where to hold and spring from, knew the exact distance between one marble plinth and another. They outnumbered the SoGa, but they out-skilled them, too. She wasn't in a battle anymore. She was in a butcher shop.

Her only job was to get through it alive. There was no point in pretending she could fight. She dropped to her knees and crawled toward Moon. She couldn't believe his confidence, the way he inhabited his body so fully with a gun in his hand. There were no shots ringing in his ears, no screaming, no clouds of dust and rubble. No fallen bears. It was just him and his focus and that moment. The suspenders cut a V shape into his body as he drew his shoulders back and fired into the destroyed hall.

As she crawled toward him, she heard a sudden click. She looked up and realized that she was in someone's crosshairs. She saw a flash of orange from the eastern trench, and followed the line of sight from the gun to her body. Suddenly, Margo remembered that this battle was not arbitrary. It was not some skirmish between PACT and their longtime enemies that she and Moon had accidentally been caught up in.

This was over her.

Her, and the watch. The thing that Captain Halvpas had apparently been tracking her for, had gone from world to world in relentless pursuit of. The watch her father had left her in his will. The watch she tried to sell to a Cash4Gold dealer, who took silver also.

He fired and she dived for shelter, finding it behind a bear's dismembered head.

The soldier knew who Margo was, and what she was worth. Perhaps for that reason, he abandoned the logic of the shootout to bolt across the room toward her. Moon fired, hitting the soldier in the leg. He went down.

Moon turned slightly to see where the SoGa had been headed. Finally, he saw Margo there.

Crouched behind the marble block. Watch gleaming, eyes wide in terror. The spell that had come over Moon while he was lying on the ground, the precision that was mysteriously available to him, dissolved the moment he saw Margo. What had been cool competence turned immediately to dread.

She, Aska, and Moon were on the far left side of the room, where the whistling bear had once stood. Dimi's troops had filed in at the other end. The fighting was now concentrated to the balancing bear's end of the hall.

Seeing that the way was clear, Moon crawled on his belly from his plinth to Margo's, keeping his head low.

The wounded soldier was down, but he was not out. Seeing Moon exposed, he began firing, his arm shaking, his body bloody. Moon rolled, guarding himself behind another pile of fallen ceiling. He was protected there, but not for long. There were still too many SoGa in the room, and at any point the Hall of Bears could move and allow in more.

Margo had no choice but to take aim. She had never in her life fired a gun before. She had not even owned a toy gun as a child. Aiming and firing meant nothing, and was nothing to her. But she squeezed anyway, her eyes closing from pure reflex, the trigger far more of an effort than she could have ever predicted.

The recoil was fierce. The first shot seemed to do nothing except blast her right shoulder backward. The force was so extreme that she was amazed the gun even stayed in her hand throughout.

She hadn't hit a thing. The soldier was crawling toward them now, determined. Mo was caught between one marble plinth and the other, the pile of rubble protecting him yet obscuring his aim.

If he rolled either way, he would be completely exposed. Dead meat. All he could do was wait for the wounded soldier to slowly gain on him, and to either kill or be killed once he did. Aska had still not seen Margo, and was now joining the fray toward the back end of the hall, clouds of noise and gun smoke surrounding her.

Margo fired again. The bullet hit a couple of feet clear of the soldier, glancing off one of the remaining bear statues behind.

She was running out of time. The room started to move again, the gas lanterns above the shattered bears swaying slightly as it did. Suddenly, an idea occurred to her. She shot into the roof, hitting the fixture that held the lantern in place.

Miraculously, it fell. It smashed into a ball of flames in front of the wounded SoGa. He fell back, stunned. Margo shot again and again, her vision too clouded to see whether she was hitting him, and too terrified to know if she had.

"Mo!" she screamed across. *"Run."*

He seized the moment. He bolted to her, and they both found shelter behind the huge marble block. She reached inside his pants pockets and felt the grimy package of axiom that he had used to make the market bomb. She took a fistful of it and threw it into the flames behind her, the fire roaring warmly in approval.

Suddenly, the combat at the other end of the room felt very far away. The world shrank down to the size of just two people, quivering in a destroyed hall. He reached for her, curling his arms around her waist, his face pressed into her thigh.

His body in that moment. The way he grabbed for her, rested on her, held fast, begged for stillness. It opened up something strong and intuitive in Margo, breathed a kind of protective courage into her that she didn't know she had. The adrenaline of holding him, of their both being alive. It made her delirious. Connected and cosmic. She understood love as a wobbling table, as a three-legged dog. You had to take the weight of a limb when it went missing. You had to hold the other person up. It was the only way you could both make it to the end.

Moon was bleeding. From the face, from the forehead, from some unidentifiable place under his clothes that made his shirt sticky. Rubble and shrapnel had cut away at his skin, but nothing seemed permanently damaged. They would survive this. They would get away. They had just killed a man. She did not know how Moon's religion regarded sins like this, but in her own, she was going to hell. They both were.

The flurry of gunshots at the other end of the hall began to dim. They had lured the SoGa into a trap, and now the guards would die, overwhelmed by PACT's force and by its knowledge of the labyrinth.

She saw the familiar figures of PACT standing, checking, examining the bright bodies of the fallen.

She traced her fingers over the bleeding cracks in Moon's lips. "We won."

It was not pretty. But it was significant. Even Margo, who knew almost nothing about PACT, could understand that. How many in the Southern Guard had fallen today? How fast would the word get around?

"Anyone alive down there?" Aska yelled.

Margo turned her face around the marble, unable to move with Mo slouched into her. She didn't say anything. Later, Margo was able to identify that she was experiencing shock, that famous soldiers' illness. Fitting, for her first war zone. She could not speak or see clearly. She merely joined eyes with Aska, the dagger woman who'd woken up that morning with the sole ambition of taking them to Khaise.

Aska bounded toward them, rifle swinging, fair hair falling all around her. Triumphant. Extraordinary. Alive.

Which was when the dead SoGa rolled over and shot her in the neck.

twenty-eight MOON

You do not join a revolution unless you are prepared to die.

Aska knew this. She must have. But I also think she probably came close enough to death a few times—had a few near misses, witnessed the slaying of her peers, even—to suspect that she was immune.

I did not know her very well, so this is speculation. But I suspect she thought as we all do. That she wasn't the type to die young. That this was a fate reserved for other, more tragic figures. People who took bigger risks. Who did not time the movements of bronze bears and hungry cats to the minute. Who were not prepared to tell the Lunati salesman to fuck off, on account of his obvious shortcomings to the mission at hand.

But of course, Aska was exactly the type to die young.

I hate myself for thinking it, even while she is in the process of dying in my arms. We never think of ourselves as the tragic figure in the story.

"I'm sorry," I whisper, the resilient SoGa officer finally lying dead beside me. How many people have I shot to death today? Four? Five? "Aska, I'm sorry."

There are a few seconds, a minute even, when I know she is still alive. Bubbles form in the wound at her throat as air attempts to push past her broken windpipe. Aska looks at me, a frown of confusion written across her face, an expression that seems to say *Really? Me? Now? Are we sure?*

Does anyone really have last words? Anyone who's killed like this, anyway? I know the stories about murmured confessions, and fatal secrets, and wise advice. But who could ask that of Aska now? Of anyone?

She blinks at me, her face slowly emptying, the muscles going slack. I have known Aska for a very short time, and yet it is a shock to see how her face appears when devoid of animation. Take away the frowns and grimaces, the wheeling and the dealing, and she is astoundingly young. Her face as smooth and unlined as a sculpture.

I remember, the night I found my parents, thinking that they looked like puppets, or models.

Margo, at the other end of the hall, begging Dimanche in a language he cannot understand. For help, for medical attention, for a doctor, for Sonne. For a miracle. As if the president of PACT has not seen young members die before. As if this is something he can undo.

"I'm sorry," I say again. "It won't be a waste, Aska. I promise. I'll get Margo to Khaise. We'll do as you said. I promise."

Aska gives me one final, hard look that is summoned from every corner of her failing body. Eyebrows furrowed. Stare direct. Everything in her eyes says that she is present, that she has heard me, and that she will be keeping a record of this promise.

Then she dies. It's not so much a fading as a sudden evaporation. A closing of the account.

And so, on.

"What happened?" Taiyo's voice from over my shoulder. He is, miraculously, still alive. When the shooting began, he had barely known how to hold a gun, and amid the chaos I had lost sight of him. He crumples to the ground beside me. "No," he whispers. "*No.*"

Neither of us has known Aska for more than a day. But Taiyo, with his godlike worship of PACT and all who dwell within it, has not lost an acquaintance. He has lost a hero. He gently raises the crown of her head into his lap, pushing the hair away from her face. His gaze travels down her body, the ugly wound at her neck still bleeding freely.

"Can't we cover her with something?" Taiyo says desperately. Holding himself tight against the threat of oncoming tears. "She feels cold. Why is she so cold? Already, Mo?"

I gently transfer Aska's body into his embrace, and Taiyo holds her tightly.

Suddenly, Margo and Dimi are behind me, their movements quiet. Dimi crouches to put a hand on Taiyo's shoulder. He says something that none of us understand, and realizing this, he stops. He puts his hand on his heart and looks down at her body.

"The best," he says simply. "Our best."

I reach into her clothing and pull out the pocket watch that she used to mark every movement, not just her own, but the machinations of Alder City and the world that exists below. It's a simple little thing, the twelve hours of the Alder day clearly marked in black lettering against a white face. The frame and lid wrought in silver plating, monogrammed with the initials *S.D.* It means nothing to me. I pass it to Margo, who frowns for a second, then gives a small smile of recognition.

"Sam Donnerstag."

Margo passes it on to Dimanche. He holds it in his palms, seeming to warm it slightly. As though it were a stillborn puppy that could be patted back to life. Then he stops it, freezing Aska's time forever.

The watch. Margo and I lock eyes. Remembering why we were followed. Why this happened. There is more than one significant timepiece in the room right now, and Dimanche needs to know about Margo's.

Only, neither one of us has the ability to speak to him.

"We need to find someone," I say quietly. "Someone who can help explain to Dimi . . . everything. The market. The watch. Halvpas."

"Go to the barracks, then," Taiyo says, still looking into Aska's face. "Maybe find Sonne. And . . . I don't know. A stretcher. Something to carry her with. Let me . . . stay with her, a minute longer."

Dimi passes me Aska's watch again. "Sonne," he says, his eyes wet, his throat heavy. I just nod and pocket the watch.

A group of triumphant PACT soldiers are raiding the bodies of the fallen SoGa, extracting papers, travel visas, guns, and ammunition from the young guards who were every bit as alive as Aska just moments ago. Dimi leaves Aska's side and begins instructing them in loud Alderian. It's hard to judge. But it's difficult to feel cheered by it, either, this supposed victory of rebels against an invading force. PACT is a use-every-part-of-the-animal organization. They have to be. It would be silly, dangerous even, to let these bodies go unexamined.

Margo and I drift past like ghosts. We are invisible to them, foreigners merely stopping by for a visit, and not engaged in the serious business of guerrilla warfare.

I have been a Lunati since birth, and a salesman since the age of twelve. Both classes of people regularly go missing without investigation, and you can't belong to a group like that and not learn to shoot. My father had me practice on glass jars in the desert. The glass invisible except for the glare of sunlight that bounced off it, almost blinding you. If you can keep your eyes open through that, he said, you can keep your eyes open through anything.

But I have never shot at a person before today. I'm not proud of it. Not proud of aiming, firing, wounding, or killing. But at least I kept my eyes open.

We wait at the spot that used to hold the balancing bear, Margo slouched against me. Our faces blank.

"That's the first dead body I've ever seen," she says quietly. And then adds, "That's the first person I've ever killed."

"Let me tell you. You don't get used to it. Dead bodies, I mean."

The slot in the wall opens. We step in. The dark passage surrounds us, the smell of gun smoke trapped within the narrow tunnel.

Suddenly, fear crosses Margo's face. "Halvpas," she says.

"Don't worry about him. We'll get a train, and—"

"No, I mean. He made it to the alleyway. Why didn't he come down?"

Was Halvpas the type of officer to send his men into a death trap while he waited above? Was that how you got ahead in the Southern Guard?

The clockwork mechanisms of Alder seem mysterious when you first encounter them. But it's simply a series of circles that rotate around one another, gaps lining up to create new routes and entries where they rest. If you lived here a week, you'd know the plan pretty well. A gap on one end of the circle will match the gap on the opposite end.

When one door opens for you, it opens for someone else, too.

But we didn't think about that when we stepped into the balancing bear's path.

That another door was opening at the other end of the room. That the other door had people behind it.

And that one of those people was Captain Halvpas.

We are halfway down when we hear the explosion.

I feel it in my chest first. A thump. A sensation not unlike a giant reaching inside your body and seizing every organ at once, gathering them together, then letting them go again. Your insides just a cluster of loose marbles.

I turn around. Ears ringing with a terrible dull whistle. There's a pause, like the moment Dimanche stopped the watch that lived in Aska's pocket. Then a curve. Perhaps a trick of the eye; perhaps real. But there's a sense that the giant had picked up not just my insides but everything. The atmosphere. Time and space itself.

It only lasts a second, but I see Taiyo turn his face to me. I watch his black head of hair flatten and prickle as the invisible wave rolls over him.

Then a great, godlike silencing.

A blinding white crash knocks us clean off our feet, cannonballing Margo and me to the back of the pathway. The hall has already begun to disappear from view as the door slides closed, debris blasting into the tunnel. The last thing we see is an orange uniform, then a gush of white smoke covering it.

Margo is screaming something, her face stricken, her hands over her ears. We're both still unable to hear, I realize, and still screaming. All we can do is run in the other direction, toward the barracks, toward the cats, toward any room that isn't currently decomposing around us. The underside of Alder rapidly becoming a death trap, while the surface of the city clicks calmly away.

As the din of explosion clears and my hearing begins to return, all that is audible is my own voice rattling inside my head, repeating the same thing over and over.

Taiyo.

Taiyo.

Taiyo.

PART THREE

KHAISE

twenty-nine

MARGO

Afterward, Margo found she had no memory of how they got on the train to Khaise. She knew, because Moon told her, that they met Sonne in the barracks as the Hall of the Seven Bears was collapsing. Words were exchanged. She couldn't remember in what order, exactly, or whether it was Sonne or someone else who helped them to the train station. There were tunnels. The smell of fallen plaster and blood drying on her clothes. She had a short, swimming memory of seeing Yaz again, of a series of bribes and handshakes taking place as they were bundled into the horse box of an acquaintance and loaded onto a train headed north.

She could not count in hours how long the journey was. The voyage was a constant kind of waking dream, where she felt asleep when her eyes were open, and curiously alert when they were closed. The light traveling through the shafts in the horse box brightened, moved, and dimmed. More than once, she woke up to nothing but blackness, and the only sound was of horses softly huffing in the dark.

They didn't talk, really. Neither of them could face enunciating what they had just been through, nor begin to parse out which parts of it were their fault. Neither could bear to say Taiyo's name out loud.

This was the longest Margo had ever spent with a horse. It was big and dun-colored, and seemed to get used to the two of them quickly, dozing and shuffling as they did. She and Mo took turns leaning against each other. There was barely space for one person to lie down comfortably, and so they found various entanglements to attempt comfort. Bodies cramped and slid together like broken biscuits. The occasional urge to piss leading to humiliating, crawling journeys to the back of the box.

A morning came. She opened her eyes, golden light penetrating through the slats in the horse box and warming her skin. Moon was awake. He needed a shave, badly, yet somehow the thickening dark stubble only made him look younger.

"Hey," she whispered, her voice hoarse.

"Hey," he returned. He was hunched into his body, his back against one wall of the box, his feet against the other. "I think we need to talk about that."

He pointed at her wrist. The morning sunlight was catching the links on her watch. The family heirloom that she had once traded for three hundred euros, and had just cost the lives of more than a dozen people.

"I had no idea," she replied, the machinery of her throat slowly beginning to work again. "I *still* have no idea. It was just a thing my dad left me in his will. I don't see how it could be important to the SoGa, or why they're mounting some interworld conspiracy to get it."

She tried to remember the history of the watch, before she inherited it. He hadn't even worn it, really. It lived in a box in his dresser, like any ordinary old watch might, and he wore one with a simple leather strap in his day-to-day life. She had only seen him actually wear the thing a handful of times.

"What did he do for a living, your dad?"

"He was . . ." She rattled her brain. It was one of those mystifying jobs that people had, and it involved going to Asia a lot. He would go to represent companies that had business there but had no sense of the language or customs, which, presumably, Richard Madden had at least a grasp on. Although she had never heard him speak a language other than English.

"He was a salesman, too, kind of. He went abroad a lot."

"A *salesman*?"

It was disorienting, how you could know a word your entire life and then have it change. Not the meaning, exactly, but the power. *Salesman* had meant nothing for so long. Buying and selling. Now it was a term so charged that electricity came off it when she reached for it with her tongue.

The market hall came back to her. The paper crane that had jumped into her hands, that had once danced on her duvet cover. The day in the tunnels when Moon pulled out his silver seeds for the first time. She knew them. It wasn't déjà vu or skipshock playing tricks with her memory. She *knew* these things. They had been in her house. The treats and toys her father brought back when she was little, the presents that she wasn't allowed to take to school. They'd stopped, eventually. Stopped when she became cognizant of the substantive difference between a self-folding paper crane and an airport Swatch.

"Margo—what happened to him?"

She thought of her father's business trips. His long absences. His disappearance. The plane crash. The body never found. She lined up her own experience with his, and how it would appear to the world she had just left: A trip. A disappearance. A train fault. A body never found.

She was not, she realized, forging new footprints here. She was stepping into ones already made.

Her father could have been traveling between worlds this whole time. Her whole childhood, even. The stories lined up alongside each other, her own and her father's, as though they were opposing exits in Alder's great rotation. It felt clear now. She was following a path. Predestined, maybe, or at the very least premade.

The blast came back to her. The terrible white light. The hot surge that pinned her to the wall and felt as if it was going to melt the skin from her bones. Just thinking about it brought a tremor into her hands, a shaking that would not stop even if she sat on them. Here she was. Margo Madden, once an ordinary schoolgirl, now part of the legions of battle-scarred skipshock sufferers who had only their survival to be thankful for.

Who and what had been destroyed when the SoGa bombed the Hall of Bears? Would she be dead herself before the answers became clear?

If she really was stepping into the footsteps of her father's life, and if he really was the custodian of a precious relic with untold value, then perhaps he was killed in the same scenario. The only reason that Margo and Moon made it out of the labyrinth alive was that Taiyo had sent them for a translator, and a stretcher for Aska's body. Perhaps her father had not been lucky enough to have a Taiyo. Almost nobody was.

The SoGa would do anything for this watch. Including going to the North; including flinging their own men into a nest of PACT militants. Their study and commitment ran deep. Captain Halvpas knew her name.

"Mo," she whispered as the train compartment shook. "I don't think I just inherited this watch."

"What do you mean?"

"I mean, I think I inherited a responsibility to keep this watch *away* from Semper. Why else would my father have left it in my world, where no one can get to? Why else would he have specifically named it in his will, when nothing else was? Not his money, not his property. Just this watch."

She stared at it again, the glass screen at the center of the watch face showing the silver cogs that turned within, reminding her of the world she had just left in ruins.

If she was right, if this was her sole responsibility—a burden her father had carried wordlessly, and for decades—what had she done with it? Aska, gone. Dimi, gone. Taiyo, gone. A score of PACT members she did not know. And who else? Who next? What did the SoGa now know about the labyrinth, and to what extent would it crush the North's hope of overthrowing Semper? All was lost. Margo had taken a nation's hopes and scattered them to the winds. And she did not even know she was doing it.

The tremors in her hands started again. The shake so violent that her chest started to vibrate.

Moon held her. "Margo," he hushed. "Margo, Margo."

They should have taken more solace in each other. Someone should have said, at some point, *Well, at least I have you.* But that kind of solace and gratitude would have required a degree of processing that was beyond her. Nothing felt like memory, or fate, or a dreadful thing that simply happened because sometimes life works out that way. Margo felt like she was still in the Hall of Bears. She started to wonder whether she always would.

"Look at your watch," he said softly. "Remember your breathing? Timing your breath to the minute."

Her breath.

Her watch.

The minute.

That was her trick, or had been since she had tried to run away. When it became clear that Donna-Anne was using therapy as a threat rather than a tool, the therapist tried to give her a coping mechanism that would take Margo beyond their one session. He had suggested the breathing. He had even said that anchoring it to the watch would help her feel connected to her father, though she rarely did. He never wore the watch, after all.

She had timed her breath when the train was stuck in the tunnel, fixing her hand on the slender timer that only ticked for sixty seconds. Then again, when they entered Alder. She had shown Moon. Started the timer. Let the minute pass.

In both scenarios, the same thing had happened. The tracks had fallen from the sky. The train had been broken for days.

"It's not me," she said, with a faint shred of relief. "Mo. It's not me. I'm not the special one. The watch is the thing that's breaking the tracks."

She explained it slowly to him, her throat still sticky and cragged from her time in the exploded underground. Though it couldn't have been more than two minutes, she felt as though she talked for a year.

Moon began to nod slowly. "The watch is the thing. The *watch* is the thing."

"How did we think that *I* was the special one?" Margo asked, the first notes of her old voice coming back to her.

"It's not such a hard thing to believe."

They smiled weakly at each other. It was almost like a joke, almost like how they spoke. But gentler, meeker. Wrecked but not ruined. Not completely. He coughed and carried on.

"I guess pretty soon we'll have our chance to test this theory out."

"How soon will we be in Khaise?"

"It's in the East; it gets hot there. Trust me, you'll know."

They listened to the rails hum. On top of the fear and exhaustion, the traumas old and new, the revelations and the reanimations of buried memory, she felt a dread sense of being a subject of history. Of being one of those people you read about. Who fled one war, and accidentally found themselves in another. Who gave birth to eleven children in a tenement building and lost five. Who survived all of World War II only to be shot down in the early months of 1945. She felt like a person who extraordinary things happened to, and when you read about them one hundred years later, all you could say was: But how did they go on? After that? After *that*?

The answer was always so beguilingly simple: because they had to.

But I couldn't.

You would.

Somehow, they had remembered to take their suitcases. Moon gingerly clicked his open, the horse swishing his tail testily at the sound of rusting hinges. He pulled a mirror and a straight razor out of his case. Some kind of shaving paste in a jar. She smiled. "You're going to do that here?"

"Yeah. Can you hold the mirror?"

"Sure."

She held it in the light, watching him as he traced the contours of his face with the thin blade. So this is how people start to go on, she thought. They start with shaving.

Soon after that, the temperature rose sharply. What limited conversation they shared dwindled back down to nothing as the humidity became too hard to bear. Her clothes stuck to her in dirty rags, unrecognizable from the clean, precise tailoring she had left New Davia with.

"Vesna," she murmured. The landlady felt so far away now, like a god from a dead empire.

"I know. We'll have to find a way of telling her. Of telling . . . everyone. Taiyo's family. He had brothers, I think."

She nodded. Of course, she was supposed to go home at some point. But when? And more importantly, how? Was she expected to just go back and start school in Dublin now, as if none of this had happened? She remembered the conversations she'd had with Taiyo the night before his death: of all the places he could live, he still chose New Davia. Still the six-hour world. He had come into Alder in a coffin, and now he would never leave it again.

They felt elevation, and the horse began to fidget and grunt.

"We're coming up to the world barrier," Moon said. "I guess wait till we're through, then push the button. Break the track."

The tracks climbed and there was a sudden burst of new air, new atmosphere, and she knew they were through. Margo held up her watch. Habit overtook her, and she began to breathe purposefully, inhaling when the third hand reached one number, exhaling on the next.

The train slowed to a stop. Moon put his fingers to his lips. They waited in sweating, humid silence for their horse box to be unloaded, and in that time, the light changed through the slats of their prison so much that it made her queasy. Two hours, she remembered. Khaise was a two-hour world.

They heard rattling, falling, commotion. Shouted words in a language she didn't know. If it had not already happened in Alder, she would have been frightened. But finally, she was able to take some satisfaction in a plan working as it should. The tracks had fallen. Khaise was at the top end of a broken train line. They had just greatly limited the amount of explosives the SoGa would be able to get their hands on, had preserved countless halls of innumerable bears. Taiyos and Askas and Dimanches in other worlds were marginally safer, because they had done this.

Moon took the money that Aska had given him out of his pocket.

"I'm glad you made me take this, in the end," he rasped. "We're going to need it."

"For what?"

"Bribes."

Her heart fell. The horse box was trundled out of the station, and when it was finally opened, a redheaded jockey type of a man was there, scowling. Moon appeared to have some of the Khaise dialect. There was bartering, sniping, then the peeling of notes. She watched 150 gens go into the man's hands, and then they were waved away.

There was no point even discussing what this loss of money could mean for Moon. The man could turn them in to the authorities, and would. They walked from the station's loading dock, their legs bent and sore, their backs twisted from their long journey.

"It's not technically a desert world," he said, rubbing at the base of his spine. "But it borders a few, so the sand gets picked up by currents of air and carried over. And it just swirls around, making this kind of . . ."

"Haze," Margo finished grimly. Beads of sweat were already trickling down her neck, her short hair curling wetly at her temples.

"Right."

Today, the haze was piss-yellow and thick, the sun shining brightly but completely obscured from view. There were gabled railings to guide them, painted white but turned dirty brown. In the distance she could see rolling gray mountains, scrubby farmland, and a gray cloud of thunder floating toward them.

Khaise had a strain of wealth that ran through it delicately, like the thin blue veins in a wrist. One-room clapboard bungalows painted in bright colors—turquoise, magenta, strawberry-milk pink—nestled next to grand houses with ivy-strewn iron gates. Skinny men went shoeless, while others were escorted into shops by valets holding umbrellas.

You could do a quick assessment on the division of wealth in Khaise by simply counting umbrellas. Margo put it at about one in twenty. For every nineteenth person whose ribs were showing was a twentieth person with a bright, fringed umbrella. The fringe was fine and shiny, and reminded her of the curtains you might find in an old lady's house. On the riverbank, she saw horse-drawn carriages that were covered in white lace. There were shadows of women in there, traveling like queens in an ancient litter, flutters of laughter emerging as they passed by.

Endless crops of strange neighborhoods that had grown, weed-like, until they connected with one another. Long streets stretched out into unseen endings. They wove through, seeing fewer umbrellas and more stalls, tables selling food and greasy metal junk. Engines, handles, and springs from ancient farm equipment. The one thing every street had in common, no matter how rich or poor, was a bell with a brass clapper fixed to a high lamppost. It was not long before one started to clang heavily.

Margo looked around, waiting to see what this clanging indicated. People looked up briefly, nodded in the bell's direction, and then resumed whatever they were doing.

"What was that?"

"End of day."

She blinked, feeling that old nausea again. "Oh."

"I know. I don't feel great about it, either."

But for all the occasional prettiness, it wasn't long before Margo felt destroyed by Khaise. The heat was too much. The effect of all the umbrellas and gauze was that the rich floated like faceless ghosts and the poor appeared before her with uncomfortable clarity. She saw starvation; she saw sores on bodies; she saw people with no teeth. Unlike Alder and New Davia, where the skies were large and clear and telegraphed the time of day with dizzying speed, the atmosphere was too muggy and muted in Khaise to know what was happening or even the time. Margo didn't know if it was morning or afternoon, or whether these concepts existed at all.

They stopped at a two-story building lined with balconies, sliding wooden doors, and a large courtyard. Its ornamental bridge slid off the busy street and ran over a tributary of the river. The water looked oily to her, iron-rich and strange. The wooden beams sweated a slimy green algae, and she made a note to herself not to touch anything unless Moon was touching it, too.

The courtyard had only one open room, a reception area where an old woman in a black lace mantilla was working. She sat at a ledger, surrounded by low-burning candles smelling deeply of rose.

It took her a moment to greet them, and in that slow second, Margo braced herself. For revulsion, for suspicion, for a stream of confusing racism that Margo still didn't know how to defend Moon from. Instead, the woman looked up, her eyes a startlingly bright blue, and smiled.

"Ahoro, Fengari!" she cried, and came out from behind the desk to throw her arms around Moon. The woman was very small, and stooped, so looked even smaller.

"Ahoro, Gara!" he replied, squeezing the old lady and swinging her around as though she were a little girl. "You miss me? Margo, this is Saffy."

"Miss you? I thought you were dead. How long since I see you?"

"Too long. Not since I first got my license."

The woman cast her blue eyes on Margo with interest. "You get married?"

Moon laughed. "Not yet. This is . . ."

"Mars," she said. She didn't know why, exactly. She did not know Aska well enough to live in permanent tribute to her. Just that the way Aska saw her filled her with a kind of courage, and she suspected she would need a lot of that, going forward.

"Mars." Saffy clapped her hands together. "Mars and Levi Evreleri. I will make special room, for a honeymoon."

It took Margo a moment to realize that this must be Moon's real name. Levi Evreleri. She repeated the sounds to herself, each sound warming her like a secret. It was a name filled with light and romance, but perhaps she would have thought that regardless of what Moon was called.

"Are you two related?" Margo asked politely, trying not to feel too left out among this happy reunion. Saffy laughed, and Margo saw she had several teeth missing.

"The boys from Khaise are not this handsome," she said, brushing the hair off Moon's forehead, tucking a strand behind his ear.

"The full moon comes around a lot in Khaise," Moon explained, allowing himself to be fussed by her. "Every fifty-eight-ish hours or so. And Saffy would always put us up, when I was a kid."

"Some people say Lunati unlucky," Saffy said proudly. "Me, only good luck when they come. Good luck and big tips. Look."

She pulled the neckline on her blouse down and revealed a necklace where a row of silver seeds hung. They had long since lost their luster, looking more like iron than silver, but she was proud of it.

"Saffy," he said, lightly touching the seeds. "You kept them? All this time?"

"I keep some. To remind me of my friends."

There was a fluster of silence as Moon seemed to struggle to tell the woman what this meant to him. But it was like he didn't know himself.

He held Saffy by the shoulders and placed a kiss on her forehead. "Thank you," he said.

Saffy looked grateful, yet embarrassed. "OK, OK," she said, brushing him off. "You two need place to stay. You come here because nowhere else takes unmarried couples, am I right? Don't worry. I don't care."

Margo interrupted. "We're not—"

Saffy waved her hand. "Please. If you are sleeping in the same bed—"

Moon tried. "Saffy, we're really not a couple. We're . . . business partners."

It was humiliating, to have this conversation now, and in front of her. For everything they had suffered, it was still unclear what exactly they were to each other. She felt strongly on the morning of the market that he was hers, her person. Now too many shadows hung around them for her to be clear who she was, much less who belonged to her.

"Woman salesman? Never. But OK. You want your woman decent." She looked through her ledger. "There's a suite. Bed and another small bed. Families take it. Free, for you."

"I'm not taking your room for free, Saff."

"Did you hear me? Free. I said free."

"I'm paying you." Moon started taking money out and laying it on the counter. Saffy pushed it away, the coins spilling on the floor, as though they were all disgusting to her. "We don't know how long we'll be here, OK? If they fix the tracks sooner—"

"No, no, no. You are like family; family don't pay."

Moon picked up the money. "Saff, you need to run this place. You've got girls cleaning the rooms, I bet."

"Of course! You think I give you dirty room?"

"So the girls do clean it. You need to pay them."

Saffy resented being cornered by this logic. "They don't need much," she replied sulkily.

"Fifty gens, Saffy."

"I won't take more than forty. Not from you."

Despite her exhaustion, Margo laughed. So much of Moon's days were about haggling people down, and here he was trying to barter Saffy up. Finally, she took the money and showed them to their suite. They followed Saffy down a set of dark, narrow corridors, wooden ceiling fans whirring brightly overhead.

"What was Moon like as a kid, Saffy?" Margo asked. She knew that Moon didn't much like direct questions about his past, but there seemed to be an amnesty on Saffy talking about it. "As a little boy, I mean?"

"Ah. Heaven. The sweetest, the kindest."

Moon snorted. "Saffy, you were never around; you had no idea who I was. Always out chasing boys."

"They chase me."

Margo laughed, imagining this old woman with a bevy of young suitors. Suddenly, Saffy looked at her, quite wounded. Moon caught it.

"We all wanted to kiss Saffy," Moon said quickly. "All of us boys dreamed of growing up and marrying you."

Saffy's pride recovered, and she let them into their room, handing Moon the key. She showed them inside, the room simple and dimly lit, the ceiling fan mercifully on. The room had a large bedroll with no blanket on it, and behind a partition wall, a smaller one for a child.

Saffy talked about the bathhouse downstairs and when they could use it, chattering on and on. But Margo sensed that the atmosphere had shifted. She still felt the sting of her own faux pas. Saffy was edgy with her, addressing only Moon, and drew the mantilla over the side of her face that Margo could see.

Saffy left, and the two of them were alone in a family bedroom.

"Moon," Margo said slowly. "You weren't joking, were you? About the boy chasing."

Moon sat on the bedroll and began taking off his shoes. He didn't answer.

"Mo."

"What?"

"The boy chasing."

Moon sighed. "When I was a little kid, Saffy was the age that I am now."

thirty
MOON

"First," I explain, "she's actually not that old."

It's true. The teeth go quick in a place like Khaise. The water is too hard, too full of minerals. You can get it filtered, but it's expensive, time-consuming. Also the sun, even through the thick mist, burns brightly. It's not exactly friendly on the skin.

"Are you telling me that woman was in her twenties *ten years ago*?"

I've seen Margo take a lot of things in her stride since meeting her on the train in New Davia, but this, for some reason, is impossible for her. She can't swallow it. I try to think back.

"Moon."

"What?"

Margo's hands flutter to her throat, as if she's trying to manipulate her own breathing. I can't blame her for being shocked. I was shocked, even though I was prepared for it. Were it not for the black veil, which Saffy has been wearing since her husband died, I would not have recognized her.

"That's not *OK*," she says finally.

"No," I agree, though it's plainly obvious. "It's not."

"Mo," she says quietly. "We were sent here to kill the tracks, right? And we've done that."

"Yes. We've done that." There's another dead quiet moment, so open and terrible that I simply add, "Go, us."

"But Aska's dead. Taiyo's dead. Dimanche is dead. Half of fucking AlderPACT is *dead*, Moon. Aska was going to find some opening to rescue us, right? How on earth is anyone going to find us? Does anyone even know we're *here*?"

"Sonne," I reply. "Sonne knows we're here."

It was Sonne who got us to the surface, and then onto a train. Sonne who had to hear from me that his closest friends had been destroyed in a blast that we were responsible for. Sonne who had behaved smoothly, efficiently, and like his heart wasn't breaking inside his chest.

"We must alert the others," he had said, as though he was planning to create a second family out of Margo and me, purely because we were the only ones left.

"No, Sonne," I had said. "We have to go to Khaise. Do you understand me? I promised Aska. I promised her."

And so he found us a way. But what did he do next? What could he do next? There were no instructions, no designated place for us to stay in Khaise. Nowhere to wait while they found the opening that Aska spoke about. I can see Margo's mind going to the same place that mine is. That we have done our one heroic deed, and now our punishment is that we will rot in Khaise forever. That she will have me, yes, but she will also rot in rapid time. And that is a deal that no one—least of all someone from a twenty-four-hour world—is prepared to strike.

"Listen," I say, taking her by both shoulders. "You need a bath."

She really does. Whatever she had to swim in to get Dimi to save our lives, it's still stuck all over her. There are traces of gray grime covering her arms and neck. I want nothing more but to take her downstairs and carefully scrub every mark away, to see if I can find the Margo from before the blast. The one who lay on the mattress with me. The Margo who had never held a gun before.

She looks up at me like it's something I might be capable of. "OK."

The baths are in the basement. You follow another long corridor, turning left for the women's section, and right for the men's. It's all academic really because the whole structure is just a big stone swimming pool with a curtain that falls between the two sides. If you were in the mood to be a pervert, you could probably squint and see the outlines of the opposite sex through the curtain. Nobody in Khaise ever would, though. Anywhere with this much dirt and dust has to have a pretty rigorous and respectful hygiene etiquette.

There are many obvious reasons not to come to Khaise. The heat, the horrifyingly short days, the lung-clogging mist. But then there's Saffy, and the other people like her. People who fought a war against the South for the right to own their fuel reserves, and won. There's a wealth discrepancy, sure, but at least it's a wealth gap between Northerners. And there's beauty. You get a place like this: the basement of a shabby boardinghouse, quietly housing a natural hot spring. It's basic, and you have to scrub yourself off with a rough rag before entering, but it's tranquil. Tapered candles burn on the walls, the hot sour smell of sulphur quickly dispersed by the heavy oils Saffy mixes in.

I get in on the men's side, and the place is mercifully empty. There's an instant unspooling of my muscles, a grateful purr in my arms and legs as the warm water laps up to my chest. The gari beads around my neck twinkle slightly in the low light. The one advantage of being in Khaise is that I'll be able to do another silver Wash fairly soon. You're never more than sixty hours from your next full moon.

From across the curtain, there's the quiet, dipping sound of Margo submerging herself in the pool. A light gasp as the water envelops her. The sound of drops falling onto her skin. I can just make out the outline of her body, the curve of her back, the shadow of her arms as she stretches them out in front of her.

It is deeply inappropriate, not just by Khaise bathing standards but the moral standards of what we just went through, to be this horny. To want to cross the curtain's divide and wrap her slick body around me, this girl who Saffy is convinced is my wife. Mars Evreleri, if you will. The wife I haven't even kissed.

"It's funny," she says. "I can't see anything, really, but ah . . . this feels . . ."

"Pretty shocking, I know."

"Insane."

"I mean, we're three feet apart."

"Yes."

"And I can't see anything."

She paused. "You can't see *anything*?"

"No." But I find myself swallowing hard, my eyes focused on the rising steam and the delicate dip in her back. Her top lip, slightly plumper than I remember it being, perfectly silhouetted by the flicking candle behind her.

"I guess . . . we are in the same body of water. If I made a ripple here, you could feel it over there."

"Try it," I say, my dick for some reason getting hard at the phrase *body of water.*

She slaps the water with her hand. The oily tide gently travels and laps against my bare chest. "There it is," I say. "Margo's wave."

I watch her shadow sink deeper into the water as she finally allows herself to relax into it. I close my eyes and try to do the same. Finally, the heedless adrenaline of survival is able to float away, because we are not going to be murdered by the SoGa, not right now, not today. We are not trapped in a horse box that could be investigated at any moment; not swimming through the various drowned corridors of Alder. All we can do is sit and attempt cleanliness. Attempt absolution.

We cannot see each other, but the atmosphere shifts the longer we sit in the hot water. The mischief dissolves. The amusement, the relief, the play-acting. We are being boiled alive in our guilt. I do not need to even look at the curtain to know it's happening to her, too. That the Seven Bears are roaring in her head as loudly as they are in mine.

"Mo," she says. "I keep going over it, and going over it, and . . . looking for something we could have done differently."

I look into the pool. My skin has caught the surface of the water, leaving a whitish glow. "We should have listened to Aska," I say simply. "I shouldn't have come."

A slight *whoosh* of water as Margo suddenly moves her arms, splashing herself. "What are you talking about?"

"She was right. I'm too visible, no matter how much I try not to be. If I hadn't been held up by all those stupid Alderians, you would have gotten to the platform with minutes to spare."

"But the SoGa were on the platform anyway," she argues. "If anything, we would have stepped onto the platform early, and Halvpas would have caught me. And well, they would have caught the watch."

I ponder this, the logic of it making sense, but the heart of it not feeling true enough, real enough. If that was the case, I wouldn't feel like this. Like I've just added countless more bodies to my rap sheet, which was not short to begin with.

"If I had just killed that *fucking* SoGa quicker," she says, turning the knife on herself. "But I'd never fired a gun before, Moon. They're not exactly common where I come from. I mean you'd *think* they are, the amount you see them in movies and on TV, but they're not. Not in Ireland. So I just shot and shot, barely looking at what I was doing; all I wanted was to be close to you. I convinced myself he was dead because I was too chickenshit to make *sure* he was dead. Can you believe that?"

She begins to cry, the bathwater sloshing as she pulls her hands over her face. "I should have stood over his body and kept on shooting until he was *nothing.*"

People contain multitudes, and within Margo there is the lost schoolgirl, the emerging revolutionary, and the woman Saffy thinks is my wife. But this latest, this Margo who wants to stand victorious over a mass of blood and pulp, is not one I'm prepared to be responsible for.

"No, Mars"—and there it is, rolling off the tongue, just like that—"you can't think of it that way."

"Why not?" she answers bitterly. "It's true, isn't it?"

"Disallowing everything but the watch for a second . . ."

I'm queasy about the watch now. I was impressed by it at first. Even enjoyed the costumery of wearing it for a few days in New Davia, the pleasing weight of it, the elegance it added to everyday movements. But now the thing is too powerful, too heavy with destiny, like an anchor dragging Margo into a place I can't follow.

"If you had killed the SoGa quicker," I continue, "and Aska had lived, then we wouldn't have left the Hall of Bears to get a stretcher and a translator for Dimi. We could have died in that bomb attack."

"Yeah," she bites back as if she has thought of this. "And instead, PACT doesn't have a president, and Taiyo's mother is down a son."

"They would have been killed regardless, Mars. The only difference is that the SoGa would currently have a watch that has the power to break trains."

Silence. Just the drip-drip-dripping of water falling off her skin. It's impossible to tell whether she is buying any of this. "There's one thing I keep thinking about," she says at last. "Halvpas. Did he just stay in the fish alley, while he sent his soldiers down to die? Then just . . . threw a bomb, once he figured out he was losing?"

"Maybe he waited till the fish alley connected to another platform where his troops were, and sent down reinforcements," I reply, puzzling it out. "But yeah. He sent them down to die, and he stood in an alley while it happened."

"He can't even have known for sure that all his soldiers were dead," she says. "And he threw a bomb in anyway."

Her face in perfect profile as she stares into the middle distance, contemplating this. What kind of man she's dealing with. What we're both dealing with.

"How could a person . . ."

"These kinds of people, Mars . . . they don't feel regrets, because it's not useful to them. They think strategically. They trap their own men like rats. And the only thing worth learning from them is . . . well, a sense of perspective. We can't change what happened. All we can do is move forward."

And who am I, really, to make a statement like that? Margo feels my voice curve. She swims to the other side of the pool. She's next to me now. The flesh of her arm smooth against the curtain, her bare legs touching mine. I still can't see her, making the whole thing feel even more like a dream. Her body transforming from a shadow puppet to a real girl, like some kind of wish for a lonely boy.

"Do you do that?" she asks. "Have you moved forward?"

"From what?"

"From whatever it is . . ." she starts, but doesn't know how to go on. "Why are you in sales, Mo? Why do I call you Moon, and not Lev? Why do you have a fake name?"

Ah, so here's the catch: you can have the girl right next to you, her face invisible, her slippery legs flush with yours, but you have to tell her everything. You have to confess, confess, confess.

"I think I told you before," I begin. "But when I was really little, the caravan trails got shut down. You remember about the caravan trails, right?"

"Yeah. Temple gateways that let you travel between worlds."

"Right. So they shut those down, then we had to get the train like everyone else. Remember, anyone could use the train then. But because we were suddenly more visible, on the train with everybody, people hated us even more. Said we were thieves, or that we smelled, or we were just unlucky. Whatever. There would be a protest whenever we rolled into town. It's bad. Then there's all these organizations, these movements to get the kids away."

"To get the kids away where?"

"Oh, orphanages, trade schools, that kind of thing. They had to save the next generation from growing up scum, you know."

I can feel Margo crunching her toes underwater, wincing at the violence of it. I have a strange sort of vision, then, one that I know I'm sharing with her. It's not as if Margo and I are telepathic. Far from it. But I'm focusing so much of my energy on how she's interpreting my story that I'm almost pretending to be her as I tell it. I feel like I can see what she's picturing, and what I picture is myself as a child.

Not a reduced version of how I am now, but how I really was.

Small, for one. I didn't get tall till I was about fifteen. Thin, underfed by whatever institution they stuck me into, all sleep dreamless, all thoughts about food and the lack of it. There was a theory, at the time, that you could get rid of the Lunati *parulta* by starving kids. And you could, I suppose. Our moon skins turned to a mucky gray, and we waited for our introductions into real society.

They never came, of course. There was no real interest in immersion. We became shadow children. Drifting in dark city corners, begging a passing crateman for a ride to wherever the next moon was. And then they started taking our gari, cutting the beads off our necks. The last step of assimilation. Taking away the rights we were born with, the ability to make our own silver. They took the beads away from you shortly after you came of age, and dumped you back into the street. Your final graduation was supposed to be a severing of everything you had come from.

"So I get taken away a lot. We'd turn up in a world that had just made some crazy law, and then they'd descend on our community with a huge fine and an order to take the kids away. They'd round up a dozen of us and dump us at an orphanage, just to show they were doing something about the dreadful Lunati problem. Then I'd run away and find my family again. It wasn't hard. No one actually cared. Then the same thing would happen, a few months later."

"How old were you?"

"Ten, eleven. Twelve you're a legal adult, so."

"*Twelve?* My mother wouldn't let me walk into the dentist alone at twelve."

"When I turned twelve," I go on, "I was in one of these institutions, and I broke out. Same deal as last time: I knew the schedule, so I knew where my family would be, but it was like everything was different."

"Different how?"

It's a hard thing to parse, exactly, especially when you've never spoken about it before. How things felt versus how things really were. I hinge my neck back, my eyes to the ceiling. My hair now fully soaked.

"It was like, there was this ragamuffin quality to me when I was a kid. You know? Like I was an annoyance, but people felt sorry for me, and they were basically kind. *It's not his fault.* You know? But suddenly I'm hitching rides with cratemen and they're treating me like a criminal. One guy turns a knife on me."

"And you're twelve?"

"I'm twelve," I reply. I don't really understand why this is such a sticking point for her. "I'm making my way back to my parents, but it's harder than ever. I'm being stopped everywhere; I can't sleep in doorways like I used to, can't shelter in churches. There's no goodwill left. I'm a grown Lunati man now, and you don't see grown Lunati men in isolation. You see them in groups, in families, and it makes people nervous. They don't want me around. So I start stealing. To survive, you know. I had to eat. I finally reach the world my parents are supposed to be in, and I can't find them in the usual spot. Turns out they've been moved out to the countryside. Typical. So I try to stay in a boardinghouse. They won't let me in. This is a cold world now, colder than New Davia. Lunati are good at cold temperatures, but not *freezing*. I ask if I can sleep in the barn. They say no. I tell them I'll freeze to death; they don't care."

"So what did you do?"

"I light their barn on fire."

"You lit their *barn* on fire?"

"I just couldn't take it anymore. You know? I hadn't asked for any of this. I was just a kid looking for his family. And these people, who didn't understand our way of life at all, they were trying to kill us. Or at the very least, they didn't care if we died. So I lit their barn on fire."

For some reason I'm talking faster, as if the door on Secret Time might close at any moment and I have to take advantage of it now.

"I killed their animals," I say fiercely, daring Margo to hate me. "I torched their grain. I didn't care, and I wasn't sorry."

"I don't think you have to be sorry," she says at last. "It was just a barn."

"Yeah, well. They didn't think it was just a barn."

"What did they think?"

"They thought it was an act of aggression from us as a group. They all remembered me, begging for a room. Assumed I had come from the tents. So they found where my parents were staying, and they torched everything. They burned it all to the ground."

The ceiling is spotted with condensation, speckling the paint. I stare up at one amorphous blobby shape, something that looks like a child's drawing of a ghost.

"When I finally found their bodies," I say eventually, "their garis had been cut off, and there were half-moons carved into their arms."

thirty-one

MARGO

"I'm really sorry," she said at last. She felt the uselessness of her own words tumble out of her, how silly and vague they all were. "That's a terrible, terrible thing. What happened to the people? The . . . murderers, I guess?"

"Them? Nothing."

"Nothing?"

"The official line, I believe, was that a landfill caught fire." He sighed heavily at the other side of the curtain, lifting himself slightly out of the water and leaning back against the side of the pool. It was like he was shaking himself out of a trance. "No one cared much. Haven't you been paying attention? Everyone hated us."

"Didn't you testify? Talk to the police, I don't know?"

"Are you kidding? I had burned down a barn. I would have been arrested instantly."

"But you were only twelve."

"There's nothing *only* about twelve, Margo."

A hatch in the wall opened, and a new fresh flush of water poured into the pool. She would later learn that the bath was simultaneously topped up and drained slightly once a day from a hot spring that lay in the mountains around them. There was a slight pull of the old water rushing out. Steam rose instantly, blinding them both with puffy white clouds.

"I don't know if this will make you feel any better," she said. "But if you were in my world, you couldn't get tried as an adult until you were eighteen."

"Eighteen?"

"Eighteen."

"And what? Nothing you do up until then counts?"

"It's not as if it doesn't count. You could get sent to like . . . a correctional school, I suppose, or some kind of juvenile prison. But you couldn't go to *prison* prison."

"So you don't judge me for the barn?" Mo asked. "Yaz is Lunati, and I know she still doesn't understand why I burned down the barn. That's why I hadn't seen her in so long, until the other day in Alder. We were brought up not to cause trouble. To turn the other cheek; to keep a low profile wherever we went."

"Of course I don't judge you for the barn," she replied, meaning it. "I don't care what you say, Moon. You were twelve. And you had just been thrown into the street by some adults who should have taken you in. What they did was basically criminal, even before they . . . before they got to your parents."

There was a silence at the other side of the curtain, like Moon was making up his mind on whether he could believe her. Margo's face became hot. The temperature in the room climbed higher with the rush of fresh spring water, the steam pushing hard on her.

"They had a responsibility to you. They failed you, Mo, as the older people. As the ones with the houses and the heat and the empty beds. You were not equals. You were not a thug. You were a child."

Suddenly, Margo was crying. For Moon, for the life he had suffered, for the guilt he had been forced to carry. But that was not the whole story. She cried for herself, too. She had been fourteen when her father died, not very much older than Mo when he had lost his family. She had suffered through so much pity in the years after, but no one could acknowledge the burdens of the years before.

Not just her preteens, but everybody's. The years when you became just old enough to recognize that other families did things differently than yours—watched different shows, had different rules around screen time, ate at different times on Christmas Day—but too young to really grapple with why.

The Madden house had been anti-noise, anti-fuss, and antisocial. Her mother was both constantly paranoid about Margo's well-being yet seemed completely disinterested in her as a person. Clothes, gifts, hobbies, and habits were filtered through the lens of what other people expected, what Richard approved of, and what Donna-Anne was comfortable enough to seek out. She hated the internet, so refused online shopping. She also hated going into town, because of who she might run into.

"I can't get stuck chattering" was a common refrain, and that was weird, too, because she was the kind of person who was always talking to herself. Clothes and food and books were bought from a reliable clutch of discreetly old-fashioned boutique stores. Evenings were quiet and strained, even when Margo was very small. Occasionally, when her father was home and not too tired, he experienced manic fits of aspiration on Margo's behalf. That she should learn to sing Italian librettos, for example, or read Sanskrit. Just as Donna-Anne could be both overly concerned yet completely incurious, Richard seemed to think that Margo was four years old one moment, and forty-four the next. He asked her if she had ever written a play. He told her that she was never allowed to cut her hair. She lived her life with the rules of a Victorian infant, but the expectations of a Rhodes scholar.

Those were the good days. The bad days were dominated by strange anger, when her father would suddenly become extremely sensitive. Glasses in restaurants were pronounced too dirty, and management would be requested to explain why. Lawnmowers employed three gardens away would become cause for screaming rages. A string hanging off her skirt would turn into evidence that Margo was wasteful, spoiled, and undeserving of the life his travels had made for her. She thought of this behavior now and wondered if it was skipshock. Perhaps everything strange about Richard Madden could be attributed to it.

Whether it was or wasn't, childhood made Margo uncertain, shy, and quiet. But slowly she began to recognize a fierce beating in her chest. It drowned out everything, told her constantly that something was not quite right. There was a rottenness, a sourness in the house she lived in. She could never say it, so instead she wrote it down. One night when she was thirteen, she lay under her dressing table in her bedroom and wrote *This is not normal* in liquid eyeliner.

After her father died, all the doubts about her family became lost under the public pressures of grief. She had to only remember the good things, to only talk about the good things. So she thought about presents and the stolen, midnight breakfasts. She forgot the problems, the insomnia, the black tar in her gut that always nagged at her.

It was only now, when telling Moon about the ways that adults had failed him, that she began to feel failed herself. And that, she supposed, was why she was crying. Her parents had raised her wrong, made her crooked, and now she had the weight of the watch thrown on her with no instruction on what to do next.

She didn't want to cry anymore. She didn't want to feel lonely or faulty, like a car that had somehow been driven off the lot with the rear bumper hanging off. She just wanted to be with him. To take the shards of their strange lives and make a mutual project of a new one, together.

There was no parting in the curtain, no split to pull aside. Khaise bathing rituals were strict, and the rules of salesmanship generally indicated that you should observe and follow the customs of wherever you had ended up as sternly as if you had grown up with them.

But Margo was not a salesman. Not really.

She swam a length out and ducked her entire body, head to toe, underwater. There was a rushing in her ears, her temples thudding with the sudden pressure. When she reemerged on Moon's side of the curtain, it felt as though the remaining layers of grime on her skin—the pond life of the tidal corridor, the blood and rubble of battle, the warm animal smell of the horse box—had finally been sluiced off.

The air prickled against her. She felt not so much cleaned as peeled away, the water not just dissolving the events of the last few weeks but the past seventeen years. The oil-infused water became sticky against her eyelashes, creating a misty, stinging film over her retinas. She blinked hard, his body coming into focus.

Moon shone in front of her, his skin like the gleaming insides of a shucked oyster.

Margo was up to her chin, observing the boy at the edge of the pool like a crocodile, her gaze low. Her body naked, if hidden underwater, obscured by the dim room.

He raised his split eyebrow. She swam closer to him, the blear of oil clearing, his body moving into sharper focus. Here and there she saw the congealed scars of the Seven Bears battle, scratchy Rorschach tests across his ribs and chest.

"You know I don't tell that story very often," he said.

With a creak, the hatch in the wall opened and let in another gush of hot water. The rising steam blinded them both and made her brave. She knew that he had been with girls before—*Not Bread*—

and that her own experience was so limited that it might as well be rounded down to nothing. She could pretend to know what she was doing as long as he couldn't really see her.

Under the privacy of the soft, lamblike clouds around them, she touched him. She pressed at the dip below his throat, the slight hollow where the shining string of beads sat. His hands closed firmly around her, the span of his fingers starting at her rib cage and ending on the pillowy curve of her hip.

The steam was so thick now she could hardly see his features. She felt for them gently, learning his face beyond the things that had simply happened to it. The strong nose, the slight wolfhound quality to his long bone structure. The wet cobweb of eyelashes. Margo touched Lev Evreleri's face and felt as all people do after they learn the person they love was wronged badly as a child. She was caught between the urge to comfort him and the vitriolic longing to travel back in time and commit homicide.

There, in the warm fog of touch and freshly aired memory, she cupped the back of the salesman's neck and kissed him. Just once. Their faces beading with condensation, their lips raw and radiant.

Margo was a haphazardly raised person whose parents did not always care for her as they should. But that didn't mean she hadn't internalized a set of standards, or at the very least stages, for how physical intimacy should go. Your first kiss with a boy you liked should ideally happen fully clothed, and before you've saved his life. Your first time naked with him should be in a bedroom tucked in the back room of a secure location, preferably a friend's house, preferably somewhere the parents had gone away for the weekend.

And, even if you ignore all these unwritten rules, the interaction should not end when you realize that you are both covered in blood.

thirty-two
MOON

It's Saffy who sews my shoulder back together.

The wound is as long as a slit on an envelope, and just as thin. It doesn't hurt, except for when Saffy swabs it with herbal disinfectant, but it does bleed. And bleed. And bleed.

I had thought it had scabbed over, and was repairing itself in accordance with its brothers across my chest and ribs. But on closer inspection, none of them are healing. The blood had stuck and hardened against the cotton of my shirt, forming a kind of gauze. When I took off the shirt to get into the pool, I ripped away the beginnings of scar tissue. The water then softened it all, and the slight flexing of my arms to hold Margo—*naked* Margo, the soft, slippering mermaid Margo who had suddenly appeared at the men's side of the pool—had ripped the old wounds open, letting them bleed freely into the pool. And onto her.

"Levi, what trouble are you in?" Saffy says, snapping a length of pale string off with her remaining teeth as she stitches the wounds.

I lie face down on the table, in a light-filled room at the back of Saffy's bathhouse. She grows plants here, makes ointments, runs her many side businesses. Things grow so quickly in Khaise. Not with the sun-ripened acidity of fruit from the South, but with a wild, pondering, witchy magic. Tall ferns spotted with fawn freckles, spiked cacti dripping with pea-green ooze. She snips samples, grinds with a pestle, makes high-smelling medicine. Despite everything, I find myself wondering if I should go into business with her, selling creams on the road.

"Why so many? Are you in fights?"

My gaze travels to Margo, chewing on her nails in the opposite chair. Should we tell Saffy about PACT? About the Seven Bears? She's our only contact in Khaise, and the only person who can help us. But can I really visit this kind of pain and devastation on her? Draw the SoGa on Saffy like we did on Aska and Taiyo, who, at the very least, had opted in for that kind of lifestyle?

"Why aren't they healing like they should?" Margo interrupts.

Saffy answers it for her. "He travel too much. Lunati are good for travel, but not this much. Now that he has you, he can settle down. Same place every day, he will get better."

"This can't be skipshock, too, can it?"

Saffy takes a spoon to the green ooze coming out of her window cactus and pours it in a pair of teacups, topping it up with hot spring water from a piped trough on the floor. She hands Margo a cup, then sets one next to me, too.

"It's the nosebleeds all over again," I explain, my mouth muffled by the table. "My blood is getting too thin to clot properly. That's why the wounds keep opening."

I feel like my dick stopped working on my wedding night. How in the world did I manage to take a situation with almost no possible downsides—naked girl, candlelit bath, no discernible threat of being murdered—and somehow manage to screw it up anyway?

"You stay in Khaise," Saffy says firmly. "Time pass quickly. Skin heal quickly. Anyway," she goes on, dabbing an herbal-smelling cream onto my back, "train closed. You must stay until open again."

Margo sips her tea, keeping her eyes fastened on mine over the rim of her cup.

Saffy continues talking.

"Very strange. You know Khaise does business with the South? They buy our fuel, our energies." She stops for a moment, finding some new wound on my lower back. She starts to examine, poking the puffy flesh, then cleans it with a wet cloth. "This one is no good. This one will be infected. I fix. Anyway. Days ago, SoGa come here. Only a few. Maybe thirty. But SoGa never come to Khaise; they order it all with cratemen. But they come to order *namakshura*. Big, big amount."

I feel something cold and metal slide into me, and my whole body tenses. "Relax, relax," she says soothingly. "Only one moment."

"Mars, what is she *doing*?"

"Tweezers," Margo replies, sounding like she's about to vomit. "They're just very, very long tweezers."

"*Namakshura*," Saffy repeats. "You know this word?"

"Gunpowder."

Saffy nods. "Gunpowder."

Margo and I say nothing. Do we tell Saffy that we know this already? My train of thought is broken by another wrenching metallic sensation in my back. This time, it's worse. It doesn't feel like poking and sliding. It feels like *digging*.

"Enough for an army," she goes on. "Fengari—we are worried. Why so much? Why now? We think they are making ready for a war. They have not needed supplies like this in many years. What are they planning? But then, before it can leave Khaise, you and your wife come and you break the train. Hold your hand out, Levi."

I hold out my palm, my arm long and perpendicular to my body. Something cold and hard drops into it, and I open my eyes to see that it's a shattered hunk of bronze plating.

She sews up the wound quickly as I feel the grimy metal between my fingertips, this man-made parasite that's been quietly threatening to kill me.

Done with her surgery, Saffy crouches to where my hand is, her blue eyes locking firmly to mine.

"Fengari," she says sternly. "How long have you been working for PACT?"

I start to sit up, grimacing, a thin towel around my lower half. I reach for my tea.

"Not long at all," I reply. "As long as I've known Mars."

I realize instantly that this sets up the wrong impression, that it paints Margo as a gun-slinging revolutionary who has convinced me into the game. But in retrospect, there's no better white lie I could have told in that moment. Saffy seizes Margo by the shoulders.

"You found a *sensible* girl," she trills, kissing Mars on both cheeks twice. "A fighter."

"I suppose I did," I reply, slightly dazed. "Saffy, how long have *you* been in PACT?"

She blinks at me, as if this is a crazy question.

"Since what happened to your mother," she says. "Since your father. Since you."

Saffy comes back to Mars. "You know how I meet his mother?"

"No." She's blinking hard now, trying to stay awake. We both wandered in and out of consciousness a lot in the horse box, but I don't think you could fairly call any of it "rest."

"Playing cards," I say, rolling my stiff, newly stitched shoulder.

"Playing cards," Saffy agrees.

My parents only ever played cards when they came to Khaise. It's funny, a place like New Davia has an obsessive relationship with making the best of the few hours they have. In Khaise, they know their time is short. They're better at accepting that and utilizing it.

Some of our best Washes were in Khaise. The stars were so bright above the mist that it made everything cool and pale silver. Two long tables were joined in the courtyard, and all the women played together. This was the thing we did, whenever we were in Khaise. The women played cards when the men were bathing, and vice versa. You never played for money. Only favors and small honors. I win this round, then I name your next baby. Or: I win this, you let me wear your ring. It was a game of closeness designed to engineer more closeness. I never understood what the game was. They played with four packs, and everyone was always holding at least ten cards.

"Your mother and father, they used to stay at the Kastilo Baths. I meet her at their card night. You were there."

"Moon was there?" Mars asks, sounding like a child lulled by a bedtime story.

Saffy puts her hand at knee height, to indicate a toddler.

"Ah."

"But I meet here, and we talk and talk, and I am pregnant with a baby. I am so sick, but we laugh so much."

I can feel the muscles in my chest contracting. It's better, really, to think of my mother as an abstract memory. A ship that pulls slowly away from land, and gets smaller on the horizon with each year she is gone. But this, the picture of my mother as a young woman, laughing over cards, feels like the boat is crashing headlong back into the harbor.

"His mother always wants me to marry again, to marry one of

her Lunati brothers. So we could be family, all together. I said I will think about it. Every time I see her, I say: I will think about it. Then the rules change. Semper says Lunati are criminals, murderers. I say, no Lunati I ever met. It doesn't matter. Semper take them all away. Every time the full moon comes I think: Where are my friends? Every time. I never forgive them for this, Lev. Never."

"Saffy," I say gently, quietly begging her to stop. "I know."

"And once the trains are closed," she presses on, insistent, "once nobody can go anywhere, Semper forget about Lunati. Why do this? Why make a villain and then forget him?"

It's something I've wondered myself. The hate I get from merchants, from tradespeople, from casual acquaintances. The shakedowns from the authorities, the condescending *"Of course, I've never had a problem with your type"* from the benign cosmopolitan well-wishers. For what? Semper hasn't put out any public decrees about the Lunati in years. There's never been an official repeal of the rules around worship, just an understanding that so few visible Lunati are left that it's not even worth policing anymore. We were a toy that was picked up for political expediency, and when that goal was reached, we were dropped face down in the mud.

"We will bring them all back," Saffy says fiercely. "Before I die, I will have a whole party full of Lunati again. Here, in this house. Only PACT will fight for this. It is the only way."

For the first time, I entertain the notion that there really are people who care about what happened to us, who saw, who remember. That maybe it isn't all pleasantries, and weak-willed regret that they didn't do better when the moment was upon them. Maybe they did their best. Maybe they want to do their best, still.

"So what now, Saff? How do we . . ." *How do we get out* is too rude a question. I rephrase. "Do you know of any openings in this world? That Semper doesn't know about, I mean? Our PACT contact in Alder said that some kind of rip had formed that PACT was able to pass through."

Saffy frowns. "I have not heard of this," she admits after a moment of thought. "This is a big thing, if this is true."

"You can ask around, though, can't you? The local PACT heads?"

Saffy bites her lip. "I can ask, yes."

I finally take a sip of her tea, gagging instantly on the taste. "Saffy, what's *in* this?"

"Help you sleep."

Oh no. "Saffy, have you drugged us?"

She tilts her head. "Only to be helpful. You so tired, both of you. So many troubles."

I look over and see that Margo is sleeping peacefully in her chair.

"Saffy."

"Drink yours. Good for your skin. Good for sleep. You need sleep."

I push away the cup. I wish I could say I was surprised. But she did this when I was a kid, too. She made a judgment on how you were feeling, then quietly fixed you something she thought would cure it. It generally would, too, but you'd still feel annoyed that she didn't ask you first.

I sigh. "Help me get her into bed."

After we've taken Margo back to the room—half leaning on my good shoulder, Saffy under her other arm—Saffy offers me a fresh cup of her magic tea again.

"No, Saff," I say, pushing it away. "I'll sleep later. I need to think right now. Margo—Mars—she's not from here. She's not my wife, either. She's from a Southern world and I need to get her back there. She's got a mother. A family."

Saffy looks dejected at the thought of hosting someone whose problems she cannot solve. She thinks for a moment, gnawing on the knuckle of her left thumb. "You said an opening? This is what AlderPACT say to you?"

I nod. "Aska seemed to think that a world expands continually, and that new openings form all the time. Like someone growing too big for their clothes and the buttons popping."

"Buttons popping." Saffy nods. "OK. Follow me."

"Now?" I look back at Margo, asleep on the floor. "I can't just leave her."

"You can. She is tough, this one. I can tell. Come now."

So I follow her. Out the doors of the bathhouse, my body stiff with stitching, my mouth filling with sand-drenched mist as the town envelops us both.

We walk the streets of Khaise, oddly empty now, programmed to whatever strange time pattern the city adheres to. They're probably bathing. Everyone likes to do everything together here. We walk on, Saffy's little figure strong and elegant through the mist.

The tight knot of streets begins to fall away as we walk uphill from the river to a scrubby overgrown patch of small farms. Goats tied to posts. Ducks wandering out of hedges. I keep my face covered in a handkerchief, wary of the thick wind penetrating my already damaged body.

"The air carries so much here," she says as she takes my hand, gallantly leading me over the wall like a knight. "Rocks and dust. Tears and blood. All around. All the time."

"All right." It's not a comfortable thought. I burrow my face deeper.

"I'm thinking about your problem, and your Mars, and your mother. About the buttons that come off when the world gets bigger. That's why I bring you here."

I look around. "To a field?"

"Not a field. You think you can grow a thing here?" She stamps on the coarse ground. "No. Only good for goats."

"Then why . . ."

She starts uphill again, and I'm forced to follow her. The hike begins to crunch at my calves as it gets steeper. My shoes aren't right for this.

"You know I'm your teyzi?"

"Yes." I've never been sure what a teyzi even is. I know it's a big deal for other people, but for us, the women who are around you are all important. It's odd to single out one.

Saffy laughs. "I know you don't care. I won the honor. In a game of cards with your mother."

"It's not that I don't care," I protest. "It's just that I don't know what to do with the information."

"Nothing. Nothing to do, for you. Only for me. I am your mother, now that your mother is gone, and mothering is more important to the mother than the son. When she is alive, anyway. Only when she is dead does the son realize."

Is this true? It's terrible if it is.

"But that's why I bring you here."

Eventually, we come to a cluster of boulders crowned by one big C-shaped rock. There is a nanny goat curled up there, and it moves, slowly and irritably, as it sees us approach.

We stand there, under the rock. I wait for something to happen. I've spent so much of the past few days crawling through tunnels and secret passageways that I feel like I'm about to plummet into a pool of sharks.

"Look," she says at last. And I look all around before I realize that she's pointing to herself. Saffy unbuttons her collar. The silver seeds, the ones from my mother's harvest, are pressed against the fine skin of her neck. She lays her fingers on them. The dull pewter color has started to turn and shimmer. The seeds are suddenly restored to their former, glittering silver.

They wink through their silver phase and turn again. They start to give off a haunting, feeble blue light.

"What's going on, Saffy?"

She takes both my hands in hers. My skin—pale during the day, luminous at night—is now dappled with blue freckles. Not sky blue; not cornflower; not midnight. This is the soft blue of light shone through opals.

I move my arm, and the blue wavers. It is not my skin that is blue, but a light that is shining onto it.

We look up at the curve of rock protecting us. There, nestled in the gray stone, is throbbing blue ore shining down on us in fragments of speckled light.

From somewhere deep in my memories, there is movement. Like a single verse in a forgotten song. Something tells me if I just sing it, the rest will come flooding back.

I trace the blue ore with my fingers. It's slightly warm to the touch. A vein of it wraps around the stone and leads me out of the shelter.

"We're near something," I say. "We're near something important."

"Yes. Yes."

The blue vein takes us around to a crack in the boulders, something the eye might mistake for a giant solid rock but is actually two slabs, separated to form an opening. Behind the opening, there are more panels of rock, but the distance is just enough to create a kind of corridor.

We follow it, keeping one hand on the ore as a guide. It is surprisingly wide, and becomes a circular path that winds inward. Big enough for two people to walk and swing their arms without touching each other. Big enough for a family. Big enough, I realize, for a pony and cart.

The caravan trails.

I was so young when they closed. I forgot that the portals were like churches themselves. This is where we gathered. This is how we found one another. These hidden temples, these openings to other worlds.

Of course. Of course. If the buttons on the jacket of the world were going to pop anywhere, of course it would be at a Lunati temple.

We follow the circle as it gets wider, and the vein of blue ore begins to expand into wide panels of shimmering sapphire light.

The last time I was in a space like this, I was riding on my father's shoulders. The room reveals itself to me like information does to you in a dream. Things are intuitive and obvious, yet cryptic and obscure. The feeling of the walls. Warm and smooth, like just-blown glass. The perpetual half-light, the atmosphere hushed and navy as twilight. The raised stone dial that sits at the center. It looks like it should host a throne, but instead it's just a simple stone archway. An archway that leads to nothing, with only the other side of the cave visible.

When the caravan trails were open, the stone archway was what we passed through to go to other worlds. The room was the temple; but the archway was the portal.

In the old days, the archway's portal held the same warped gateway that the train's world barriers have. Now it's empty, showing nothing but the dark room. Where, to my surprise, a selection of wilting flowers sit in glass vases. Saffy has been tending this space as though it were an empty mausoleum. All this time. All these years.

She reaches into her pocket, takes out a brand-new deck of cards, still in their box. She places them on the archway, using both hands, as though handling a religious relic.

"I do not know the openings," Saffy says. "But your mother told me about the Lunati. That the silver on your gari kept the caravan trails open, but believing made the silver full of power."

"Believing?"

"Believing. It's important."

We look at the archway, empty of power, starved of belief.

"We believe in Khaise," she says, "that you must give your sadness and your love into the air. You must speak it out loud."

She is so hopeful, just then. That one word from me could reopen the portal. Saffy is not a witch, exactly. She knows her herbs and potions. She knows her legend and her faith. She has a kind of belief in the divine magics of the world, not cards or crystals, but the inexplicable sorcery found in coincidences, chance meetings, and dramatic ironies. But she has no sense of it herself. Just an instinct that something *should* be a certain way, even when it often isn't.

But I have already spoken my sadness into the world today, and it did not reactivate any old pathways, any lost cultural inheritances.

"Speak it," she demands. Little foot beating off the floor.

"I miss home," I say. "I miss my family."

"Again. More."

It tumbles out then. All stream of consciousness and completely free of context that Saffy might understand.

"I'm afraid. I'm afraid I'm going to get sick and die just like Heck, in that lonely room in Vesna's house, and taken out to be buried in the snow. I'm afraid I'm never going to be with Margo, not properly, not without the world's problems in the palm of our hands."

I can't stop, all of a sudden. If the Khaise air really does take on the truth of spoken word, the pollution is about to get a whole lot worse.

"I'm afraid she'll go back to her world and get old and get married and forget about me, even though, if you think about it, that might be the best-case scenario for everyone involved. I *hate* being everyone's worst-case scenario. I hate being the scrubby, scummy little Lunati salesman with the briefcase and the funny face. I want to be loved, just like everyone else gets to be loved. And I want her. Not anybody else. I want her to stay with me, and I don't want her to go home, and I'm terrified that if I saw a half-good opportunity for her to get home I would kick dirt over it, lead her away by the hand, tell her there was one more thing that needed doing. And that's not love, is it? That's hoarding. That's kidnapping, really."

Saffy has my head in her hands now, her fingers on my neck, her palms at my ears. Holding my skull together to stop it from exploding.

"I'm afraid I can't love anyone properly."

"Why, Levi, why?"

"Because I don't know how. Because I loved my parents so much that I killed them, just trying to get back to them. I'm afraid I'll do the same to Margo. I don't know the difference between love and just wanting something, like a child wants a toy. I'll kill her, Saff. I'll kill her just by wanting her too much."

There it is. My terrible truth, added to the mists of Khaise.

But too many terrible things happen in Khaise every day. My confessions do not, as it turns out, amount to a hell of a lot. The archway stays dead. The buttons on the suit remain in place. And I go on standing there, crying in the arms of my mother.

thirty-three
MARGO

Margo woke up alone, feeling as though she must have been asleep for a hundred years. She was so deeply rested that she felt like she had crossed some invisible line between the living and the dead, in a blissful pink world where nothing was needed from her. There was a pale lilac robe embroidered with golden flowers folded and waiting for her. She drew it on herself, her skin clean and soft from the baths. She felt brand-new, just born, yet the smell of the oiled water made her feel rich and womanly and strange and calm.

Mars slid the wooden door open to a narrow balcony outside. A gauzy screen protected her from the haze, and she sat in a slatted armchair that looked onto the street below. There was a light rain falling, the remnants of a storm she must have just missed that left deep puddles in Khaise's many potholes.

There was a line outside Saffy's place. Two girls stood at Saffy's bridge handing out linen bags, and a little boy was selling paper fans outside the bathhouse walls. *Oh, that would be nice,* she thought. A pretty paper fan to keep the steam off you as you sat and soaked your problems away.

She peered closer and saw that there were a lot of young families in the queue. The girls with the linen bags gave children special tickets, and though Margo didn't understand the language, their calls seemed to imply that this was a kids-go-free time at the Khaise bathhouse. It was family time. Margo watched, marveling that she could be so far from home but that certain things were the same everywhere. There would always be families, and family deals, and merchandise stands that erupted around those stands like weeds.

The tea haze finally clearing, it occurred to Margo that this was a very busy time for Saffy. And here she was, lounging around on a balcony.

Bristling with embarrassment, Margo looked around for her suit. Instead, she found a white linen-type dress, airy and loose, that fell to her feet. Also in the clothes cubby was a pair of wicker slippers, and a padded blue jacket that tied at the waist and disguised the fact that she couldn't find her bra.

In the lobby, she found Mo at a table, working already. He was packing each of the linen bags, quickly and carefully, with a small towel and a gray scrubby sponge thing. He folded each towel, packed the bag, tied the drawstring, and passed it to one of the girls, who would then pass it to another girl out in the line.

Margo stood there, watching him. The activity was so plaintive and wholesome, so lovely in its way. She briefly forgot about Khaise's terrifying two-hour day and imagined for a second that Moon was just an ordinary boy, helping out at a family business. The kind of small job you do on a Saturday for extra money between being a student and having a life.

"Hey," she said. "Can I help?"

He noticed her at last, smiling widely as he saw her. "Look who's up."

"How long have I been out?"

He hesitated before answering. "A few hours."

"You mean a few days."

He didn't reply. Just packed another bag.

"How many?"

"Three."

Three. She had been asleep for three days. If she was in her own world, that would qualify as a coma.

"Look, don't freak out. You needed the rest. And you haven't missed anything."

She came behind the desk where he was filling bags. "Yes, I have," she said, touching him lightly on the arm. "I've missed you entering a new line of work."

Margo leaned over and kissed him on the cheek, just below where his tattoo began. She knew it was too forward, too familial, too established a gesture. But she wanted to play this game, too. Pretend that they could be local kids working at a local business, and terribly in love at the same time.

He blushed. She felt like she was in a cartoon.

Margo started filling bags with him, and after a little while, collecting the used ones from people as they left the bathhouse. Babies waved at her. Young parents apologized when their toddlers ran behind the counter. She learned to stop looking so shocked when so many of the mothers were her age. Then she stopped being shocked altogether.

There was a scream from outside. The sound of splashing, then struggle. They both looked up. Saffy, who was passing at that moment, gestured to a long stick behind where Margo was standing.

"Give," she ordered calmly. "Someone always falling in."

Margo passed her the stick, noticing the long metal hook on the end of it.

Margo and Moon followed Saffy into the courtyard. She was right: a boy had fallen into the stream below Saffy's bridge. A pudgy little guy of about seven or eight. The recent rainstorm had made the water higher than it would have been, but even still, he could dog-paddle easily enough. A rockery of gray boulders should have been his route out—a grapple, a climb, a hoist, and he would be on land again easily—but this was currently proving impossible.

Because the Southern Guard were there, drunk, and making a game out of batting him away from the riverbank. There were six of them, and four bottles of brown liquid being passed between them. Whoever was not currently holding a bottle would prod at the boy with the butt of his gun, pushing and probing as though he were a dead toad in a swamp.

"Come on, now," one called as the boy fell back into the water again. "We've already established you can't get up this way. Use your *ingenuity*, for god's sake."

But there was nowhere else for the boy to climb to. The bank was too high and muddy. His only option was to swim to the other side that bordered the road, but a strong, deep current was running through the stream. The boy didn't look like he fancied his chances of swimming across.

He was starting to panic now. Everyone could see it. Every few seconds he would lose his footing and his face would half sink into the iron-rich water. He gulped and spluttered as more water went up his nose and down his throat.

"Stay here," Saffy instructed Margo and Moon. "I am serious, Levi, you and Mars are not safe."

"Neither is he," Moon argued, pointing at the boy.

"Yes. But he is not Lunati, and not a wanted criminal."

Saffy strode across, reaching out to the boy with the long stick that she kept for aspiring drowners.

At this, the SoGa yelled with all the indignation of boys having their game interrupted by a teacher. Their entire manner seemed to suggest: *Really? You're going to ruin this for us, too? Don't we have things hard enough?*

The Khaise bathers were all filing out of the bathhouse and beginning to bottleneck in the courtyard. The soft sweetness of family hour was rapidly turning into a fierce and protective tension. None of them wanted to cross the bridge while the SoGa were still present. Not with their children.

"Put it *down*," the SoGa said. "Or I'll break it in half."

Saffy did not put it down. She instead reached her stick into the river and encouraged the boy to reach for it. The boy's cheeks were bright red now. His arms flailed for the rod.

The Khaise day bell began to ring. Margo had spent three days asleep, and one day folding towels. For a second she forgot about the scene at the river and felt gripped by dread, of the hourglass of her life trickling away too fast and without her permission.

She was not the only foreigner who felt this way.

On hearing the bell, the SoGa's mood began to turn. They were no longer arrogant boys, bullying a younger child before they became bored and moved on. They were a police force sent to Khaise to escort a military shipment, and now they were stuck. Indefinitely. They had all grown up in worlds of twenty hours or more, and they were angry.

The SoGa who had told Saffy to put down the stick reached for her neck and slammed her into the river. Margo saw Saffy's body flail and the black mantilla come free from her hair.

Moon pushed his way through the crowd to get to her. Margo threw herself ahead of him, knowing that the SoGa would be looking for a boy with a moon on his face. She grabbed hold of Moon around the waist, her grip suddenly iron. "No," she commanded. "Mo, no. You can't."

"Let *go*."

She dragged him by the waist until he fell to the ground on top of her, his back crunching on top of her chest. A space cleared around them. Fortunately, everyone was too terrified by the SoGa to care whether two bathhouse employees were fighting.

They got to their feet just in time to see Saffy swimming across the river with the boy riding on her back. Her gray hair wet and loose around her, her arms strong and lithe.

The bathers started to cheer as Saffy reemerged on the other side of the river, the boy spitting out water but clearly safe. Clearly fine. He looked up, waved at his parents, and then vomited into the grass.

Everyone cheered harder, and it was funny, because by all rights vomiting in front of everyone he knew should have been the worst moment of the boy's life. But he looked oddly proud of himself. He took a deep bow, and everyone laughed more. The SoGa had set an unfair game, but Khaise had beaten them anyway.

A shot rang out, piercing Khaise's thick atmosphere. The SoGa who had pushed Saffy fired into the air. The bathers cowered, shrinking their bodies back under the courtyard's awning. They weren't used to force like this. They were left alone in Khaise, mostly. Nobody ever wanted to come to Khaise, and that was what was good about it.

They marched into the courtyard, all six of them. Their drunken bodies were suddenly snapping into military sobriety.

"Who is the owner here?"

Saffy hobbled over the bridge. She had been hurt by the fall. Margo could see that now. Saffy limped on one leg, her hand on the ballast. The crowd parted for her, rippling like straw.

The SoGa gave no acknowledgment that this was the same woman he had tossed into the river. He simply nodded at the sopping older woman before him.

"The Khaise bathhouses are closed until further notice. Additionally, we have suspended gambling, communal gatherings, and any social activities outside the home."

Audible gasps from the crowd.

Saffy only nodded. The SoGa seemed annoyed that she was not giving him any pushback, so he carried on anyway.

"As you may have heard," he went on testily, "the train lines are experiencing . . . faults. The Southern Guard are here to make sure that there is no sabotage, as important shipments from this world are required elsewhere."

Murmurings, confirming yes, everyone had heard this.

"Khaise is under suspicion of sabotage. Semper hopes this is not the case, given the long trading relationship our two nations have enjoyed. But until such time as that sabotage is either uncovered or dismissed, Khaise is under martial law. Please, do not leave your home unless for food or medical reasons. You will be subject to interrogation, and potentially, arrest."

Never mind that they were drunk, or that there was no proof of this decree. No missive, no newspaper, no bulletin. There was no way of telling whether this threat was real, or something this soldier had come up with after being embarrassed by Saffy.

He looked into the appalled crowd.

"That is all."

The SoGa left. Shortly after, everyone else did, too. Family hour was over.

Over the next few days, Margo helped Saffy clean the empty bathhouse. With no business coming in, Saffy could not afford to pay her workers, and the upkeep of the place—even without customers—was immense. The constant swilling of hot water left grime, limescale, and spores of mold all over the hotel's shabby rooms. She was always standing on a chair and scrubbing, or on her knees and scrubbing. The skin on her hands became rubbed and raw.

She didn't complain. With just the three of them at the bathhouse—"like three old peanuts in a can," Saffy's words—Margo found herself to be the only truly fit one among them. Saffy had been injured quite badly from the river. Her legs were scratched and scabbed, her movements careful and stiff. She didn't want sympathy about what had happened, and seemed very embarrassed when Margo brought it up at all.

Moon, too, was still recovering. As his skin gradually knit itself back together, his pain only seemed to increase. He couldn't raise his arm above his head without rupturing his stitches, couldn't lie down without smarting the wound on his lower back. He dozed fitfully in chairs, unless Saffy had drugged him. Margo would find him lying on the floor on his belly, his face pressed against the cool tiles.

The SoGa had been serious. The city was under lockdown. Every hour or so, another report drifted into the bathhouse like steam. The SoGa had raided a house, taking all the jewelry they could carry. They were roving the streets, drunk, and looking for things to get them high. Lots of things in Khaise could get you high, she was learning. The frequent rainstorms, terrible heat, and mineral-dense soil sprouted all kinds of strange things. Most people in Khaise had a casual relationship with it—special occasions only—but the lockdown and the SoGa unrest had started an underground drug trade. It was beginning to get competitive, and soon after that, violent.

"You're telling me a drug cabal has formed *already*?" Margo said, astounded. "It's been two days."

"People act quick here." Mo shrugged. "They have to."

By the following week, things had become more frightening. The SoGa had beaten a man half to death for visiting his neighbor. Some shops in town were looted. And finally, the most terrible story of all: a woman in labor was not permitted a visit to a hospital, and was told to give birth at home. She died the following day.

Margo's period came. Badly. She had to ask Saffy what women in Khaise did with their periods, and the answer was a kind of reusable tampon made of a marshy substance that she did not question the origin of. Her last period had finished the day before she left for boarding school.

She couldn't quantify how long she had been away in her own world's time, when you added the New Davia days, the Alder days, and the Khaise days together. Maybe a little less than a week. Her poor mother. That's all she could think about. *My poor mother.*

Moon was another concern altogether. Perhaps it was his injuries, or maybe he had simply changed his mind about her, but Moon had become harder to locate. Not just because she worked so much or because he was drugged so often. There was an absence now, in the way he looked at her. He seemed to look past her, like he had caught his own reflection in the wall behind. She was starting to think she had imagined the moment in the pool. It wasn't a hard thing to believe. It had all the erotic unreality of a dream, of something you wished would happen to you.

Then one morning, he came to look for her. She was on her hands and knees in the main pool area, scrubbing at some mildew in the dark tiles. It was insulting that he would come looking for her there, the site of their aborted attempt at a romance.

"The Wash is soon," he said. He looked nervous. She put her scrubber down.

"Oh?"

He knelt on the floor, his knees in the soapy water.

"I'd really like you to do it with me."

"Oh."

She didn't quite know what to say. Except: "Is there any tangible way that I can fuck it up?"

He thought about it. "Not really, no."

"OK then." Then she stopped, because what was the point in being coy, really, when a Khaise drug cabal could form in two days? She didn't have the time to be coy. "Lev, is this a date?"

It was an experiment. An experiment in being direct, and an experiment in calling him Lev. He seemed to take both well.

"Yeah." He smiled. "Yeah, Mars, I guess it is."

He leaned across the wet floor and kissed her. A light little thing, a brush, a flutter. But all him. All there.

The door to the baths cranked open. Saffy stood there with a pile of towels.

"I need you both," she said, her voice uncharacteristically stern. "You are going to a party."

They sat with Saffy in her parlor. Conspicuously not drinking anything.

"Big problem," she said. "Namakshura is missing."

"What? The namak they ordered for the army?"

"Namak for the army. They store it at the train station, guarding it all the time. But then somehow they move it. Fifty big crates. Poof. Gone."

Moon wrinkled his brow. "That doesn't make any sense. And what, you think it's at this party?"

"A party. Yes. There is a woman in town here, Countess Shura, the one who is selling them the namak. She is holding a big party for the SoGa. You will go. You will find out where the namak went."

Margo was utterly perplexed. Every time she got accustomed to the new demands of her strange life, the terms would shift again. First she was a boardinghouse maid, then a PACT foot soldier, then a bathhouse assistant, now a spy.

"Can you . . . tell me more? Why us? I don't even know Khaise."

"This is it exactly," Saffy said, with some delight. "You are a stranger here. But you are young. You are clean. You have your teeth; you are healthy. You speak the Traders Language. All the first families speak it also, even at leisure."

"I'm sorry, the first families?"

Moon answered. "The families that own all the fuel and resources in Khaise. We saw them on the first day."

"The white lace carriages," Margo recalled. The gauzy, slightly menacing serenity of the rich. Their beaded umbrellas. Their distance. "But how many first families are there?"

"Twelve. But then they have cousins who are more like second families."

"But won't they know me? Or, you know. Know that I don't belong?"

Saffy shook her head. "You must remember, we are in Khaise. Babies grow quick. Rich children go south for school. Faces change so much. You will slip in just by looking like this. And you will listen. And you will learn."

"But who would talk to me?"

Saffy's eyes slid over her. "People."

"Men," Moon interrupted. "She means men."

Margo felt herself flush. "Oh."

"You will sit with men, be interested, ask questions. They will all think you are the niece or daughter of someone they know. They will talk if you ask. And the SoGa won't know any Khaise at all. You must prioritize them."

"Saffy," Margo said slowly. "With great respect to the profession, I'm not a whore."

"No whore," Saffy protested. "Just listen."

"She's not doing it, Saffy. It's too dangerous. She's already a wanted person using a fake name and the sales license of a dead man."

All of this was true, and valid, and yet Margo knew she would do it. She had spent long enough in Khaise to understand how rare an opportunity she represented. She had all her teeth. She spoke the right language. She wasn't visibly malnourished.

"I have just heard that the SoGa are in baths now. Raiding all the old houses. They will find me soon. They will find you soon. We need to know. For your safety, and for ours."

"The SoGa have been raiding *bathhouses*?" Moon exclaimed.

"There are not many soldiers so they do it slowly. And Khaise is big. But they are working through them, like dogs chewing through bones."

"I'll do it," Margo said. Then turned to Moon. "Look, it's dangerous, but you were doing worse when you were twelve. It's just talking. I can handle it. I promise."

Saffy looked slyly at Moon, like they shared a secret. "Someday," she said, "you will be together without all the world's problems."

As usual in the North, important decisions were made quickly. Saffy immediately brought her to a bedroom cluttered with pictures, dried flowers, playing cards, and matchboxes. She extracted a bundle of pale blue silk from the mess.

"Take off clothes," she said, not unkindly. She had learned that nothing Saffy said or did was unkind, really, but done in the spirit of love and brevity. Margo pulled the smock dress over her head.

The silk was nothing but a huge rectangle, but Saffy started measuring it and pinning it to Margo. After a few pins were put in place so that it draped like a Grecian statue, Saffy pulled a mirror out.

Glass was so rare in Khaise that Margo spent a moment looking at the mirror as an object, rather than the reflection within. But there she was. A young woman with hair that curled in soft waves around her ears. She was covered in blue silk. Now she understood why silk was always silk, always valuable, always synonymous with luxury. The way it clung to her body made her look at herself. Really look at herself. Her boobs, which had sprung up at thirteen and been roughly the size of an apple cut in half, had rippled outward, protruded in a way they never had before.

At first, Margo was sure this was some kind of optical illusion, created by a combination of the blue silk and a dirty mirror. But she looked down and saw herself in the full light of Saffy's dressmaking space. She had changed. She had filled out for one. There was a soft layer over her stomach, a thickness to her thighs, a widening in her hips.

A body cannot change very much in a month. A regular month, anyway. But the skipshocked body is different. A teenage one even more so. Hormones become confused; pituitary glands receive mixed messages; adrenal glands have their say. The result was this. Margo had lost her remaining girlhood. She always knew that she was losing time. But she also assumed, on some level, that she had a lot of it.

But no. Not anymore. She had crossed some kind of threshold, and there was no going back.

"You are OK?" Saffy asked. Margo's face was completely drained of color. Her knees trembled and she lost her balance. Saffy steadied her. "Sit down, baby, sit down."

She sat in Saffy's chair and, in the full light, rolled up the blue silk to the top of her legs. There, scratched like cave paintings, were deep red furrows on the inside of her thighs. "Oh my god," she whispered. "Stretch marks."

Saffy, who had seen so many women age and die before her, suddenly understood the kind of existential horror Margo was being confronted with.

"Head between knees," Saffy said. "I make tea."

"Saffy, no."

"Normal tea. I promise."

Saffy went away and came back, a clean flowery tea in her hands. She watched Margo drink it and offered no advice at all, no wisdom, no soothing. Things changed. Then they changed again. The body most of all.

Saffy sewed quickly where she had placed the pins. Margo sat with a towel around her, sipping the hot tea in silence. The whole thing was finished in minutes. She slipped the dress back on, feeling as exposed and new as a peeled fruit.

"OK," she said after a moment. "What now?"

"Now," Saffy said. "More clothes."

Saffy produced an incredible array of clothing and accessories, all of it scrounged or saved or traded or resewn or dyed to match the blue silk. Possibly a hundred parties had occurred while they were in Khaise, but Saffy had been quietly getting resources together. Lord knows how, while the city was in lockdown. The important thing in Khaise, she told Margo, was to look the part. Everything else followed after that.

On top of the silk, Margo put on another dress that buttoned at the back. It, too, was blue with a panel of pink embroidered flowers. Over this came a thin transparent veil made of fine gold thread, and over this a white lace veil that looked just like the ones she had seen on the street. And all through this, Saffy briefed her.

"Your name is Ariella Yvina," she said. "You are a distant niece of the countess. You go to school at Calibaba in the Southwest. Your father is in the iron trade."

Another name. Another identity. "Is that a real person?"

"No. But there are so many Yvinas, and so many Ariellas, that you will be fine."

"Surely I need to know more than that."

"No. Girls are shy. Or they are meant to be." Saffy carried on pinning and veiling. "You will be greeted. You will go to a small room to take your outside layers off. You will give them to Moon, your servant. We will cover his face. This is normal in Khaise. Then you will be at the party. You will listen. This is all."

Margo looked in the mirror, everything so entirely covered now that there was no scope to feel strangely about her body, let alone see it.

"That's *all*?"

"You think I don't tell you enough," Saffy said at last. "Truth is, I do not know what these parties are really like. I know a little, but not everything. I am putting you in danger. I cannot pretend I am not. I am sorry to do it."

She looked sad then, because what Saffy did for the love of PACT she did at the expense of her own soul. "But you are a big chance for us, Mars. Khaise is sending weapons to a war. We must know how."

Saffy had to guide her by the hand into the courtyard. Margo felt like a cart horse, blinkered and heavy with tack. Before she even saw him, her hand was placed into Moon's. Margo had to tilt her head slightly to see through a gap in the gauzy lace, where all she could see was Moon's own head wrapped in layers of muslin.

"Are you *in* there?"

"Yes. Are you?"

"Just about."

They crossed the bathhouse bridge, the sound of running water louder to her now that her vision was so strangely obscured.

"Watch your step," Moon said, and only then did she understand that they were stepping into one of the veiled carriages.

"Where did they get this from?" she asked as they sat within the odd, womblike walls of the carriage.

"Better we don't ask, I think."

"Moon?"

"Yes."

"What the fuck is about to happen to us?"

"I don't really know. But I can guess."

They were starting to move. No one had told them how long the journey was going to take. She could feel herself starting to sweat through her carefully arranged layers.

"Guess, then."

"Well, you'll feel like an alien. You'll be incredibly uncomfortable, and feel like everyone is wondering what you're doing there, and as if you're about to be found out. But then you'll realize that this is just how people feel at parties anyway, and the quicker you do that, the better spy you'll make. First rule of sales, take what you have and turn it into an asset. If you're nervous at the party, play the part of a girl who's nervous at a party."

This was far more useful advice, and far exceeded the "do your best" or "you'll be fine" that she was expecting. It made her less nervous, to know she didn't have to cover her nerves.

"Have you crashed a lot of parties?"

"One or two. Sometimes they want a guy standing in the corner showing off his exotic wares from all his dangerous travels. It's like cheap entertainment to them. Just don't get drunk, and don't stop listening."

"OK."

"And don't talk to me, either. That's the most important thing. I'm supposed to be your servant. I'll always be behind you, but you can't turn and look for me. OK? Don't make it look like we're friends. That's the only thing that will make them suspicious."

Another Orpheus trial.

"So treat you like dirt."

"Yes."

"Fun."

"Don't get too excited."

They trundled on through the winding streets of Khaise. The driver did not seem to speak the Traders Language—funny, how Margo was already coming to think of English that way—and kept quiet throughout the journey. Eventually, the carriage passed through a set of gates. Margo could make out a palace in the distance, huge and terra-cotta, the color of a plant pot. They quickly joined a line of carriages. They moved slowly, and the palace became clear to them a little at a time. It was a huge, single-story structure, but with a series of high domed roofs that shone with gold detailing.

When their carriage finally reached the palace entrance, the carriage doors swung open and a valet put out his hand to Margo. She stepped out, wobbling slightly as she did.

"All right," Moon said. "Showtime."

thirty-four

MOON

The lockdown, it seems, was only for regular people. The first families were never going to stop partying. Not the second ones, either.

No one looks the slightest bit curious about Ariella Yvina or her cameo at a Khaise house party. I suspect that a lot more went into the planning of Margo's appearance here than we can even comprehend. That Saffy herself was just given a scrap of information, and that all of us are simply single cogs in a wide infrastructure gearing toward a singular goal. The People's Action for Common Travel. Such a stupid name for such a benign, impossible request. The people want to travel. It's everything the Lunati believed in, everything I should believe in, too.

A dream I believed was too fanciful before I stood in the Lunati gateway, the doorway to the long-dead caravan trails. Before something awoke in me again. I now understand what Yaz was trying to tell me. She's older than me; she remembers what it was like. Things change. They can change again. Maybe I'm aging out of cynicism. Maybe it really is for the very young, people who have only had one or two sets of circumstances befall them, rather than the constantly shifting fortune that time inevitably shoulders on you.

Things change.

They can change again.

A narrow hallway creates a sort of roaring traffic of conversation.

This is the kind of house that has a women's entrance. If you didn't know anything about the first families of Khaise, you'd assume they were some kind of highly modest bunch of merchant aristocrats, with all this veiling and ceremony. In reality, no one gives a shit about modesty. The women enter through a separate corridor because everyone wants their first appearance to be breathtaking.

There's fifty women here at least, all smothered in various contraptions of white lace. Some old, some very young. Some holding on to one another like schoolgirls, some moving through hallways like ghosts preparing to sail through walls. They are led to an antechamber, which has its own personal bath and changing-room scenario going on, hooks for the women to leave their outdoor clothes. They are expected to enter through the women's entrance and leave through a separate door into the main body of the party. Margo steps ahead of me, disappearing into the web of them, and to her credit—does not look back.

The male servants are expected to wait, silent and at attention, on the other side of the antechamber, the door the girls are supposed to walk out of. I've been to houses like this before, and am dimly aware of the etiquette. Nothing prepared me for how strange it would feel, watching veiled phantoms enter through one door and nymphs exit through another. It's hard not to think about abattoirs, where cows trot in one side and mincemeat comes flying out the other.

Then Margo comes out.

Looking more naked than she did when we were both sitting in the dark baths. There, we talked until our fingers and toes wrinkled, and the thrumming heartbeat of *Margo is naked Margo is naked Margo is naked* sounded under every quiet thought. But those moments were private. And now here she is, in clinging blue silk, for everyone to see.

Her eyes scan the waiting area for me, her expression worried and fraught. She finally settles on me, my face almost totally covered by the muslin wrap.

Then she remembers. Remembers that I'm her servant, and that girls like her don't talk to people like me at parties like this. So she moves to a large gold fountain that other girls are using to wash their hands. She's already made a friend. Younger than her, a head shorter at least, and chattering to Margo ceaselessly as Margo nods and smiles. She looks glacial and womanly next to the other girl, and it scares me.

It's not that I'm amazed she can wear a dress. It's that the dress makes me notice the rest of her, the constituent parts of Margo that have subtly changed since she arrived here. I mean, she had breasts and a waist when she arrived. She wasn't a child, but there's a dimension to her body now. A sturdiness, a fullness. And I want to touch her. I want to measure the width of her hips with my hands, and the feeling is so uncomfortable that I have to mess with the change in my pockets.

My Khaise-spoken fear that supposedly got carried by the air comes back to me again. Margo going home. Margo growing up and getting married. Margo, just some woman who has moved on with her life. I want to vomit. I've never felt simultaneously so horny and so nauseous.

I trail her and the girl to the next room, another room in a sequence of endless rooms, and finally we're in the main gut of the party. Which is to say: there are men in this room. Not just servants but men. They sit on low couches, each smothered in cushions and cool silks, smoking and drinking and playing a kind of board game where flat carved pebbles are the bounty. And every man, when waiting for their turn, sits back and watches the women's entrance.

They watch each new girl come through, shimmering in pale blues or yellows or pinks, their sheer gold veils pulled back off their faces and over their hair. I can see now why Saffy was not particularly worried about Margo "belonging" here or not. It's blatant how little it matters if you have fresh, creamy skin and the right airs.

Margo plays it perfectly. She nods; she laughs. She keeps her eyes glued to the floor a lot, presumably because she doesn't want to accidentally look at me, or appear too amazed by anything around us. The carved walls, studded with precious stones. The woman walking a swan on a leash. And in the center of the room, a cluster of SoGa soldiers, chain-smoking army cigarettes and looking absolutely furious.

The servant next to me is a much older man, looking straight ahead with a fixed, dull expression. His eyes, however, don't leave the SoGa. Even when the swan starts rearing and squeaking; even when a man flips the pebble game after accusing another man of cheating. The old servant keeps his eyes on the young soldiers, his face never betraying the remotest interest.

I decide to try him, to keep things light.

"Heard anything about the train?" I ask in my best Khaise.

He shakes his head. His eyes briefly flicker to me. "Still closed," he says.

"I bet they're not too happy about that," I reply, and neither of us have to clarify which "they" I mean.

"Hmm," he replies, noncommittal.

I look for Margo. The smaller girl has taken her into a group with some other girls, and I get a little nervous. The last thing we want is a big conversation about who knows who or who has mutual friends, and big groups almost always revert to that kind of chatter. We want clusters of two and three.

I scan the group, and find myself strangely proud that Margo is the prettiest one. Or is she? Do the girls with the long fair hair just seem obvious and stupid next to Margo, and do the leggy girls just seem gangly, and do the petite ones just seem lacking? Have I spent so much time with this girl that she is now the paragon of what good is, the standard by which everything is automatically judged?

"You are new," the old man says. "Your girl is new."

"Just back from school," I say dutifully.

"Hmmm," he says again.

Margo's group, all in their mid to late teens, starts to move. Slowly, the group seems to be floating toward the cluster of SoGa. Girls start to fix their veils and smooth their dresses. They take turns in discreetly swiveling their necks around to see the young, furious men.

It's then I realize why they're so interested. The SoGa are the only young-looking men in the vicinity. Almost every other man in the room appears middle-aged. They have big bumpy noses. They have burst blood vessels, shining bald heads. They have soft bellies and turkey necks. And here, I suppose, is the rift in Khaise social life. The rich men have to stay and run things. The rich girls are sent to Southern boarding schools so that they might better decorate a room, and brought back for party season. Then they graduate, become third or fourth wives, then mothers, then graduate to first wives after the original wives die. Then widows, after which they do not go to parties anymore and spend their days taking carriages from one woman's card game to another. The SoGa must seem exciting at a party like this. The girls must see them as heroes, celebrities. A rescuer, even. You can see it.

These parties. This being looked at. The silk dresses and the rooms to disrobe in. This is meant to be the peak of a rich Khaise woman's life. Which isn't to say the men have it much better. They've inherited this weird cultural practice of partying with teenagers. Most of them don't seem to be enjoying it all that much.

"They have seen her," the servant next to me murmurs.

He nods toward Margo. He understands that Margo is the only *her* in the room, at least where I'm concerned, and possibly where he is concerned, too. Is he in PACT? Has he sidled up to me on purpose? Does he know exactly who I am?

Margo's group is beckoned over. There's no more inch-by-inch moving now, but long goddess strides from everyone, each a contestant for the prize of a SoGa husband. They settle next to the men in orange uniforms, all the soldiers looking far less upset now that they have some beautiful girls for company.

I know that it's better that Margo sits with the SoGa. They are far less likely to see holes in her story, and more likely to give her information about the namak.

"She your girl?" the man next to me asks. Margo folds herself into the low cushioned chair, knees together, protecting the rippling mass of blue silk from bunching where she can.

I nod very slightly. "She's my girl."

thirty-five

MARGO

As a broad category, it turned out that teenage girls were more or less the same everywhere. They all wanted reassurances on their hair and clothes. They all had heard of a better party happening elsewhere. And they were all sick of the men they knew, and captivated by the ones they didn't.

The last time she had met anyone from the SoGa, they were murdering her friends. The Southern Guard here had less of a sadistic streak, but only because they hadn't grown into it yet. They were boyish, seeming strangely close to her own age. They had golden faces, shiny hair, and fresh stubble. They were trying, they said, to grow their beards out for the first time now that they were in a time zone that allowed for the growing of beards. It was a competition between them. There were many competitions, many bets, many little games they had created to pass the time. They were marooned here, just like her.

"We have this thing going with the cards," one explained to her. They were sitting close together, the soft, low cushions pulling them down to the ground. "They love cards here."

"We do," Margo said, resting her cheek against the cushion and staring up at him with sleepy interest. It was easy to pretend that she was in a party in her own world, if she ignored everything else about the party except the boy in front of her. "We love cards."

"There must be five packs in the house we're staying in, all mixed up together. Every time we deal, it feels like the seven of spades comes up. We're going crazy, how many seven of spades we're getting. So I start putting the seven of spades on Ori's pillow. Next day, I'm biting into my sandwich and my teeth hit the seven of spades. The fucker has hidden it in there! Suddenly, all the guys are in on it, hiding the seven of spades everywhere, waiting for someone else to find it."

"So fun."

"It's funny," he agreed. "They're funny guys."

"How long . . ."

"We don't know," he replied. "The train engineers can't figure it out."

"Are there people working on it?"

"Can we not talk about the train today?" he said, his smile disappearing. "It's bad enough that we have to talk about it in the house all day, and with the fucking Khaise council, I don't want to talk about it at a party, too. They're not going to seal Khaise, OK? It's a technical fault."

"I'm sorry, I'm sorry," she said soothingly. She touched his hand. "It's just, we're all so scared, we're hoping you guys will have the answers. And. You know, I'm hoping to get back to the South soon, too. For school."

He nodded, softening. "Well, it's not really South where you go, is it. It's more like Mid-Axis."

"It's Calibaba."

"See, that's Mid-Ax," he said, almost pityingly. "What, fourteen hours, you get there? That's not really South."

"It's South to me."

"Yeah. Yeah. I guess it is. I guess." He took a deep sip of his drink and, while examining his ice, started to peer down her dress. "You won't ever be like this again, will you? I mean, you'll probably be old in about a year. One of my years." He paused. "Weird. So weird."

How was a Khaise girl expected to respond to this? "Yeah," she agreed. And then, in a fit of genius. "We only have tonight."

She didn't know where she was going with this. Just that it was something to say that would make him feel closer to her, and if he felt close to her, then he might tell her something. No one had taught her how to be a spy, so she was mostly guessing.

He perked up. "Yeah?"

"I don't know when I'll be at a party again. This will probably be the only time I'll ever see you."

He edged closer, his hand on her leg. The silk was so fine that she could feel the sweat of his fingertips on her skin.

"They have birds outside. Have you seen them yet? Big orange ones, size of dogs. They're trained."

"No."

"Let's go see them," he said, moving to get up.

It was obvious what he was trying to do. Parties really were all alike. "I have a chaperone," she said. For the first time in the conversation, she had an excuse to look for Moon, and there he was standing with the servants, his gaze firmly on her. He could see the hand on the leg. She hoped he didn't judge her for it.

The SoGa's eyes flickered over. Clearly, he was unconcerned. If Margo's life was too short to even really account for, then Moon's was irrelevant. "It's fine," he said. He took her hand. "Come on."

Margo wasn't sure what to do. She knew this could be her only chance to acquire real information. But she also didn't know how much it would cost, or if this boy even had information to share. There was also her identity to protect. Would a well-brought-up Khaise girl ever step outside with a stranger at a party? Would stepping out risk too many eyes on her, and the eventual revelation that she didn't belong at this party at all?

"Let's stay," she said, a little too desperately. "I could get in trouble. And so could you."

He scoffed. "*Everyone's* going off with girls."

He sounded about twelve.

"Everyone?"

"Everyone. Most of the guys are in brothels. No one says anything. I mean, the girls are happy for the business, with the lockdown and everything. It's like all the rules are out the window." He paused, regarded his audience. "I don't go into brothels," he added.

"All the rules are out the window," she repeated. Not because it really meant anything, but because the music of agreement tended to make people talk more. She remembered her father saying something like this. All people want is a mirror, he said. A mirror to how they already feel. Another oddly salesman-like expression. She dog-eared the memory.

"Yeah," the boy agreed. "They spend all day in there sometimes, or they go to bars and say they're working. And they can pass it all off as investigation."

"Investigation of what?"

"Of the girl." He sighed. "Of the girl and the watch."

Margo felt her heart stop.

"What do you mean? What girl? What watch?"

She had never felt more grateful that she wasn't wearing it. It was at Saffy's, under the spongy cork mattress. Even so, she felt its weight on her wrist. Like invisible handcuffs, like a phantom limb.

"Shit. Never mind." The boy flushed deeply and drained his drink. "We're not supposed to . . ."

He quickly looked up and down the row of seats, where his friends were still chatting to the other Khaise girls. Everyone was laughing and touching, and talk of orange birds flowed in every direction.

What was happening? How had she become a factor in the SoGa's appearance in Khaise and their stockpiling of ammunition?

The boy was panicking a little. He wanted to remove himself from Margo, to quickly absorb himself in a new conversation, to forget that he had ever let anything slip.

"It's OK," she said. "I know."

"You *know*? How do you know?"

She bit her lip and remembered Moon's advice about how the best way to play off nerves was to dial them up, not down. She wasn't nervous because she was about to potentially ignite a bomb of information. She was nervous because she was a girl talking to a boy.

"The watch that breaks the train," she said.

He grunted. "God, can anyone keep a secret these days?"

"My dad's in government," she said slowly. "He's on the Khaise council."

"Right." He looked into his drink. "I mean, if that's the only thing it did, we'd be fine."

"Excuse me?"

"Nothing."

His face shut down. He was uncomfortable with her now, uncomfortable with himself. Margo's mind darted around his comment. The watch did more than just close the train? She had barely wrapped her head around it destroying train lines.

Margo had to prove she was a safe bet for conversation. The only thing better than a secret was finding out that someone else knew it, too, and that you could dissect it in private. But she couldn't by any means feed him new information. She couldn't lead him back to Moon, or Saffy, or anyone else who had helped her so far.

"She's young, right?" Margo said slowly. "The girl. I don't know. It's a big thing at school. Because she's, y'know, our age."

"It's in *schools*? Damn." He raked a warm hand through his hair. "I mean. We don't know what to make of it. Just that she's some skinny kid with a watch who was kidnapped by Northern terrorists."

Margo felt an odd pang at *skinny kid*, knowing that she no longer fitted that description, and never would again.

"So you think she's in Khaise?"

"That's the thing. We were just here for the namak trade. But then the tracks broke. So we figure that Khaise PACT has this watch, probably killed the girl weeks ago, and now they're using it as a weapon. Which means they have to be in Khaise. We've been tearing through every fucking underground bunker and cave we can find. *And* we have to keep moving the namak around, in case they get ahold of it."

"Namak. Are you guys starting a war or something?"

She tried to sound as dumb as she could, like war was a thing on the news, and for other people. Which it always had been, in her old life. It wasn't a hard role to play.

"What? No."

Since her first full day in New Davia, the supposed war that Semper was starting was all anyone in PACT could talk about. But this boy was confident, and he was telling the truth. There was no war, not as far as he was concerned.

"This is just the beginning of the extraction process," he said. "PACT has found new ways to travel, or at least that's what we've heard, and the watch will help them do that. Listen. It's a good thing you're going back to school soon. But if I were you, I'd try to get farther below the Axis. Maybe you can study hard and get a scholarship or something. I don't know, do they do that?"

"Why do I need to go below the Axis, if there's not going to be a war?" she asked. "And what do you mean, extraction process?"

The boy looked at her, really looked at her. For the first time in their conversation, he seemed to understand that she was a person. Not a collection of pleasing yet quickly expiring body parts, but a person who might be cared about.

"Once we find this watch," he said, "the trains are over."

"What do you mean the trains are over?"

"We've been instructed to take as much out of the North as we need, and then . . ."

She felt her heart stop.

"And then?"

He had said too much. He would get in trouble. He was worried, now.

"Please," she said.

"They're going to seal the North," he said at last. "The whole thing."

thirty-six

MOON

Margo rises slowly, the low couches so sunken that she has to put her hands on the floor to get purchase. The soldier she's talking to looks drunk and annoyed. You don't need to know how to lip-read to figure out what's going on.

Something like: *Where are you going? You can't leave, just like that?*

And she responds in the vein of: *I'll be back in a minute, I swear.*

Her hand over her heart, an oath of friendship. But the boy looks scared. He's extremely young. Or maybe he isn't, but everything about him ripples with inexperience. He's clearly said too much. He wants to stuff his own words back in his mouth. Margo's been a perfect spy, and now all I have to do is get her out of here without drawing too much attention to ourselves.

Margo floats casually back toward the women's entrance, to the gold fountain where all the girls washed their hands before descending on the party. There's a stack of hand towels near the doorway, and I appear silently at her side, giving her one.

"We have to go," she whispers. "Now."

I've just realized that we were not briefed on an exit strategy. We don't know where the veiled carriage came from or when it would be appearing again. Presumably at the end of the party, which could be two days from now.

The old servant, the one who kept his eyes so firmly trained on the SoGa soldiers, approaches us. "A pleasure." He smiles, shaking my hand. "So sad to see you go, and so early."

He moves away in one casual sweep, leaving a coiled note in my hands.

Female changing area. Green curtain.

There's no time to question it. We are already a mistress and her servant spending rather too much time standing together at a society party.

We move quickly, past the corridor with the gold fountain and to the women's changing area where I collected Margo not long ago. It's a milk-colored, powdery room with a high floral aroma. There are gold fixtures and rows of changing cubicles against a back wall. There must be fifty, each with their own peg, shelf, and bench to sit on. Silk dividers separate one cubicle from the other.

"Green curtain," I say to Margo. "Where's the fucking green curtain?"

We run down the cubicles, me on the left side, Margo on the right. Each silk curtain a different color, red and yellow and pink and—but not green, never green.

"Here!" Margo yells from the other side of the room. "Follow my voice!" I stumble toward her, charging through the silk curtains as they slip coolly over my head. I put my arms over my face, as though I'm being attacked by bats.

I'm moving so quickly that I almost slam into Margo, knocking her off her feet. "Sorry, sorry," I say, putting my arms out to steady her. Her skin is bare and warm, and I'm suddenly aware of how close we're pushed together by these swaths of jade fabric. We're both breathless, both amazed we've escaped the party, our eyes scanning each other wildly for safety. *Kiss her,* I think. *Tell her she's done well. Tell her how good she looks.*

"Green curtain" is all I say.

"Green curtain," she agrees. Her breath a little heavy. I can see the cracks in her lips, the dip in her neck. Shit. "What now?"

"I guess someone comes to get us."

We listen for a moment. Nothing. No footsteps, no running water. No servants. The party hums in the next room.

"His hand," I suddenly blurt out. "His hand was on your leg."

Margo looks up at me, face flushed, the adrenaline of it all putting her blood up. I can hear her heart beat, I think. I can hear her heart.

Not just adrenaline. No. Not just that. The sudden awareness of herself, in the blue dress, of being in a room full of people who want the girl in the blue dress. A power she now has, over me and over everyone else, too.

I step toward her, my hand feeling her body through the thin material, my breath on her neck. I don't kiss her. I physically can't, not with the wrap around my head.

My hand widens to match the span of her leg. My thumb spreading so it can land just below her crotch. I pull her close. Her back exposed and damp from the humid party, despite all the hosts' attempts to keep it cool. I run my hand down the knuckles of her spine, and press my covered mouth to the cleft of her neck, where her hair is sticking gently to her skin. A bead of sweat has made its way there, and I can feel it, salty and damp against the gauze. Margo shivers. The dress is so thin that I can feel every breath rattling through her, all of her body working at once. I've never, not once in my life, wanted a person like this.

She looks up at me, firmly encased in my arms now.

"They're going to seal the North. That's what the namak is about, and all the other resources they're buying up. They know

PACT has new openings. They know they can't hold the North back much longer. So they're sealing everything."

"What?"

She sounds manic, like she hasn't quite processed what this means yet, but needs to say it anyway.

"They call it extraction."

"They call *what* extraction?"

There isn't an eyelash of space between us. Pressed against the back changing wall, my hands on her hips, her waist.

Click.

The wall gives way. Suddenly, there are raindrops on the backs of my hands.

"Oh," she says. "So this was the way out the whole time."

We're standing outside the huge, dusky-orange building. The recent rain has lightened the atmosphere, and the ever-present haze has finally lifted. The moon is out, fat and pale. In a few hours, it will be full again. Which means I'll have to do the Wash, and Margo and I will have been traveling together for a little over one month.

"Carriages," I say. "Let's go find them."

We're forced to creep around the whole side of the palace to make it to the main gates. It takes longer than it should, both of us silent, hovering behind pillars and plants as we wait for various party guests to clear. The path is finally empty when we dash for the gates. Margo with her shoes off, her feet silent on the excessively watered grass.

"Hey!" I hear. A voice. A man's voice. "There you are."

I turn and there he is: the SoGa who had his hand on Margo's leg. The same leg that I had my own hand on about three minutes ago. The closeness of these two events means that I can only think about punching him in the brain.

Margo turns, and he sees the shoes in her hands, the wild expression. In the flicker of a second, she attempts to smooth her face, back into the kittenish girl he was sitting with just moments ago. But it's too late. His eyes move quickly between me and Margo, to her bare feet, to the muslin cloth that is starting to unravel. Margo does not look like an elite Khaise woman, and I do not look like her servant.

This SoGa may be young, but he knows what deception looks like when he sees it. From the inside of his jacket pocket, he draws a gun.

"Don't move."

There we are, completely still. Frozen until he decides what to do with us. There's a horrifying moment of silence. It is impossible to parse how much of this boy's reaction is an officious response to Margo being a spy, or simply anger because he really thought they had something going.

Margo decides to risk it, and speak. "I'm sick," she says lamely. "I was feeling sick. I didn't want to bother you. I need to go home."

The SoGa grimaces and lifts his gun to us.

"Don't lie to me."

He sounds like a child scolding his own mother.

Suddenly, there's a blinding flash of light. Someone, somewhere has turned one of the garden spotlights right on the SoGa's eyes, shrouding Margo and me in darkness. He winces, covers his face.

"Run."

We bolt. Charging the two-foot distance to the gate, waiting the whole time to be shot in the back. Outside, the lace carriage is waiting for us. Empty, but equipped with two horses. I haven't driven a pony since I was eight years old and sitting on my father's lap, but I'll have to improvise. I get up in the driver's seat, take the reins, and go. There's no traffic on the way out, all the other drivers waiting patiently in the stables until the party ends.

All the same, these carriages are heavy. They don't move fast. I force the horses into a trot, but it's not enough. In moments, the SoGa could be on horseback, galloping along the wide road and blocking us off.

"Margo," I shout. "Can you ride?"

"Can I ride?"

"Horses. Can you ride horses?"

"Um . . ." There's a silence from the back, where Margo is being bounced around like a pebble in a boot. "Only in theory."

"Theory?"

"Books, you know?"

I peer into the dark, and manage to spot a narrow bridleway where we can pull the carriage in. We turn in, and I halt the horses behind a scraggly bush. "Quick," I say to Margo. "Take the lace covering off. The white will attract light. Ball it up and throw it in a ditch. I'll unhitch the horses. We can ride from here."

Margo slides out and starts untying the covering, feeling her way in the dark.

"Ride where? To Saffy's?"

"We can't go to Saffy's. They might follow us there."

"We have to go back," she says, panic in her voice. "Moon. We have to. The watch is there."

I have just narrowly avoided being shot. Margo has just told me the world is going to end. I don't know whether to kiss her or turn her upside down until the information falls out of her pockets.

The lace covering slips off. At least now we'll be less visible.

"Margo," I say, taking her bare shoulders in both hands. "Come on. You have to tell me. What happened? What did he tell you?"

"The watch. It does more than just break trains."

"What? What do you mean?"

"I'm not sure, exactly. But Semper knows about the new openings PACT has found, and they've decided they're going to seal the Northern worlds."

"So—what? They're going to rape the North for resources, and doom everyone who lives there?"

"And they're going to use the watch to do it. I don't know how exactly, but it's a big part of the plan. He was cagey about it. Honestly, I don't know how much he even knew."

My mind stutters on the information as my gaze returns to the terra-cotta palace on the hill. The spotlights are up now, no longer festive and scattered but roving, stalking the ground for criminals. The alarm has been raised. The party is over.

"Then we have to move."

thirty-seven

MARGO

They took just one horse. They left the other still hitched to the carriage and tied to a tree in the middle of the road, infuriatingly in the way of any SoGa who wished to follow them. It wouldn't stop them, but it might hold them up a few seconds. The morning was breaking already, or whatever counted as morning in a place like Khaise.

Margo couldn't ride, and so she found herself in front of Moon on the horse. No saddle, his arms tight around her as he held the reins. Here, then, was the "good with horses" Lunati stereotype she had heard so much about. Moon had never mentioned riding himself, in all the time they had known each other and discussed horses. But here he was, guiding a strange animal and charging it through the wild country that surrounded Khaise. He was good with horses.

He was good with her, too. Whispering into her ear, the wind too heavy for real conversation, simply murmuring things. *I'm here,* he said. His voice softer than she had ever known it. *I'm here. You're safe. It's OK.*

The blue slip rode up to her hip, and while she wasn't naked, she wasn't far off, either. His legs pressed against hers, her skin exposed to the wind. Moon kicked the horse on, and she felt all his leg muscles work, squeezing at the animal's soft belly. She was aware, on top of everything, that some women dreamed their whole lives about sitting on a horse with a man like this. Here Margo was, getting it, at seventeen, and at the end of the world.

I'm here. You're safe. It's OK.

It was not safe. She was not OK. She was the domino that could fall and end up closing the North. Every world estranged from one another, every link forgotten in a generation or two. And for a watch she had never even liked.

Suddenly, every bell in Khaise was ringing at once.

The day bell clanged often in Khaise, its presence necessary yet resented, but she had never heard them like this. They clanged on and on, not a brief reminder but a sickening chorus. They were weeping, nauseating, terrible. The alarm had been raised. Everyone in Khaise was awake now. Everyone knew something was wrong. Rumors would spread quickly.

They finally reached Saffy's, charging their stolen horse across the bridge, its hooves heavy on the wood. This poor animal that had only ever ferried rich people from one party to another. It was not made for late-night dashes across uneven, rocky land.

Saffy rushed out, her hands over her ears, the ceaseless tolling of the bells reverberating around the courtyard. They slipped off the horse's back in Saffy's yard, and Margo remembered the gun that was raised at her, just moments ago.

She did not matter in any of this. It was the watch only. The watch that needed protecting. They would murder her, Moon, Saffy, and the stolen horse if it meant getting to the watch. They wouldn't think twice.

"We need to get our stuff," Moon shouted across the din. "Saffy, can you hear me? We need to go to our room and we need to get our things and we need to leave. We're in danger now. OK?"

Saffy just nodded, taking the horse. "Go to your people's place," she said. "Go, no one find you there. I can bring food when things die down." With that, she slapped the horse hard on the rear, allowing it to bolt hard into the town.

Everything in their room was how they left it. Their briefcases neatly stacked in the corner, the famous watch stowed under the cork mattress. Margo slid it onto her wrist, the chain feeling heavier this time than ever before. Their salesman suits waiting for them.

It felt good to be back in proper clothes again. Margo left the silk dress on the bedroll. She hoped Saffy could repurpose it for something. They patted themselves down, checked that everything was where it should be, and fled the bathhouse on foot.

The bells still ringing. And ringing. And ringing.

She followed Moon, her mind hot with thought, barely registering the farmland or strange rough terrain that they trundled over.

He guided her over ditches and fences, his hand in hers.

They came to a large curved rock, and Moon's pace quickened, his grip on her hand frantic.

"Where *are* we?"

He laughed. Stood still for a second. "Look," he said softly. "Look at me."

Blue light, the same shade as the dress she had just discarded, shone down on his face in spattered freckles.

"What? What is this?"

He led her down a narrow stone path that gradually widened. All the while, the blue light became stronger, the rock turning to slick glass.

They were standing in a temple. A temple with a stone archway mounted upon a swiveling blue dial. There was no outside light except for a small, circular hole in the ceiling, blowing in the heavy Khaise air.

"It feels . . . holy," she said. "Like a church."

"This was how we got around," he said, his voice soft. "Before all the . . . stuff started."

He put his hand on a glowing blue panel.

"I always thought, you know, why did they bother? Why didn't they just do the same as other families, and stay where they were? Stay in one place, like regular people did. But *this* was the way of life they were protecting. It wasn't just because they liked traveling. This is our religion, you know?"

She had heard people speak, several times now, about the various conflicts that had led to the strained, difficult way of life they were forced to lead. Margo had assumed that the chief injustice in all of this was how time zones were hoarded: how people were forced to age faster, live harder, die younger. But that was only a very tiny part of it. She had gotten used to two- and six-hour days. But it was the erasure of things that broke people. It was Vesna, realizing she would never go home to Sopilka. It was Moon, knowing his tattoo might technically allow him the benefits of travel, but the true Lunati traveling life that was his birthright was lost forever.

But here they were. The spectrum of Moon's own identity was rushing to meet him, and he was felled by it. She knew he was an acquired taste, as a person. He was difficult, brooding, and frequently impatient with people. He was self-centered, sometimes, and neurotic. He always looked a little rumpled, regardless of what he was doing. But she had acquired him.

"How did it work?"

Moon pointed to the blue dial. "The disc beneath the portal door is movable." He indicated a series of stone handles that lined the side. "The ponies were hitched to the notches, and they would pull the disc around. See the markings?" Moon gestured to the engravings that bordered the edges. "It would work like a compass. North, northwest, west, southwest. You lined up the archway with the direction you wanted to go in." He looped his body through the archway, his hands on the pillars. He looked boyish all of a sudden. "You could go anywhere like this."

"No visas," Margo said.

"No visas," he agreed. "No tickets, no visas."

They were silent then, regarding each other on either side of the archway. The secrets were melting away now. There was just one left.

"Margo," he said. "Who *was* your dad? How did he end up with this watch?"

She shrugged. "He was . . . I think he was a salesman, honestly. He traveled my whole life. To different countries, in my world. It was mostly my mum and me, and she was kind of obsessed with him, but also . . . kind of afraid of him?"

She was surprised at herself for saying this. She had never said it before.

"He died, over two years ago, while he was away on one of these work trips. But he left the watch to me in his will, and that's all I've really had to remember him by." She laughed to herself. "I tried to pawn it once. That's weirdly how I ended up on the train. I tried to sell it so I could run away and start a new life." She looked around. "Which I guess I did."

"Yeah," he said. "I guess you did."

He stepped toward her, his arms clinging to the highest point of the archway. His hair shagged over his eyes, and suddenly he seemed so much bigger than her. He had never seemed so big before. She suppressed the urge to kiss him. This was a holy place. She would never have kissed someone in a mosque, and she wouldn't kiss them here, either.

They simply stood there, suspended in the moment. However fast time in Khaise moved, the world seemed to slow down just for this.

But it could not stay slow for long. The hole in the ceiling suddenly shone with brilliant white light. Night was here again. A whole day had passed in escaping the party. The moon cut a strip across the middle of the room, illuminating the salesman until he shone. Mo let go of the archway. A new persona seemed to envelop him, neither the stern salesman nor the freak she had come to love. He was something else now. Serious.

"It's the full moon," he said, taking off his jacket quickly. He started prizing at the top buttons of his shirt. "Help me get my gari off."

"Your beads?"

"Yes. Hurry, if you can. We'll only have a moment to do this."

The room was flooded with moonlight now, the silver beads shining blue under her fingertips as she unpicked the clasp. The skin on his neck so bright it almost blinded her. The chain slid off in her hands.

"Welcome to your first Wash," he said. He shook the gari from its chain, and each silver bead came away into his palm. Moon knelt in the strip of white light and placed each bead before him, lining them up like a child lines up his most precious treasures. Starting left to right, each bead was put into a pair. Moon murmured prayers as he went, all in a language she could not understand. Within the minute, there were fifteen sets of two arranged in a semicircle around him.

The moon that had been so focused on the salesman now split its attention among the fifteen pairs of beads. Margo watched the long shaft of light separate into individual panels. It was like the light was a maypole, and each bead had taken a ribbon.

Margo didn't quite know what to do with herself. She understood she was in a quiet, holy place. She knew she was watching someone engage in a private thing. She wanted to be invisible, to melt into the walls, to observe him as though she wasn't really there at all. Because the truth was, she was fascinated. She had been fascinated by this process, this gift of making your own silver, since the moment he had told her about it. Now she was afraid that her very presence in the Lunati temple was rupturing the ritual, spoiling it somehow.

A small pile of silver seeds plinked before him like rain, and he did not look up to see them fall. They were blue too. The fresh silver supercharged by moonlight. Margo fell back against the wall.

He was all change now. A stillness came over him. He was motionless, like his brain and heart and soul had gone to some other place, someplace where she could not follow. She was jealous, then. An hour ago she was pressed up against the walls of a women's changing room, his body hard against hers, and she was sure that he belonged to her completely. But no, he would always belong more, much more, to this other thing. This bigger thing. She was jealous of the thing for having Moon, and jealous of Moon for having the thing.

She slumped against the temple walls. Feeling too impure, too muddy. Why was she here? Why was this allowed? The heavy watch, the source of all this drama, jingled against the smooth blue glass. She fiddled with it, careful not to mess with the third hand, and noticed something.

The watch was blue.

Blue as the new-minted silver, falling like raindrops on the dais. Glowing.

Her father's watch, she realized, was made of Lunati silver.

thirty-eight

MOON

Last month, in New Davia, the silver Wash produced eight seeds. My lowest yield ever. The month before, it was nine. The month before, ten. I log every yield carefully. Everything goes in the notebook. Spikes in growth annotated carefully, theories jotted down, outside factors noted. Nothing could prepare me for this, though.

Thirty seeds.

Thirty solid silver seeds.

I blink. *How can I have thirty fucking silver seeds in front of me?*

I touch them, expecting it all to be a trick of the light. But no, here they are. Real. New.

"It's not like this," I splutter to Margo. "It's not usually like this. Not at all."

"So many?"

"So *many.*" I bless each of them, before gathering them into my pockets. "Maybe because I've never done a Wash in a temple before. I don't know. It must be stronger here."

Margo is shaken by all of this. I suddenly realize how strange this must be to her, this quaint little ritual that somehow results in thirty pieces of silver before us.

"Maybe it's stronger because you're here," I offer.

"But I'm not Lunati."

"Yeah, but . . . you're honorary, I guess." You can marry in, I remember. You wouldn't be genetically Lunati, but if your kids have one Lunati parent, they will be. You wouldn't get excluded or anything. At least, you wouldn't be excluded if there was anything left to be excluded from. I have a sudden image of Margo as a Lunati woman, back when that meant something. What if it could mean something again?

"Is Lunati silver like all silver?"

"Huh? No. That's why it's so hard to sell. People can tell. The light."

"Would all silver shine blue in here, though?"

"What are you talking about?"

Margo lifts her wrist. The watch is glowing blue, as though just cut from the moon.

"Why is it doing that?"

A strange nausea comes over me. People with skipshock are supposed to avoid surprises. It's why so many salesmen have such a don't-give-a-shit demeanor. We can't handle it.

The watch keeps glowing blue, and for some reason the shine is louder than every bell tolling at once.

"Why is it doing *that*?" I repeat.

A watch would not do that unless it was made of Lunati silver. But why does Margo own a watch—a highly sought after, war-making watch—that is made of Lunati silver?

"I don't know. I don't know why it's doing that. Does all silver do this?"

"No." And to prove it, I reach into my suit jacket and pull out Aska's pocket watch. The one I've been carrying since Alder and somehow didn't give to Sonne in the panic.. It remains dull gray in the darkness with no light to bounce off it.

"Margo, why did your dad have a Lunati watch?"

"I'm telling you. I don't *know*."

"Was he Lunati? Was your dad Lunati?"

"No. He wasn't."

Of course he wasn't. If her dad was Lunati, then Margo would be, too. You would see it.

"Are you saying it's a stolen watch, then?"

She steps away from me. "My dad wasn't a thief, Moon. He was a businessman. And he's dead."

"Why have you been so fucking secretive about him if he's this innocent businessman, then?"

Why am I swearing at her? Is this even fair? It feels fair. Margo has been carrying around something that was made by Lunati. Something powerful. Something important.

"Just because it's made with Lunati silver doesn't mean he stole it. He could have bought it. You sell Lunati silver all the time. It's how you first made your living, isn't it?"

I take her wrist and turn it over. The glass watch face has turned to match the silky blue glass of the temple.

"You think he *bought* something like this?"

"Maybe! I don't know."

"I feel like there's something you're not telling me."

"Moon, there's nothing I'm not telling you. What could there *be*?"

I'm upsetting her now. I try to calm myself down, to keep the panic out of my chest, but it won't go away. Why does she have this? And who does it belong to?

"It's been in the family a long time," she says. "I don't know what you want me to say."

She massages her temples, as if trying to figure out how best to manage me. "Listen. Calm down. Nothing has changed."

"It kind of has, Margo. It kind of fucking has."

Suddenly, I can see my parents' bodies, their arms carved, their garis torn off. The children at the reform school, their garis carefully snipped off with bolt cutters before graduating.

"Here's what hasn't changed, Mo. We're still partners. We're still in danger. We still have the watch, this thing the SoGa are willing to go to war over. You can't decide I'm the enemy now. We're the only thing we have."

She's right. Of course she's right. But my brain won't settle on the notion, can't stop thinking about how Margo's father came to own a Lunati watch.

"I need a minute," I say at last. "I'm going to take a walk."

"You can't just *take a walk*," she snaps. "We're on the run, remember?"

An hour ago, all either of us wanted was to be alone together. Now we're dying for space, claustrophobic in this tiny temple. We stare at each other, all hurt and fury. Both confused as to how this happened and how we can't seem to go back.

"Here," she says, unclasping the watch. "Here. Take this. Throw it into a volcano, for all I care. I don't want it, Moon. I never wanted it. I don't know how it came to my father, but it's yours. If you think it's a Lunati watch—and I think you're probably right—then. Well. Take it."

She places the watch in my hands. I've held the thing a dozen times, but not like this.

The last thing I held that felt this significant was Margo.

"I'm sorry."

But the damage is already done. We've had arguments before, but it's never felt like this. I've accused her dead parent of stealing from my dead parents. It's hard to come back from that.

"I can't take this," I say, although—can I? Is it actually mine? Or not mine, but you know.

"Well, hold on to it." As the cool silver touches my skin, I can feel the rage start to ebb away. It's not Margo's fault. None of this is. Not what happened to the Lunati, not my parents, not the stolen gari, nothing.

"I'm sorry. Look. Margo. I'm being an idiot. Take it."

I try to hand back the watch.

"No," she says firmly. Those big eyes again. "I want you to have it, Mo. I'm serious."

And to prove she really is serious, she closes her hand firmly around mine. Her hand on top, the watch, and then me.

Behind us, the portal suddenly shimmers to life. The atmosphere beneath the arch begins to move and sway, the air marbling before us. We watch it, mouths open. It swirls, then finds its own momentum. Drawing out the blue from the temple stones, looking more and more like a splash of violet oil traveling across water.

Margo is the first one to speak.

"If this watch can close pathways," she says, fixing her sharp green eyes on my face, "it can open them, too."

There is nothing left now but to walk through it.

"I must have done this all the time, as a really little kid," I say. "Using the portals like this. But I don't remember at all."

And I don't. Maybe my mother carried me through. Maybe I was old enough to walk, by the time the trails were finally closed. Whatever memory should exist is missing.

Margo laces her free hand through mine, and I realize I'm shaking.

"Together?" she says.

"Together."

We step through. And in a rush of heat and dizziness, the caravan trails are open again.

thirty-nine

MARGO

The room they stepped into was almost identical to the Khaise temple they had just left. The circular stone space glowed with blue light, the circle beneath them complete with granite etchings. For a moment, they wondered whether they had imagined the shimmering formation of water and light that swirled underneath the proscenium archway. Had they walked through nothing? Had they traveled nowhere?

But the sky told a different story. The Khaise temple was ensconced within a bouldered cave. Here, they were outside.

They looked at the sky as though it were the roof of a painted chapel. Their eyes open, their arms held aloft like children. The stars were somehow closer than they had ever been.

When their eyes finally met, they started to laugh. Then they couldn't stop. They had *won,* somehow. Everything was against them winning, and yet, here they were. They had found a way to travel. Their papers would not be flagged by the Pigs; not reported to the Southern Guard. They could go on evading the SoGa forever, if they wanted.

They hugged each other tightly, still laughing, each staring at the sky over the other person's shoulder.

"We did it," she said. "We actually *did* it."

She knew that Moon had felt victories in his life, but none like this. His successes were focused mainly on quick sales, good deals, and new products. He had no emotional dictionary for this kind of jubilation. And so his mind turned, quickly, to a kind of awed panic.

"*How?*" he kept on saying. "When they closed them down, it was . . . it was supposed to be forever, Margo. Not even my parents dreamed of them opening again. When something is closed, it's *closed*."

"Or not," she said, lifting up the watch. "Be *happy*, Moon. It's OK to be happy."

He looked back at the archway. It was still swirling with color. She slid the watch onto his wrist, fastening it. She felt strangely calm about the idea of leaving it with him, possibly forever. It suited him so well.

"Margo . . ."

"It was always yours," she replied. "I was always meant to just hold on to it. Until it found you."

Moon took her face in his hands and kissed her, very gently, on the forehead.

"Why isn't it closing?" he suddenly asked. "It's only supposed to be open for a few moments. I mean, that's what happened with the train tracks, right?"

They stared at the portal. If anything, it was gathering more color and fluid, like a thick puddle of oil paint. The button, which had popped back up within seconds of being pushed the first time they used it, was now sticking in place.

"Your father, Margo . . ." he started. "Is there any chance he was . . . Well. Like *me*?"

"Lunati?" She thought about it. It was such a strange thing to consider, like asking if her father was really Batman. "I mean. He traveled a lot. But he didn't have your glow, or anything. He was just, you know, an ordinary brown-haired white guy."

She tried to pin down her father in her memories. It was getting harder and harder, the more things that happened between his life and now.

"He could have used axiom, or something. Or he could have had different coloring than me. This is Lunati magic, Margo, I'm sure of it."

Just as Moon instinctively knew that they had discovered the caravan trails, Margo knew that her father was not part of an ancient race of nomadic people who charmed silver and kept ponies. She had a queasy sense that however Richard Madden had come to possess a Lunati watch, it wouldn't have been through being Lunati himself. He had been a certain kind of man, with a certain way. "Your father is conservative" is how her mother had put it, whenever Margo was frustrated. "He likes things how he likes them."

And he did. He liked his house quiet, his tea black, and his daughter well-behaved. She could think of nothing that might link him to the Lunati, which must mean that his possession of the watch was a kind of theft.

"We need to get back to Vesna," Margo said. "She needs to know this is here. If there's going to be some kind of mass sealing, we need to get people out, Mo. And quick."

He laughed. "This was one of the reasons they closed the trails in the first place, you know. Illegally transporting refugees. But you're right. We need to get back to Vesna. So we need to figure out where the hell we actually are."

They both had to pull on the notches to get the platform to move. It was not easy. The dial hadn't been used in almost fifteen years, and it was so stiff that Moon had to open his briefcase to see if he had anything in there that could help. In the end, they just had to pull.

Eventually, the platform started to grind and move. They had to stop every few paces, their muscles screaming as they pushed their entire weight into moving the heavy stone. But they did it. They moved it northwest, eventually. They'd found a way of getting to New Davia without leaving a paper trail.

"Yaz," Moon panted. "Yaz can get us horses. And it wouldn't just be for Lunati people—god knows there aren't many of them left—but it would be, you know, for anyone who needed to travel. It would have to be secret, obviously. We just need to make sure they don't get ahold of the watch, and we're fine. They can get one of us, but they can't get us all."

Margo's limbs were on fire as her mind jumped from future to past. This would undoubtedly make an enormous difference to PACT, and to the freedom of everyone in the North. But it didn't change the central mystery: Just how had her father, Richard Madden, ended up with a watch like this?

"And we'll be able to find your world. The sealed world. We can find it through the caravan trails. I'm sure we can. Your father must have used some kind of corridor between our worlds and yours."

Margo was silent a moment.

"We don't know anything about what my father did."

They stepped through the portal again and found themselves in another temple. This one was marble, with a slight chill in the air. Moon took out his train map and a pencil, trying to plot which world they were now in.

"What do you see, Margo? Anything you might call a defining feature?"

"Uh . . . a couple of sheep skulls."

"Delvan," he replied, triumphant. "An agricultural world with near-constant rainfall! That's from the salesman test, Margo, I had to memorize it. We're doing it. We're actually *traveling*."

They went through the portal again. And again. Each time, Moon spoke about the years he had spent scraping gens together to afford train tickets. The endless, grinding poverty. The bone-deep exhaustion from relentless skipshock. *This is how it should be,* he kept saying. This was how it was meant to be.

They arrived in New Davia.

They emerged on the coast, not far from the tunnel networks. She could smell the ocean from the temple chamber, an underground portal that felt like the inside of a sarcophagus. It was completely dark. Their hands groped at the glowing blue panels, and they felt their way to a doorway covered by layered slates.

"Should I close the portal?" he asked. They each regarded the blur of oily light.

"It's your watch now," she replied. "Seriously, Moon, this watch clearly belongs to your people. However my family ended up with it . . . I'm sorry, OK? I'm really sorry."

She broke off then, and started pulling out slabs of stone carefully from the doorway. Specks of daylight began to shine into the chamber. Slowly, the New Davian coast began to reveal itself.

The ocean was roaring, waves rising high, pushing the deadly cold to the city. It cut through them both. They hugged their clothes to their bodies, their faces and fingers numb.

"Remember when we first did this walk?" Moon suddenly asked.

Of course she did. She had been picked up by the throat. She didn't want to think about it.

"You know," she said. "I used to live a twenty-four-hour day, in a seven-day week, in a three-hundred-and-sixty-five-day year. I had a breakfast and a lunch and a dinner. I slept for eight hours every night, and longer on weekends. And . . . I was unhappy, Moon. I was miserable. I used to wait for the day to end so that eventually enough days would pile up and I would be old enough to leave home forever. I hated my hometown. And everyone would tell me, every day, that it was just a phase, and it would pass. But every time a phase passed, I would just find myself in another even worse phase."

She kicked the ground, stones scraping her feet.

"But now I live here. And I don't sleep enough and I don't have regular meals. I have less of the things that are supposed to keep a person alive and yet I feel more alive than I ever have. And I don't know what to do with that, really, Moon, because someday we're going to find a portal back into my world, and it will all return to how it was. And how am I supposed to do that? Knowing what I know now? The way things really work, the way things *really* are?"

He looked at her. "What are you saying?"

"I don't know. I don't know what I'm saying. Except that I meant what I said before. It's you and me, Mo. We're a two-man operation, indefinitely, as far as I'm concerned. Where you go, I go."

She knew what she was giving up. Years of her life, potentially. But did it matter? Years and the number of them meant nothing. She thought of her life before the train, the life before New Davia, the life before him. She would turn her back on it forever, if that's what it took to be with him. To keep living this life, where she felt alive and relevant.

Vesna's house came into view. Glowing red, the white spirals even more brilliant against the murky gray sky. He slid his frozen hand into hers.

"Will you go in with me?"

"Yeah," she replied. "I'll go in with you."

PART FOUR

HOME

When we get to the boardinghouse, Vesna and Ani are in the kitchen. I know the ticking of Vesna's house well enough to know that Ani will have just gotten here to start prepping dinner. They're both standing at the counter. Vesna at her ledger, Ani carving up vegetables.

"Margo," Ani says right off the bat. "You're still here."

I had forgotten, in all the machinations of our travels, that the original plan was to send Margo home.

Vesna comes toward us and hugs us both, squeezing us to check that we're healthy, looking squarely into our faces in her officious landlady way.

"Do you need food?" are the first words out of her mouth. She does not wait for an answer, but starts a volley of more important questions. "We were so *worried.* What happened? I mean—when we heard about the tracks in Aldercarr, I knew you'd be stranded for a while, but I was going out of my *mind,* Mo. Was Margo OK with Heck's papers? Did you get in any trouble? Where did you stay? Were you at a boardinghouse? Do you want ham?"

She starts carving a joint of smoked ham, her brows knit in anxiety, her questions relentless. I try to answer, but she just keeps talking.

"I said to Ani, a boardinghouse in Alder, that will bankrupt them.

Even if Moon sells everything he has. And poor Margo, she's been away from home so long; Margo, are *you* OK? You look different."

Vesna's gaze falls on Margo again. On our hands together. She seems to be thinking thirty things at once.

"Ves," I say softly. "Can you give me a second to at least *answer* any of these?"

Vesna nods silently, and in that silence, I see her eyes fill with tears.

"Oh, Ves," I say, letting go of Margo and holding her in both arms. "Come on, now, I've been gone longer than this . . ."

"I was so *worried*. I thought you two were dead." Then a stillness. "Where's Taiyo?"

We are then forced to tell her the story. Of Taiyo, the Seven Bears, the way he cradled Aska's body, the bomb thrown in by Halvpas. The image of Halvpas in the fish alley, waiting for his troops to die, visits me again. His cruelty, his callousness, the depth of which is almost certainly boundless.

Vesna inhales sharply, as though I have stabbed her beneath the ribs. She sits down. How long, in New Davian time, since she had taken Heck out of his room to be buried?

"I suppose," she says, her voice heavy and choked, "it's the kind of death that someone like him dreamed of. In the middle of everything."

She is trying her best to be leaden and ironic, because the only other option is bottomless tears. And she doesn't have time for tears. After the dinner service, maybe. When she's alone.

"Out with a blaze of glory," I say.

"Taiyo doesn't need a blaze of glory," Vesna replies, and then she hides her eyes from us.

I bend over her chair, taking her shoulders in both arms. Her face falls into the crook of my elbow, my shirtsleeves growing damp.

Ani takes over on the ham and carves off some thick pieces for me and Margo. Vesna quickly straightens up, wipes her face on her sleeve, and looks at me.

"How did you get back?"

And so we tell them. We tell them about Alder and Khaise, and the party. The realization that the watch, while temporarily effective on interworld train tracks, seemed tailor-made to suit the Lunati portals that have been empty and vacant for so long.

Vesna starts to pace the room, her voice trembling. "You're telling me you walked *through* those portals?"

"I've seen the old caravan portal by the sea," Ani says in wonder. "It's just a stone archway."

"I'm telling you," I say slowly, deliberately, still savoring the miracle of this. "We bounced through four or five worlds and got here in less than an hour. That's from Khaise, Ves. All the way east."

"With no paper trail," Margo adds. "No SoGa on our tail, no way of them telling where we are."

The room falls quiet, the miracle of this discovery washing over them.

"So people will finally be able to get home," Vesna says finally. "On . . . on sealed worlds?"

"I don't see why not." I squeeze her shoulder. "You can go back to Sopilka, Ves."

"You could lead an army this way," Ani says. "You could attack the SoGa, smuggle weapons to rebel armies. This is guerrilla warfare. Getting them before they can get us."

I raise my eyebrow.

"I thought you weren't in the revolutionary business, Ani?"

"I'm not," she says. "I'm just saying."

I start to really consider what this supposed war might look like, if the North could move and mobilize. Northern worlds might be poor, but there are more of them. The few revolutions that have popped up over the years have been quickly quashed largely because rebel factions could not communicate with one another, by virtue of so few people being able to travel.

"People could actually unite," Margo says. "People in different worlds could come together *against* the Southern Guard."

Vesna nods. "Filter people through the basement caves, and then send them wherever the SoGa are currently terrorizing."

Suddenly, maps are out, doors are bolted, and between bites of smoked ham, Margo and I are asked to explain again and again how the watch works.

"The worlds with the strongest rebel armies," Vesna says, now stabbing a train map with toothpicks, "are Aldercarr and Bostow."

I wince. "Maybe not Alder, anymore. I'm not sure who's left."

"There's got to be some. You said twenty people might have died in that blast. Including . . . including Taiyo." She pauses briefly, shifting her body to carry this new pain. "But. There's hundreds of them. We assemble a few more of our side together. We take them to Alder, we meet the leaders of their PACT branch. Whoever has taken over from Dimi. And then—working *together*, Moon—we coordinate an attack on one of the Southern headquarters. Somewhere near the border, where the time speed is starting to get a little hasty, which is never where they send their top guys. We take a Southern world. Then we spread out from there, influence the worlds just north of the border, get some diplomacy going—some of them will be loyal to the South, but not as many as you think—and from there, Semper falls."

"Semper falls," Ani repeats drily. "Just a hop, skip, and a jump, and we're a liberated people by next week."

"All right." Ves puts a hand up. "All right, this is just me brainstorming. And sure, it will all take months. Years. But it can afford to take that long. It's that important. And we have *this* now." She holds up my arm, the candlelight catching on the silver. "If we can travel, that means we can mobilize, and if we can do that, we can do anything."

It's hard not to feel swept up by her energy. Ani, Margo, and I all look at one another. She's speaking in broad strokes, but it's easy to see how it might all work. Especially if the rebel armies in other worlds are as strong as she believes they are.

"That's if Semper doesn't seal off the entire North first."

"Well they can't unless they have the watch, can they?" Vesna puzzles it out. "They're still hunting it. They would have sealed us off already if they really could."

The watch. Its glass face is still looking up at me, quietly humming with potential. The watch made of Lunati silver, that Semper somehow crammed the power of worlds into. Margo laces her fingers through mine as I examine my own wrist, her fingers small and slender.

"I'm guessing," Vesna says slyly, looking over us both, "that you're not joining the other salesmen for dinner?"

And we agree that we will not be.

forty-one

MARGO

When Margo had worked at the boardinghouse, Moon's room was the only one she had never cleaned. This was a fact universally understood throughout the house, that Vesna only ever dropped off linens at his door, and that he kept the cellar room clean all by himself. Margo could never figure out whether this counted as an insult or special treatment.

Now that she was inside, she saw that it definitely counted as special treatment. Certainly, the room was damp, and got almost no sunlight from being belowground. But it had its own fireplace, its own entry, and its own working tap. None of the other rooms had this.

"Why *do* you always get the cellar room?" Margo asked once they were inside. She felt awkward all of a sudden, full of chatter and questions, picking up objects and setting them down.

"I think I met Ves during a very particular time," he replied. He was crouched at the fireplace—and began sparking at kindling. He was nervous, too, she realized. He couldn't get a match lit. "She worked here after she left Sopilka, and then she inherited it from the old lady who owned it. Ves was so excited, owning her own business. She couldn't wait to send for her sisters, her mother. Then they sealed Sopilka. She needed family."

"And that was you?"

"In a way. I was cut off from Lunati; she was cut off from Sopilka. We both felt like members of a club that was dying. I think she understood that I needed a place that felt stable, like home. I've always been grateful."

He finally got the fire going. Margo sat on the floor next to him, holding out her hands against the flames. They were still crackling and spitting, chewing through kindling like teething babies.

"And so you were just friends?"

She couldn't help it. She was jealous of the story. Jealous that Vesna had known him longer, jealous that any other girl could know anything about him.

He smiled at her, the fire in his eyes. "We were mostly just friends."

"Oh, come on! Are you serious? Did you guys sleep together?"

"No comment."

She was furious with herself for asking, and furious with him for completely harmless sins committed long before he had met her. "How many times?"

He scratched his head. "Look, you're getting the wrong impression."

"What impression is that?"

"That I'm a serial seducer of my friends, or that you're one in a long line of women who I've connected with over our terrible lives."

"Back home we have a term for that. It's called trauma bonding."

"Wow." He paused. "You know, all this time I've imagined that your world was idyllic, but it must be pretty bad if you have a term just for that."

"Yeah. We have terms for a lot of shitty things." She shook her head, annoyed that he was steering her from the point. "How many times?"

Why was she being such a little bitch about this? Vesna was her friend, after all, and there was clearly nothing between them now, if there ever had been.

"Twice. Once when we were drunk, and once again as a sort of experiment, to see if there was anything there."

"And was there?"

"No."

The room was starting to warm up now. The flames in the grate were flickering to themselves reliably, a black space of heat growing between the wood and the fire.

"Are you actually annoyed about this?" he asked. Clearly, this was not how either of them thought their first moments alone together would go. They had escaped the Southern Guard, Captain Halvpas, a citywide lockdown, and a bloody battle. Were they really going to fall out over two isolated experiences, shared several years ago?

"No." She thought about it. Pondered what she was really anxious about. "When I told you that I would stay with you, no matter what," she said timidly, "you said nothing."

"Because I'm a Lunati salesman with a Northern visa, Margo. I've got advancing skipshock and bad habits. You really want to spend the rest of your life trailing around with me, selling axiom to idiots, a few good memories and then be dead at forty?"

Margo shrugged. "You're forgetting that we're going to save the world. Worlds."

"Oh yes. Saving the worlds. I had forgotten all about that."

The heat of the fire, already burning her shoulders, finally pushed her forward. She took off her suit jacket, then was struck with an idea that tingled her blood. They sat across from each other, both cross-legged on the rug. Two salesmen, hashing it out.

"You know," she said, slowly unbuttoning her shirt, "I never did see my bra again, after that first day at Saffy's. It was one of the only things I had from my world. I've had to learn to live without it."

His expression did not change. It was that old salesman's approach of not tipping his hand. Of not showing how badly he wanted something, or how afraid he was that it might go away.

Margo was very interested in the limits of this. She slid the shirt off and let it lie on the floor. She held his gaze, daring him to respond. He understood the game completely. Moon studied her but wouldn't let his face flicker.

She felt so resolutely female, so confident in her ability to capture him. There was a girlish part of her that might have worried how he felt about her body; but the stronger, louder, woman part knew he was helpless. Doomed, really.

But Moon had been in sales so long that it always took him time to accept the terms of a good bargain. There was always something wrong. Some hole in the deal.

You had to convince a person like Moon that you weren't out to make a deal at all. That what you had, you were willing to give for free.

She swiveled around so her back faced him, then lowered herself backward. Once again, they were looking at each other upside down. The day of the haircut, the night of her tattoo. The Seven Bears. She leaned into the cradle of his crossed legs, and took his hands. Margo kissed both his knuckles, then slid them down her body, and under her waistband.

There was a shivering gasp then, the feeling of warm thumbs against tender places. Her body felt like new territory, with wilds and frontiers that she had not thought to imagine.

"You know," he murmured, stroking the soft skin of her belly, "the first time I saw you, I thought you were on drugs."

"And now?"

"Now I'm sure you are."

She laughed, and as she did his silver gaze changed again. She turned up her face to meet his.

Finally, he kissed her.

It was difficult to tell whether Lunati kisses were fundamentally different from the kisses of ordinary people, but Margo felt as though the raw silver in Moon's bloodstream was now ticking through hers. Like his lips were sending light to the farthest corners of her body, from the tips of her fingers to her toes.

Or perhaps that's how it felt, regardless of whether a person was Lunati or not. Maybe that was just what being in love felt like.

She sat astride him, a knee on each side of his hips, her mouth lost on his. The fire began to whimper and die, a dog they were too distracted to feed.

"Lev," she whispered. "Take me to bed."

So he did. Her body laid out on the boardinghouse sheets, her lips raw. He loomed above her, the gari beads lightly touching her neck as he kissed her.

He tried to be a gentleman. She did not make it easy.

"We can wait," he murmured. As if they were not naked already. As if she could not already feel him against her. "We have time."

"Respectfully," she said. "We don't."

She drew him into her. And with all the countless worlds that Margo was expected to help save, she knew this was the only one she would really risk her life to defend. The world of him and her. They were a subculture and a population. The were the census and the forwarding address. They were lovers, and then they were asleep.

For the first time in their relationship, Margo woke first.

There was so little light in the room that she couldn't tell what time of day it was. But she was conscious, suddenly, of the sticky feeling between her legs.

She was on her period again. The Khaise cycle had been so short that her body had once again become confused by the time change. She should be glad, because it would at least limit the possibility of her being pregnant, but it wasn't ideal all the same.

Margo shifted her body, checking underneath herself for stains. Feeling her movement, Moon reached for her waist, pulling her close, as if this were one of a million mornings where they did this. And it was, she realized. Or it was about to be.

He kissed her without even opening his eyes.

"Shh," he said, his lips pressing on the warm skin of her chest. "Sleep."

But all she could think about was stains.

She dressed and got out of bed. "I need to get something," she whispered.

"Hey," he said, sitting up. He was suddenly worried, his voice clear of morning haze. "You're coming back, right?"

She grinned, leaning over the bed frame to kiss him. "With food."

She was out the door before she realized that she had put on his clothes by mistake. There was something undeniably sexy about having two sets of clothes that were identical. She wore her boyfriend's clothes, and her boyfriend wore hers.

It was an unusually bright day in New Davia, the sun shimmering a reflective glare on the pale snow. Margo shielded her eyes as she walked around the house, her footsteps crunching, as she hoped that the kitchen door was open. There was a chance that no one was awake yet, and she could ask Vesna what solutions New Davia had for periods.

Through the screen door, Margo could see Vesna's reflection in the mirror she kept above the countertop. The mirror she had spotted Margo in on the very first day when Moon brought her to the boardinghouse.

As she came closer, she saw that Vesna looked different. At first, she thought it was because the sun was hitting the mirror strangely, and the glare was shedding a strange purple light on her.

But no. The closer she came, the more she realized that this was Vesna's face.

And that Vesna had a black eye.

She was making something, some kind of drink, and her left eye was destroyed. This woman, six foot tall and the color of bricks, was bleeding out of her lip. Vesna. Their Vesna. Their refugee landlady from a long-closed world. Someone had beaten her, and beaten her hard.

The eye that was still open raised slightly, observed Margo, and carried on with what she was doing. Margo stood in the snow and watched Vesna quickly lean forward and trace her finger on the mirror.

ИUЯ

Margo turned and fled.

She ran aimlessly, knowing she needed a plan. She could run toward the woods, and lose whoever was after them, but knew she would only get lost herself. She could veer toward the road and find the market. But what about Moon? Would they get him, too?

Perhaps if she had been more sure about where she was going, had a clearer direction of travel, they would not have caught her so quickly. It's hard to say. She was not a particularly strong runner in the first place.

A shot rang out, startling birds and shaking the frost-covered trees. She kept running, the thick snow slowing her down. Every step was like the heavy struggle of running in a dream. A second shot came, and suddenly she was face down in the freezing snow. She tried to get up but realized, with a small measure of pain, that the bullet had penetrated her leg.

Like all normal people, Margo had often wondered what it would feel like to be shot. She thought about the pain, the blood. But this felt like nothing; like not having a left leg. Maybe this is what people talked about when they described their body going into shock. She pulled herself forward, her hands finding the frozen rocks, knowing already that it was useless. That whoever wanted her, had her.

She heard footsteps coming toward her. Heavy, masculine. She didn't even turn to see who it was. She knew. He had been tracking her since her first day on the train, and would have tracked her until he died, if that's what it took.

"Miss Madden," he said evenly. "Would you like some assistance in turning around?"

Margo pressed her hands to the snow, like she was doing a push-up, and managed to slowly flip her body around. She was lying in the snow, looking up at the man who shot her.

It was Captain Halvpas, in all his perpetual youth and terrifying seniority, aiming a rifle at her head. Halvpas, the one who had pinned her to the wall on her first morning in New Davia.

"Thank you," he said. "Now: the watch."

She could put up a fight, and he could shoot her in the head and take it. Or she could give it willingly, pleasingly, and perhaps be left alone. There was always a chance.

Margo reached for the familiar weight in Moon's jacket pocket, and immediately felt the click of the trigger.

“Easy,” he said sternly. “Tell me which pocket.”

She thought quickly. “Left pants.”

Halvpas knelt down. There was no one behind him. Maybe they were in the house, or perhaps he had even come alone. He dug into her clothing and Margo seized her moment. She clasped one of the frozen rocks and aimed for Halvpas’s skull. He weaved, and she got his neck. He reeled, and she grabbed his rifle by the butt, wrestling it off him in his split second of weakness.

Margo fired immediately. Taking even a second to think would cost her too much time, and she just needed a bout of fire and violence to put distance between herself and Captain Halvpas. The shot went directly into the snow, but was loud and close enough to his ear that he instinctively covered his face.

Margo stumbled, her hand and shoulder trembling from the recoil. She could not stand with her leg, but she could prop herself on one knee, as if she were proposing marriage.

And so: here she was. Once again pointing a gun at a man’s head.

She cocked the rifle, determined not to get it wrong this time. She was about to kill a man, and she knew that she would never regret it. She would not look away this time. This was simply a thing that needed to be done.

“Hold on there, gunslinger” came a man’s voice.

Margo looked around her. There were four members of the orange-clad Southern Guard surrounding her. One, she realized, who must have been in the woods already, and possibly waiting for a chase like this one.

And every one of them had a gun trained on her.

“Drop it,” said one of the other men.

Halvpas looked up at her, a familiar timepiece resting in his hands.

"Drop it, Margo," he said. "We have the watch now, so rest assured, we *will* kill you."

She didn't drop the gun. "You'll kill me anyway," she said. "Why not have one less Captain Halvpas in the world?"

She meant it. She would go down in a blaze of gunfire, if that's what fate had in store for her.

"Because," he said, "we'd rather not kill you, Margo, if we can help it."

"And why is that?"

Halvpas smiled.

"Because of your father," he said. "He's very much looking forward to seeing you."

In her half second of desperate shock, Halvpas seized the gun's muzzle. He then forced the butt of it, battering-ram style, straight into her forehead.

She was immediately knocked unconscious. Her wounds were dressed quickly and quietly in the snow.

I must fall back asleep while I'm waiting for Margo, because I have one of those dreams that feels too much like real life.

In it, we're in a thunderstorm. I'm holding her under the shelter of a curved rock. She's talking, but the sky is grumbling too much to hear a thing she's saying. Then the lightning hits.

It's all so loud that I wake up, briefly. Then I turn over the pillow, curl the blanket around myself, and drift off again.

forty-three
MARGO

When Margo woke up, she was strapped to a chair in a beautiful room. She was not at Vesna's. She could see snow out the window, so she figured she must still be in New Davia. The landscape started to move.

She was on a train.

Nobody had ever mentioned the existence of a first-class train car. It was essentially a small, incredibly well-appointed studio apartment. There were two chairs and a tea table set up by a roaring grate, shielded with an ornate woven fire screen. There was a formal dining area—again, set up for two—dressed with thick white linen cloths and heavy silverware. There was a little shelf of books, their spines all gold-embossed and strangely blurry to her. Her vision collided with itself as she tried to take in her new surroundings, her right and left eyes tripping on each other.

The inside of her mouth had turned to cotton and the heat of the fire made her lips feel cracked. She reached for the tea tray and only burned her hand on the side of the boiling silver pot. She had been drugged at some point while unconscious in the snow. Pasadol perhaps, or some cheap imitation of Saffy's pleasant potions.

"Let me get that for you," Halvpas said, pouring a short cup and then wedging it firmly in her hands. He guided it toward her face and she drank, too druggy to realize it was probably more drugs.

He sat in the chair opposite her. It felt unnatural for such a big and dangerous person to be with her in such a small and ornate space. It was like being forced to play backgammon with a deadly animal. She tried to fix him with a resentful glare, but she only looked sloppy and unfocused. He did not look much older than her or Moon, but in the South that didn't tell you anything.

The train started to move.

"How old are you anyway?" she asked, slurring her words. "Twenty-six?"

He didn't answer, but looked somewhat offended by the guess. "You should sleep."

"Where's the watch?"

Halvpas allowed himself a smile. He took a small box, the kind you get from a jeweler, and briefly brandished it in front of her.

"You really put me on the run for this, didn't you?" he said, rattling the box briefly. "I won't hold it against you."

She heard another set of men's feet from behind her.

"And I won't hold it against you, Captain, for it taking so long," came a low, eerily familiar voice. "Thank you for staying with her."

Some whispered murmurings, an urgent debrief, was exchanged between the two men. Margo felt very far away from anything, like the conversation behind her was a radio frequency she was only sometimes able to tune in to.

Eventually, the other man came to sit in the chair opposite her.

"Darling," her father said. "If you only knew all the trouble we've been going to, just for you."

Richard Madden sat pleasantly in front of her, as though returning from yet another one of his long business trips. The jeweler's box that Halvpas had been holding was now resting in his lap.

Words failed her. Margo felt as though her mouth was filling with cement.

"I know, sweetheart," Richard said. "It must be a terrible shock for you. But if you had just stayed on the train, and not been taken by that awful . . ." He broke off. He didn't want to get into it now. He had been worried about her. Her father, who had been dead since she was fourteen. He had worried.

Seeing that she had no ability to respond, Richard Madden finally opened the jeweler's box in his lap. He frowned.

"Halvpas," he said, pulling out Aska's pocket watch. "What is this?"

forty-four
MOON

The most common response I get when I tell people what I do for a living is: I couldn't do a job like that. What they mean is they *wouldn't* do a job like this. We are twice as likely to be alcoholics, three times as likely to die by suicide, and infinitely more likely to disappear without anyone caring at all.

But all I ever say is—you're right. You *couldn't* do a job like this.

You couldn't find a lost girl on a train and end up changing your entire life around her. You couldn't throw a bomb for her. Couldn't break a train for her. Couldn't admit that everything you've ever believed about life and how to live it, up until the point of knowing her, was completely incorrect. Absolutely stupid. Incoherent. Childish. Dumb.

Because here's the thing.

Every so often—for every one in a hundred of us, I suppose, or maybe fewer—you meet someone who does care when you disappear.

And then they disappear.

Even though she was with you just a moment ago. Even though your pillow still smells of her hair. Even though you can still feel her breath on your skin. She disappears. You don't get to know why, or how, but the cave in your chest is so deep and wide that you can't swallow; can't sleep; can't think. All you can do is try to find her. Call in every favor. Take every route. Hurl yourself at the iron wall that fate has erected between you until your body breaks against it.

So I put on her suit. I affix the watch she once tried to sell. And I get moving.

Most people, I think you'll agree, really couldn't do a job like this.

ACKNOWLEDGMENTS

The saying is "Rome wasn't built in a day," but they should change it. It should be, "Rome wasn't built by one person." I'm not comparing this book to the Roman Empire, but it is *my* Roman Empire, and I built it with a group of people whose commitment to it has been unparalleled by anything else I've done in my career. I'm so grateful for them, and grateful for the opportunity to thank them here.

Bryony Woods, Susan Van Metre, and Gráinne Clear are the brain trust of this operation. Thank you all for the conference calls, late night email chains, and five-hour lunch meetings that helped iron out everything, from the fiddliest bits of time logic to the grandest moments of adventure. Thank you also for letting Sylv join in. Thank you, as always, to Sylv.

Thank you to Jamie Hammond, Deb Lee, and Pam Consolazio for their beautiful work on the art for this book, which has gone beyond anything I could have imagined.

Thank you to Jenny Bish for double-checking everything.

Thank you to the true world-hopping salesmen of publishing: Karen Coeman, Lara Armstrong, and everyone at Walker and Candlewick who spends hours standing up at the Frankfurt, Bologna, and London Book Fairs, selling their hearts out.

Everyone in my life calls Andrew Mills "Showbiz Andrew" because he rings me up and says things like "finished the book—I'm thinking movies. Big, big *movies*." Thank you, Showbiz Andrew. Whether or not the movies come calling, I still appreciate that you're thinking movies.

Thank you to Meg Wassell for doing the decidedly unglamorous work of answering my emails and seizing my social media while I finished this book.

Natasha Hodgson was the first person to read even the smallest scraps of this book. Tash, thank you for believing in this adventure from the very beginning, and thank you for taking me off the train.

Ella Risbridger has been thanked in the acknowledgments of every single one of my books and, with luck, will be thanked in all of them. Ella, thank you for being not just my first reader but my second, my third, and my thirty-third. Thank you for every note, even the ones I get grumpy and quiet about.

Sarah Maria Griffin, thank you for coming to an off-season spa hotel with me so that we could eat cream cheese sandwiches and finish our freaky little books. Your dedication to freaky little stories continues to make me feel more legitimate about my own, and I hope you know the power that has.

Jennifer Cownie is a Swiss Army knife of a human being. Thank you for jumping on trains all over Europe with me so that I could better understand the salesman's life. I cannot fall asleep anywhere, haggle in a language I don't speak, or wake up like a dog—but you can, and I'm deeply grateful for that.

Gavin O'Day, you are my husband and the only reason I am qualified to write any kind of love story. You are also the only person qualified to talk me down after I have threatened to give up, and I threatened that quite a few times on this one. But one time, when

I was deep in despair about the whole thing, you said, "Just so you know, I think it's really cool that you're writing this book." And the first thing I thought was, *Oh my God, Gavin thinks I'm cool!*

To my family of salesmen: my mother, who could charm the stars; my father, who could talk his way out of a sunburn; Jill, who could make anyone give up state secrets; Shane, who could sell ice to a polar bear; and Rob, who could probably knock over a bank. It's not hard to write characters when you come from a family of them.

This book was written over many years, and there were many times when I lost confidence with it. Many, many people asked me, "You still writing that time-travel thing?" and then would have to listen to long updates about how it was going. Thank you to Tom McInnes, Dolly Alderton, Ryan Farrell, Harry Harris, Katherine Rundell, Sam Sedgman, and everyone else whose name temporarily escapes me and for whom I will always regret not including, but let's face it: there's a deadline for turning in these acknowledgments and my editor Susan has been very patient already.

It is impossible to write a book that is about moving and traveling without thinking of your own history with the subject. I am in a global club of people who have moved alone in order to make a life somewhere else. A life isn't built in a day, and it isn't built by one person, either. It was built by a thousand people who were kind to me, who gave me a job, or who let me join in.

To those people, thank you.

is the author of the *New York Times* bestseller *All Our Hidden Gifts*, the first book in her Gifts series. She is also the author of novels for adults, including the international bestseller *The Rachel Incident*, now being developed for television.

An Irish author, journalist, and host of the acclaimed podcast *Sentimental Garbage*, she has contributed to *Grazia*, *The Irish Times*, the *Irish Examiner*, *BuzzFeed*, *Vice*, and *The Times* (London). Caroline O'Donoghue lives in London with her husband and dog.